RAVAGE

Raegan of Ruin Book One

A. L. Rook

PLAYLIST

The Hunted - The Rigs
Kids in the Dark - All Time Low
No Roots - Alice Merton
Runnin' - Adam Lambert
Follow - Saint Phnx
Bulletproof - La Roux
Arcade - Duncan Laurence
Enemy - Imagine Dragons
Lifeline - Layto
You Don't Own Me - SAYGRACE
Habits (Stay High) - Tove Lo
The Time of Our Lives - The Venice Connection
We Can't Stop - Miley Cyrus
Cheap Thrills - Sia
When We Were Young - Andy Black
Numb - 8 Graves
Nightmare - Halsey
Chandelier - Sia
I Just Wanna Run - The Downtown Fiction
Gods & Monsters - Lana Del Rey
Armor - Landon Austin
Don't Start Now - Metrixx
Ride - ZZ Ward
Teeth - 5 Seconds of Summer
Just My Type - The Vamps
She's a Lady - Forever the Sickest Kids
Love It When You Hate Me (feat. Blackbear) - Avril Lavigne
Guest Room - Echos
Genius - Written by Wolves
An Unhealthy Obsession - The Blake Robinson Synthetic Orchestra
I Miss You - blink-182
Infra-Red - Three Days Grace

Listen on Spotify

This book is dedicated to my husband.
Thank you for supporting my dream and pushing me to hit publish
when imposter syndrome was at its highest. For not questioning my
crazy when I'm in "the zone" while writing or lost to a daydream.
You're my lobster.

TABLE OF CONTENTS

Chapter One

RAEGAN

A SHORT, WIDE BUILDING sits unassuming before me in the dark of night. It's three stories of worn and chipped brick, with metal-barred windows on the front, and large black numbers over the double doors. The buildings on either side of it are at least eight or nine stories and tower over it, shadowing it almost completely from view on this narrow, dead-end road tucked away on the city outskirts.

If not for the specific address scribbled on the card I'm holding, I'd never have noticed it existed.

It's the perfect hideout for the shadow organization that I'm hunting.

One that's also hunting me.

Gifted Enterprise, Inc.

They kidnap people, particularly children, who exhibit powers that should be impossible. They brainwash and then use them for power and control over a society who still has no idea that people with these powers, like me, exist.

They stole me from my grams when I was only eight. In the beginning, they made me believe that I was taken for a special training program so I could one day help save the world. Like some superhero. I was sixteen when I learned that we were being trained to be mindless soldiers to do their dirty work from the shadows. And those who never complied became lab rats attached to tubes and machines until their bodies gave out.

Even though I've been free of them for five years, they've left me with scars that will never heal.

The card that led me here was in the pocket of one of their men that I'd dispatched in the last city. I'm hoping this is some facility for testing or maybe a drop-off point for the kids they kidnap. So far, it looks like an abandoned apartment building, but Gifted Enterprise has already shown me how deceiving appearances can be.

After stashing my backpack of supplies in the tight alleyway, I grip the gun on my hip and pull it free. I count the entry and exit points around the building. Windows and double doors in the front, windows on the side, a single door, four balconies and windows in the back.

I triple check there's no one around before sliding through the shadows to the back door. I pull my lock picking kit from my pocket and get to work. It takes longer than usual with the extra locks on it, but finally, the click sounds.

I could always use my gift to break in faster, but the last few times I've used it, GE found me within days.

The door creaks and squeals as it opens. Cringing at the loud noise, I leave enough room for me to slip through before closing it behind me.

The space reeks of rotten food and piss, and I immediately switch out the lock picking kit for my gun and flashlight to scan the room and check for squatters. It's large and open, with a stairwell on the right and a set of entryway doors opposite me. There are mailboxes mounted to the wall on the left, confirming my theory that this was once an apartment building.

The floor is layered with unfinished food, wrappers, an overturned chair, ratty blankets, cans, empty glass bottles, and what looks like a still-wet puddle in the corner.

Gross.

I wrinkle my nose and focus on the path from where I'm standing to the staircase. It doesn't look like anyone has been here in a while, aside from that puddle, and it's the first time I'm forced to consider the possibility that this is a dead end. Why would the GE goon I killed in the last city have this card on him if this place had been abandoned? It makes no sense. Or maybe they're looking to buy this building and turn it into a testing or storage facility?

I'm grateful I'm wearing thick, army-style boots as I step deliberately through the mess, careful to avoid any food or debris that might stick. The single flight of stairs ends in a narrow hallway with two doors.

The nearest one is a plain, boring nude color with a gold knob. There are no numbers or letters to indicate the individual apartment. I flick my light down the hallway and to the other door, and it's bare as well.

I clutch my flashlight between my teeth and pull out the lock picking kit again. Pressing my ear to the door to listen for noise, I count to sixty, then insert the tools into the keyhole until it clicks.

As soon as the tumblers turn, I swap the kit for my gun and open the door.

My flashlight reveals solid hardwood floors that are clean and polished. The smell of lemons permeates the space as if it was freshly wiped down. There's a coat rack on a short wall, a boot tray below it, and a small door on the other side that I'm assuming is a coat closet.

The contrast between this and the rest of the building is like night and day.

I cautiously move further inside, closing the door behind me, and the space opens on either side. There's a cozy living area directly to my left, complete with a full sectional, rug, and entertainment center. Across from it on the back wall is a U-shaped desk stacked with computer monitors. A hallway of closed doors splits the two areas on the left wall. The rest of the open floor plan flows from a dining area to a kitchen with another hallway through it to the right.

Based on the size of the space, this has to be most, if not all, of this side and floor of the building.

I follow the hallway at the end of the living area first, nudging each door and sweeping the flashlight across the rooms for signs of movement. Bedrooms. Spacious ones, with a walk-in closet and private bathroom in each of them, which I check for hidden occupants before I move on.

I'm still trying to wrap my head around what the hell I've stumbled into. It went from a homeless hangout to a recently updated, penthouse-style apartment in the span of thirty stairs and an ugly door.

After three bedrooms and a locked door, I make it to the last room at the end of the hallway. Origami in various shapes litter the nightstand next to the bed. I step closer and holster my gun to pick up the one in the shape of a crane.

My chest constricts at the memory of a naïve girl collecting origami animals like this on her shelf from a sweet, quiet boy. Of the first paper crane he ever gave me.

The memories thicken my throat, reminding me I'll never have anything close to what I had with him, and the others again.

I ruined that.

Then GE ruined me.

I toss the paper bird back to the nightstand. It's been five years since I last saw the guys I'd grown up with on the island where GE kept us. It'd be best not to think of them when it only reminds me of happier times followed by years of pain and remorse. I need to keep my focus on my mission.

I yank the top drawer open and rummage through stacks of paper and a bag of hard candies before shoving it closed and going for the bottom one.

"Don't you know it's rude to pry through a guy's drawers without permission?" a husky male voice murmurs teasingly, his breath heating the back of my neck.

I grab my gun, spinning around and swinging my arm out. The stranger moves back effortlessly, like some ninja, but my finger is already on the trigger. The gunshot rings through the room. I focus my flashlight on the dark figure to see if I got him, but there's no sign of him being injured.

Something pale appears out of the darkness in front of him—*fingers*, I realize—when they pinch the air. He's wearing black fingerless gloves that meld with the rest of his attire. It looks like he pockets what he grabbed—which I'm having an oh shit feeling was my bullet—and then something clicks behind him.

Light bursts in the room, and I recoil into the nightstand and squint my eyes at him. He doesn't move, thankfully, and I blink furiously until I can get a good look at him.

He's much taller than me, close to a foot, and wearing nondescript clothing. Black jeans, boots, and a hoodie that shadows his face.

I hope he's not some Gifted Enterprise assassin who can control metal. The lower ungifted goons were easy. I haven't come up against one with a gift yet.

"Who are you?" I keep my gun trained on him.

He chuckles, and the sound sends a shiver rippling through me. It's cold and hollow. Nothing like the warmth that normally comes with a person's laughter. No, his sounds more like a dark promise of all the painful things he enjoys doing to others. But there's a niggling familiarity in it that tugs at my chest, and I don't fear hearing it like a person with any self-preservation should.

He raises his hands slowly, palms out, and then pushes his hood back to reveal himself. He tugs down the gaiter from his face until it's bunched up around his neck. The lighting reveals raven-black hair with an almost bluish tint. It's cut short on the sides and left long and messy on top. He has a full, pouty bottom lip that would be pretty if his mouth wasn't twisted into a smirk while he eyes me intensely. As if he'd enjoy nothing more than to chase and devour me.

He cocks his head, reminding me of a confused puppy. A large, deadly puppy. And then it hits me.

The origami animals.

His laser-focused attention.

It's been five years, and he's fucking *grown* since I last saw him, but it's definitely him.

"Jackson?"

His smile returns.

"What are you doing here?" I ask, my breathing thin.

He doesn't seem surprised or upset I haven't lowered my gun, even at knowing his identity. He tucks his hands into his hoodie pocket and shrugs. Like seeing each other after so much time is no big deal. Even after what I'd done that caused him and the others to hate me. They hated me so much they abandoned me on the island with GE and didn't look back.

But maybe that wasn't enough.

Are they here to hunt me down and kill me?

If only they knew how much I'd suffered by the hands of GE, by *him*, after what I'd done, they'd know I've already been punished beyond repair.

"This is my room," he answers matter-of-factly. His voice is low and quiet, but it's also so calm and confident. It's exactly how I remember it, and that twists like a knife in my heart at how much I miss it.

"Why did a GE goon have your address in his pocket? Are you working with them now?"

Smirking, he leans casually back against the wall. For what he thinks is going to be a long catch-up session, no doubt. "Because I put it there."

My expression slackens as I realize the implications of that. He used a Gifted Enterprise lackey to lure me here. I tighten my grip on my gun. "Do you all hate me so much still that you sought me out to kill me, then?"

"No…" He pauses, cants his head to the side as if in thought, then adds, "I don't hate you. I never have."

But the others do.

The unspoken words hang in the air between us.

"But you'd kill me for them?"

This time, his smirk looks closer to a smile, and I catch the dimple in his left cheek. "No."

Exasperated, I huff. He never was the verbose one. "So, what am I doing here then, Jack—Jackson." I correct myself immediately when his nickname slips out by mistake.

He flips a business card out from his pocket and holds it up. "I have a gift."

It's a non-answer if I've ever heard one. Jackson never lied. He's not a coward with his words or at saying exactly what's on his mind; whenever he shares, that is. But it's been five, no, actually *six* years, since we were last together.

People change.

I have.

"Not interested. If that's all, then I'm leaving." I click the safety back on my gun and lower it.

Jackson chuckles softly and flicks the card at me. When it should fall and spin through the air, it remains flat and steady as it cruises its way over to me. He used to send me his origami animals this way back on the island, using his gift to create a controlled current of air around them and guiding them where he wanted.

It pauses in front of me, and I stare at it. "You've gotten better," I comment, though we both know I'm referring to how he stopped a bullet traveling at a high velocity in a short distance rather than this business card.

"Of course. I'm not the same weak kid you remember." There's still a smile on his face, but darkness consumes his gaze when he delivers the words. A darkness that now looms like a shadow. If I could afford to care about him or the others anymore, I might wonder what happened to him in the time we've been apart.

But I can't.

"I've changed," he finishes.

His words only remind me of all the things GE did to me and I did for them in our year apart on the island. Nausea slides up my throat like reflux, and I swallow the burning memories back down.

"So have I," I deadpan. Ignoring the card still floating before me, I walk out of the room. Thankfully he doesn't stop me, and I make it out the front door.

I'm not accepting a gift or anything else from him. He may think he's changed, but he doesn't know what I've been through. Even when I was still within arm's reach of them, I'd been changed. Broken and remolded into the foundation of who I am today.

I'm no longer a naïve little girl thinking she's some kind of hero.

I've accepted that I'm a villain.

CHAPTER TWO

RAEGAN

Six Years Ago on the Island...

Tick. Tick. Tick.

I fidget under the covers while keeping count with my bedside clock.

9:57. 9:58. 9:59.

A smile spreads across my lips.

Ten o'clock.

I sit up slowly, careful not to disturb my roommates who are already asleep. Tara is still awake in the corner of the room with her flashlight shining on her book. She doesn't acknowledge me when I slip out of bed. Only she knows where I'm going and so long as I keep stealing books from the library for her, she'll keep my secret safe.

The hallway is dark and eerily quiet. There are no windows or lights on in this corridor at night. I'm not sure if they think that's somehow a strong enough deterrent to keep us all in our beds at night, but I've never been afraid of the dark.

Besides, I've been here long enough that I could get anywhere with my eyes closed.

Instead of tip-toeing to the door directly across from mine, I creep down the hallway to the stairs.

I promised the guys I'd bring us snacks from the kitchen tonight.

I move my bare feet quickly, but methodically, down the stairs. I know just where to step to avoid the creaks and groans that would give me away and force me back in my room.

I had to do that a lot in the beginning of my time here, but now, I'm a pro. The master ninja of the manor. Only the guys know of my skill because I'm always the designated kitchen thief.

Jackson would obviously be a better choice in staying quiet and collecting things, but we've found that I get off far easier on punishments if I'm caught. At most, I'm chided and escorted back to my room where the door is locked to keep me in. Sometimes, the staff lets me keep one of my prizes before returning me to my room.

The guys are given chores or something like that. They never cared to really talk about it, so probably something boring.

I'm halfway down the first-floor hallway to the kitchens when a hushed moan breaks the silence. I freeze and look behind me.

No one's there.

Another moan erupts, louder this time, and curiosity turns me around. I keep myself on the uppermost pads of my feet and sneak closer to see who's going at it so I can tell the guys.

There's a door that's partially open, and I press myself against the wall to listen.

I hear a smacking noise and then a crash. "Shut the damn door first."

My heart leaps into my throat, and I debate running to the kitchen before I'm seen, but a familiar voice makes me abandon that idea.

"Whoops, sorry!" A soft, but slightly nervous laugh follows.

I'd know that voice anywhere.

I have to look. To see it with my own eyes.

Vera, Dane's sister, is in a staff member's room at night. And now I'm freaking out about what that crashing sound was. I can't leave now. Not until I make sure she's okay.

I move in front of the door and put my hand against it, getting ready to open it all the way when it pushes back against my hand. Vera steps around the door, and her eyes widen when she sees me.

My expression probably matches hers as we stare at each other, wondering what the other is doing here.

"Vera—"

She steps into the hallway, forcing me back while she tries to close the door enough behind her that I can't see into the room. "Are you spying on me?"

"What? No. I heard something and then I heard you and wanted to make sure you were okay—"

"You heard something from all the way upstairs?"

I thumb toward the kitchen. "I was going for a snack."

Her eyes narrow at me like she has an internal bullshit-o-meter that can tell whether I'm lying through my teeth or not. But I don't know why she would think I was following her around. Well, not that I wouldn't if I thought she was in trouble.

"What are you doing?" The door is yanked from her hand and

flies open, as do Vera's eyes when she looks back over her shoulder.

Gordon, one of the scientists who's been training us and studying each of our gifts, scowls when he sees me. "Get in the room." Vera scurries inside and when I hesitate, he adds in a commanding tone, "Both of you."

This time, I do as he asks, and he closes and locks the door after me.

There are rules he has to follow with disciplining us for stepping out of line. I'm confident that he's only trying to avoid any other intrusions until this is sorted.

The room is the same size as mine, but for one person rather than four. The bed is nearly three times the size of one of ours, and there's enough room for an entire living area. My gaze sticks on the broken lamp and knocked-over side table.

"She saw us," Vera confesses. She closes the distance between her and Gordon and fists his shirt. "She knows."

He grabs her wrists and pulls them away. "Then fix it. Or I will."

Vera sets her determined gaze on me. "Look, Rae. This isn't what you think it is."

I look between them. *What do I think this is?*

Extra training? Or is it like how I sneak to the guys' room at night to spend time with them? But the crash. The *moaning*. Were they...?

Vera had been offering to give me advice on boys and kissing, and I wondered how she knew about all of that. I never saw her hanging out with the boys in her class.

Unease churns in my gut at the direction of my thoughts. She's only a year older than me at seventeen. And Gordon...well, he's got to be at least twice my age in his thirties, if not pushing his forties because of the silvering of his dark hair.

"What is it, then?" I ask hesitantly.

She takes a breath and then lays it all out. "When we were doing our one-on-one sessions for training, we started talking about the goals of Gifted Enterprise and what we're going to be doing in the future. He told me about all the horrible things happening in the world today and how we're going to stop it. We'll be saving lives once we've mastered our gifts. We just need to try harder and do what we're told."

She shoots me a look, as if she thinks I haven't been trying with my gift. I give her one right back because I freaking *do* try. Hers doesn't hurt her like mine does.

"I asked him to give me more training so I could start helping more. I don't want to waste any more time when we could be helping. So, we started spending more time together, figuring out more things I could do with my gift and...well..."

It's weird seeing her so embarrassed. Vera's always strong and confident. Nothing rattles her. I looked up to her when she and Dane first arrived, before she was moved up into different classes from us.

"What?" I push, the unease getting heavier the more she continues. But I have to know what's going on. For her. For Dane.

Vera looks to Gordon before her gaze snaps resolutely to mine. "I kissed him. He stopped it, of course, and told me why we couldn't. We tried to stay away from each other for a while, but we couldn't do it. We fell in love."

I bite my lip to keep my face from showing the discomfort and *ick* that I'm feeling. I can't pin down the reason, but something doesn't sit right.

Gordon's watching me with a neutral expression. I can almost see the wheels turning through his stare, but I have no inkling as to what it's about or how he feels about this admission.

"Does Dane know?"

Vera shakes her head and grabs my hands. "No, and he can't know."

"But—"

"*Please*. He won't understand."

"Ver, *I* still don't understand."

"You don't have to," she snaps back. My eyebrows shoot up with surprise at her tone, and she softens it before she continues, "This isn't about you or Dane. It's about me finding someone and not wanting anyone else to get in the way of that. You get that, right? I see how you are with my brother and his friends. They may be a bunch of blind idiots, but I know you have feelings for all of them."

I press my lips together and don't answer.

She nods like I've agreed with her. "Exactly. None of my business. I need you to keep this quiet for me. I'll be eighteen soon and then it won't be such a big deal to everyone. I'll also be done with training and classes here and I'll get my clearance to leave the island."

Her turning eighteen doesn't make me feel better about any of this.

Can I keep this from Dane when I have such a bad feeling in my gut?

I consider it for half a second before I know that I can't do that. But I can at least give her the chance to do it herself first.

"You have to tell Dane."

"I will. After I turn—"

"No," I cut in. "Tomorrow. He deserves to know what's going on with his sister."

Vera frowns and drops my hands. She looks back to Gordon for support, but he just looks at her like he's expecting her to make the decisions on this. It should be a good sign that he's not trying to control what happens with this, right?

My gut tightens in disagreement anyway.

"A week. Give me a week to figure out how and when to tell him," she finally replies, though, she doesn't sound happy about it.

Tough luck, because it will be hard enough for me to keep a secret from Dane for a whole week when it's about his sister doing who-knows-what with one of the people keeping us here. Hopefully, she rips off the Band-Aid and does it tomorrow.

"A week," I confirm.

"And just Dane. His friends don't need to be in my business either. He's the only one who can know right now. And he doesn't even need to know that you know either."

I don't understand why she's making such a big deal out of this if she planned to tell him once she turned eighteen in a few weeks anyway. But I drop it. If she's happy and her brother knows about what's going on, then it isn't my business to get involved any further.

I nod reluctantly and then glance back at the fallen furniture. She follows my gaze and then rolls her eyes. "You'll learn when you get older. Now, are we good here? If you don't mind, I'd like to pick up where Gordon and I left off before you poked your nose in."

My nose scrunches before I can help it, and she glares at me. Well, gross.

Gordon unlocks the door and opens it so I have to duck under his arm to leave.

"No snacks on the way back," he tells me just as I'm between him and the door. "Straight back to your room."

I scurry out and almost forget to watch my steps on the stairs until a faint creak snaps me out of my head. I re-focus on where my feet land on the stairs until I'm back on the second floor. I debate returning to my own room to avoid seeing Dane or the others. I haven't even seen them yet and I already feel the burning need to tell them what just happened.

But if I don't show up, they'll come looking for me anyway to make sure I didn't get caught.

I push and pull at my cheeks, smushing my own face around to remove any sign of whatever expression that whole encounter left me with.

Okay. I can do this. Just act normal and not like I have a huge secret that belongs to one of their sisters that they should definitely know about.

I swallow and turn the door handle slow enough to keep from making any noise. I step into the room and turn to softly close it.

"Where are the snacks?" Dane asks, peering over my shoulder.

I jump on reflex and fall forward into the door with a thud that's loud enough to send me into a panic.

"Woah, what's wrong?" He grips my shoulders and guides me to face him. His golden blond curls fall in a messy tangle across his forehead and at his temples, but his original brown color is coming back in at the roots. He'll likely be dyeing it again within the week to match his sister's natural golden blonde.

There's concern in his amber gaze as he looks me over. He doesn't drop his hand from my shoulder, which would be comforting if he wasn't the *exact person* I'm trying not to spill the beans to.

I duck my head and skirt around him further into the room before my face can betray me until I get a handle on it. "Nothing. I'm fine."

Kellan drops from the bar Aiden mounted in the middle of the ceiling and lands in front of me. He wipes his face with the bottom of his shirt so I get a clear view of his naturally tanned and sculpted abs.

I swallow.

I mean, I'm pretty sure his body and metabolism already gifted him with what would make any girl fan herself. Why he continues to work out and make it even more droolworthy is a continuous point of concern between me and my hormones.

Then he's covered again, and I blink back to reality. His blue-green eyes twinkle under dark brows while he smirks knowingly at me. "She seems good to me," he drawls.

I shove playfully at him, but he grabs and yanks me in for a hug. My body instantly sinks into his warmth and the safety behind his arms. Not only is he tall and broad, but he's impervious to my terrifying gift.

I'm safe in his arms because I could never truly hurt him with it.

"She looked spooked when she first came in." Dane's voice is still laced with worry.

I try to wriggle my way out, but Kellan tightens his arms and refuses to let me go. "Did someone catch you trying to get the snacks, beautiful?"

My fingers tickle along his inner elbow, right where I know he's sensitive. He jolts at the contact, and I slip out of his reach. "Something like that," I tease back with a grin. It's not that far off base, really.

Kellan laughs and shakes his head at me. "Well, aren't you being mysterious tonight? Aiden's been the same way. You guys sneak off together to do something we should know about?" He waggles his eyebrows.

Dane scoffs and folds his arms. "Of course not."

Rather than getting involved in that conversation and the possibility of me giving away that something *had* happened between Aiden and I, just not tonight, I ignore them to seek out Aiden in the room.

He's sitting on his bed, one leg bent and his arm dangling over it. He's facing us, but it's almost as if he's looking through us. Like he's so lost in thought that none of us are in the room with him. Or he isn't in the room with us.

"Hey." His head jerks up as I approach his bed. "Are you okay?"

He gives me a look that I've never seen before. Icy tendrils curl around my heart and squeeze. "Yeah," he mutters, then turns his head so he's staring at the side wall.

Um, okay then.

I try to remind myself that we'd been fine in class earlier today. That this has nothing to do with what happened between us last night. Something else must have happened tonight.

Even as I repeat that reminder in my head, it doesn't stop the heart-shredding fear and pain from this blatant rejection.

I touch my lips the barest amount as I remember his blistering kiss and how he'd left me breathless. My heart pounds at the memory and then crushes when he doesn't so much as look my way again.

Is he regretting it? Or did I mess it up somehow?

Fingers entwine with mine and close in a gentle squeeze. Dane's giving me the same look as when I first arrived. "Are you?" he echoes my own question back at me.

I force a smile on my lips. "Why wouldn't I be?"

Vera better talk to Dane soon. Really freaking soon, because I can't keep this secret about his sister when I have such a bad feeling about it. We've all been there for each other for years growing up in this place. We were taken from our families at a young age to keep us safe and train us to use our gifts. But we still missed our families and had times where we tried to escape and get home together. It's always been us against them.

And now one of us is *with* them.

And it feels like I'm with *them* the longer I know about it and Dane doesn't.

I pull my hand gently from his and make my way over to the last one of our group. The one who's usually quiet and keeps to himself, but watches everything all the same. The one who won't question or push me on anything.

Jackson has both knees up with his arms and chin leaning against them. His sky-blue eyes follow my every movement across the room until I stop next to his bed. He pulls the sheets back and holds them open for me in invitation.

He knew exactly what I was coming over for. I smile at him and climb in on the side against the wall. He has a thing about always sleeping on the outside of the bed, which is fine by me.

Dane and Kellan murmur quietly to each other, but thankfully they don't press me on anything else. For tonight at least. Tonight, I want to curl up with one of them—Jackson in particular—and relax enough to sleep.

The lights flick off, and I curl on my side, facing the wall. Jack's breath is warm on the back of my neck, but he's careful to still give me space. I share their beds for comfort, but there's no spooning or funny business.

His fingertips graze across the fabric of my pajamas. Up and down. Down and up. Long, soothing circles I can still feel even as sleep takes me under.

The last thing I remember is his voice in my ear. "I'm here," he whispers. "Whatever you need, little one. I'm here."

Chapter Three

RAEGAN

There isn't anywhere for me to go tonight. I left the last city and my temporary living arrangement behind. I need to find a place to stay at least until tomorrow and then figure out my next move from there.

All I know is that I can't stay here. Not if Jackson and the others are here.

My chest aches as Jack flashes in my mind again and how much he's grown from the sixteen-year-old I once knew. I'm worried about the darkness in his expression, but the smile he gave me, the genuine curve of his lips that pokes a dimple in his cheek, was everything like I remembered it.

I wish I could catch up with him and them like old times, but it's a foolish dream.

I destroyed the bonds we shared. I don't deserve to get to know who they are now. It would be best to keep my distance from them. But being so close and yet so far from them is a torture all on its own.

Once I've grabbed my backpack from the bushes, I take the long walk back to downtown, where the city is still alive and active, even in the early hours of the morning. People are dressed for the nightlife as they meander down the sidewalks, coming and going from bars, pubs, nightclubs, and whatever debauchery spots are open.

My lips curve into a smile as I take in the view. Vibrant neon signs cast a blue-purple glow on the streets and buildings, creating their own light enough that plain street lamps aren't needed. Chatter and the rumble of engines are a steady background buzz that is comforting in its constant noise.

I can't sleep or relax in silence.

It's a beautiful city. One I would have loved to explore more if not for the discovery of Jackson.

My phone vibrates in my back pocket, and I pull it out. Something flies out with it and tumbles to the ground. I narrow my eyes at the small rectangle and bend down to retrieve it, twisting my wrist around to see the front side. There's another single address on it just like the last one that led me to Jackson's apartment.

His gift, no doubt.

The impulse to toss it twitches my hand, but curiosity grips me before I can follow through. What sort of gift would he give me? A trap? He had me at the apartment if that was what he wanted, so then why bother sending me elsewhere?

Sighing, I look back to my phone to find a warning that my monthly plan is almost expired.

Great.

I pocket the card and my phone, shifting the one arm of the

backpack I'm wearing further up my shoulder. I keep walking until I find an electronics store to buy another month of data and minutes. I stop by a pizzeria that smells too good to pass up, and once I've finished my meal, I finally bring the card back out.

I search for the address on Maps, and it appears twenty blocks away and most definitely on the outskirts of the city again.

Seems fishy, but I can't help the need to know what sort of gift Jackson would be leaving me after all this time.

Maybe I shouldn't seem too eager by rushing over there anyway.

It's just after one in the morning. Nothing more unexpected than putting it off to the next day, right?

"—a liability. She never should have existed in the first place. Just kill her and be done with it," an unfamiliar voice echoes outside the door.

"We can't throw away a gift this useful. I can get her to control it." *I recognize this voice, but I don't care enough to place it.*

I'm a murderer.

A monster.

My arms tighten around my knees. I bury my face deeper into them as another sob escapes past my lips.

The tears don't come.

I've gone through them all, wasted them in the first few days I've been locked away in solitary. In the pitch black, concrete room that leaves me with only my thoughts as I replay the moment I killed Vera over and over again.

I'm trapped in a Hell loop of my own making.

"It's a waste of time. Don't bother anyone else with this experiment of yours. If it fails, it's on you," the first voice answers.

"Of course."

Light spills unforgivingly into the room as the door opens, blinding me in its harsh brightness.

"Get up!" Boots stomp across the floor, and a hand grabs my upper arm roughly to yank me up. The voice curses viciously. "You're as ripe as a dead body."

I stiffen when the image of Vera's lifeless gaze immediately fills my mind. My chest constricts until the air in the room seems thinner, and I grab onto the arm of the person trying to force me to stand instinctively.

"Don't touch me!" he snaps, smacking my hands away and pulling again until my feet are under me. "You're lucky I'm the one getting you out of here after what you've just cost us. You'll never be able to do what she could, so you'd better find a way to make yourself useful before I do exactly what they want me to do with you."

I stumble onto my feet.

Fingers dig into either side of my face and jerk it until I'm staring blankly at Gordon.

"Are you going to be a good little pet for me, or should I toss you away now?"

My cracked lips press together in preparation to speak. "Pet?" I croak.

He scowls at me. "Yes. You'll do exactly as I say without question." He leads me from the room and my feet follow on autopilot while my eyes are still adjusting to the light of the hallway. "Starting with a shower and some food so we can begin your training."

By the time I'm able to open my eyes, I don't recognize where we are. We're passing by a long window that looks into another large room filled with beds.

And people.

"What's that? Where are we?"

Gordon doesn't look at me or the room when he answers. "The lab where failures go to donate their gifts until they die. You'll be lucky to go there if you fail me. If they're successful in extracting your gift, they'll keep you alive longer. But"—his grip on my arm tightens hard enough that I cry out in pain—"don't fail me, pet."

He brings me to a training gym and opens the storage room where a medical bed on wheels sits in the corner with a floor lamp and clothing rack beside it. "This is your room now. You'll shower in the locker room. Be ready every morning. You're not to leave this gym without me." He releases my arm and starts to leave.

"But—why?" Why am I here? Why can't I leave? What's happening?

Gordon tsks and shakes his head. "You really think we're going to let you get close to anyone else after you killed someone so easily?"

"I didn't mean to—"

"Don't. Lie!" His hand whips across my face, and my body crashes into the storage door before dropping to the ground. He storms over to me and grips my hair in a punishing hold. "Vera was the key to us taking the next step and you ruined that."

My face contorts with pain, but even when tears are beckoned to my eyes, nothing comes. "She was going to kill Dane. I just wanted to save him. I didn't want to hurt her. Please..."

"You're a fool. You think that boy is going to thank you for killing his sister? You think he's going to believe anything you say after he learns that you're the one who did it?"

Fear chokes me at the thought of Dane or the others finding out about this. Of what I've done. Would they believe me? Maybe. If I had time to explain everything. But then...how can I tell Dane that Vera was helping GE? That she wasn't the sister he thought he knew? She wasn't the girl who showed up on the island.

I can't.

I squeeze my eyes shut as the realization sinks in. I can't let them know what Vera had become. How twisted and apathetic she was when she wasn't with them.

I'll never tell them. They can keep their good memories of Vera while I hold on to the real her as penance for what I did.

As long as Gordon doesn't tell them first.

My eyes snap open with a new resolve. "Don't."

"Excuse me?"

"Please," *I amend.* "Don't tell them."

His smirk is cold and malevolent. "Them? Oh, right. The others who hang around him. Should we go tell them together?"

I try shaking my head, but his grip is too strong for it to move much. But it's enough. He laughs and tosses me back. "Then be a good pet and go take a shower. I'll be back with food and you'd better be finished before then." *His dull brown eyes leer down my body with a smirk pulling at his lips.* "You'd hate to find out what happens if I'm back first."

Revulsion coils in the pit of my stomach, and I curl in on myself as if to protect myself from him.

His smirk intensifies at my reaction. He leans in and drags his thumb down my lips. "Give it time, pet. You and I are going to have a lot of it."

My body drops a few inches, and for a second, I feel like I'm falling. I grab at whatever's closest while my stomach's busy getting lodged in my throat and I'm choked by painful memories resurfacing in my dreams again.

Then I smell the sweet, delectable aroma of hot coffee.

My panic dissipates instantly because...coffee.

I can't be falling from the sky if that's what I'm smelling.

I try to peel my eyelids back, but they're heavy and thick.

"I know I said you could sleep here last night, but I'm not sure I was prepared for how long you sleep," a deep voice drawls above me.

I find the strength to snap my eyes open and then hiss at the brightness of the room. I move back on instinct, realizing I'm lying in a bed, and then stare blearily at the man sitting on the edge with a coffee mug in his hand and a look of amusement in his expression. He's wearing gray slacks, a white button up long-sleeve shirt, and a tie. His dirty blonde hair is mussed back from his face.

He extends the coffee toward me, keeping his distance but offering this olive branch between us. As I'm reaching for it, the sheets slide further off of me and expose my naked torso.

Ah. Of course, I did.

It all comes rushing back now. Changing into my one skimpy dress in the pizzeria bathroom and then hitting up the nearest nightclub. Then finding a guy who looked interested and getting him to buy me drinks and bring me home with him so I didn't have to waste my money on a dirty motel or expensive hotel for the night.

I must have slept with him.

Good times.

I don't bother covering myself up once the sheet falls. He's obviously seen it all before, and I reach for what's important right now. That coffee.

The man's gaze travels down my exposed flesh, but there's nothing leering or rude about it. He doesn't give any indication if he likes or dislikes what he sees either, which might set others off, but I'm an absolute realist. This was just a one-night stand that got me free drinks and a room for the night, and I'm satisfied with the turnout of all that.

I take the mug and try to remember what he'd said when I first woke up. "What time is it?"

He smiles and checks his watch. I didn't realize people still wore those anymore with cell phones being in everyone's pockets, but nope, he's wearing a shiny-looking black watch with fancy dials and everything. "Three in the afternoon."

Oops.

I bring the mug to my lips and let the coffee burn my tongue and throat on the way down. My eyes close of their own accord, and I groan. It's fucking *wonderful*. When I open my eyes again, he's watching me patiently, like he has all the time in the world for some weirdo to crash his home and sleep in until mid-afternoon, drinking his cup of coffee.

Who is this guy?

"Sorry about that. Your bed must be comfortable."

"You must have been that tired," he counters.

I shrug one shoulder and take another deep gulp. "Maybe. Do you always bring coffee to girls who sleep over and stay past the respectful time?"

He chuckles. "Certainly not."

Hm. Red flag.

My brow arches in question.

"You seemed to need it," he answers as if that's a normal reaction to an absolute stranger who openly admitted to him she was using him for the night. "I can help you if you want to share what brought you to a nightclub to look for a place to sleep at one in the morning."

I hum after drinking more coffee. "I don't share. I also don't do relationships if that's where this is going. I had a good night, I appreciate the bed and the coffee, but once I've finished this cup, you'll never see me again."

"Fair enough." He stands and tugs at the cuffs of his sleeves on either arm. "I'm not looking to pry, but if you do need a friend, or a friendly acquaintance, in your corner, let me know. I have resources that I built around me for something like this, so I'm more than happy to offer them."

I bite my tongue at the *something like this* comment. What situation does he think I'm in? Some homeless girl who can't get a job and was disowned by her family? I mean, it's not totally off, but it's missing the key points that make having me around more dangerous for him than for me.

People die from being around me because of GE's hunt to get me back. Death by bad luck, I guess, because they don't care about unnecessary casualties to get what they want.

"Resources?" I question instead.

He nods and gestures to the room. "Other apartments and places to stay. A job. Assistance with...finding answers."

Well, that was cryptic. "Am I supposed to know what that last one means?"

He smirks. "You can't have all the secrets." His hands settle into his pockets. "You know where to find me now, so if you decide to take me up on any of those, just knock. You can also find me in the nightclub downstairs most nights."

The nightclub is downstairs? Well, that was convenient. I finish the last swig of coffee and set it down on the nightstand on the far side of the bed from him. When I look back up, he has my backpack and the dress from last night on the bed for me. "You work there?" I take the dress and tug it over my head, then stand on the other side and pull it down over my bare backside as far as it goes.

"I own it."

I snap back up to look at him. Resources, huh? I purse my lips in thought and then shake my head. I don't trust anyone. Least of all, someone I met at a nightclub. "Thanks, but I'll be out of this city before the end of tonight anyway."

"What's your name? Will you give me that at least?"

I hunt for my boots, which are on his side of the room, and flop back on the bed to yank them on. "What's yours?" I counter back. This guy is a stranger and should stay that way. The less he knows about me, the better.

"Elias."

I wait for a last name, but he leaves it at that and then raises his brow for me to reciprocate. I raise mine back with a smirk. I never said I'd offer him mine; so foolish of him for thinking so. "You got a bathroom, Elias?"

His pale blue eyes flash like he thinks he has me. "I do. In exchange for your name."

I grab my backpack and shrug. "Fine. I'll piss in the alley."

He makes a strangled noise in the back of his throat. "Fuck, don't do that. It's that door over there." He points to one of the *many* doors in this room. "Feel free to use the shower if you'd like. I have to be out of here in an hour, so that's how long you have before I'll escort you out. Use whatever products you want." He leaves me to it without pressing for my name, and I wonder what I said that freaked him out so much.

Chapter Four

RAEGAN

I TAKE UP EVERY minute of the hour he offered me to pamper myself for the first time in a long while. The hot, soaking shower was at least half of that time. Then blow drying my blonde hair with soft curls and adding some makeup, another chunk. After my needs are met, I snoop.

I mean, he can't think that I wouldn't, right? Something about him sets off warning bells.

He's too *nice*.

No one is that nice without wanting something.

He already had sex with me, so unless he knows exactly who I am, which I doubt considering how calm he was around me, I don't know what else he thinks I have to give him.

I decide by the second empty closet in this room that it's a guest room. There's no dresser and no clothes in the closet. No personal items. The bathroom was stocked with items that any guest might need. Even shaving sticks and cream for men and for women.

It's weird to sleep in your guest room when you bring someone home for sex, right? On second thought, that's fucking smart. No personal items, less important things to steal, and not to mention more time to clean the sheets. Genius.

Elias walks into the room while I'm cramming myself under the bed, my ass in the air and dress riding up above it, in search of a secret box or safe or *something* that might clue me into this guy. He clears his throat. Startled, I jump, and my head smacks against the metal frame.

"Ow! Fuck, that hurt!" I shimmy out from under the bed, even if that means my dress only rides further up my waist in the effort. I focus on rubbing the injured spot on my head first. "Can't you walk a little louder?"

He's still in his suit, but he's wearing a matching gray jacket now as well that's buttoned at the middle like he's ready for business. Which, I guess, he is. Amusement flickers in his eyes rather than annoyance at my snooping which, again, screams that something is not right. "Is that what you really want? Or would you rather I hand over whatever it is you're searching for under the bed? Buried treasure, perhaps? Weapons?"

Standing upright, I finally straighten the dress. "If you're offering, I wouldn't mind the weapons. Are you a serial killer or something?"

"Oh? No treasure?"

That wasn't a no to the last question. Or a yes, either. My mouth twitches into a smirk. "Too heavy. I travel light." Though I wouldn't mind extra cash. I have a decent amount from bartending in the last city I'd been in, but it won't last me long. I lift my backpack and loop one arm through.

Elias eyes it for a long moment and then brings his gaze back to me. "Interesting." He turns and flexes two fingers over his shoulder in a *come-on* motion. "Let's go. I need to lock up."

I follow him out and check that the hallway's clear while he's busy pushing buttons and turning keys on his door. "Well, it's been fun," I start while turning away to leave.

"I can walk you out," he offers, but I wave it off.

"I can see the stairs from here, and I'd rather get going." *Better to leave while I'm ahead and before the status quo changes.* I shoot him a smile and then make a beeline for the stairs to put some distance between us.

I meant what I said before. I probably won't ever see him again, as interesting of a character as he was. After I check out the supposed gift from Jackson, I'll be hitching a ride or hopping on a bus across the country. Any city that's as far away from this one as possible.

I've only seen Jackson one time, and already my nightmares are bringing me back to a time that I wish I could forget. I don't need the pain of seeing him or the others and reliving everything I've done and everything I've been through.

Between stopping for food, buying a new outfit to change into, and walking the twenty blocks to get to the address, it's nearing eight at night, and the sun has set.

The address brings me to a warehouse in the middle of a manufacturing district. There are small, rectangular windows along the top of the building that would barely allow any light into it during the day. It's all wall and garage doors, with a single man door at the front left corner.

After dropping my backpack in a corner, I pull my gun and

flashlight from it and then lockpick my way inside. Heavy breathing, followed by the cloying scent of copper, floods my senses. *What the fuck am I walking into?*

My hand tightens on my gun, and I raise my flashlight with the other hand to sweep over the area. It's a single, open space with a concrete floor. A man is tied to a chair in the center of the room, with rows of chains piled on the floor ten feet from him. His shoulders quake with the effort of his labored breathing as his head hangs forward.

I shine the light over the rest of the warehouse again to make sure there are no other entry points or hiding places aside from the door I entered and the closed garage bay doors. Satisfied, I close the distance between us and squat to get a look at the prisoner. There's dried blood pooled at his feet and spattered over the concrete.

How long has he been here? At least a day, considering when Jackson gave me the card. And he's been sitting here waiting for me. *Oops.*

He tilts his face up to look at me, and it's swollen and bloody.

"Are you here to rescue me?" he whimpers.

I smile, resting my arms on my knees and angling the flashlight into his eyes so he can't get a good look at me. "No, I'm not. I'm here for answers."

There must be a reason Jackson left this guy for me as a gift. I don't recognize him, but I have a good guess he's related to Gifted Enterprise.

The man simpers, and I curl my lip when snot drips from his nose. "I'm just a recruiter. I don't know anything you're looking for except for the upcoming gala. You'll be able to get what you need there."

My attention perks up at that. "Tell me everything about the gala."

He mumbles about already telling my buddy everything, and I press the barrel of my gun against his kneecap to regain his focus.

"O-okay, okay! Rich socialites gather to donate to their cause. It's being held at the Reynard Museum of Art on the twelfth of the month. You need to have an invitation to get in."

My blood chills. Were these going to be all the investors of our misery? I planned on going after the board of directors and anyone directly involved in the project, but what about those who gave the money for it?

"Are they investors of Gifted Enterprise?" My hand with the gun shakes in anger against his kneecap, and his eyes widen.

"W-what? No, most of the donors don't realize what it's for. The organization is fake. It's a front for helping children with mental illnesses and birth defects."

One second, I'm seeing red, and the next, the guy is screaming, and my ears echo with the sound of a gunshot.

Whoops. Too bad I don't care about hurting people who kidnap children and then brainwash and torture them.

Or kill them when they don't get what they want out of them.

Agonized, he screams and wails. I stand and point the gun at his face. "Quiet, or I'll shut you up permanently." He bites his lips to stifle the cries, and I count to thirty before I continue, "How do you know all of this if you're just a recruiter?"

"No outsiders are allowed. Only employees can do catering and serving."

Fuck. There's no way I can get an invite, but I thought I'd at least be able to pretend to be staff.

"How can I get in?"

"What? Y-you can't," he sputters, spittle flying.

I push the gun into his forehead. "Think harder. Are there *any* non-staff members aside from the invitees?"

Sweating, he mutters incoherently under his breath, and I force myself to take a deep breath of my own. Even though the warehouse is thick with the smell of his blood, I've learned how to breathe through it. When it's the blood of my enemies, it doesn't bother me so much.

Being a recruiter means being the lowest on the totem pole in the hierarchy of Gifted Enterprise. They find "problem" children, kids who are put in extra programs or maybe mental illness facilities when they show strange behavior, or those who do things that can't be possible.

It started by stealing them off of the streets and out of parks. But when the parents went out of their way searching for them, and one set of parents recognized their kids years later, brainwashed, it brought too much attention to the organization. Now, there can be no loose ends.

Instead, the recruiters kill the family and steal the gifted child.

They drop children off at a facility and collect their paycheck based on the age and type of gift.

Rinse. Repeat.

They may not actively participate in what happens to the children from there, but they sniff them out and steal them away. They take everything away from the kids so they have nothing and no one to return to if they ever escaped and found out what happened.

Like how I found out that Grams was dead by the time I made it off the island.

"Time's up." I nudge his forehead. "How can I get in?"

"Invite! Steal someone's invite or get invited yourself! That's the only way."

I roll my eyes. "If this is a common event, I can't impersonate someone that other people know. Strike two." Also, no way in hell I can get my own invite. I'm not entirely sure if I exist anymore. No license and no legal ID. I don't even know the day of my own birthday; just the month and my age. It's why I rely on more creative methods for making money and getting a place to stay for a few weeks or a few months at a time.

When he doesn't offer an alternative, I *tsk*, and my finger pulses over the trigger.

"W-wait! Wait! Guest! Be someone's guest! They get a plus one." He's hyperventilating now, sweat streaking down his face and into his eyes that he has to blink away while his hands are tied.

I shift the barrel back enough to see the small circular impression on his forehead. "That's not a bad idea. I think I can work with that. So, who are some of the invitees?"

"I don't know any names, I swear! I always worked in the back kitchens or as a valet. The servers aren't recruiters, they're guards. They are the ones who know."

Even if I had a guard's name, it wouldn't help. My search engine skills are basic, and most name searches return nothing true or accurate unless the person is in the spotlight. An investor with a lot of money? Yes. A person meant to hide in the shadows for illegal activity? Definitely not.

"So, basically, you have nothing more for me," I conclude. His eyes widen just before I fire a shot between the eyes. It's a clean kill and more than what scum like him deserves, but I now have a deadline of two days to get things in order for this gala.

Find a place to stay.

Find someone with an invite and somehow get the guest spot.

Find a dress.

Make money.

I flip the chair back with my boot, forcing the dead recruiter over to the ground. I'd clean this up, but I'm hoping to keep Jack and the others busy to avoid any other run-ins. I've already got Gifted Enterprise looking for me, which is why I avoided using my gift on this guy and leaving my signature. I'd do it if I planned on leaving right away, so I'm long gone before there's anything they can do about it, but now, it looks like I'll be staying here at least a few days longer.

It means there's a chance I'll run into Jackson and the others if this guy already gave them the information on the gala, but that's a risk I'll have to take if it means getting closer to my end goal. It's been a slow process on my own, trying to take them down, and I'd be an idiot to look this gift horse in the face.

Hopefully, this isn't some long game to get back at me. I don't know why they would go after GE after they escaped them, though. The best idea is to stay hidden and try living a normal life. I'm the reckless one trying to get my revenge on them for what happened with Vera and the year after because I have nothing and no one left anyway.

They still have each other.

Chapter Five

JACKSON

THE GUNSHOT ECHOES THROUGH the open warehouse without any insulation to buffer the sound. I'm sure it can be heard clearly from outside if anyone were walking by, but I've already set up a perimeter to be sure I'm alerted if that were the case.

Since Raegan isn't aware of that, or me, it was a reckless move. A knife could have taken care of the guy just as easily without the noise if she doesn't have a suppressor for her gun.

My lips twitch to a smirk. None of that matters anymore. It's concerning that she lived this way for the last five years and could have been caught by either the police or the GE scum, but that's in the past now. I don't get hung up on something that's already passed, and I had no control over.

Now that she's in my sights again, I'll be the guardian angel she always should have had.

Though, maybe guardian demon would be more accurate.

I stroke my thumb over the smooth wing of the paper crane I created as she uses wet wipes to clear away any blood or dirt on her skin. The temptation to send the crane down to her fills me with adrenaline at the sweet nostalgia of being able to share something between the two of us again.

"Hi! I'm Raegan, but you can call me Rae. What's your name?"

The girl smiles up at me where I'm perched on the back of the chair, my shoes sitting on top of the desk. She's tiny for this age group in the class, and from up here, she looks even smaller compared to me.

The teacher has yet to arrive, so others in the class are congregated in their little cliques as they whisper and gossip about the new kid.

Me.

Little do they know that I can hear them all anyway.

My lips twist into a smirk at that nugget of information that I'll never share. The look on my face brings on a whole new wave of whispers from my new classmates. Their words are more familiar than anything else here has been since I arrived on the island yesterday.

"He's so weird…"

"That look gives me the creeps."

"Why is he on the desk like that?"

"Can you believe he kicked Mikal out of his desk?"

"Who does he think he is?"

Only three others and this girl are staying quiet. I notice that two of them, both of the guys, are watching her interaction with me.

Interesting.

I cock my head at her, as if studying a creature I've never seen before and trying to determine if it's harmless or not. "Don't you think I'm strange?"

She mirrors me by tilting her head like mine. It's a silly move, but I smile at it anyway. "Why would I?" she questions back with a finger to her lips.

I shrug, not willing to give her reasons if she hasn't found any yet.

My fingers keep folding the square paper even with her interruption. I've made these enough times that I could do it with my eyes closed, and it's become a comfort to keep my hands busy with this instead of using my gift.

But while they're busy, my mind races.

"I have a question for you, little one." She doesn't get upset over the impromptu nickname, which compels me to continue. "Is it better to be feared and left alone, or noticed and used?"

Her nose scrunches as confusion paints her face. "Why are those the only two options? I don't like either of them."

My smile sharpens. "Then what are you doing here?"

"What?"

She doesn't understand. None of them do. I was feared in my foster home. By my foster parents. By my foster siblings and classmates. It meant that I was ignored or talked about behind my back, but I came to accept that.

Until a few days ago when my foster parents sold me to this company.

Who knows what they want with me, but I'm sure it has something to do with the power I have that scared them. Better to give me up and make me someone else's problem. Getting paid for it probably didn't hurt them, either.

I'm betting everyone here is a pawn for the company that paid for me like some show horse. Are we just here for show or something more?

The girl tugs at my sleeve, bringing my attention back to her. She doesn't look frightened when I look at her like others do. She smiles brightly when she has my full attention now.

"What are you making?" She points to the paper in my hands.

I finish the crane in a few more folds, then lift it in the palm of my hand and blow behind it. Once the air is there, I use my gift to guide the lightweight object to her cupped hands that formed as soon as she saw it take flight.

She gasps when she catches it, and I wait for her to say something about my gift.

"It's so cute! How did you learn to make this? Can you show me? Can you do any other animals? Can I keep it?"

I blink slowly at her while taking in her reaction. The flush of her cheeks as she studies it from different angles with excitement. The rapid words falling from her lips as if she can't wait to get all of her questions out before taking another breath. The clear blue of her eyes that are wide in amazement.

"Sure."

Her smile grows as her hands wrap protectively around the paper bird to keep from crushing it. "Thank you...?"

"Jackson. Or, Jack."

"I love it, Jack! Thank you!"

I made hundreds more origami animals for her after that day, and now I can't make one without thinking of her. But then, she's never been far from my thoughts.

I would gladly share this one with her now, but it's too soon.

If I've learned anything over the last two weeks of watching her, she no longer trusts anyone. Least of all, those of us from her past.

I don't blame her.

She needs time to process seeing me again and what, or who, she's already realized will follow. I need to use the time I've lured her here for to prove myself to her. The others can do what they want, but this time, I'm not letting her go, no matter what it takes.

Raegan finishes cleaning herself up and leaves out the main door without ever looking up.

People never look up.

I swing forward and push air beneath my feet to help me switch from a sitting to squatting position on the metal bar I've been perched on since following her here. I pocket the crane and walk steadily across the one-inch bar to the high window I left unlocked for myself. Even if my body starts to lean to one side, I easily shift the air around me as a buffer to keep myself balanced.

Once I'm outside, I stick to the rooftops as I follow my little one. The buildings are close enough together that it barely takes any of my gift to keep me aloft and complete the jump.

She returns to Hype, where she'd been last night. I wouldn't trust this type of location for her to be in without someone watching her back, but it's the nightclub owned by Elias Thorton.

She'll be safe here.

The monster in me stirs at the thought of Elias touching Raegan, and I let its hunger for violence swell in my chest and spread through my veins like poison. My eyes close, reveling in the darkness as I soak it all in. I won't hurt Elias, not tonight, because I haven't even begun to prove myself to Raegan to be worthy of her. But I can feed the monster what it wants to keep it sated for now.

It's time to get back to work.

The guy's already cold when I get back to the warehouse, even though it's only been a couple of hours since I left. I should have cleaned him up first and then caught up to follow Raegan, but the thought of her wandering this area of the city, unaccompanied for even ten minutes, didn't sit right with me.

It was a chance worth taking for her.

If anyone found this place while we were gone, I'd have taken care of them and any trails that led back to her or me.

The cabinet in the corner contains a small portion of my clean-up supplies, so I grab what I need and stalk over to the body. The recruiter scum's eyes are still wide open, but they're glazed and empty now.

He deserved far worse than a simple headshot. I'd saved a four-year-old girl from GE's clutches when I grabbed him. Who knows how many others he'd taken in his time with the company? One little girl out of possible hundreds means this isn't really a win for our side.

They have so many recruiters that they'll hardly notice the loss of one.

I've taken out enough of them over the years to have slowed their progress substantially but not stopped it.

They'll never stop so long as those in charge are still there to brainwash and coerce others to join them.

It's why we're now aiming for the top.

After we escaped the island, we took some time to adjust back into society. Two years ago, we realized that we may have gotten off the island, but GE was still around. We, and other people with gifts, would always be hunted by them. There are other islands and other gifted people who didn't get the opportunity we did to escape.

The least we can do is help free them and end this group before they achieve their goal of controlling the world from the shadows by using people like us to do it.

I shove squares of gauze into the holes in the guy's head and knee to stop the blood that's now oozing from the wounds. At least I'd gotten some pain out of him before I'd gifted him to Raegan. And now I'll make him disappear like he'd never existed. No one to miss or mourn him and certainly no one to ever find him.

Gone like ash in the wind.

Stepping back, I wave my hand to send a rush of air beneath him and the chair, then hold it in place to keep them hovering off to the side as I get to work clearing the blood from the concrete.

My special concoction of bleach and corrosive chemicals spills out of the jug I'm holding and over the blood and sweat and whatever other possible evidence might be on the concrete. It bubbles right away, foaming and hissing as it eats away at what it finds in a sound that's so familiar it makes me smile.

After a good few minutes, it leaves wet concrete in its wake. I dust my second concoction over top in a fine white powder that will absorb any moisture over the next hour before I can sweep and dump it.

With that taken care of, I climb the walls to the metal bars along the underside of the roof and then open the unlocked window. The dead recruiter in his chair follows behind me, floating, as I slip back into the night, moving from rooftop to rooftop further away from the heart of the city.

Once the recruiter has been disposed of, I decide it's time to return to my brothers.

I barely open the door into our primary apartment, the Loft, before Dane whines, "Are you fucking kidding me right now?"

My mouth quirks into a smile as I move further into the room, then plant myself behind where Dane's seated on the couch and cant my head to the side as I look at him. Most people shrink back with fear when I give them this look, or even just by having my attention trained solely on them, but he's known me since we were kids and moves back out of righteous indignation rather than fear.

"Jackson. Back the fuck up. You are *covered* in dirt and blood, and I don't know what else, and you reek of gasoline and smoke. Why didn't you stop at the safe house for a shower before coming here? Hell, swim in the lobby's fountain on your way up for all I care. We don't bring that shit here." He twists around on the couch to glare at me while simultaneously adding more space between us.

I shove my hood back off my head, revealing my black hair which is a stark contrast to Dane's dyed blond hair. The blond is a reminder for himself and to all of us of who we lost. But also proof that he doesn't know how to move forward from the past.

It's annoying.

"If we're dropping the rule for not bringing work back here, then I don't want to hear shit about cleaning up here after my nights out," Kellan drawls from further down the couch, his eyes still locked on the video game he and Dane are playing.

I may be covered in shit, but Kellan looks it. His self-care has gone out the window as his brown hair and beard grow wild, and the scent of alcohol wafting from his body is strong enough to taste it on the back of my tongue. It's been a couple of months since I've seen them, and while he's been riding the self-destructive train for a while now, it looks like he's recently taken it to the next level.

I'd feel guilty for being gone so long if there was anything I could do about it, but years of trying have proven that the problem can only be fixed by him if he wants it.

And he doesn't.

Kellan's avatar dies in the game, and he drops back into the leather couch, his hand fisting around the neck of a bottle of whiskey as he guzzles it down like it's water. Only after he's polished it off does he whip out a cigarette and plant it between his lips.

"Oh, hell no." Dane dives over to snatch it, but Kellan grabs him by the face to hold him back. "You are not smoking in here."

I look to the high-backed, winged chair where Aiden is sitting exactly where I expected him to be. Rather than watching the spectacle of the other two, his brown eyes are locked on me.

I raise my eyebrows at him in question of what he wants.

"Find anything of value while you were gone?" he asks, still ignoring the ruckus happening on the couch just feet away from us. It sounds like Dane tried using his gift to stop Kellan, but the guy runs and participates in fight clubs as a hobby. Dane doesn't have a chance against him.

The second I smell cigarette smoke, Aiden's eyes snap over to them. "Take it outside, Kell."

Kellan chuckles and stands, taking a deep drag from the cigarette and then exhaling it at Dane. "Calm down, Rapunzel. You know I'd never stink up your tower." He stumbles toward the balcony and shoves the door open, then collapses into the chair out there.

Dane's jaw ticks while watching him, then he pins his glare on Aiden. "I'm taking his gift and stabbing him next time he does that."

My face remains blank when I look back to Aiden. I hadn't realized things were getting this bad between us. There was a moment when we all came together, and it seemed like we would be okay, but the past year has shown me that isn't the case. We were like broken pieces of glass. We fit together, but it was unstable. Just as easy to cut each other than it is to line up all of our jagged edges.

We were missing the glue that kept us together.

Raegan.

I finally answer Aiden. "There's a gala happening on the twelfth at Reynard. Only Gifted Enterprise employees are in attendance, aside from the invited donors to their cause. There's a hefty buy-in to attend and then a silent auction to support different research or specific kids."

I have everyone's attention now. Even Kellan's, whose gaze I can feel through the open balcony door.

Dane nods sharply, back to business. "Right. I'll get you an invite, Aiden." He gets up from the couch and moves to his workstation, where he spends ninety percent of his time. It's a long, L-shaped desk with three rows of three monitors, each curved in front of him. He taps away at the keyboard a mile a minute.

"It's black tie formal, and you'll need a mask," he calls out once he has Aiden's invite up on the screen.

"Probably to protect their own identities, but it works out for us too," Aiden muses, his thumb and forefinger rubbing at the light brown stubble along his jaw. "We'll do the usual. Dane on overwatch and Kellan on standby outside."

I nod and move past them toward the hallway that'll lead to my room now that my message has been delivered. That's my job, pulling information and then taking out the trash. The other three handle the rest from there.

It's a process that Aiden put in place once we started working together to take down GE and got the resources to make that happen. Getting this building, a stockpile of money, and different revenue streams allowed us to focus on helping others and trying to work our way up the chain of Gifted Enterprise personnel. Seeing Raegan broke and on her own is a reminder of where we could have been if not for a lucky break and Aiden's overachiever business sense.

I flex my hands to soothe the building frenetic energy tingling beneath my skin. I need to rest so I can get back to helping her.

"Wait." I stop just before the hall at Aiden's voice. "Don't you have something else to share with us?"

My lips twitch upward. Nosey bastard. Of course, he knows. How he knows and Dane doesn't is a surprise, though. I turn on my heel to face the room again and shrug, but the smirk stays on my face. "Not particularly."

It'd be better to give myself more time with Raegan before the others find out about her. But Aiden, being the control freak he is, can't stand me keeping this secret from the rest of the group.

"Who broke into our safe house the other night, Jack?" he presses on, his forehead furrowed with frustration that I'm not just coming out with it.

"No one broke in."

Aiden pins me with a look. I've known him since childhood, so

I'm immune to it. I hold his gaze, my smirk widening as he struggles with maintaining his control beneath the façade he wears. "Fine. Who did you let into our safe house?" He breaks first, and now my smirk is a full-blown, maniacal grin that's as much mirth as it is a baring of teeth.

"Raegan."

There's a crash and the sound of glass shattering, followed by Dane swearing up a storm. Kellan's back in the room, cigarette dangling from his open mouth in shock. And then there's Aiden, still sitting in his fancy chair and staring at me as if he's waiting for me to spill all of my secrets to him.

He should know me better than that.

I start to turn away from them and pause again when Aiden speaks. "Is that it? You're not even going to share what happened or why she just so happens to be in this city?"

"No." My gaze alternates between the three of them, then lingers on Dane a bit longer. He's taking deep breaths, and his hands are clenched in his hair.

"What the fuck, Jackson?" Kellan finally spits out. He throws his cigarette out the open balcony door and storms up to me, fisting my hoodie. I can't help that the grin is still there, even if I can see that it's pissing the others off. As much as this news upsets them, it's what I've been waiting five years for, and I'm excited as hell about it. Nothing they say or do will change that.

There hasn't been a day since getting off the island that I haven't searched for her.

I know there's more to the story with Vera, but the staff never gave us a chance to talk again after we found out. And then the island was destroyed and we were forced to escape before I could find her.

"What do you want me to say?"

Dane's voice cuts in before Kellan can respond. "Get rid of her." His voice is low and dark but fierce in his resolve.

The darkness in me rears up in defiance at the threat toward her, and my body stiffens. It's a sign only my brothers recognize as me preparing to strike when I'm angry, and Kellan's grip on me tightens. "Don't," he warns under his breath so only I can hear him. But it doesn't matter because *no one* threatens Raegan around me.

The knives under my hoodie are out and in my hands in seconds. Kellan shoves his body against mine until the blades sink into him to keep me from sending them at Dane. He grunts from the pain but doesn't budge, keeping me pinned against the wall and gripping my wrists, so I can't pull the knives out or go for more. It's a painful trick, but effective, as his gift will heal him anyway.

"He's right. She could still be working for GE and may be looking for Dane. We just need her to leave this city without finding out he's here," Aiden reasons, like Dane's comment was merely saying to kick her out of town.

We all know he meant killing her.

I'll have to keep an eye on him as well now to make sure he doesn't go rogue in his personal vendetta if he's already prepared to kill her.

"That's not—" Dane starts, but Aiden cuts him off.

"No one is killing her, Dane. As long as she's not in our city, we agreed to leave her alone."

Dane jumps to his feet. "But she's in this city now! Why are you still defending her? She's one of them!"

"Are you telling me you'd have no problem hurting her? Even after everything we'd all been through?" Aiden asks slowly.

"Everything on that island was a lie. She wasn't *real*! You're protecting the memory of a girl who never existed in the first place," he snaps back coldly.

Kellan's hands tighten on my wrists. I don't think he realizes he's done it. It's an involuntary reaction to what Dane's saying that speaks volumes to where he stands.

"What if she's here to kill one of us next?" Dane adds angrily. "She was willing to kill my sister, after all."

Aiden's tone is firm when he answers without hesitation, "Then, I'll handle it."

I already know none of that is true. She looked ready to run when she saw me. And she killed the GE recruiter instead of saving him. I'd bet she's been fighting them all this time like we have.

I don't bother saying anything when their minds are already made up. I'm going to find out why she killed Vera on the island and what happened in the years since then. I doubt they'll listen until I have that.

There's a stretch of silence where I'm sure there's a stare-down happening between them, but Kellan's bulky frame blocks my view.

Dane makes a noise of frustration and drops back onto the couch.

Aiden picks up where he left off. "Jackson, will you be able to handle getting her to leave, or do I need to do it?"

I know he's hoping to keep it a secret that the rest of us are here, but he also knows how obsessed I've been with her since we were kids. All of us wanted her back then, and we each fought for her attention in different ways.

I'm the only one who never let go.

Kellan looks at me, and I can see the conflicting emotions battling in his eyes before he locks it down to his default devil-may-care attitude. I shove at him, driving the blades further into him to get him to back off of me, but he just grins at me. "Or maybe I should do it?"

Prick.

As if I would risk them actually scaring her away when I just found her.

I smirk at him. "I'll talk to her. Now. Get. Off."

He pulls back, and the knives, which are still in my grip, slide out of him. I wipe them on my hoodie and slip them back into place. His wounds are already healing and turning a hard gold when I move past him and the others to the balcony. I start my controlled descent from balcony to balcony until I can make it to the roof of the nearest building.

There's no chance of me hanging around the Loft now that Raegan's name has been dropped, so I'll have to go to the safe house for a shower and change of clothes before I check in on her again.

Not to threaten her away from the city like they want. Little do they know I brought her here, though I'm sure Aiden suspects it. He thinks time and what happened on the island may have changed my mind about her. I haven't spoken a word about her since we left the island to give him a reason to believe otherwise, but the idea of me growing out of my obsession is laughable. It's stronger than ever with the years lost between us that I need to catch up on like I need air to breathe.

At least tonight confirmed that Aiden doesn't want to hurt her, even if Dane does. My little one won't be scared away by Aiden or Kellan if she has a mission in this city, so their threats mean nothing so long as Dane is left out of it.

I just need to earn her trust before then.

Chapter Six

RAEGAN

The thumping of the bass in the nightclub echoes in my chest and vibrates down to my feet. I close my eyes and smile as my body becomes a part of the music, and my muscles twitch with the need to dance and drink the rest of my night away.

But I have business to deal with before I can let loose.

The bar is long and translucent, so the lights bouncing off the walls and floor are reflected across the counter in various colors. Four people are working behind it when I squeeze into a tight space and lean forward to make eye contact with the closest one. She's small and skinny, with the top of her dark hair pinned up in two messy buns and the rest of it flowing down to her lower back. There's glitter on every inch of exposed skin, which is everywhere except her nipples and ass, that sparkles under the lights.

When I catch her attention, her entire face lights up with a smile like the world is made of unicorns and rainbows. The saturation of innocence around her stuns me for a moment.

"What can I get for you?" Her voice is sweet and soft but somehow loud enough I can still hear her over the music and crowd around us.

"I need to see Elias. He told me I could find him here."

"Oh, of course!" Her smile somehow *brightens,* and I decide this must be what it looks like if someone grows up in bubble wrap. Is it bad that I'm torn between wanting to protect that and pop it at the same time?

She points further into the club and then angles her finger back. "His office is down there and to the left. Take the stairs up, and he'll be the last door at the end of the hallway." Then she looks me up and down. I'd normally snap back at her for it, but there's no judgment in her gaze. She's not sizing me up or picking apart my appearance. Just taking me in. Not so different from Elias when I woke up this morning. "Do you want me to make you a drink to take with you?"

Yes, please. "A gin and tonic." I smile at her because hers is freaking contagious, and I dig into my bra for cash.

"Great! It's on me." She mixes the drink and slides it over to me, then takes on her next customer before I can thank her.

I watch her for another minute as she flits around from customer to customer, mixing drinks and sharing her glowing smile with everyone she meets. Like a sparkling butterfly or something.

Huh.

The drink is perfectly mixed.

Of course it is.

When I make it to the door, I knock three times and open it after Elias calls out to come in. He's sitting behind his desk and computer, still dressed in his gray suit and looking just as put together as he did first thing this afternoon.

He looks up from his computer when I plop myself down on one of the two sofa chairs in front of his desk and raises an eyebrow at me after taking me in. Then he leans back and steeples his fingers together over his leg he's crossed over his knee. "Welcome back, Girl-with-no-name."

I take another sip from my glass and then set it down on his wooden desk. His eye twitches as he looks at it. "Elias," I greet him with a nod. "I'm here about those resources you offered me. Are they still available, and what do they cost?"

His gaze doesn't move from my glass like it's offended him for being there. He leans forward, pulls something from his drawer, then picks up my glass to wipe the condensation from the desk and places a coaster beneath it before setting it back down. He shifts back into his seat as he was before and answers me without missing a beat.

"What resources are you in need of specifically?"

I scoff and roll my eyes. "Really? You're a neat freak and you own a nightclub, of all things?"

He chuckles. "The two aren't mutually exclusive. I can have a clean nightclub."

"Sure, whatever. It looks like I'll be in town for another few days, but it may be longer than that. You mentioned something about a place to stay? I can work in the club most nights or clean during the day. You can keep me off the books and make money off of me if I can use one of your apartments rent-free. And I'd like to keep any tips I make."

His eyebrow raises, and he taps his steepled fingers together. "Do you have experience working in a nightclub?"

"I do. I can bartend, barback, dance, clean…anything but cook." It's the same arrangement I had with my first boyfriend. I had to dance and bartend at his club to cover my side of the rent and utilities, but this time, I'm keeping one hundred percent of my tips.

Elias watches me carefully and then nods. "I have an open one-bedroom apartment on the fourth floor. Use it for as long as you need. You can also work when you need cash to get tips, but don't worry about rent. All I need from you is your ID, so I have proof you're over twenty-one."

Ah, fuck.

He sees the look on my face and sighs. "No ID?"

I smile cheekily at him. "Nope."

"How old are you?"

My shoulders lift in a casual shrug like none of this bothers me.

It does. A little.

"Twenty-two. Give or take a month."

"Eventually, I'd like to hear your story. Hopefully, my resources can earn a bit of your trust in me, so I can actually help you."

I squint at him because I just can't figure out his angle. Why would he be bending over backward to help a complete stranger? Why would he care about me when I've given him nothing? "You first. Why are you helping me? I can't trust you if I don't understand why you would offer so much to someone who could be a serial killer for all you know."

Which I am, technically. If it means someone who kills multiple people. And there being a trend for the victims. Because my targets are all tied to Gifted Enterprise. I've honestly lost count of how many people I've killed.

For and against GE.

I'm the villain here. Exactly as they wanted me to be, except for one key detail. I'm aimed at them instead of their enemies.

Elias nods and smiles. "Understandable. I'll share my story with you then, with the hope that you'll give me a bit of yours. It goes without saying that whatever we're sharing right now remains between the two of us, correct?"

I simply nod and pick up my drink again in case I'll need it.

"Good. I was born with the gift of Truth. I can tell when someone is lying, when they are omitting information, and I can also see who has a gift or not."

"What do you mean, you can see it?"

"It's hard to explain, but I guess I'll go with calling it an aura. Someone with a gift emits an aura around them that I can sense. It doesn't tell me what they can do, but I can get a general idea of how strong they are when I compare the feeling with others." He shifts forward and waves a hand toward me. "You, for example, your aura feels heavy. What's normally a tickle is more like the beat of a drum. But unsteady. No real rhythm, as if you haven't found the right beat yet."

Unsteady. As if I needed someone to confirm who I am by comparing me to a musical instrument.

My walls go up, and my posture stiffens now that I've officially been outed for having a gift. It's rare. Selected politicians and organizations are obviously aware of us, but even they are keeping us a secret from everyone else. So they can use us against others like weapons. And we're too afraid to out ourselves out of fear for what the general population would do to us.

The Salem witch trials are proof we wouldn't be accepted.

That was the first time people like us had been discovered. And they were hunted. Tortured. Friends and family looked at them with hate as they were burned at the stake.

We're the generations later from those who survived. Still trying to survive.

It doesn't matter that Elias admitted that he's gifted like me. It doesn't make me feel any safer. Keeping this secret is paramount to survival. The more people who know about me, the more in danger I become. And I'm already on the top capture list from a worldwide organization full of powerful people with unlimited resources.

I shift in my seat so I can spring up and out of here at a second's notice if I need to. I can use my gift against him if I have to in order to escape, or if I can't trust he'll keep my secret, but I'm not ready to use it just yet. He hasn't actually said anything that insinuates he will rat me out or that he knows who I am. Just another gifted in the world.

Elias watches me as if he can read every thought in my mind. I freeze. "Can you read my mind?"

He chuckles and shakes his head, but it isn't until he speaks that I relax a little. "No. I'm pretty good at reading body language, but that's not a component of my gift." I nod, and he continues, "Someone close to me was hurt because of people hunting us, and there was nothing I could do to save them at the time. I worked to build myself up until I could get them back, but when I did, there was a stain on their soul I could never erase. I've sworn since then to help as many gifted as I come across. Either to keep the same thing from happening to them or to help them recover and get back on their own two feet."

Elias pauses and then inclines his head. "I believe you're the latter, so I'd like to help you as much as I can. I'd be able to help you better if I could learn more about what you're going through or trying to accomplish. But I also understand if you don't fully trust me either."

Well…I swallow the words I'd normally say in self-defense. Do I believe him? Not completely. I'll never blindly put my trust in someone else ever again. Not after having it broken and crushed to fine pieces that'll never fit back together again. The only person I can trust is myself. But I could use the help that he's offering me.

I started fighting back against GE three years ago, and I hate to admit that I haven't gotten far. One person with no support, no extra money, only my stubbornness and ability to survive whatever I've come across, can't realistically take down a worldwide organization.

I know that.

I've had too many close calls. Too many times where they found me because I had no idea what I was doing. I've only made it this far through luck and trying to learn from my mistakes.

But I'm far from where I need to be.

"Trusting people in the past hasn't worked out so well for me." Thoughts of my first boyfriend, who'd found me broken and alone on the streets after escaping the island and then took advantage of me, come to mind first. They're followed by the others who died just because they'd been close to me. Or who had given me up the second I told them about my gift.

He nods, accepting my truth.

"But I'm also not making much of a difference on my own. I can't keep going the way I have been and succeed." I take a heavy breath. "I think you actually have these resources that you talk about and you seem genuine. I can't trust you completely, not yet, but I could use some help."

When I don't continue, Elias presses gently, "What difference are you trying to make?"

I bite my lip. My survival instinct screams at me to keep my mouth shut. Not to involve anyone else, for keeping myself safe and them if they wind up as a casualty because of me. But...what more can I do on my own? Three years, and what do I have to show for it? Dead recruiters?

"I'm trying to take down a group that uses people like us."

His eyebrow raises. "How so?"

Ugh. I'd hoped that would be enough for him. "I was kidnapped when I was eight and taken to an island with other gifted kids. It was mostly school and one-on-one sessions to learn about our gifts at first, but I learned later that they were conditioning us to use our gifts for them. For their agenda. And if anyone refused, they were tied to a bed and experimented on until their bodies gave out. Or just killed. I've seen some of the people who were brainwashed by them. They think what they're doing is for the greater good, but they're just killing people or doing horrible things because it benefits the people in charge."

Surprisingly, he doesn't look shocked by what I've said. "You're trying to take down Gifted Enterprise." It's not a question, but I nod slowly anyway.

His index fingers tap as he studies me.

I'm afraid this is where he'll either draw the line and rescind his offer, or call in a tip to GE that I'm here. I tense, preparing again to fight or run, but he lowers his hands to his desk and nods toward my glass.

"Have another drink before you bolt on me. I'm surprised that you're going after such a big fish all on your own. How long have you been doing this?"

I take the drink without further prompting and finish it off. I definitely need the liquid courage to stay in my seat. "Three years."

Elias sighs and rubs his forehead. "Either you're extremely lucky, they want you alive, or you have a serious gift that can help you hold your own."

Shrugging, I place the glass back on the coaster. "Probably a mixture of all three."

"I've run into them a few times over the years, but my focus has been to remain off their radar. I work to keep others like us safe and hidden. Not shine a light on us by putting everyone I've sworn to protect in their line of fire by fighting against them."

I shift forward in my seat. "I'm not asking for you to put anyone else's lives in danger. This is still just me. If you can help me with information, then I'll do the dangerous part. I've been stuck only finding the recruiters, and they aren't getting me anywhere. Or, there's a gala coming up in a couple of days that could have actual board members attending. If I can somehow get an invite or be a guest, then I might be able to jump higher up the ranks and make some progress."

His pale blue eyes that are almost silver study me. "And once you're higher up the ranks, what then?"

"I—" Any words die in my throat as I realize I have a plan, but I don't actually have a *plan*.

He nods. "I see. You have a wish list. But you're lacking in a plan of execution. And unless you're some badass assassin who can fight groups of trained soldiers, *gifted* soldiers..." He pauses with a look, and I shake my head to confirm that's *not* the case. "...then I'll need you to promise me that you aren't going to run in there, gift blazing, the second you find someone higher up."

"Why? I mean, I know why I shouldn't do that, but why would you want me to promise you that?"

"Because I'm not investing my time and resources just to help you get yourself killed. If we come to that point, then you'll come to me and we'll figure out a plan together. I may not have a team of fighters under me, but I'm sure we can work something out that gives us the advantage." He taps his fingers against the desk again. "Although, the Guild may have those resources."

"The Guild?"

Elias stands and walks over to the window. He points to a tall, silver building that towers even over all the other skyscrapers. "They were taken over by new management about two years ago, so I can't say with great confidence where their loyalty lies. But based on the jobs they've been taking up lately and where I've seen some of its members involved, I'd guess they're enemies of GE."

He turns back to me. "Regardless, I'll do what I can to assist you. Without"— he holds up a finger—"involving anyone else. For now, at least."

He smiles at the shocked look on my face. "Don't look so surprised that I'd help. They've taken people from me as well, but I didn't have the resources at the time that I do now. And when I did, it was more pressing that I helped those I kept encountering first. This is a good opportunity for a partnership against a common enemy. Besides that, I have a good feeling about you. And I always trust my instincts."

"Um, I don't know what to say. Thank you? I mean, this all sounds too good to be true—"

"Don't get too excited. I'm helping with information and networking more than anything. The hard part is still on you," he reminds me.

Still, it's more than I could have ever hoped for, to have someone like him in my corner. Not to mention, the job and apartment that he'd originally offered me. I'm starting off much better here now than I ever have since being on my own.

I liked the freedom of going wherever I wanted, whenever I wanted. But now that the burden of worrying about a place to sleep, food, getting the information by myself is gone, it feels like I can breathe for the first time in a long time.

I stand and try to figure out the best way to thank him for...well, everything he's willing to do for me. A stranger.

Elias chuckles softly and shakes his head. "Whatever you're thinking, stop. You're making me uncomfortable and you haven't even said or done it yet. I'll look into the gala to see if there are any strings I can pull. I'll need a contact number so I can let you know my answer to that. And for any other communication, so you don't have to come find me here any time you need something."

Right.

I hold out my hand for his phone instead of offering mine. He's promised a lot of good things, but I'll need to see them in action more before I can trust that he will actually see this through and not just report me to GE for compensation or to protect his hide.

He doesn't seem put out by having to hand his phone over and easily places it in mine. "The gala is happening at the Reynard Museum of Art in a couple of days," I tell him, giving him the last bit of information I have on it. I type out my current number and send a quick text to it so we'll have each other's numbers and then...I hesitate.

I could leave it like this, just a simple phone number, but I could at least give him something to call me. I add myself to his contacts under the name "Rae." I'll respond to it, but it isn't my full first name, and there's no last name either for him to try looking me up. It's good enough.

I hand the phone back to him, and his brows quirk when he sees my name. "I'm sure it'll be a pleasure working with you, Rae. Don't hesitate to let me know if there's anything else you need. I'll text you the room number and code to get in for the open apartment next and then look into the gala." He walks me to the door and opens it for me.

It still feels too good to be true to have someone on my side and with the resources he has. But I can handle myself if this goes sideways. "Sounds good. Thanks again."

Chapter Seven

RAEGAN

"Mrs. Callahan!" Kellan's raised voice announces just outside the doorway to the teacher's lounge.

My hand jerks and coffee spills over the cup. Crap! She's earlier than usual.

I finish pouring both cups of coffee and then grab the nearest towel to wipe up the mess. My heart is pounding in my chest at the chance of being caught, but the adrenaline merely brings a wild grin to my face. Kellan will keep her out; I'm sure of it. He has my back.

"...and you look so, so...nice...today. I love the floral print." Kell schmoozes in his deep voice that would make even the most uptight of teachers breathless.

I'm used to it enough to keep my focus, although I won't deny a certain heat sparks beneath my skin whenever he uses that tone.

It makes me happier than I'd ever admit to him he refuses to call anyone beautiful *but me.*

Once both cups are made with sugar and creamer the way we like it, I sidle up to the wall next to the door and wait for Kell's gaze to check on me. He smirks when he sees me, then turns back around to face Mrs. Callahan.

"There's something I've been meaning to ask you, actually. Can we talk in here? It's...private. I don't want anyone else to overhear." He lowers his voice conspiratorially while waving his hand behind his back for me to slip out.

I hurry out in the opposite direction of them, counting on Kellan's large frame and off-putting words to distract her. I sneak a glance over my shoulder to see him using his body as a shield for me while he guides her into the teacher's lounge.

He's only fifteen, but already he's reached six feet and looms over most of the staff and students here. His shoulders are broad, and his muscles developed from either a crazy metabolism, or as a side effect of his gift, which he only helps by working out daily on top of it.

Pair that with his bronze skin tone, messy dark-brown hair, and roguish grin, and it's game over.

I make it to the cafeteria and slide into my seat next to Dane with the end seat open for Kellan.

Vera leans over Dane to look at my spoils and then rolls her eyes at me. "Really? You'd risk detention and extra work for that crap?"

My arms wrap protectively around the two Styrofoam cups on the table while I hover over them to keep them from view. I lift the one for myself and bring it to my lips. The hot, earthy bitterness sweeps over my tongue and nearly burns down my throat in my rush to drink it. I moan softly at the taste I haven't had all week and have been missing.

It's not fair that only the adults are allowed to drink this stuff.

Kellan stole me some once, and I was hooked. But getting any is always a risk, so we try to limit it to once a week.

Vera huffs and sets her drink down on the table. "If you're going for discreet, you're failing with all of that moaning." She stands and moves behind me, leaning down to whisper, "Unless you're hoping for a different type of attention."

My head pops up from my coffee. Jack's giving me a small smile across from Dane, and Aiden's no longer focused on the latest business book he's reading. His chocolate gaze is locked on me.

Dane smirks, leaning his elbow on the table and his head on his hand as he watches me. "Back off, Ver. She can make whatever sound she wants. If anyone else dares to say or do anything, we'll take care of it."

She chuckles and ruffles her brother's hair. "Oh, I'm sure you will, little brother."

"Hey!" He knocks her hand away, but she's already whispering in my other ear to keep her words private.

"Let me know when you're ready for some girl talk, Rae. I think it's time, don't you?"

My cheeks heat at the insinuation. I bite my lower lip and turn my head to look at her. She tosses me a wink and a wave and then struts away from the table.

I'm not sure how she seems so confident about boys. Maybe when I go visit the guys at night, she's spending time with someone in her class?

The breakfast hour ends with no sign of Kell.

"Relax, Rae. I'm sure he's fine," Dane tries to soothe me while we stand and clear our table. I cling to Kellan's coffee cup that's already gone cold.

"He should've been here a long time ago. Did he get caught?"

Dane shrugs. "Maybe he and Mrs. Callahan are still fucking."

I smack his arm. "Don't even joke about that. He wouldn't—" My words cut off when I catch the smirk on Jack's face. I rush over to him and tug at his sleeve. "Do you know something, Jack? He isn't banging the teacher, is he?"

He pushes the hair in my face behind my ear, his smirk growing wider. "Why do you ask? Would that bother you, little one?"

"Yes! I mean...because it's a teacher *and...does that mean he is?"*

Jackson chuckles. "Right. Only because it's a teacher." His blue eyes twinkle mischievously, but I don't bite. That is *the only reason I'm concerned.*

One hundred percent.

Maybe more like ninety...or seventy. Whatever!

"Do you want me to check on him?" he asks, canting his head to the side to watch my reaction while waiting for my answer.

"I'll find him and make sure he's okay," Aiden cuts in, snapping the book closed and passing it to Jack with a nod.

Jackson sneaks the books out of one of the teacher's rooms one at a time, returning the previous one after Aiden's finished with it. The books in our library are about things we'll never find useful. Like learning about weather and mitochondria.

Aiden has higher aspirations once we turn eighteen and get off this island.

If they actually do what they've promised us.

The guys don't quite believe it. I'm starting not to either.

"Hurry up and get to class and I'll meet you there," Aiden adds. We nod, trusting that he'll fix any problem Kell might be in, and start walking. I drop Kellan's coffee cup in the trash regretfully at the door.

"Wait." Aiden grabs my wrist to stop me. Both Dane and Jackson

stop too, but he waves them on. "Give us a minute."

Once they're out of hearing range, or at least Dane is since none of us know Jackson's actual range, Aiden turns to face me.

"You and Kellan need to tell me when you're doing things like this so I can make sure you both don't get in trouble." His voice is low and smooth like melted chocolate. It's pure ear candy to listen to.

I smile playfully up at him. I've had the biggest crush on Aiden for years, and it seems the only way to get more of his attention is by pulling stunts like this. Doing things he wouldn't 'approve' of just so he can pull me aside to tell me not to do it again. "But the risk is half the fun."

His hand slides beneath my ear with his thumb resting on my cheek.

My body stills at the contact. Tingles radiate down my neck, and I suppress a warm shiver. He leans in, stealing away the oxygen between us.

"I don't want anything to happen to you. We know there's more going on here than they're telling us, remember?" he croons softly.

I nod the barest amount. I can't speak right now. All the breath has been sucked from my lungs.

He smiles when I comply. "Good. If I catch you and Kell doing something like this again without warning me, then I'll have a punishment of my own for both of you."

My knees wobble. Why does that sound more like a promise than a threat? Is it both? Can I want both? It feels like my skin is on fire and my heart is melting into a puddle between my legs. Is this normal?

"Well?" Aiden prompts when I don't respond.

I'm not sure how I'm supposed to reply to that, so I just nod to avoid anything strange coming out of my mouth instead.

His thumb strokes my cheek, and it feels like a reward, before his hand disappears and I almost release a sound that I know I'll regret.

"I'll find Kell and make sure he's okay, so don't worry about him."

"Okay."

He waits for me to scurry back to where Dane and Jack are waiting for me before he goes the opposite direction to find Kellan.

My heart hammers in my chest, drowning out anything else as we walk.

I don't think Aiden's realized the effect he has on me. If that was what I got for sneaking some coffee without telling him about it, then I am definitely doing that again.

A knock at my door startles me out of my memories. I've been thinking about my time on the island far too much since seeing Jack again. I'm sure it doesn't help that there's a high chance I'll be seeing him or the others tonight at the gala, and it's almost all that's been on my mind when I'm alone.

I've tried to distract myself downstairs at Hype by giving Elias as much information about Gifted Enterprise and how they operate as I can and working the bar in the evenings.

Elias got an invite for himself with the information I gave him about GE and his own connections, or maybe it was waving around enough cash, so I'll be his plus one.

There's another knock, and I grab my gun from the counter. I click the safety off as I approach the door and peer through the peephole. Elias stands there in a suit with a bag hooked over his shoulder.

I open the door, my gun still steady at my side but aimed at the floor, and frown at him. "You're early," I say in an accusatory tone.

He takes in my dress and sighs. I'm wearing an A-line red dress that lands mid-thigh and poofs out with extra tulle under the skirt. There are fake diamonds sewn haphazardly all over it in no discernable pattern, and its sleeves are just two pieces of extra tulle draping down my arms. I'm pretty sure it's a crappy prom dress from ages ago, but I found it cheap at a consignment store and figured the fake diamonds glammed it up enough for a *gala*.

Based on his expression, I guess not.

He whips the bag in his hand out from over his shoulder, and it crashes into my chest. "Absolutely not. Put this on. You've got twenty minutes and then we're out the door." He brushes past me into the apartment and takes a seat on the living room sofa as if he owns the place.

Well, I guess he does.

I glance at the see-through bag and shrug. Maybe I can pawn this navy blue dress off at the consignment store with the red one after I'm done. After clicking the safety back on my gun and closing the door, I retreat to my bathroom to change.

This one is a long, navy-blue sheath dress with a sweetheart neckline, the barest of sleeves, and a flowing train behind me. The glitter or whatever is sparkling in a thin layer over the blue fabric is beautiful rather than tacky. It's mesmerizing. I never would have been able to afford this. So maybe I'll give it back to Elias when I'm done as a thank you for letting me wear something so nice once in my life.

Maybe.

I'd be tempted to keep it if it wouldn't take up so much space in my backpack.

I switch up my hairstyle to a fancy updo with soft blonde curls and waves framing my face and then fix my makeup with a smoky shadow to make my blue eyes pop.

I'm back in the living room with a couple of minutes to spare. Elias gives me a once-over and nods his approval. I'm expecting some heat between us; anything, considering we've slept together before and now I'm all dolled up, but he looks at me like this is just business, and all I can see is a nice guy helping me out. Just...nada. Zilch.

I shouldn't be disappointed that we won't be sleeping together after what I'm sure will be a heck of a night between getting close to employees of Gifted Enterprise and seeing old friends who despise me, but there it is.

Somehow, Elias feels more like a reliable friend than an ex-bed partner.

"I'm glad I got the measurements right. I'm usually good at guessing those, but dresses can be a bit more complicated."

It fits like a glove.

He stands, pulls a box from his suit jacket, and opens it to reveal two silver dangling earrings and a matching necklace with a sapphire teardrop. "This is just on loan, so I'll need these back," he clarifies while my mouth waters at the prospect of how much these might go for. He taps my chin to close my mouth, and I swallow.

Right. Just borrowing them.

"Got it."

He moves around me to place the necklace on my neck while I fiddle with getting the earrings in place. They're heavy fuckers, and I'm wondering again how much they're worth. And how much my current alliance with Elias is worth.

Unfortunately, his help in getting me closer to GE has been more valuable than anything I could pawn the jewelry for, so he wins.

He's a perfect gentleman and escorts me downstairs, where a black town car is waiting for us with a man in a suit holding open the back door. Elias helps me in first and then goes around to the other side to take his seat.

"So, what's your plan for tonight? Is there anyone in particular you want to speak with? I've no problem talking to anyone, but if you're looking to start a fight or a fire, I'm a bit more limited," he begins after the car starts moving and the divider is up between us and the driver.

I rub my hand against my thigh where I can feel the strap that's holding my gun and a blade between my legs. I wish I could have fit more weapons than my gun and three knives, but this dress and the strappy heels made those a challenge. This is the closest I'll be to this den of monsters in five years, and no number of weapons I wear in there will ever feel like enough.

I was broken when they had me, and I'll never let them touch me again.

"This is just intel gathering. So, names, faces, rank, or roles." I debate telling him about the possible complication I might encounter, and my hand involuntarily squeezes my thigh.

"What else?" he prompts me to continue. I look up at him and see him eyeing my grip. I quickly release it. "There's obviously something else on your mind. If you want support in there, tell me."

I close my eyes and take a deep breath. "I'm pretty sure some people from my past will be there as well. There's...some animosity between us. I'm hoping to avoid them if that's at all possible, but if not..."

Elias nods with understanding and finishes for me. "You need someone to get you out of there?"

"Just out of the confrontation. I'm not going there for them, so I don't want this to interfere with my mission. If you can get us out of the conversation, then that should be enough." Hopefully. I have no idea what they think of me after these years. If the hate burns just as strongly or even more so than when we last saw each other.

Aside from Aiden and now Jackson, I haven't spoken to Kellan or Dane since I was forced to tell them I killed Dane's sister.

If I have to bump into any of them tonight, let it be anyone but Dane.

I don't know if I have the strength in me to stop him if he decides to kill me.

Please let me escape this city without seeing him. I can handle the others. Just...not him.

The car pulls up in the line in front of the museum, and we wait our turn to get out. There are bright lights and cameras flashing when Elias opens my door, and I grip his arm more tightly than I intended to. I've spent the last few years in hiding and keeping my face out of pictures or the public eye to avoid being found.

Now here I am, having my photo taken for some stupid gala.

Great.

Elias seems to notice me curling myself into him more to avoid my face being captured, so he wraps his other arm around me and hustles us through. I can hear him greeting those around us with a smile on his face, but he keeps everything short and moves us along until we're inside.

He drops his arm and then tilts my face up, his eyes analyzing my face.

"I'm fine." I release his other arm and step back. "Stop searching for shit."

"Lie," he counters smoothly, reminding me of his gift. He pulls two sleek, black masks from his jacket pocket and hands me one.

"You believe GE will see your photo and come after you before you're ready?" he surmises in a hushed tone.

I nod solemnly and put the mask on. He's observant as hell.

"I apologize. I should have considered that earlier and given you your mask before we left the car. That's on me." He relieves a passing server tray of two champagne flutes and hands me one.

Shrugging, I take a sip while scanning the arriving guests. The masks vary from animals, to jesters and royalty, to over-the-top accessories that spread well-beyond their heads.

The masks are great news for me, but it will be harder for me to memorize faces if all I can see are their eyes and mouth. Some masks cover their entire faces, and with makeup around their eyes to blend into the mask, it'll be impossible for me to know what they look like.

As if reading my mind, Elias leans down to whisper in my ear. "I'll keep an eye on body language when we meet with people, but getting them to share about themselves is going to be your best bet." He offers me his arm. "Now, time to mingle?"

I down the rest of the champagne in one go, exchanging it for a fresh one from another server's tray. I have a feeling I'm going to need the buzz to get through tonight and loosen up a bit. "Yup. Mingle time. If I keep disappearing, it's to write information down for myself for later."

His blue-grey eyes sweep me from head to toe, and he gives me a puzzled look.

"My thighs," I answer his question with a teasing tone, and when he blanches, I straight up cackle at him. "I brought a pen and paper. Relax."

Elias grins and shakes his head. "I never know what to expect with you."

I pat his arm. "That's probably for the best. Keeps you on your toes."

Getting information out of people becomes easier as the night wears on and the drinks keep flowing, doing the hard work of loosening tongues for us. The donors are the easiest to speak with because they're oblivious to what they're actually giving their money to. A waste of time, really, so we move on quickly once we've identified that's all they are.

The GE employees we come across are more tight-lipped, but Elias is charming, and he can get a few to share bits of information that I'll piece together later. I have a handful of names to research after this, and I take it for the win it is.

On my way back from the restroom to jot down the latest name and information into my notes, I hear a scuffing noise and freeze. The hallway around me is clear, but I've been on the run long enough to trust that I heard what I did. I slip around the corner into a dark hallway and curse Elias for the long dress as I gather it up and out of the way, reaching for my knife when a hand covers mine over my thigh and another covers my mouth.

My body reacts on instinct, jerking to throw the person off of me and jabbing at their midsection to aim for their kidneys. There's a faint grunting noise—male—and then my arm is pinned to the wall with his body.

"I just want to talk," a familiar, velvety voice murmurs into my ear. He smells like cinnamon and freshly baked apple pie, which throws me for a second until he speaks again. "Let go of the weapon, Raegan."

Aiden.

I knew they would be here tonight, but I'd been so consumed by talking to everyone possible that I'd forgotten.

Jackson may be willing to let me walk away, but my last encounter with Aiden didn't end well for me.

I play along and relax myself, pulling my hand away from my thigh holster as he loosens his grip on me. As soon as I'm free of him, I shove off the wall and slam my shoulder into his chest to knock him back and then tear down the hallway.

My hands scramble at my dress as I run and try to get under the heavy fabric to reach for my blade again. Fuck long dresses. I'm never wearing them again. I finally get it out of its sheath when arms wrap around my shoulders and waist from behind, yanking me back into him.

I kick my foot back to try and nail him between the legs, or at least stab him with my heel, and he shifts in time, so I only catch his thigh. He curses and shoves into the backs of my knees to drop me, then pushes me against the wall while I'm off-balance. His body covers mine, pinning my legs and arms against the cool wallpaper.

"For fuck's sake, Raegan," he hisses. "You always make shit more difficult than it has to be."

He huffs at me when I glare in his direction, even though there's hardly any light to see by. I can't see if he has a weapon aimed at me either. If he thinks I'm going to go down quietly, then he has another thing coming.

But then, my mind and body don't always work on the same page.

Even with my life possibly on the line, my body comes alive at the feel of him against me. At his hot breath and smooth tone in my ear. At the almost sweet but delicious smell of him around me. I have to fight the urge to grind back against him. Fuck it. Maybe I'll do just that to scare him off.

I shift my ass the tiniest bit so that it's leaning into him, and he grips my hair. I'm forced to suck in my lips to keep any sounds to myself while also cursing him to the moon and back in my head for affecting me like this. This is *not* a turn on. And especially not with *him*.

Not when it reminds me of all the times he'd been close to me like this before.

When he'd kissed me senseless.

Even after all the time that's passed and the guilt that weighs heavily in my mind, my body is transported right back to how it felt being near him before as if no time has passed.

"What are you doing?" he demands. Like I'm a crazy ho rubbing up on him when he's trying to...I don't even know what yet. Kill me? Threaten me?

Shit. That's exactly what I'm doing, isn't it?

Why does he have to smell so good and feel so good, though? Why can't he smell like trash?

Why can't my body forget him?

His breath tickles the back of my neck and it's goddamn hard to suppress my shiver, but I manage it. "What are you doing in this city, Raegan? Are you working on a job for GE?" His voice is like cognac. Smooth and strong and so easy to get drunk on.

I focus on his words instead. On the confirmation that he still believes I'm working with the enemy.

I don't know why seeing Jack again made me think things might

be different after so much time. That maybe they'd realized something had to be wrong. Did any of them ever question what I said
and wonder if there was more to it?

Tears threaten to choke me, but I force them back.

*It's better this way. I can't tell them the truth about what happened
back then.*

"I'm not working with them," I tell him, steel in my voice. "I'm
hunting them. Let me do what I need to do and then I'll be gone
before you know it."

There's a pause like we're both holding our breaths before he
breaks the silence, his voice soft and deadly. "Am I supposed to
believe you've changed sides? That GE was worth killing Vera for,
but something else changed your mind?"

Gritting my teeth against the truth, I force out, "Believe whatever
you want. I'm telling you that I'm here against GE."

His fingers tighten in my hair, drawing a subtle gasp from my
lips. "Unfortunately, you've already broken my trust before. I'm not
taking that risk again where someone else gets killed. Leave this city,
and I'll leave you alone. But if I see you again, consider us enemies."

A stab in the gut would hurt less than the words he whispers like
poison that floods my veins. I knew if I ever saw them again, it would
be like this.

It doesn't matter whose side I'm on now. It doesn't erase what I
did.

This is the way it should be.

I harden my heart and fortify the wall between me and them.

"We already are," I whisper, my voice thick with emotion.

"Is everything alright over here?" Elias interrupts, and Aiden
quickly releases me and steps back. Light suddenly fills the hallway

from an open room where Elias has turned it on to better illuminate us.

Aiden's hands are already perched in the pockets of his black pressed slacks as if we'd been standing in the dark having a casual conversation. His brown hair is short and styled back, but aside from height and build, he looks just like he had when I'd seen him last. His eyes are cold as he looks at Elias like another enemy. Do they know each other?

"Everything's fine. Just old friends catching up," Aiden answers smoothly.

Elias moves to my side almost protectively, and Aiden visibly stiffens. Annoyed that I may have an ally? "I see. Well, I've been looking for my date for a while now, so I hope you won't mind that I'll be stealing her back." He smiles tightly and takes my hand in his. I let him because there's nothing more I have to say to Aiden anyway. He squeezes my hand, but I'm not fluent in what the heck that means, so I squeeze it back to say that I'm fine.

Elias pulls me away from Aiden without another word. My neck prickles with the feeling of him watching us all the way down the hall. I hate giving him my back after just declaring us as enemies, but it's also good to show him that I'm not scared of him.

Not now. Not ever.

Chapter Eight

RAEGAN

Elias doesn't ask me about what happened, and we continue on our hunt for information. But my mind isn't so forgiving and keeps running back over what Aiden said, and I'm only getting more and more distracted as it stews and festers. When I make a snarky remark to the current person we're talking to, Elias apologizes and excuses us.

"Go take a breath outside. Or are we done here?" he asks calmly. There's no hint of sarcasm or annoyance at my behavior. This man has the patience of a saint.

I nod. "Let me take a quick break, then I should be okay to keep going."

"There's a side exit over there that should be quiet. I'll wait just inside the door to make sure no one follows you out."

Ugh. Why was I attracted to Aiden shoving me against a wall but not Elias being considerate of me?

I'm definitely broken.

He guides me to the door and stands off to the side. I open it and am instantly hit with the soft, cool breeze of the evening. I take a gulp of fresh air and already feel like my head is clearer. I keep walking away from the building until there's some space around me. A single light above the door illuminates the area I'm standing in while the rest of the alley is dressed in shadows.

I clench my fist to my chest, trying to calm the frantic beat of my heart that hasn't settled since being near Aiden. He's thrown me off my game. I can't concentrate on what I'm supposed to be doing here, when all I can think about is how my body reacted to him. How it was drawn to him as much as it always had been. Like coming home.

And then having reality slap me in the face with the undeniable truth of all I am to them now.

Their enemy.

I *knew* I had to stay away from them. Hearing his voice one more time, feeling his body against mine...that's all it took to stir up the longing and regret I've been avoiding since I last saw them.

I slowly bunch my dress up to check for my weapons, only to feel something strange where my gun should be. I pull it out and then stare at the disfigured metal that comes out instead.

What.

The.

Fuck.

How dare he use his gift to warp my one good weapon. I stole it from the first Gifted Enterprise goon I took down on my own three years ago. It's my only long-distance weapon. The one that's gotten me out of too many bad situations to count. My *one* gun I used to keep myself safe and take out the recruiters. Aiden, that son of a *bitch*!

I throw the mutilated metal away from me and start cursing him eight ways 'til Sunday.

Now how am I going to get out of close calls without it? While I'd like to say that I've gotten better at this, I know I still make mistakes. But at least I had that to get me out quickly and have the chance to escape and start over again somewhere else.

Not only is he distracting me, but he's putting extra road blocks in my way.

"Aiden make that piece of art for you?" a deep voice drawls from the shadows.

I reach for two of my knives and turn toward the, unfortunately, familiar voice. I'm expecting a man of six feet to come out of the darkness, but a built, six-foot-four man steps out instead, wearing Kellan's face.

There's a cigarette dangling from his lips and a full bottle of whiskey clutched in his right hand. His beard is long and overgrown, his dark brown hair shaggy, and I'd call him a mountain man or Yeti if I didn't recognize the twinkling blue-green eyes staring back at me.

He looks...terrible.

There's a second of hesitation as I take that in while comparing him to the Kellan I remember. What happened to him? Why did Aiden look put together while Kell looks like he's been through hell?

I shake those thoughts from my mind as I think back to Aiden. I'm their enemy and I can't let my guard down. I've already lost my focus and my one gun because of Aiden. I can't afford to lose anything else with Kellan.

I raise my hands in a fighting stance with my knives poised to strike if he takes another step closer. "You look like crap," I tell him honestly.

He takes me in while sucking on his cigarette and then smiles, smoke billowing from between his lips. "Aw, don't be like that, beautiful."

The old nickname stabs at my chest, and I grit my teeth from the painful memory. "Don't call me that." *Don't make this harder than it already is.*

His face twists and darkens, but I don't understand what I've said that could have possibly upset him. He wanted nothing to do with me anymore, right? So, why make this more painful by rehashing old nicknames and memories?

By calling me the one thing he never called anyone else. The nickname that made me *feel* beautiful. Special. Wanted.

And we both know that's not what I am to him anymore.

He draws on the smoke again, and even though I tell myself that I shouldn't give two shits about him or why he looks like he does, I can't stop the words from tumbling out. "Smoking is a nasty habit. Maybe start with fixing that. And a haircut."

"I don't need advice from *you*," he sneers, taking another deep drag and getting closer to me like he's going to blow smoke in my face. I bring my blades against his gut and throat.

"Don't you dare blow that at me. I'll stab and leave you here."

Kellan turns his head to expel the smoke and chuckles darkly. "Oh, you could do so much better than knives. Why are you bothering with them when we both know the real weapon is *you*?"

He snatches my wrist and pulls it closer to him until a line of red wells up between him and the knife. "We both know you can never hurt me, but it's cute to see you try." He drops my hand and raises his arms up. "Go ahead. Do your worst. Let's see what you've got."

I yank the knives away, and if I slash his skin while I'm at it, then so be it. "What's the matter with you? You turn into a masochist or something?" I scowl at him and wipe the bloodied blade against the inside of my dress.

He scoffs and tosses his cigarette to the ground, then steps on it. He raises the bottle to his lips and drinks like he's gasping for air. It stretches out his torso, though, and I get a clear view of the scratch healing itself and then changing from skin to...something else. We never figured out exactly what it was. Just that it was hard and impenetrable once it filled in.

His gift made him invincible. Any injury would self-heal and then be covered in golden scales and impenetrable skin for the next hour that nothing could pierce through or scratch. He was right; I couldn't hurt him. No one could.

But that was one of the reasons why I'd leaned on him so much when I was younger.

He was safe from me. Always.

But now, he doesn't look at me like someone he wants to protect. He looks at me like the bad guy.

And I am.

"Good to know you spent your freedom doing nothing but smoking and drinking your life away." I funnel my anger at this entire situation that I've gotten myself wrapped up in tonight at him. I can't take much more of this. I need to push them away so we can all keep our distance from each other.

Kellan smashes the bottle on the ground and turns on me.

Okayyy. He may look like shit, but he's also huge. His body blocks out the light when he faces me until I'm lost in his shadow. "You don't know *anything* of what I've done these last five years."

"Of course not! You all left me behind. Whose fault is that?"

"Yours!" he roars. "When you betrayed us!"

"I didn't, I—" I slam my mouth shut and look away. I can't let the truth slip out. No matter what they say.

His hands grab my shoulders. "Tell me. Give me a reason that we can put the past behind us, beautiful." Kellan's expression is almost desperate. I've never seen him like this; like everything in the world has narrowed down to this one request.

I squeeze my eyes closed. I can't look at him without wanting to break my promise. I knew it would be hard. But knowing did nothing to prepare me for this.

If I told them, it would all be for nothing. The year I endured with Gordon. Keeping Vera's image preserved for Dane's sake.

It doesn't change the fact that I killed her.

I don't deserve forgiveness after everything I've done. Knowing Kellan, he'd probably give it to me anyway.

I can't give in just because seeing them again is hard. My promise to own what happened and protect Dane from Vera is stronger than this.

"I can't," I gasp out. "I made a promise."

"A promise?" Kell growls. "Is a promise more important than us? Than me?"

Yes. Breaking the promise would only hurt them more.

Kellan's face shuts down with disappointment when he sees my firm resolve. He releases me and steps back.

My chest tightens. *I'm sorry, Kell.* My only goal in life now is my revenge against GE.

It takes all of my willpower to keep any tears in check as I finish with, "There is no future for all of us. I've already moved on from the past. You should too."

I brush by him to the door, and he scoffs. "Oh yeah? You move on with GE?"

"I'm here to take them down." I twist my head to look at him over my shoulder, but he doesn't bother turning after me. "We're leaving," I tell Elias when he glances over to me walking in. "There's nothing more for me here."

Chapter Nine
RAEGAN

"You have something?" Hope blooms that I've actually done something right and made progress in my mission. I'm leaning against the door to his office in Hype, where we've been meeting almost daily to discuss GE.

Elias leans back in his seat and laces his fingers over his crossed legs. "It's not exactly what you were hoping for, but it is something." He waves me in. "Sit down, Rae. You aren't running off the second I tell you anything, so get comfortable."

I try not to let the disappointment show on my face, but I can tell from his expression that I failed.

It's so hard to hide anything from this man.

"Well, I'll still take something," I admit while moving to one of the chairs in the room. All the while I keep fiddling with one of my knives on my leg. Elias watches it for a moment before dragging his gray gaze back up to my face.

"Do you know how to use that?" he questions while gesturing to the blade.

I flip the knife up and snatch the handle in one smooth motion. "Enough. I'm pretty good at throwing them, at least."

That was easy to practice on my own. I'm not so good at fighting up close. I'm just as likely to cut myself as my attacker, so I try to keep my distance or go for a surprise attack when I can. It's hard to practice fighting an opponent with a knife when you have no idea what you're doing.

Pointy end in the bad guy? Easy.

Using the knife to block and attack without letting them use it against you all while moving? Nope.

He nods and leans his face into his hand. Even as he looks like he's getting settled in to listen, his posture and the air around him makes me think of a prince on his throne. One that cares about his people and who listens, but is of a higher breed himself all the same. "And why do you have it out now? You didn't in all of our previous meetings. Should I be worried? Did something happen?"

I huff out a laugh. Because he looks far from worried. Either he trusts me so much already, or he has a secret that gives him the confidence to not be worried sitting across from me when I've told him I'm good at throwing knives. His gift is Truth, which doesn't help in a fight. So, is it trust then?

"My gun is...broken. Can't be repaired. Which means I'm back to using knives, and I've been a bit out of practice. I'm just getting my hands used to them again." I cock my head to the side as a thought occurs to me. "Would you be able to get me another gun?"

He smiles sympathetically. "I'm afraid that's something I can't help you with."

"Why not?"

"You would use it against Gifted Enterprise, of course, and if you did wind up killing someone with it, the gun that's registered to me would come back on me. I can't have that kind of tie to something."

"Black market?" Elias blanches as if I told him to kick a puppy, and I sigh. "Sorry, I just figured you had those types of connections."

He runs a hand down the front of his three-piece suit. "Of course not. I came into some money at a young age and invested it in real estate and a few other things. It took some years of buying and selling to get me where I am today, but I assure you, I have everything I do through completely legal means."

Ugh, the one person I've allied myself with walks the straight and narrow, while I'm trying to kill and take down a shadow organization.

Good choice.

He nods, like he can read my mind. "It's why I can help you, but I can't *help* you."

"All right, got it. Let's get back to that guy at the gala, yeah?"

He pulls out a manila folder from his drawer and drops it on the desk between us. I reach over to pick it up and find a man's profile sheet, some photos, and employment records inside.

"Are you sure this is the right guy? It says he's a paramedic," I muse while flipping through the pages.

"You're correct. I had my doubts at first. This doesn't seem like any higher tier member of the organization. I almost couldn't find any connections between him and GE. And then I was able to pull the GPS history on the ambulance he works in."

"You were able to do what? How?"

"Not me. I know someone who could." *Right. Connections.* "Once we had that and the 911 dispatch call history for the days he worked, we found more than half of his stops weren't from emergency calls."

"So, the guy kept taking a break in random locations?"

"That's most likely what his employers believe, if they do track their ambulances. But once we add the times and locations to a map, it looks like he's going to very specific places. There's hardly a break between an actual call and going to these locations. And he doesn't stay there for long at all. Almost as if—"

"He's picking something up and dropping it off between calls," I finish. Or some*one.* "He's the one that grabs the kids from the recruiters to take them to the testing site." The reason that questioning recruiters means nothing is because they just take the kids to a random drop site and call it in and then the children disappear.

Elias nods. I whip out the map to look at the noted locations he and his "friend" worked on. "That's what we suspect as well. The downside is that every location is different. He never dropped off at the same place. So even if you go to one of the sites, they'll be long gone and using another one."

Damn!

I close the folder. "So, what you're saying is, I need to ask this guy for the next drop location or find out how he gets that information in real-time."

"That, or wait to see if I can dig up anything else."

I'm not great at waiting around. But I've also learned not to jump right into chasing someone down without doing my homework first. I need to follow his routine to find when he's alone, then come up with my plan to question him.

I stand, and Elias immediately follows. "Thank you again, Elias. Let me know if you find anything else on this guy or someone else from the gala."

"Of course, Rae. I promised to assist you in any way I could." He buttons his jacket and slides his hands into his trouser pockets. "Before you leave, I should warn you that there's a chance I'm being followed. I'll be keeping a low profile here for the next few days while it gets vetted out, but keep an eye on your back as well in case someone is onto us."

My heart sinks. They couldn't have found me so soon. And Elias wasn't supposed to be in danger by helping me behind the scenes. Could it have been the gala?

This is why I should work alone. I knew people getting close to me put them in danger, and now that I'm starting to care about Elias, I can't let anything happen to him.

He gave me another lead, and I'll have to make the best of him and do the rest on my own.

"Stay safe, Elias," I offer with a small smile before walking out. He tries to say something to stop me, but I'm already walking to my apartment before he can try to change my mind.

A week passes of following the paramedic and learning his routine. Elias keeps trying to check in on me and get me to stop by to see him, but I ignore his texts and calls. He's smart enough that I know he's figured out what I'm doing. I can only hope he'll get tired of that soon and go back to finding other people to help.

He doesn't.

He shows up at my door.

I'm tying my hair up in a ponytail when the distinct beeping sound of the buttons to enter my apartment goes off. I know better than to assume it's Elias because knowing Aiden, he'd somehow be able to find out my apartment and code to threaten me again, so I withdraw my longest blade from my thigh holster and cover myself behind the wall of the bedroom where I can still see the door.

I mentally curse him for the millionth time for ruining my gun because I'm now back to close combat fighting as my only real option. Asshole.

The door opens, and Elias calls out, "It's just me. I know you're here, so stop ghosting me."

I sigh and lean on the bedroom doorframe so he can see me. "If you know I'm doing it, then you obviously aren't getting the point."

He pauses when he sees my outfit and frowns. I'm in black cargo pants, boots, and a tight long-sleeve Henley with a gaiter wrapped around my neck. The gaiter can either cover the lower half of my face or come up to cover my entire head except for my eyes. Then his gaze falls on the dagger in my hands. "Am I interrupting something?"

"Yup. I was just heading out. What can I do you for, Elias?"

"Out? Do I want to know what for, dressed like that? Never mind, I don't. I can already guess." He strides to the couch and sits, leaning against the back cushions with his arms outstretched on either side and one leg propped up over the other. "Is there anything I can do to help?"

I sheath my knife. "I'm better off doing this particular job alone." I join him in the living area and choose one of the chairs to sit in to the right of the coffee table between us.

He nods like that was the answer he expected. "I'm heading out of the country for a few weeks. The person who was following me wasn't from Gifted Enterprise, but from a contact I have in Europe trying to reach me discreetly. There's someone he needs help with and asked if I could come out to get it all sorted."

I nod along with a straight face. I respect him even more for how he literally flies all over the world to help others out, and then I feel guilty that he's been helping me when he could save others. I've been fine on my own so far. I've escaped all of my nasty situations *alive* one hundred percent of the time, so I'd say that's a good record.

"I don't want to leave you while you're in the middle of—well, everything with Gifted Enterprise. If you need me to stay, I will. I have friends who can go out there for me to help until I can get there."

I blanch and shake my head in earnest. "What? No! Go. I'm fine here. Really."

Elias smiles. "I knew you would say that, especially since you've been avoiding me. Still, my offer stands if you change your mind. I don't abandon those I'm helping. Our arrangement will remain for as long as you need it. I do have friends in the city if you ever need help. I'll be out of touch, so you'll need to go directly to them if something happens. I can leave you with an address of where to go. Someone is always there, just tell them I sent you and they'll get you what you need."

The offer is tempting, but I won't take it. GE may not be following him like we thought, but it was a harsh reminder that I shouldn't have involved anyone else in my personal vendetta. Elias is too good of a person to get mixed up with me.

The people closest usually wind up dead.

I smile at him anyway, and his brows draw in as he pins me with a *look*.

"Don't give me that fake smile. Promise me you will use the help if you need it."

He reads people way too well. I sigh and roll my eyes. "Fine. I will." *If I'm dying and I have no other choice.*

Elias holds my stare for another minute and then pinches the bridge of his nose. "I've never had someone so difficult to help before. In any case"—he drops his hand—"I'm also here to ask a favor of you."

I cock my head to the side, and my hair sways with it behind me. "A favor?" What could he need that he can't get himself?

"There's...someone...I'd appreciate you keeping a lookout for while you're around."

That piques my attention. "Who?"

He rubs the back of his neck, and it's the first time I've ever seen him look uncomfortable. Or not in complete control of himself. "She works at Hype downstairs. I'm hoping you can just check in every now and then to make sure she's there and okay. She works every night shift, so it doesn't matter when."

I raise my eyebrows, and a smirk tugs at the corner of my lips. "A girlfriend? Or crush?"

Elias clears his throat. "Neither. Just...a friend. I'm looking out for her, and she tends to draw unwanted attention frequently. The security in the club already watches over her there, but she won't let them escort her home."

Definitely a crush. My smirk stretches to a full Cheshire grin. "I see. Sure, I can check in on your girl. What does she look like?"

Are his cheeks pink? Ugh, this is too adorable, and my black heart can't take it.

"Brown hair. Short, around five foot two. Green eyes. You can't miss her. She always has a smile on her face and lights up whatever room she's in. Even at the nightclub."

"Wait. Glitter girl?" I break into a fit of laughter and slap my knee. "The girl who dresses like a rainbow and smiles at everyone like they're the nicest person?"

His mouth is turned down in a frown, and if I didn't know better, I might think he's glaring at me. "Her name is Portia."

"Right. Portia. Okay, yeah. She'll be easy to spot and check in on."

"Thank you. I wouldn't have asked otherwise, but she knows my friends, and she would notice if they kept showing up at the club while I'm not there."

I nod, the grin still splitting my face. "Understood. It's a *secret* crush." He's about to say something, but I cut him off with a more serious tone. "If I can't contact you, what do I do if I need to report something about her?"

Elias looks torn between defending against my claim and answering me, but finally, he pulls an envelope out of his inner jacket pocket. "Go to this address, and the person there will be able to find me and get in touch."

I take the plain envelope from his hand and check inside for the slip of paper. There's an address, apartment number, and the word "Kit" written on it.

"Got it. Anything else?"

"One more time. Are you sure you don't need me around here for a bit longer? It looks like you're about to go out to fight GE. Are you questioning that paramedic now? I can stick around in case something happens."

"I'm positive. I've been doing this for years. Don't worry about me. Now, I at least have access to quick cash and a place to sleep every night. I'm better off now than I've ever been," I promise.

It's sad that it's actually the truth.

We walk to the door, and he pauses in the hallway. "Be safe, Rae."

I nod and smile reassuringly at him, then close the door.

The worst thing that can happen is that I die in the process of fighting for something I believe in.

That's far better than where I could have ended up.

Chapter Ten

RAEGAN

Now I'm running late.

I pocket my phone, double check all of my knives are in place, and then head out.

The paramedic should be asleep in his apartment now, based on the routine I've been tracking the last week. He works the day shift and sleeps alone in his apartment. It's a relief he doesn't have a family or roommate with him. Now, I can use his apartment for some one-on-one time.

Once I make it there, I slip around the back and begin my climb up the metal balconies. They're all independent of one another but close enough that I can stand on one and jump to pull myself up to the next one. I have to take it slow to keep from making enough noise to draw attention, which only adds more time to the plan. It's an exhausting exercise, and I'm glad I took a city bus to this area rather than walking.

The last thing I need is to be too tired to get this guy restrained and wind up getting myself killed because of poor planning.

I really wish I had my gun.

I count the six balconies that I've climbed and carefully step down on the metal floor so as not to make a sound. I peel off one of my gloves to expose my hand and then hold my palm against the glass door.

My gift warms in my gut as I call on it, pulling it to my exposed hand until it burns. Fuck, does it burn. I don't let my enemies know that it hurts me to use my gift. That I'd rather use a gun or a knife than pull on this little trick to destroy whatever I touch. But I'll also use it when I need to.

I grit my teeth and thrust my gift out from my palm in a rush. If I do this too slowly, the glass will crack and make noise as it falls apart. If I do it fast and hard, I can force the glass to dust in a matter of seconds with minimal sound.

The burning pain spreads down my arm, but then the glass is gone, and crystal dust falls in front of me like ash. I shake my hand in the cool night air, but it'll take a good fifteen minutes before the burning pain stops.

I carefully tug the glove back on and then flex my hand to make sure I can still move it through the pain. With my right, I grab a knife and point it ahead of me.

Then I push aside the curtain and step inside.

The apartment is dark, as I'd planned, except for the thin line of light under the bedroom door at the end of the hallway.

Fuck. Is he still awake?

I creep closer, focusing on silence and stealth more than speed, then freeze when I hear bone breaking followed by a groan.

"—where it is. One bone every time you don't answer the question," someone growls from inside the bedroom.

"Did you know there are 206 bones in the human body?" a nonchalant second voice adds.

Son of a bitch.

The first one roars with laughter. "Did you hear that? Sounds like you have 203 chances left. I guess we've got some time together still."

Kellan and Jackson.

I turn the door handle and throw it open. There's no point trying to sneak in. Jackson would kill me before I could even see the room. At least this way, they'll see me before they act.

I'm taking the risk, though, because neither of them tried to kill me the last time. So far, it seems like we want nothing to do with one another, and that's it.

I can handle that to avoid missing out on this lead.

I just wish they would stop showing up wherever I go.

The man that was supposed to be *my* victim is zip-tied to his gaming chair in front of Kellan and Jackson. He's covered in blood, bleeding profusely through his nose, and littered in bruises already blooming over his face. One of his legs is bent at a weird angle, which explains why they didn't bother tying his legs up.

I shift my gaze to Kellan, who's standing in a wide stance, his arms crossed over his chest and a scowl on his face. The bit of knuckle I can see on one hand is already scaled over, meaning he bloodied his fist and his gift took over to protect him. Apparently, he's using that armor-like skin to continue beating the guy. Kellan's jeans are ripped, his shirt maroon and tight across his chest and arms, accentuating the pure muscle he's developed.

Jackson is dressed like the first night I'd seen him in the city. All black, hood up, but his piercing blue eyes almost glow through the shadow of it as they lock on me.

Kellan looks like a pure enforcer, while Jackson looks like the God of Death, just waiting for Kellan to be done with him before he whisks him away to the afterlife.

"What the fuck, Jack?" Kellan growls at his friend. "You knew she was here, didn't you?"

Jack shrugs, which makes it difficult to tell if he knew and didn't care I was here or if I somehow surprised him.

Since my target is already bound and helpless, I yank my gaiter off my head. "What are you doing here? This guy's mine." I jab my finger at the guy whose head is bent over while he sobs into the carpet.

"I didn't see your name on him anywhere, beautiful," Kellan drawls in his deep voice.

My teeth clench as he uses the nickname for me again. To torture me? If so, it's working. It feels like a punch in the gut, winding me with memories and old feelings of safety and being cared about. And then it all slips through my fingers when he stirs those emotions up, because I may be physically close to them, but I've never been farther away.

"Well, I've spent weeks getting to this night. I'm not letting it get fucked up because of you," I snap back.

This is also my last lead that Elias worked hard to get for me before leaving on his trip.

I have to make this count.

Kellan scoffs and steps up into my space. I hold my ground, my hand gripping the knife at my side tightly. One wrong move, and I'll stab him in the dick.

Wait, would that scale up like everything else? Become an armored dick?

Fuck, not important. Focus.

He leans over me, because he's a giant compared to my five-foot-four self and smirks. "Not my problem. Now, skedaddle before *you* become my problem. Or more of a problem than you already are by being in this city." He smells of blood and musk, rich and dark and so delicious; my body heats with excitement at his proximity, even as angry as I am with him. I really need to get my mind and body on the same page.

"I didn't realize you owned this city. Where's your name stamped on it?" I snark back.

"Oh, it's on it. Trust me. You just need to listen a bit harder." He bares his teeth in a grin, and I'm tempted to stab him over it. Prick.

"Look. I'm not leaving until I get some information. Either you let me stay or—"

"Or what? You'll fight me? Don't waste my time." Kellan turns away from me, and I take that moment to lunge forward. He spins, prepared to block my attack, but I pivot and wrap my hand around the back of the restrained guy's neck. It doesn't matter that my glove is still on. It'll disintegrate first, and I can buy new ones.

"Fuck, you wouldn't," Kellan growls at me. Then he turns to snap at Jackson. "Are you really just going to stand there?"

"Or," I continue as if he never cut me off, "I kill him. Then none of us get the information, and we're all back to square one."

Kell swears viciously, and his face turns thunderous. "This isn't a race. Both of us losing only means they're winning. Let him go."

At least Kellan can't read my body language so easily to tell that

I'm bluffing. "Let me stay."

Jackson *tsks* and finally moves from his spot to stand in front of the guy in the chair. He squats down and leans his face into his fist as his elbows rest on his knees. "See what you've done? She might just kill you out of spite because you won't tell us one location. And when she does, believe me, it'll hurt far worse than anything he or I could do to you." His voice is husky and low but calm as ever while he talks about murder. Then he smiles, and a full body shiver takes over the man.

He continues, "Do you know what she can do? Her gift allows her to break down the molecular structure of things she touches. Primarily inanimate objects, but it works on people too. You see, people don't just turn to dust like other matter. It attacks your organs first. Breaks them down internally. Then it hits your skin, and it begins to crack. It splits apart. And finally, your heart bursts. It's all in a matter of minutes, but I'm sure you can imagine it'll feel like an eternity when it's happening to you." Jackson's smile is sharp and wicked, the gleam in his eye making it look like he's lapping up the fear he sees in the man.

"Would you like to give it a try? You can let us know how it feels. The others are usually too busy screaming, so we've never gotten a clear answer. Maybe you can do better," he finally finishes.

Even I have goosebumps on my skin at the threat, and it's *my* gift he's talking about.

Definitely broken.

The man is bawling now, his entire body wracked with sobs. "P-please no! I'll tell you! Anything. Just—" Another sob. "Not that. Not that!"

Jackson pats the man's cheek with a condescending smirk. "Good man. Let's hear it then."

"235 West Fillmore Avenue," he sputters as blood, snot, and tears hang from his face and lips. "That's the next drop off location. The burner phone they contact me with is there, on my desk. W-will you let me go now? I have nothing else. I swear it!"

Jackson stands back and nods. "I believe you."

Kellan steps up in front of the man to draw his attention. "You won't speak any of this to anyone. If I hear so much as a whisper that you opened your mouth, I will personally hunt you down. And believe me, there's nowhere you could go—"

I can't believe they're going to let this man go just like that. They've broken three bones and he's seen their faces. I learned the hard way, more than once, that leaving someone alive gives them the opportunity to go after you or rat you out. It's also how GE came to find out I was still alive and is now looking for me. I came *this* close to being killed because of that mistake.

I won't make it again.

Kellan's speech is the perfect distraction for me, so while he's reading him the riot act of how exactly he's going to get all of us in trouble, I take my dagger and drive it up and through the back of his neck and out his eye.

It takes strength to get it in there, but as long as you hit the spot right, it slides right through.

The man is dead in an instant, which is nice, considering the circumstances. I could have used my gift just as Jackson explained, but I don't know the full extent of his involvement in the organization. Being involved gets him dead. But only certain involvement deserves my gift as punishment.

There's a roar, and when I look up after tugging my knife out, a body slams me to the ground. Pain blooms into my side at the same time the wind is knocked out of me, and all I can focus on is trying to breathe.

"What the fuck?!" Kellan shouts in my face. "He was just a lackey. We were letting him go." I gasp for air. He pulls back the slightest bit when he realizes I can't breathe. He doesn't apologize, just glares at me with what looks like betrayal and disgust.

Right.

I suck in air and cough until I can get my lungs working again. "...kill you...later," I wheeze, trying to explain that the guy will come back or tattle which will get them killed later, but then I'm coughing again. Sharp stinging pain stabs into my side again, and I glance down. There's just enough space between us that I can see my knife is stuck between us, the blade on either side digging into each of us.

He hasn't even noticed. Or, at least, he's so used to the pain that he isn't even affected by it. But our blood is slowly joining and then running down my side to the carpet beneath me.

Fuck.

Evidence against us.

"Kill us? I thought you said you were after GE or are you here for us too? You just murder everyone you don't like now? Is that part of this promise that's so important to you?"

I pinch my eyes closed so he can't read the pain in them.

Murderer.

Monster.

Villain.

His weight is suddenly gone, and when I open my eyes again, Jackson's pulled him up and has stepped between us. His eyes are narrowed at the blood leaking from my side and the pool of our DNA now soaking into the carpet.

Fucking Kellan.

I yank my gaiter off to press into my wound to stop the bleeding, then groan and curl onto my side. My other hand presses into the blood-soaked carpet. My eyes close when the steady burn of my gift returns. I try to focus on the bloodied area of the carpet, but my control over my gift isn't what it used to be and it clears out a wider area than I'd planned.

Well, hopefully it's good enough.

I at least got to it and the padding beneath before any blood reached the floorboards, so aside from having no good explanation for why a chunk of his carpet is gone, at least our DNA isn't all over this crime scene.

I slowly make it back to my feet, retrieving my knife and wiping the guy's and now our blood on my pants before putting it away. There goes another pair of pants that I'll have to destroy and replace.

"You're welcome," I grit out through the pain.

Kellan's still glaring at me with eyes narrowed, so I just huff and decide not to bother helping with anything further. I wore gloves the entire time and now my blood has been removed from the scene. There's nothing here linking me to this man. Whether or not Jack and Kellan took the same precautions is on them; unless they know of a way to get rid of the body completely. No body means no murder.

When I check in on Jackson, he doesn't seem fazed. He's watching me carefully, but his face is blank, and he hasn't reacted at all to what I did with killing the guy or cleaning up Kell's mess.

I turn and freeze when pain lances through my side. Gritting my teeth, I force myself to keep moving through it. I leave without another word between us, and the silence echoes louder than anything else that could have been said.

CHAPTER ELEVEN
RAEGAN

A SHOWER DOESN'T WIPE away the misery that has me in a choke-hold.

Murderer.

Even though I'm trying to do the right thing, even though I'm doing what I must to survive, I'll never get away from being exactly who Gordon told me I was.

A murderer.

A villain.

If only the guys knew what our enemy had done to me in our year apart. What Gordon made me do. For him. *To* him.

Don't think about it, I remind myself before I spiral into those dark memories. I shove them back down, locking them away and repeating that Gordon is dead. He can't hurt me anymore.

My fingers shake as they probe gently at the cut on the right side of my torso. It isn't deep enough to need stitches, thankfully. I patch it up with first-aid items Elias has stocked in the apartment and tape a long stretch of gauze over it. I wince at the touch, but there's no blood on the gauze at least. Better.

Now that my thoughts and emotions are both haywire, I decide that I need to drink or dance until I'm ready to collapse if I'm going to have any chance at rest tonight. I can make money dancing and check in on Portia while I'm there, too, so it's killing three birds with one stone. Thankfully, Hype is still open for a couple more hours.

I put on a short, tight sheath dress with a halter top and sweetheart neckline. I've been able to buy a few dress options in my weeks here working the club at night with no rent to pay, and once again, I send another mental thank you to Elias.

Even though Elias's security personnel are all throughout the club, I still pack two knives. Complacency is a fast road to death in the world I'm in.

I leave the apartment and head downstairs to the nightclub. The only way to get to the apartments is through a back door in the club, which is a great way to avoid unwanted visitors and I'm sure was Elias's intention since he offers them to most workers in the nightclub.

It's late in the night, and the club is still packed, so I have to push through to make it to the bar where I know I'll find the sweet, glittery girl.

Portia is mixing a drink behind the bar. I head over there and walk behind it, deciding to barback for a bit to listen in on her and have a reason to be close. I start with topping off the ice trays, then work on restocking anything that's low or out.

She's chatting away with everyone who orders drinks, but after the third customer, I realize it's all surface conversation. By all appearances, she's being sweet and personable, but she's also quick to move on to the next person and end the conversation, so no one even realizes it wasn't them that did it.

When there's a lull in orders, and she starts wiping down her area, I move up next to her and start drying glasses. "Hey there, Glitter."

She turns to me with a smile, but it isn't until she recognizes me that her face lights up. As if her first smile was the one that she pastes on for anyone who speaks to her, but this is her real one. "Rae! I'm so happy to see you!" What's crazy is that she actually sounds like she means it. "I have to say, you are one of the hottest dancers up there. Your box fills with money faster than anyone I've ever seen," she gushes.

I focus down on the glass I'm drying. "Oh. Thanks."

"Elias told me you were just working to get some extra money, but you could really make a career out of dancing."

I burst out laughing and set the glass down. "For shaking my ass? No, I don't think they pay for that. Maybe strip clubs, but I'm not doing that." Not unless I have to.

She shrugs. "I don't know. Maybe you could work with Elias to set up some sort of show that has you and other girls doing a routine up there together timed with the music and lights."

That...actually sounds cool. Dance routines aren't something I've done, but it can't be that bad, right? Just one song.

I shake my head. Nope. No time for that.

"That does sound fun, but I don't think I have the time right now. Besides, Elias isn't here to pitch the idea to anyway," I add, hoping to steer the conversation in his direction.

Glitter tosses her used rag into the corner pile and then pulls out two shot glasses.

"Yeah. He didn't say where he was going or for how long," she muses softly.

I instantly feel bad and open my mouth to tell her what I know and then snap it shut when I realize what I was almost about to do. Damn, did she do that on purpose?

She looks at me with another smile. "I guess it's a secret, huh?"

I blink at her, thrown off by what's happening right now. *Is* something happening right now? No, I'm just overthinking it. "Um...I think it's just private business."

Some emotion flashes across her face, but it's gone before I can recognize whatever it was. "Oh, okay." Portia finishes filling the two shots with whiskey and then hands me one. "Here's to a good night, Rae."

We clink the shot glasses together, and I toss mine back at the same time as her. I'm confused as hell, but when she takes the glass back from me, she smiles brightly and then moves down the bar to take a customer's order, and I suppose she's letting me off the hook of responding to anything else.

Right.

Time to dance. That always clears my head.

There are glass boxes suspended in the air by steel cables with string lights inside along the seams that change colors and flash along with the music. Tubes, like the ones at banks, are lined along one wall with numbers that correspond with the numbers on the corners of each box. Customers can fill them with cash, and it'll shoot into the box so the dancer is dancing amongst their tips.

That's my favorite way of making money.

Anyone can go in them, even regular customers. Then they dance like crazy to see what tips they'll get. The dancer is untouchable in that box. Suspended over the dance floor, the beat vibrating through the glass, and lights pulsating with the music—it's perfect.

I've had too much experience with dancing on a stage and being grabbed or touched at my first boyfriend's bar.

Once one of the staff helps me into the box, I close the glass door, latch it, and then let the music take over my body.

I don't even pay attention to the bills that fly through the air around me. I close my eyes and bump and grind and twist until I'm one with the music. Every once in a while, I open my eyes to smile down at the view of the crowd moving below under the flash of lights.

I'm sweating by the time I'm ready for a break. I collect the bills, finding tight places in my dress to store them until I get home, and then press the button that lets staff know I'm ready to get out.

Portia waves her arms wildly at me, jumping up and down to get my attention from behind the bar. I laugh at her excited energy and lean against the bar.

"Girrrrl! That was so hot! You have to teach me how to move like that! Please, pretty please!" She's still bouncing up and down, and I notice the eyes around the bar all zeroing in on her jiggling tits. I still know absolutely *nothing* about this girl, but her innocence and excitement are damn refreshing, and I'll do apparently anything to protect it. For Elias and for myself.

I reach for her arm to stop her. "Okay, okay! Just...stop bouncing, or I might have to stab some eyes out, and then Elias's security will probably have me arrested."

Her eyes widen at the stabbing threat or me being arrested, I have no idea, and then she nods vigorously. "Got it. No bouncing." She slides a tray of shots over to me with an eager grin. "Not tonight since I'm working, but do more shots with me. It'll help calm me down."

I quirk an eyebrow at her, but she just giggles and picks up a shot without further explanation. I'm in such a good mood myself that I shrug it off and clink my glass with hers. Soon, she gets flagged to make another drink. She waves me off and says she'll see me later, and I check my own mental box that my task is done for the night of looking in on her. I've also made some good money and feel fucking *wonderful*, thank you very much.

I rarely let myself get this hammered when I'm on my own, but this is Elias's club. With security. Of all the places I've ever been, this feels the safest. Besides, I'm just another face in this huge crowd. The chances of GE knowing I'm in this city, in this nightclub, among all the people here, are slim.

I turn and lean back on the bar as the alcohol washes through my veins, and a warm buzz tingles across my skin. I stay there for a bit, letting the alcohol do its thing and having a few more drinks.

I debate going back out to dance, maybe getting lost in the crowd or finding some dance partners this time, when I get the feeling of being watched.

By luck or sixth sense, I glance over to one of the booths across the dance floor to find Jackson watching me.

Nope.

Nuh-uh.

I flip him the finger, hoping to keep him away and stumble-walk to the bathrooms. There's a hallway to the back left of the bar for employees only that I take full advantage of. I make it two steps into the women's restroom when a lock clicks behind me.

I reach for a knife at the same time as I whirl around, but the world spins faster than I expected it would, and I stumble off-balance. A hand catches mine and pulls me back up before I fall, but then I'm falling the other direction until I thump into them.

I know I should shove myself off of them, but everything is turning around me, and I need a second to close my eyes until my brain catches up with reality. That the world isn't moving like the tilt-a-whirl carnival ride.

I take a deep breath, and the smell of autumn, of crisp leaves and a cool, clear night fills my nose. My hair is gently pushed behind my ear, and I shiver at the contact.

"Come on. Let's get you back to your apartment," Jackson murmurs in my ear, tickling the hair there until I'm weak in the knees. He lifts me in his arms.

I want to argue with him, but the second I open my eyes to do so, the room shifts, and nope. No. I still need a minute.

The movement up the stairs forces me to focus on small breaths to control my nausea until I'm set down on my feet again. I'm at least leaning against something so I don't immediately topple to the floor. *Joy.*

Something cold presses against the back of my neck, and I sigh with relief at the coolness. It takes another minute until I'm ready and then I open my eyes.

We're standing in my apartment. I'm calm for about a second until I realize what that means. I groan and push slowly off of him. The cold item on the back of my neck disappears, but his other hand remains on my back while I wobble into balancing on my own.

Not only did he know how to get to these apartments, but he knew which one was mine *and* the code to get in.

"Stalker..." I grumble under my breath.

He doesn't deny it. I should be freaked out. Concerned, at the very least. I wait for those feelings to come, but they don't. I just feel...warm.

Must be the alcohol.

I glance up, and oh, look. He used his knife to cool me down. I mean, I guess that's something he always has handy on him, and it *is* cooler than my overheating body, but no...*Stop it. Stop rationalizing what anyone else would see as crazy.* "Most people use a wet washcloth," I mutter while looking at the knife.

He looks at it, then shrugs and puts it away. "This was on me. I wasn't leaving you."

Now that my equilibrium is somewhat returned, I'm able to focus more on the situation. He's stalking me. After he witnessed me murder someone a few hours ago. "Why are you following me? Are you reporting back to Aiden now?"

"No. Why were you at the nightclub tonight? You should be taking it easy."

I squint my eyes up at him. Out of confusion and because there are two of him, and I'm trying to get them to merge into one. "Why do you care? What does any of this matter to you?" I step away from him, and his eyes dart down to my dress. "I just messed up your job and killed someone. Are you here for revenge?"

Jackson touches my side, and I flinch at the sharp sting it causes. He holds his fingers up to show me the blood on them. "You didn't even notice you started bleeding while you were dancing, did you?"

I touch my side to see that, yup, I'm bleeding. But my dress is black, so unless you're looking closely, it'd be hard to tell. How did he—?

"I'll help you re-bandage it." He reaches for me again, but this time, I'm ready and slap his hand away.

"Don't. Just...don't." If he touches me, I don't know what I'll do. Hurt him? Hug him? Kiss him? Honestly, any of those options is a possibility, and none of the fallouts will be good when I'm sober. He shouldn't be here anyway. Not here to help me. He should be angry with me. Trying to get back at me somehow. That's the only thing that makes sense.

I take another step back from him. And another. "Why are you really here? You just watched me murder someone tonight. And now I'm out dancing. Because that was *nothing*." Lie, but he doesn't need to know that. Not when I apparently need to give him another reason to stay away from me.

"You've seen proof now that I'm a killer. So, what are you going to do about it? Are you going to kill me before I kill anyone else? Because you should, you know." I don't even know the words falling from my lips, but angry tears spill from my eyes as I try to make him leave.

He stalks toward me, and I don't know if it's the predatory look in his eyes or because I'm scared of what might happen if we get close enough to touch, but I move backward until I hit the wall. I fumble over all my hiding places to check for a weapon, and my breath stalls when I come back empty. Did he remove them at some point?

Jackson slams his hand into the wall over my head, his body crowding over me until it feels like he's sucked the oxygen out of the room. He's staring at me like I'm the only person in the universe. The only thing that matters.

"You can say or do whatever you like, little one. It's not going to change anything for me. I know who you are." Jackson's voice is low, but it's calm and confident like always. No ounce of doubt in what he's saying. Just simple facts.

There's no way I can look away from his eyes when he watches me like this. Like I'm someone *precious*. It cuts me to be so close to something I know I'll never have. I don't deserve love after all I've done. And no one would love me if they knew.

I push against his chest to give myself space, but he doesn't budge. Even knowing my gift, that I could kill him with a thought now that I'm touching him, he doesn't so much as flinch. His body returns the same pressure back against my hands, so there's absolutely no space between us there.

I tear my eyes away from his with effort and gaze at his lips instead. I'm not sure it's much better, but I'm able to speak again. "I'm a monster. The villain they wanted me to be," I whisper.

He lifts my chin, but I refuse to be caught in his intense stare again and close my eyes instead. Jackson's thumb strokes my cheek while keeping hold of my face. "No. But even if that's what you believe, then I'll be your demon. You won't scare me away. I've done things that nightmares are made of. You want to burn the world down? I'll give you the match to do it. And I'll kill anyone that gets in your way."

My heart stutters, and I open my eyes at his declaration. It's a lie. A trick. If he felt that way, then why did he leave me on the island? Why would he feel that way after what I'd done? I fist his hoodie, then take a shaky breath to get ahold of myself.

I twist my lips into a smirk and give a breathy laugh. "You expect me to believe that? You *left* me on the island. I *killed*—" I press my lips together before I can say it aloud. We both know I'm talking about Vera. "Just because I popped back into your lives doesn't mean you get to mess with me. If this is your version of revenge, then it's a pathetic attempt."

This time, when I shove at his chest, he steps back and drops his arms to his sides. I take a lungful of air and then shiver at losing his body heat. His face is solemn rather than angry at being called out in his lie.

"I didn't want to leave you there. I've spent all these years searching for you. I didn't stop."

"I don't believe you!" I yell. My body quivers in anger that he would play such a dirty trick on me. I wish they would forgive me and things could go back to the way it was, but I can't let myself hope. It's over between all of us. I'm trying to accept that. Why is he making this harder?

Why?!

He just nods and offers me a sad smile. It's full of pain and regret, and my heart breaks a little. "I know. I'll do whatever it takes to prove myself to you, I swear. Just watch me."

Jackson turns and moves to the window, stopping with one foot on the ledge. "Take care of your side, or I'll be back to do it for you," he says calmly, then slips out into the night before I can tell him not to bother with his promise.

There's no way he can fix what's already broken.

CHAPTER TWELVE

RAEGAN

THE EXHAUSTION AND HANGOVER means I sleep in past my alarm the next day. It's a race to the address the paramedic gave us, and I've just given the guys ample opportunity to scope it out first.

I pray they're just as tired from whatever clean-up they did at the guy's apartment, but considering Jackson visited me last night, it's unlikely. The silver lining is that I should miss them completely, at least. I could use a break from running into them. I'd love to never run into them while I'm here, but again, I have to be realistic.

The address takes me to an abandoned auto repair shop.

It's not what I expected for a drop off point for kidnapped kids, but I guess that's the point.

When I peek through the garage door windows, the shop area is empty. No cars, no tools, nothing. The office door doesn't have a window, and the blinds are down, but there's no sound coming from inside, and it's the middle of the afternoon on a weekday.

I check the area one more time and then pull my lock picking kit out and get to work. It's an easy lock, so I'm in within the minute and slip inside before anyone can see me.

The desk is bare, as is the rest of the office. I check the filing cabinet and drawers just in case, but the guys wiped it clean, if there even was anything here. It could have been empty already, which is why it was chosen as a drop off location. But I'll never know if it was or if something valuable was here because I'm sure the guys made it here first.

Well, fuck.

A dead end.

All because I couldn't get my shit together last night and get enough sleep to wake up early.

No, I should have come here straight away after leaving the paramedic's apartment while they were still cleaning up.

Ugh. That's *exactly* what I should have done.

I've never had to race someone to my next lead before. Now, I need to find *something* to get me back on track.

I slam the open drawer closed with a huff. Something blue tumbles to the ground, and I bend down to pick it up. Just as my hand closes around the small paper—a sticky note, I think—a gunshot fires from behind me.

My heart jumps into my throat and then slams back into my chest as I wait for the inevitable pain of wherever I've been shot.

"I guess it comes down to me to take out the traitor, huh?"

Cold dread slips through my veins and locks my body in place. I can barely breathe.

Even though it's been years, even though his voice is drenched with malice and disgust, I still recognize it. It's a mockery of the voice I was once so familiar with. The voice that laughed with me and soothed away my troubles. I'd heard him say nasty things to others before, but always as a defense for his family. Never toward me.

"She can make whatever sound she wants. If anyone else dares to say or do anything, we'll take care of it."

After I had to tell them I killed his sister, Dane never spoke to me again.

Until now.

I slip into fight or flight mode. My heart rampages in my chest at a dizzying pace, its thundering beat drowning out all other sounds. I manage one shaky step after another, my muscles vibrating with the instinct to bolt, until I'm finally facing him.

The gun is aimed at my chest from a mere four feet away. There's no chance of missing me if he fires now. He's close enough that I can see the flecks of green in his amber eyes. The sharp angle of his jaw and the tic of its muscle. His hair is shorter than how he used to wear it when we were younger, though its dyed color is the same. He's in jeans and a blue shirt that reveals a sleeve of tattoos on his left arm that hadn't been there on the island.

"Dane," I breathe out.

"Don't talk," he barks and waves the gun at me.

I bite my lips and hold my hands up so he knows I'm ready to cooperate. The best I have on me are knives, and even if I could get them out before he pulled the trigger, what would I do with them? I killed his sister to *save him*.

If I turn and run, I'm dead. Step closer to him, dead. If there's anyone in the world who wants me dead, Dane is at the top of that list.

Self-preservation tells me to shut the fuck up and do what he says until I can see an opportunity for me to escape.

He rubs his face with his free hand. "Fuck. Why did it have to be you?"

It's obviously a rhetorical question, so I keep my mouth shut.

He glares at me. "Why did you do it? I want answers. Then I'll decide what happens to you."

Holy shit balls.

I'm going to die.

I swallow to give myself more time to decide how to respond. I know that I'm fucked no matter what I do. Even if I told him the truth, he wouldn't believe me while he's still buried in his grief. And I still want to hold on to my promise.

But if I lie to him, he'll know and probably kill me. If I keep my mouth shut, he might kill me out of frustration.

How the fuck do I get out of this?

When I don't answer right away, he steps forward and yells, "Answer me! Why did you kill Vera? Why did you kill my *sister*?"

I take an involuntary step backward and bump into the filing cabinet. Damn it, this office is too small. There's nowhere to go if he keeps getting closer.

"She was my sister too," I say finally, avoiding the actual question that will probably get me in trouble. She was the only girl I talked to on the island. The one who talked to me about boys. About kissing. She meant something to me too, which made her betrayal hurt that much more.

Because she'd turned her back on *all* of us.

His face reddens, and it's like seeing a bomb about to go off.

Fuck me.

"How dare you say that!? You don't get to say that after what you did to her! You killed her! And she was mine by blood. I was supposed to protect her. I just didn't think I had to protect her from *you*!"

I hold my palms out in front of my chest in a placating gesture. "Dane, please. Put the gun down so we can talk about this."

"How long did you plan on killing her? Were you just playing all of us to make us care about you so you could get close to her? Or did she try to stop you when she found out about you, so you killed her?" Another step closer. He's a step away from being able to reach me now.

"No, it's not like that! Dane. Please."

The rage turns manic in his eyes. "I know you were with GE all along. I've seen the proof. You tricked us. And suddenly, after all this time, you just appear in our city and keep bumping into us? I don't buy it. What do they have you here for? To get close to the others again so you can take me in? Are you going to kill them like you did her if they get in your way?"

Proof? What proof? And why does he think GE wants him?

My brain barely has time to register what he's saying before he reaches out and snatches my wrist. He shoves my palm against his chest and holds it there. I try to tug it back, but his hold is immovable. Then the barrel of his gun pushes into my forehead, and I freeze. "Go ahead. I want to feel what Vera did in her last moments before I shut you down."

I take a shuddering breath, but I don't look away from him or close my eyes to hide from his pain. I did this to him. But there's nothing I can say or do to fix it.

My gaze meets his, trying to convey how sorry I am for what I did.

Moisture gathers in my eyes, and I have to bite my lip to stop the fine tremble that's taken over me out of fear of what's going to happen next. I try to focus on Dane instead. His eyes. The feel of his heart beating beneath my hand. His signature citrusy scent that I used to tease him for smelling sweet and tart at the same time, just like his personality.

A new emotion flickers in his glare, but before I can think anything of it, something flies in front of my face, and the gun clatters to the ground. Dane's grip on my wrist loosens, and I pull it free as we turn to see where it came from.

Jackson's lying on his stomach in the air vent above us, a throwing star between the fingers of one hand while he rests his face against the other. He looks calm and unaffected by the heightened emotions in this small office, but also like he's been watching us this entire time, and we were too preoccupied to notice.

Which we were.

Dane glares up at him and then moves back toward his gun, but another star flies down so hard that it pins the trigger guard to the ground, and he can't lift it up.

Jackson *tsks*, then easily twists himself around and drops between us. "I'd hoped to leave you both alone to sort this out."

Dane's still trying to yank the star out of the tile and growls up at him. "Then stay the fuck out of it."

"I would if I could." He shrugs with a smirk, calm as always. "But hurting Raegan isn't an option." Jack keeps his body and eyes aimed firmly at Dane, even when he addresses me next. "Leave now, little one. I'll take care of this."

"You're seriously taking her side? What the fuck, man? She *killed Vera*! She's an *enemy* of our family! A threat! Leaving her alive is just asking for her to kill us too. She should be the number one enemy that we're fighting against." Dane gets up and tries to go around him, but Jackson sidesteps and blocks him until they're face-to-face.

I'm too busy absorbing the deep cuts and brands from Dane's words to react to anything else. I know then that that's how he feels. How Aiden probably feels. Maybe Kellan too. I'm still not sure I can trust anything that Jackson told me last night. I'm *worse* than the enemy we've all been hunting in parallel.

"Raegan, *go*," Jackson reiterates, and I finally snap out of the spiral of thoughts I was trapped in.

Right. Leave before Dane tries to kill me. Again.

I move around Jackson, who angles and shifts himself to remain between me and Dane until I'm at the door. Dane calls out one last time, just to make sure he's hammered the nail in the coffin.

"You'll never trick us again. Do you hear me? You're dead to us!"

I feel like doing something reckless.

It's probably not the smartest move I could make, but I'm not sure how much I care in this moment. There's something about being a second away from death that makes me crave doing something foolish and crazy to remind myself that I'm alive.

For however long that lasts.

Best to seize the moment and have a little fun once in a while, right?

Almost like what Kell and I would do on the island. We would sneak around, break rules, pull pranks, do things that definitely could have gotten us hurt if not killed. All because we *could*. It was one of the few ways to feel like we took control back over our lives.

Now I just need to find the right place to go tonight to get that thrill.

I'm sure someone at Hype will know of a good spot and make my way there. Staff are working to get the place set up for opening, but even without the music and customers, the workers are rowdy and there's a general feel of relaxed fun in the air. I'm tempted to stay here to drink and dance my troubles away like usual, but brush the idea aside as soon as I have it. I need more than that tonight.

I try the bouncer that Elias introduced me to on my first night working in the club. He watches me approach, arms folded over his chest, but doesn't say anything even when I stop in front of him.

"It's...Bryant, right?" I ask hesitantly, hoping I didn't fuck up the name even though we'd only met that one time.

He nods stoically.

"Great. I'm not sure if you remember me. I'm Rae, the new temp working here for Elias?"

"I remember."

"Okay..." I had hoped for some sign he was good with me and might open up, but it's like pulling teeth. "I'm still new around here and don't know of the best...spots for a bit of late-night fun. Do you think you can help a girl out with some recommendations?"

Bryant looks me up and down. "And what exactly are you looking for?"

I hesitate. I'm not sure of what exactly I'm looking for. Something with danger. Probably illegal.

"Oh. Um, any underground groups that do anything fun after the sun goes down?"

Was that too vague?

"You looking for the Dragon?" Another staff member walks over to interrupt with a grin on his face. Bryant gives him a warning look, but the other guy is unperturbed.

"Um...I'm not sure about a dragon," I start, looking between the two workers.

The guy laughs and shakes his head. "Not *a* dragon. *The* Dragon. Best fighter in the cage."

"Cage?"

"Yeah. At the Pits. You been?"

"Uh, not yet. Is there something going on there tonight?"

"Nah, it's street racin' night."

My heart rate picks up at the possibilities of racing. *Perfect.* "Right. Where's that at tonight?"

"Down at the old airport by the docks. They won't be there until after midnight, so I wouldn't bother going until then. Do you need a ride? I'll be heading there after my shift."

"Don't start any trouble while the boss isn't here, Stefan," Bryant grunts at him, though his eyes stay on me.

"I'm sure she's no trouble if she's working here," Stefan easily defends me with a wink.

"Thanks." I give him a small smile. "For the information and the offer of a ride. I'll make my own way there, but thank you."

Stefan shrugs, but his smile doesn't falter. "No problem. Have a good night!" He waves and jogs back to the bar.

I call a taxi to bring me down to the old airport just after two in the morning and then wander until I can hear the revving of overly modified engines. It's the dead of night on the outskirts of the city, where even the neon lights are gone from sight. The only light is the soft glow of the moon overhead and a sprinkling of stars. The air here is permeated with the smell of rubber and gasoline mixed with salt water and garbage, so I know I'm in the right place.

I walk through an open metal gate and then head toward the unmistakable sound of cars racing. There are cars and trailers everywhere. Most are in the back and empty as I walk by them, but some trailers still have cars in them while last-minute modifications and tinkering happens between races.

The runway stretches toward the water, but it's at least a mile out. Most attendees are clustered here at the starting line. They're standing around in groups, filming or taking pictures, placing bets, and rooting for various cars.

The throttle of engines draws my eyes next, and at the flash of a light, they tear down the runway in seconds. The sound drowns out everything else, even the cheering of people around me now that I'm in the thick of them. Smoke billows from their tires until all I can see are red tail lights glowing in the dark.

"Shredder and Guillotine, you're up!" someone shouts over the clamor, and two more cars roll up to their places in line. "Nightmare and Dark Vengeance, you're on deck!"

Without any further preamble or instructions, the cars surge forward at the flashlight signal, matching each other for a few seconds before one overtakes the other.

I keep moving through the crowd until I can see the drivers of the next race. I'm impressed by the speed and organization with which they're running this. I suppose it's necessary to get through as much racing as they can before cops roll in.

I check out the drivers of the two cars lined up and ready, and—Oh shit. My breath catches. There's Kellan, one arm draped over the wheel while he takes a swig of a forty.

Is he seriously drinking while doing this?

A small part of me wondered if he'd be here. He made some comment about having his name all over this city, but I was too focused on needing the adrenaline rush to care. Now that I see him, I debate staying or leaving.

He was always the one coming up with the wild ideas for us to try. The one who brought the smile to my face even when I was feeling down. Did I seek this out for the rush, or because I knew he might be here?

The flashlight lights up and then he's gone. Both racers are meeting each other speed for speed, one nosing in front of the other before it switches. And then Kellan shifts gears or something because he jumps forward and zips past the other car, passing the end marker with car lengths to spare.

There's cheering and the next racers being called out, but all I can focus on is Kellan as he drives around and parks to the side with the other cars on standby. He stands from his car, bottle still in hand like it's been permanently attached, shirtless and grinning. He's wearing jeans, but his feet are bare as he walks across the pavement to clap hands with Stefan.

His arms are tattooed from shoulder to hand. One side continues up the side and back of his neck while the other curls around his back shoulder blade.

I wonder how long it must have taken him to get all of that ink if his skin kept trying to heal itself over before they could finish.

My feet are frozen in place as I'm captivated by him, by his every movement and expression, while his attention and ire aren't aimed my way for a change.

The need to feel like his partner in crime, to go along with his crazy ideas that take my breath away and set my heart racing...it wells up in my chest until it's ready to explode. Maybe just for one night, we could have that again.

Kellan turns around with a wide smile that I see through in an instant. Even with years apart, I know the difference between a genuine Kellan grin and what's there now.

His eyes meet mine, and my heart stutters. I can't tell if he's still pissed with me or what, because he stares without a word until I can't take it anymore.

"Kell..."

CHAPTER THIRTEEN

KELLAN

THERE WAS A TIME when nothing could beat the adrenaline rush of a race. Just two cars, no limits, and pure speed. There's always a risk in street racing. If the car is pushed too hard or not rebuilt properly, it could catch fire or fall apart during the race. If the driver doesn't have full control of the car, it could spin out or flip from the smallest thing because of the high speed.

Some drivers wear helmets or have a five-point harness installed in their seats. Or they strip their cars and rebuild them around a steel cage to keep the driver protected.

But not me.

I live for this shit.

The risk. The danger.

For putting my body on the line and hoping it might make me *feel* something for a change.

To have that split-second *oh shit* moment where even I don't know what will happen next.

I wait for that moment as I shift into my last gear and smoke the car behind me. The finish line passes me, but I don't slow down. The victory tastes bland and empty. At the very least, I'll make good money tonight, but I've now reached the point I knew was coming.

Boredom.

Last time, I started and built up an underground fight club. I lived for the fight and beating my opponents down. Until it wasn't enough anymore, and I needed to find something new.

And now, street racing is losing its shine.

I jerk the wheel to the right, riding and balancing on two tires for a few seconds before I crash and bounce back to the ground. I take long, drawn-out gulps to heat my blood and numb my mind.

Two chances.

Raegan had *two* chances to give me *something*. I'd take fucking anything from her at this point to prove us wrong. That we were missing something and she hadn't betrayed us.

I barely believed it even when she told us.

Now, there's no Gordon, no island, no reason to hold back.

And all she gave me was a bullshit excuse about some promise.

Then she killed our mark.

It feels like she's betrayed us all over again.

Once I'm back in the line-up on standby for the cars participating in the next round of races, I throw my door open. The asphalt is cold on my bare feet, but it's a nice shock to the system compared to the warmth swimming through my veins.

Stefan calls out to me from his car, and I grin so wide my teeth are a threatening flash of white behind my thick and overgrown bush of facial hair. My brothers keep telling me to cut it already, but now I'm finding sick pleasure in pissing them off by leaving it.

So, looks like Yeti-Kellan will be around for a while longer.

I clasp hands with Stefan as he congratulates me on my win or something to that effect because I'm not entirely listening. Everything around me feels out of focus. Like I'm here, but I'm not really here.

And then the world sharpens in an instant, and I freeze.

But she can't be standing there. She wouldn't be. Not unless she went out of her way to find me. And after what happened at our last encounter...

"Kell..." Raegan starts.

Her voice snaps me back to the present like whiplash, and I scowl at her. "The fuck are you doing here?"

There's a flash of some emotion in her clear blue eyes before it's quickly covered up by a nose scrunch. She used to do that when she was *annoyed, but not angry*. Little did she know that we adored that cute gesture and would annoy the fuck out of her to see it again.

Seeing it on her now, all grown up and more beautiful than I could have ever imagined she'd be, wakes the beast in me. No one else has ever compared to the memory of her.

Even in the harsh headlights that illuminate the lot, she's perfect.

Long, blonde hair that looks soft to touch and begs me to slide my fingers through it. Vibrant, wild blue eyes lined by dark lashes. Full, pink lips that I've imagined running my tongue across too many times to count.

She continues, unaware of the unwanted effect she has on me. "I didn't know you were going to be here," she answers defensively.

I snort and shake my head, then gulp the hard liquor from the bottle. That's hard for me to believe. I already told her I own this city. And she would know best that would include any of its illegal activities. The question is why she would seek me out. The time for talking has passed. I know now that I meant nothing to her. Not as much as this *promise* of hers. It sounded like there was nothing more to say after that, and she moved on.

Then I find out earlier today while working on my ride that Dane disappeared. Jackson was nowhere to be found either, as usual, so it was down to Aiden and I to orchestrate a full-on man-hunt for Dane to make sure GE hadn't gotten ahold of him.

They've been hunting him ever since we left the island. Any time he went out, they would show up within days or even hours. They almost snatched him one time when he was out alone. We killed the guys who had him before they could get far, and now we've kept him under house arrest ever since.

His disappearance from the Loft was a red alert, all hands on deck situation.

But no. He was safe.

He'd just tracked Raegan down and pulled a gun on her.

And Jackson had gotten between them and dragged Dane back to the Loft, where Aiden has him back under house arrest.

It's been a fucking *day*, and she wants to act like everything's fine?

"I heard there was racing happening here tonight." She crosses her arms over her chest, but I can see the vulnerability she's trying to hide behind. "Are you going to let me stay? For old times' sake?"

I know exactly what this is about. She's looking for danger and something fun to take her mind off it all and, even with the years and bullshit between us, she came right back to me.

Something stirs in me at that realization, but I shut it down.

I'm not her backup partner only when she needs it. That's not a partnership. She's already moved on, right?

I cross my arms to mirror hers and raise an incredulous eyebrow. "For old times, huh? I thought we've already moved on, beautiful. At least, that's what you told me. So, how about you fuck off to wherever you've moved on to? This is my turf, and you're not welcome."

Her nickname rolls off my tongue uninvited, but it's too ingrained in me when I see her to stop. Her face flushes at the memory, probably out of anger, and I kinda like seeing that.

My mouth stretches to a devilish grin at her expression. Her lips thin to a flat line, and then when I think she's about to turn and walk away, she jumps at me instead. I catch her wrist before she can grab my arm like she seemed to aim for.

I yank her up against me, wrapping my arm with the bottle around her lower back to keep her trapped. She feels so small and fragile in my arms, and my body tightens on impulse, like I'm about to protect her from everything around us. It's what I did so often as a dumb young kid—wrap her up in my arms and she could just let go.

But we aren't those kids anymore. And I won't be fooled by her this time.

I lean down to her ear and lower my voice. "Nice try, but we both know you won't use that with all of these people around. And it wouldn't hurt me anyway."

She tilts her face up to look at me, and her eyes are lit with a determination that should worry me, but I feel a hit of adrenaline instead. She should be scared of being at my mercy like this. She knows what I can do. And she knows what she *can't* do to me. And yet she's looking at me like she's won this little game, and I don't even know it yet.

It's hot as hell.

"You're wrong," she replies with a smirk of her own. And fuck, if that look on her face doesn't get me hotter than any alcohol ever could. "People will make up anything to avoid acknowledging weird shit happening before their eyes if it's done right. And second, it does hurt you before your gift takes over. Tell me..."

Something moves at my thigh and then her hand grabs my dick through my jeans. My hard, interested dick.

Fuck.

I know it's a threat. I know it would hurt like a *motherfucker* before my gift kicks in to heal whatever damage she gets in. I know I should be pissed or worried, but...

Raegan is touching—no, *gripping*—my dick.

It lights a fire in me I thought I'd long since extinguished, and my body instinctually presses her more tightly against me. A smug smirk pulls at my mouth, and her confidence falters for half a second because I didn't crumble right away at the threat.

"Don't get the wrong idea," she snaps at me, and my smirk grows.

"Shouldn't I be telling you that? You seem to have gotten distracted, beautiful."

We're in dangerous territory, but I can't find it in me to stop it or pull back. I know I should hate her. I should say something nasty and throw her away so she'll never pop into my life again, but I can't think of any of that while her soft, warm frame fits so well against mine. I inhale, and her vanilla scent sends my dick into overdrive. *Does she taste like vanilla too?*

Her grip tightens on me, probably intended as a warning, and I groan obscenely, not caring about what she thinks or anyone else around us. "Fuck, beautiful. If that's what we need to finally say our goodbyes, then I can make some time," I growl.

Raegan tries to shove away from me, but my hold on her is solid. She's trying to dig her nails into me, but my jeans block them from making any difference. It's enough to tell me that she's uninterested in what I'm offering, though, and while I may be a complete asshole, I would never force myself on anyone.

I drop the forty to the ground, letting it shatter at our feet. Raegan startles, and in the distraction, I grip her hair and yank until I have full control of her head when I make her look at me. "If you're not offering, then let go of me. I've got a line of girls who are ready and willing for me. I'm just fine saying goodbye and fuck off for good like this."

Heat sears through my jeans and to my cock. My skin begins to burn and I react in an instant. I shove her back, and she stumbles a step, but then she's laughing hysterically and pointing at me. There's a hole in my jeans to my boxers. My dick, thankfully, appears unharmed.

"Are you sure this is how you want me to remember you, Kellan?" The little she-devil pretends to smile sweetly at me. "Or did you want to go for that ride and then you can change your clothes? I didn't realize the risk of street racing meant your pants could catch fire. Or have you just been telling some naughty lies?"

There are a few snickers around the crowd, but no one brave enough to actually laugh at me. Fucking cowards. This shit is funny.

I grin and plant my hands on my hips, even arching my back to push my pelvis out to draw more attention to it. She wants to play? I'm game. I've never been embarrassed before, and this? This is nothing.

"You can remember me however you like. Though I'm pretty sure the feel of my dick is more memorable than a peek of skin."

Raegan touches a finger to her lips like she's actually thinking about it and then shrugs with a smirk. "Nope, not for me."

I don't falter, even though now all I'm thinking about is bending her over my car and showing her just how *unmemorable* my dick can be. "Well, you'll still be thinking of it either way when you think of me, so I'd say it's fine we leave this as is. As you can tell, I've got something to take care of and another race to win," I say with a shrug and start to turn away.

"Wait."

I turn my head over my shoulder just enough to see her. She's gnawing at her lip and looking past me to my car.

"You wanna go for a ride, beautiful, then you'll owe me one."

"Owe you what?"

I give a noncommittal shrug of one shoulder. "I'm not sure yet. Think of it as an IOU that I'll call in at a later date and time of my choosing."

She sighs. "Fine."

Raegan never was one to turn down anything before, so I shouldn't be surprised that she'd be willing to accept an open favor for a race. I still am. Good to see that some things didn't change with her. Even though *other* things did.

Aiden and Dane are going to be pissed about all this, but she came to me, not the other way around. Which they would both find suspicious. Her persistence in trying to spend time with me is too, but I also couldn't care less if those are red flags. I'm not afraid of her or what she might do.

No, I'm excited by it.

"Let's go, then." I wave her after me and return to my seat in the car. She follows to the passenger's seat and goes to reach for where the seatbelt should be.

"Where's the seatbelt?"

"Oh, I got rid of those a while ago."

"Are you crazy?!"

I scoff.

"Of course. Aren't you?" I grin madly at her.

There's the smallest hint of a smile tugging at the corner of her lips before she squashes it and tries to cover it up with an eye roll. "I guess we'll find out if you actually want me dead or not then, huh?"

It's true, this would be an easy opportunity for an accident to happen. But I could never kill her, even after all that happened.

Something about her killing Vera or working for GE just doesn't add up to me. I don't care what Aiden or Dane say. The girl who used to be my partner in crime wouldn't have done that without good reason. Or she's lying and didn't kill Vera.

She's definitely hiding something, and I plan to find out what that is.

"Guess so," I offer back with a wink. I turn the key in the ignition, and my car roars to life.

"Is there anything I can hold on to at least?" she shouts over the noise of the revving engine, looking around almost frantically for something to cling on to. Raegan finally looks at me and, seeing my smirk, snaps, "Don't even say it. For fuck's sake, Kellan. Is this how you treat all of your enemies? By trying to get them to touch your dick?"

That sparks a howl of laughter out of me. Damn, I forgot how good it felt to laugh. We drive back into the queue for the next round of racing once I hear who my competitor is and move up beside them. "Beautiful, you grabbed it all on your own without me doing anything."

I pull up to the line, my hand on the shifter, and gaze now focused on Roger with the flashlight. I rev the engine and let the tires warm on the pavement until the light flashes. We launch forward like a rocket ship at blast-off. Raegan squeals, but a quick side eye reveals her smiling face and the excited look in her eyes now that we're on the move.

She always had been one for danger. Ready to do anything on a dare or get the heart pumping and prove to ourselves that we're alive. That, for one small moment, we were in charge of our own destinies. Even if it ended horribly wrong, it was our choice.

I can feel the need to shift when it's time, and when I thrust us into the next gear, we're thrown back into our seats. Raegan's gasp changes to breathless laughter, and I can't stop the wild grin from spreading across my face. I'd forgotten how much more fun things had been with my partner in crime.

We whiz past the competition in seconds, eating up the pavement like we're starved for it and passing the finish line while leaving the other car in the dust. I don't slow down, though, ripping toward the end of the strip and the black, open water of the bay.

When she realizes I'm still not making any move to stop the car or turn away from the water, she warns, "Kell..."

"What? You scared, beautiful?" I challenge and turn to face her instead of the shrinking road.

Her blue eyes lock on to mine. "Never."

My heart gallops at the fierceness of her gaze and the tenacity in her voice. It beats louder than I ever remember it before. Like she's kickstarted it back to the rhythm it was always supposed to be and had forgotten. I tighten my grip on the shifter and hold her stare even as I see the edge approaching out of the corner of my eye.

My foot jumps to the clutch, and I yank on the emergency break. My body moves on autopilot to swing the car around, the back tires skidding along the edge of the pavement before I gun it to the left.

I snicker and finally break our staring contest, pleased to see that she didn't crack once. "Good to see you've still got your guts."

She smiles, but catches herself when she realizes what she's doing. She hurriedly turns to look out her window, the coastline of the bay whipping past us as I drop down a gear. We're still moving fast, because she didn't come to me for a slow ride, but at a more manageable speed as I turn us out of the airport and onto the city streets so our ride doesn't have to end just yet.

"This good enough for old times?" I prompt teasingly.

I know I shouldn't do this; that this will all come back to bite me later by giving in to her random and impulsive urge to pretend everything is okay, but it feels like I'm riding a high I haven't felt in a long time.

She hums, but the sudden quiet quickly becomes disconcerting.

"What?" I ask roughly.

She shakes her head and focuses her attention back on the side exit I'm taking to get us back into the city. "Nothing."

I hate that word.

There's no such thing as *nothing* with her. Not to me.

Knowing my luck with her, it'll be some ruthless commentary that'll kill the moment and rip my soul out. "Spill it," I growl, already on the defensive.

Rae settles back into her seat and looks at me. My blood heats under her scrutiny and, not for the first time, I wish I could read her thoughts.

"I'm sorry. This was a mistake."

My breathing slows. "What?"

"I shouldn't have come here. To you. It wasn't right, and I'm just making things worse," she says in a breathless rush that I can barely keep up.

"What the fuck are you talking about?" I demand, my voice rising and my foot pressing more heavily on the gas.

"This! I don't know what I was thinking. It was stupid—"

I grind my teeth. Hanging out with me was stupid? She's regretting this already while I was dumb enough to fall for it, for her, again.

The car skids against the curb and slams to a halt. "Here you go. Either stay and stop talking stupid shit, or get out if that's what you really want."

Her mouth pops open as she stares at me. "Here?"

"I'm not your chauffeur. Either you're riding *with* me, or you're out of my car. Pick one," I growl. I'm done playing games. Part of me hopes she proves me wrong. That she'll tell me that it was all a bad joke and she's staying. The other part knows that there's no way she'll stay. She's already backed out of what we had. I was a *mistake*.

Raegan's eyes narrow at me and my ultimatum, and I hate that the neon lights are illuminating her just right to give her a hauntingly blue glow. She looks like a dark goddess hellbent on ruining me, and my chest constricts until I can't breathe.

I know then that I'm never going to love anyone else. I'm cursed to love someone who betrayed me and who I'm supposed to hate.

I'm already addicted to the way she makes me feel, even when she does shit like this, and I know I'll be hunting her down for more when I need my next hit.

I wait her out, impatient for her to make her decision.

Pick me, my inner voice roars, but my lips remain sealed. This is her choice. This will tell me what she wants.

"Fine," she concedes sharply. She throws the door open to get out. Her head swivels, to find any familiar landmark, and when she finds none because we are outside of the city center, she picks a direction and starts walking without looking back.

I clench the steering wheel until my knuckles are white and the leather creaks.

There's my answer.

Again.

I throw the car in gear and slam my foot down, speeding past her in my fury.

It's mere minutes of racing through the city streets before I'm pulling into the parking garage attached to the Tower. The looming skyscraper lined with steel and glass is just as cold and empty as I feel when I take the elevator up to the Loft where my brothers and I live.

The Tower was already decked out with most of its fancy features when we took it over two years ago, but Aiden and Dane made a few special enhancements of their own. Our Loft received the biggest changes.

I scan the tattoo on my wrist when the elevator reaches our floor for it to open. When Dane had first thought of using tattoos for access to this floor, I'd thought it had been a joke. I mean, the GE scientists had tattooed our skin with barcodes to keep track of us. Like we were products to be made and sold. And he wanted to do the same thing?

But this one was different. It was hidden within the sleeve of tats that extended from my chest, over my shoulder, down my arm, and to the back of my hand. Unless you knew the exact tattoo to look for, you wouldn't know it was used for this at all.

The doors open into a foyer and then another door uses facial recognition to unlock and bring me into the living room. It's late, so I don't expect anyone else to be up, but Dane is cooking something in the kitchen with his face drawn tight in thought. Aiden is sitting at the dining table with a coffee in one hand and his phone in the other.

I walk further into the room and find Jackson sitting on the balcony railing, floating origami animals above one hand and sending them into a dance around one another.

Aiden looks up first and then blinks as if I've surprised him or something.

"What?" I growl.

Dane brings plates of French toast to the table and then looks me up and down. "Where's your pacifier? I can't remember the last time I've seen you so far from a bottle."

Shit, what had happened to it? Did I leave my spare in the car?

Well, I've no interest in them digging too deeply into that, so I stride to the liquor cabinet and grab another bottle out.

To ease their worried souls.

"Finished it on the way up." I toss the cap over my shoulder, grinning at Dane's glare, then drag a chair out at the table and sit before taking a drink. "So. Did we already talk about Rapunzel escaping his tower and putting us all at risk today? Or almost killing one of us?"

Not that Dane would have actually followed through with it. I know he's angry, but I also know his history with Raegan. I don't think he'd do it.

Doesn't mean I appreciate him testing that theory.

"She's not *one of us* anymore," he snaps out automatically.

I don't react immediately to his temper. I get that years going by doesn't change that he lost his sister to someone he trusted.

But I can look at this more objectively. I liked Vera. She was fun sometimes and I had no problem looking out for her when I could out of respect for Dane. But she and I had never been close. Not like she had been with her actual brother. And Raegan.

Hearing about her death hurt, but more because of the impact it had on my closest friend. And that it was *Raegan* who admitted to doing it.

I've had a lot of years to think about her and what she said. I wasted the first few in a haze of alcohol and self-destruction; her words that she was with GE and killed Vera running on an endless loop. And then, one day, I started to wonder if there was more to it.

I can't believe that all our time together was fake. Either GE had something to do with what happened and why she said that, or else she is with them like she says and she wound up falling for us as much as we fell for her. Tonight proved that she's the same girl as the one on the island. That was real.

Even if she is with the bad guys, I'll win her over.

I dig into my early morning breakfast and then point my butter knife at Dane. "You threaten her like that again, and I'll stab you with this knife."

His chair screeches against the hardwood floors as he jumps up. His hands are already fisted and glowing with his gift. "Let's go, then. I haven't been sitting here every day for years twiddling my thumbs. You know what I'm capable of."

Aiden sighs and sets his mug and phone down on the table but doesn't bother interrupting.

I smirk at Dane and shove another forkful of toast into my mouth before responding. "And you know what I'm capable of. You really think you can take me on when I'm being serious?"

Jack pockets his paper creatures and hops down from the railing, then slips inside and sits on the table. Not between us, though. No, more like he wanted a closer seat to the fight that might break out.

There's a moment of silence, but I can feel the brewing violence like electricity in the air.

Dane rushes me while I'm still seated, but I catch his fist before it can strike me. I squeeze it and bare my teeth at him. "You'll have to do better than that."

He smirks, and something wraps from his wrist to mine. I drop his hand and pull away, but whatever he's attached doesn't loosen. He grabs my hand back and mutes my gift. What should be warm and steady in my gut is now quiet and glaringly void. I hate the feeling, but I've felt it before and have learned how to move past it. I have to remind myself that it's temporary.

I yank my hand back, pulling him to me, and then slam my other fist into his stomach. He grunts and folds forward. My elbow drops into his back, and we both fall to the ground. I flip him over and pin him down with my other arm at his throat, growling in his face.

"That was a cute trick, but now you need to learn how to use it. Until then. Don't. Touch. Raegan."

"Since when do you care?" he spits at me as he struggles to find an opening to get out from under me.

There isn't one.

His fists pummel into my sides, but I'm built of solid muscle, even without my gift being able to come into play.

"Since I saw who she really was tonight. The same girl we knew on the island."

"And that girl killed one of us. Who's to say she isn't here to finish the rest of us off? To lure you back so she can kill you too? I won't lose another one of us!" He continues to fight against me, and I press down more until he's forced to grab at my arm instead. The bracelet around my wrist—that looks like a slimmer and less clunky version of handcuffs—drops to the ground. "We never meant anything to her. She'll never care about you. Your protection is wasted."

His words echo the doubt that has taken me hostage since she returned, and it sinks like a boulder in my gut. I stand. He coughs and rubs at his neck as he sits up.

"That's my business. Not yours."

"Is it also your business as to why there is a gaping hole in your pants?" Aiden finally intervenes.

Oops, forgot about that.

"Sure is," I drawl.

Jackson cackles and picks up a piece of French toast to take a bite. No syrup, no silverware. Just eats it like an animal. "I'm sure our little Raegan had something to do with that. Couldn't get your clothes off fast enough or trying to maim your dick?"

Fuck, do I wish it were the first one.

"None of your damn business. Are we done here? We can consider that piss-poor attempt at a fight as me spanking Dane for leaving, yeah?"

Aiden nods and drinks more of his coffee. Seriously. Caffeine at four in the morning, and I doubt any of them have slept. And they say I have drinking problems.

Chapter Fourteen

RAEGAN

Boats tap together on either side of the pier as the gentle pulse of the ocean beats against them. The sound should be soothing, but it's too ingrained in my childhood memories to make me feel at ease as it should. Even the smell of salt in the air is a reminder. It makes me wonder how Aiden and the others can bear to live here with the ocean so close to them.

Unless I'm the only one of us still haunted by the past.

It's those memories that brought me here tonight. After a poor attempt at going to bed early for a change, I was plagued by nightmares.

I woke up desperate to see the ocean and prove to myself that I'd escaped. I can come and go from anywhere as I please now.

I draw the whiskey I picked up on the way to my lips to take another drink. My legs dangle over the edge of the pier, and my feet move back and forth through the water.

The sea looks so peaceful tonight under the waning glow of the moon. The waves are big and soft, pitch black, so I can't see anything but the moon's reflection. I close my eyes and lean my head back as my mind drifts off to pick right back up in my memories where my nightmare left off.

The smell of smoke and burning bodies permeates the air. My chest heaves in a desperate grasp for air, even as the taste makes my stomach clench and protest.

Everything hurts.

Another piece of concrete crashes to the ground nearby. Where there was once ceiling above me, there's blue sky.

What have I done?

I force myself to a sitting position. An involuntary sob slips out at the pain of doing so, and then again when I see the blood on and between my thighs beneath my skirt. W-where is he?

The room, no, the manor, has been destroyed. Piles of concrete and debris fill the room and area around me where a wing of the building no longer stands. There's a thick coating of dust on my skin from the wreckage, but I'm somehow unscathed from the collapsing building.

There's no sign of Gordon.

There's no way he escaped. He's been crushed.

Tears slip down my cheeks at the slow realization of what he's done.

At what he's taken from me.

I'd thought I had hit rock bottom when he forced me to pleasure him. But this...

A sharp scream grabs my attention, and I swing my head around to the rest of the manor.

The guys!

I shove off of the bed, falling to the ground when my legs don't hold me as I'd hoped. They wobble and shake from both pain and fear, but I can't just stay here. I have to find the others and make sure I didn't hurt them too.

I don't know how, but I'm sure that I did this.

My gift did.

As I push myself upright, part of Gordon's lab coat that's stuck in the rocks catches my attention.

Relief overwhelms me and threatens to take control, but I force it down. Not right now. I'll break down later over everything.

I steady myself back on my feet, gritting my teeth to hold on to the strength to find my way to them before I pass out. I take a few tentative steps first and then push until I'm hurrying down another wing of the manor that's still falling apart. I jog down a ravaged hallway where cracks are spread like vines through the walls. This side of the mansion isn't in as rough shape. There's nothing left of the building on the other end. It's a mausoleum now.

Even so, the fire that started there is spreading to this side, filling it up with smoke and burning anything in its wake.

There's a loud crack, *and I bolt forward into a run just as the ceiling comes crashing down behind me. I keep going through other rooms and corridors until I find the stairs, taking them two at a time while my body screams from pain and exhaustion. The adrenaline helps mute the pain and keeps me going. I'll be done for once I stop moving.*

I slam into the closed door of the room I want, not wasting any time.

"We have to go—" I take in the empty room.

Were they on the other side of the mansion? Are they hurt? Or were they taken away already?

Where are they?!

Movement out the window catches my eye, and I jerk toward it, my chest heaving with exertion now that I've stopped moving for a second.

I see Kellan first, running around on a boat at the docks like he's getting it ready. Dane is helping untether the ropes, while Jackson and Aiden are talking with each other.

I breathe a deep sigh of relief.

They're all safe.

My chest aches as they all work together to escape the island. Without me. Of course, they would. It's been a year since Vera died and we've even seen each other. Would they let me go with them if they knew what Gordon put me through?

I push away from the window.

They wouldn't. I'm still responsible for Vera's death.

I can't go with them, but I can do what they're doing. I can escape the island. Just because Gordon is gone doesn't mean someone else won't try to use me. Or perhaps they'd just kill me this time, since I was only worth the trouble to Gordon.

I make my way down the stairs and outside toward another pier, determined to get on a boat while I still can.

"Stop!"

I stumble upon hearing Aiden's voice. He's standing a few paces away.

His brown eyes take me in, and for a heartbeat, he looks worried about me. I know I'm covered in blood and dirt, my clothes are torn, and I'm honestly not sure how I'm still standing and moving. Maybe he'll realize I've been through hell and let me come with them. Maybe, deep down, they still care about me too.

Then his gaze hardens, and his face flattens to something cold and angry.

"I can't let you leave this island."

"What?"

He moves forward, and I step back, but he keeps going until he's grabbed me by the shoulders. I'm careful to keep my hands at my sides, but my entire body tenses while my mind is still catching up with what he's saying.

"I can't trust you. And you're too dangerous to be on their side. I'm sorry, but we've agreed this is the only way."

"Aiden, what—"

Something hard slams into the side of my head, and everything goes black.

Wood creaks behind me, and I spin around to catch five guys dressed in black and with guns trying to creep down the pier.

Fuck.

They've found me again.

It's faster than the last time, even though I haven't used my gift on anyone. How do they keep finding me?

They break into a run now that I've seen them, and I take one last drink before chucking the heavy liquor bottle at them to slow them down. Then I slide off the edge and into the water.

I swim underwater below the pier a good distance before resurfacing.

"Nothing over here," one of them calls out.

"Negative," adds another.

"Well, fucking find her then," a third voice snaps.

It's at times like these that I wish I had a non-tangible gift.

I hope Jackson knows how lucky he is that he can fight from a distance.

And Aiden owes me a fucking gun.

Heavy boots move up and down the pier as they search the ocean. I move quietly through the water under the pier, careful not to make too much noise to give me away. All it will take is one of them to smarten up and look underneath, and I'll be trapped.

My feet skim the sandy beach when I draw closer to the start of the pier, but I curl my legs up and keep swimming until I can stand with the water at my waist. Then I wrap my hands around one of the large posts and call on my gift.

There's a fire in my gut when I call on so much at once, building it up and stoking it until I release it into my hands all at once. My hands glow and *burn*. The post cracks once, loud and clear for everyone to hear.

There's a split second of silence.

"Get off the pier!" the one still on the beach commands, but it's too late.

My gift thrusts out of me and into the post, spreading up and across the planks like wildfire. The thick wood disintegrates before they can take two steps and then they fall into the water.

I run at the one guy not in the water, fisting my hands at my sides and keeping my gift active and at the ready for him. My weapons are useless until I turn this off, and I'm not willing to lose the advantage I have now that I'm warmed up.

He curses and widens his stance while angling to face me. His body blurs for a moment and then there are five of him.

Shit. Not just a regular goon.

A gifted goon.

I keep running at the one who'd been standing there first. He can multiply all he wants, but as long as I keep my eyes on the first one, the others don't matter.

Or so I thought.

Two leap and tackle me to the ground, breaking my line of sight. Sand scrapes against my cheek. I reach back for anything I can touch, and I grasp whatever I feel behind me.

He screams when I make contact. He tries to pull away, but I latch on to make sure I finish it.

Something sharp sticks into my back, and I buck and push onto my hands and knees, then spin around while reaching back to the syringe sticking out of my shoulder to yank it out. It doesn't fall apart in my hand right away like I expect, and I check in with my gift. The stab broke my concentration on it, but I hadn't even noticed with how my hands are throbbing with pain.

One of his clones is dead on the ground. His skin is split, and there's blood leaking from his eyes, mouth, and ears.

By now, I can hear the others splashing out of the water to join us.

The clone who'd stuck me grabs me by the throat and shoves me back onto the ground. "That fucking hurt, you stupid bitch."

I slide the thin blades from my thigh holster while he's busy spitting crap at me for losing a fucking copy of himself. I grip them all in my hand at once and then slash them across his throat as hard as I can. Blood spurts and then sprays over me as he chokes, wide-eyed.

I shove him to the side and scramble to my feet just as something latches around my wrist. I swipe my blades across it without thinking. I don't care who or what it is. Anything or anyone who touches me is an enemy.

Turns out it came out of one of the other goons who'd been in the water. He sends another rope-like appendage after me, and I'm able to dodge it.

Then it curves.

For fuck's sake.

Time to start throwing knives.

I aim and pitch the first one at the guy with the weird, growing limb. It embeds into his chest, and he staggers back just as his appendage wraps around my thigh. It drops to the ground, and I heave a second knife at another guy.

This one only hits his shoulder, and aside from roaring in pain or anger, he doesn't seem fazed by it.

I'm down to one more throwing knife and my dagger in my boot.

Against five more guys.

Someone grabs me from behind, and I cry out when my arms are yanked painfully behind me. Another jab from a needle bruises my neck.

Nope.

I'm done.

I don't care how much my hands hurt; my body hurts. I don't care that it feels like I'm burning myself alive inside my skin right now.

I draw every ounce of my gift up under my skin until I'm a goddamn lightning bug and listen to the screams of the man who'd been holding me. The syringe in my neck crumbles to the sand. The knife in my hand is gone too, but it's a loss I'll take over the possibility of being knocked out by whatever is in these syringes.

I leap at the next guy, wrapping my body around him.

His screams of terror pierce my ears, and he punches and claws at me, drawing blood from my arms, but I don't relent. The others move up around us, but they don't intervene. What can they do? Pull me off and risk my gift?

Once this one is well and done, I drop down and run at the next one.

A gunshot rings in my ears, and concentrated fire sears into my shoulder. My gift flickers and dies as I stumble and reach for the injury. I pull my hand away, and there's blood on my fingers.

Ah, shit.

I yell and run at them anyway, refusing to give up until my last breath.

One of them falls to the ground, but I'm too preoccupied with pulling out the dagger in my boot and launching myself at one of the guys to see what happened to him. I aim for his eye, but he grabs my wrist to hold me back. His foot kicks out my legs, and he falls on top of me, pinning me to the sand.

My arms are shaking with the effort to stab him, but he's much stronger than me and not only holds me back, but starts to twist my wrists to the side at a painful angle. I cry out and release the dagger.

He drops on top of me, and all the breath in my body leaves me in a wheeze. I pause for a second when I realize he's not moving and then peek around him.

Black combat boots greet me.

The guy on top of me rolls away, and I take a deep lungful of air.

A hand in fingerless gloves appears before my face, and I reach for it. A cool breeze sweeps across my heated skin, and I remember that my gift might still be charged. I push off of the ground instead.

Jackson doesn't get angry or snap at me for refusing his offer. He merely tilts his head to the side and watches me. His cerulean gaze is intense and laser-focused on me. It's not asking or demanding anything from me. He's just...there if I need him.

I swallow and hold my hands to my chest. Even though he didn't ask, my gratefulness for his help loosens my tongue. "Sorry. I'm not sure I'm...off...yet."

He smiles at me, the kind where it exposes the dimple in his left cheek, and brings his hand up to my face.

I step back on reflex, baffled that he'd try to touch me after what I'd admitted.

"You won't hurt me," he murmurs softly. I don't understand how he can have that much trust in me after everything I've done. And after not knowing me over the last six years. How can he believe that?

"I might, Jack. You shouldn't touch me yet." I'm not sure why I added 'yet' at the end of that. He shouldn't touch me at all.

But I'd be lying if I said my body wasn't trying to push me toward him. I'm drawn to his self-assuredness and calm confidence. I want to wrap myself up in it like a blanket and take a long, deep breath that I've gone years without. To wear his inner strength like armor where nothing and no one can touch me.

He's like a boulder in the ocean, standing tall and strong no matter the temper of the sea crashing against it. That's what Jackson feels like. And for once, I'd like to hold on to something that won't break under the waves and will keep me above water.

Jackson's smile tilts to more of a smirk, and he touches his palm to my cheek anyway.

I'm tempted to jump back, my body trembling from both fear of hurting him and exhaustion. I try to check in with my gift, make sure it's fully contained and dormant, but when he doesn't show any sign of pain, I release a breath.

"Jack—" I start to chastise.

"You should trust yourself more, Raegan." His thumb grazes

across my cheekbone. Then his hand slides down to my neck, leaving warmth and tingling in its wake. My pulse beats erratically against his hand. He's stepped up close, so there's barely any air between us, but only his hand is actually making any contact.

"I know you'd never hurt me like that." His eyes lock onto mine, and it feels like he's peering straight into my soul. "You can trust yourself with me. Like you used to."

His other arm presses into my lower back, and he pulls me against him. I stiffen at the unexpected, but familiar, embrace. He buries his nose in my neck and inhales like he's taking a drag of a cigarette.

But it's of me.

A shiver rolls from my neck to my toes and forces them to curl to do *something* with the feeling.

Jackson wraps himself around me while I'm frozen like a rabbit in the eyes of a wolf. The smell of autumn surrounds me while his clothes block out any light from the moon or stars until I'm enveloped in him. His hold tightens, and while I'd think that would make me more concerned, it has the complete opposite effect, and my body melts into him instead.

I press into him, my hands burying themselves in his hoodie as the fear and adrenaline begins to drain from my body.

"Come back to the safehouse with me. You can get cleaned up there, and I can patch you up."

"If the others are there..."

"They're not. We live in the Tower." He points to the tallest building in the city skyline that's visible from nearly everywhere in the city. It's also oddly the one that Elias had pointed out as where some Guild works out of.

He holds my arm, and I look at the bullet wound. It just grazed me, which is good news. But when I check Jackson's expression, his face is pulled down in a frown.

I can count on one hand the number of times I've seen him frown. "What?"

His eyes snap back to mine. "This shouldn't have happened. I should've been here sooner."

I scoff and step away from him. "I'm surprised you were here at all. Thank you for that, by the way." He still doesn't look any more reassured, but I'm not sure what he expects of himself. He's not my babysitter, and ordinarily, I don't need one. I may have made it out of that encounter with my life, but it was a little too close.

They're coming at me harder than before. More goons, better gifts.

The beach is now littered with bodies when I finally take the time to survey the aftermath. "What about them?"

Jackson shrugs and smiles. "I'll take care of them in a bit." He waves his hand, and one of the men lifts into the air. One by one, he moves the bodies into a boat. They're all out of line and banging together now that the pier is gone and their ropes are floating on the water.

My knives come floating back, and I pick them out of the air and return them to their holster. "Which asshole had the gun?"

He raises his eyebrows at me, and I roll my eyes. "Aiden disfigured mine. I could have used a gun tonight." He nods and takes my hand without hesitation, pulling me with him to walk closer to the boat with the bodies. That simple touch sends me right back to the island. His familiar hold on my hand makes me feel precious and protected.

He leaps toward the boat, using his gift to keep him aloft until he lands perfectly on the edge. Even as the vessel tips and rolls over the waves, his balance doesn't waver. He picks through the guys and then sails back through the air. Jackson hands me two guns.

"You should have told me. I have plenty of weapons if you need them."

I tuck them into my pants, double-checking first that their safeties are on. "Duly noted." I smile, and his reciprocal smile is heart-melting.

Gah.

I don't know what to believe about him anymore. If he hated me, why would he have come all the way out here to save me? Why is he acting like no time has passed between us? Like I didn't kill Vera?

He must see the confusion in my expression because he chuckles and shakes his head at me. "You can ask me anything you want. I'm an open book." Jackson pulls his hood up to hide his face again and sticks his hands in his hoodie pocket. For someone claiming to be so open, he sure looks closed off and untouchable from the outside.

But he always had, hadn't he? He kept to himself, making his origami animals in our room or hanging back in class. He was more like a fly on the wall in every room, present but not making himself stand out. No, that's not right. Maybe more like a raven. Always watching and observing everything happening in the room until he knew anything and everything about everyone. Ready to strike if needed, but content to do nothing until that time came.

"Why don't you hate me? The others do, and I get it. But not you. I killed Vera. I've admitted it to you multiple times. She was one of us. Like a sister to both of us. But...you haven't batted an eyelash over it."

Jackson nods and runs his hand back and forth over his hair under the hood while gazing up at the stars. "Mm. Right. That." His face angles back to gaze at me, his signature smile still there, and he shrugs. "I trust you."

There's that word again. "I don't know why you do, but anyway, how does that answer my question? I'm tired of vague answers, Jack. Just...help me understand why you're here right now. Why you just saved me or care at all about me."

"You wouldn't have done it without a reason. You said it yourself. She was like a sister to you. Her death must have hurt you as much as it did the rest of us." His smile drops for a second. "Except for Dane." Of course.

"So, when you admitted that you'd killed her, I knew there was more to it. I figured you needed some time to grieve, and then you would come find us and tell us what actually happened. When you didn't, I went to find you, but GE had separated you from us after that. I had to wait until we were both moving between rooms so I could catch you, but before that ever happened, the mansion collapsed."

He believed in me? And still does? I'd thought...he had turned his back on me. Like the others. That was all I'd wanted from them. Some shred of belief or trust in me after all we'd been through together.

Instead, they'd left me to GE.

To *him*.

I fight for control of the wetness in my eyes to keep it from spilling over. I clear my throat and press on because that's not everything. "If you believed in me like you said, you wouldn't have left the island without me. You wouldn't have abandoned me there with...them," I choke out bitterly. A rogue tear escapes down my cheek, and Jackson catches it with a bent finger, then brings it to his lips.

"No. I went to look for you, but Aiden asked me to help guide the boat with my gift. He told me he would find and bring you back." There's a long pause, and I wonder if Jackson knows what Aiden actually did.

He *did* find me. But he didn't bring me back.

He left me defenseless and alone with our enemies.

"By the time he came back, he was alone and being chased. He had to dive onto the boat and we had to speed away before they could catch us. Once we were out on open water, Aiden said he couldn't find you, that another boat was already gone and you must have left without us. I didn't learn you were still on the island until years later."

Aiden did this? On his own?

Why? Why not just ignore me and get on their boat? Why did he hunt me down to leave me vulnerable like that?

Jackson watches me intently as if he's trying to pry open my head and see what's going through my mind now. He's not angry or upset with Aiden. That tells me he has no idea what his "brother" has done.

I could tell him and the others, but what would it change?

Jackson might kill Aiden.

The thought startles me. Shit, would he? Over me? After everything he's been saying, I can't rule that possibility out.

Which means I can't tell him. Not yet, anyway.

I have unfinished business with Aiden first.

"Are you going to share what you're thinking, little one?"

I smile at him with a faux-sweet look that he sees right through based on the twitch of his lips. "Nope," I tease, popping the 'p'. He looks disappointed, and now that I know how he's felt about me all of this time, it feels right to playfully nudge him and start walking back toward the city. "Not yet," I amend.

He nods, and his lips curve upward. "Yet," he echoes like a promise.

Chapter Fifteen

RAEGAN

The chorus of "Chandelier" by Sia pierces through the fog of sleep. I moan and fumble my hand around blindly in search of an alarm clock snooze. The chorus starts up again and then I realize that alarm clocks don't play old hit songs.

My new burner phone does.

Well, it plays run-of-the-mill nagging ringtones, but when I gave Portia my phone to add her number, she apparently downloaded a bunch of songs and set up various sounds in it for different notifications.

Wait.

Portia.

I jolt upward and scramble for my phone, the last cobwebs of sleep in my head blown away in a panic. Portia is the only person who has my current number while Elias is out of reach.

I check the time on my phone before hitting answer as a third round of the chorus begins. Just after one in the morning. Which means I'd barely been in bed for an hour.

"Portia?"

"Rae? Oh, thank goodness you're okay!" She sounds relieved, but it's the hushed tones that tell me something's not right.

"What's wrong? Are you okay?" I swipe my hand across where the wall and light switch should be and hit air. I shift closer, and my knees knock into something hard instead.

What the—

"There are people here looking for you, Rae," Portia whispers.

I stop my hunt for the light and straighten. "Where are you?"

"At the club. They're searching the crowd and asking around for you. Someone told them you work here," she hisses. I'm shocked at the anger in her voice, especially because it's on my behalf.

"Okay. I'll be right down, and I'll take care of it. Just pretend you know nothing about me and get out of there if anything happens."

I can't believe that GE would start a big commotion at a night-club, so as long as she keeps working and doesn't mention knowing me, there shouldn't be an issue. I'll just have to draw them out of there and figure out what to do after that.

"Hey, you!" I hear through the phone and freeze. "Is that her? I hear you're friends with who we're looking for."

"Hm? Oh, no. Mm-mm. I'm talking to my...girlfriend. Not girl *friend*. But, like, this girl I'm seeing. You know?"

I drag my hand down my face in secondhand embarrassment. "We need to work on your cover-up skills," I murmur softly into the phone.

"Oh yeah?" The male voice gets louder, and I hurry back to finding the light switch so I can get dressed. My fingers finally run across one on the other side of the room, and I'm momentarily blinded before an unfamiliar room is revealed.

Wait, not entirely unfamiliar.

"Well then, why did I just hear her on your phone?" he continues, and my stomach drops. "Trying to coach you on what to do?"

Does he have that good of hearing, or is he gifted?

"I've gotta go, babe. I'll talk to you soon."

"Wait, no—!" I shout into the phone just as she hangs up.

Dammit!

I look around Jackson's room at the safehouse where he'd taken me to let me shower and clean my wounds. I must have fallen asleep at some point, and he'd moved me to his bed.

"Jack?!" I run through the safe house, checking each room in only a shirt of his that barely hits my thighs. I must have been thoroughly beat for him to have convinced me to wear this, but most of the night after the fight is a blur of pain and exhaustion. "Jackson!" I shout again.

Nothing.

He must still be out disposing of the bodies.

The washing machine has my bloody clothes in them, clean and washed but soaked.

I snatch a pair of sweatpants and a hoodie of Jackson's and pull those on for now, rolling up the waistband on the pants to keep them around my waist. I get my guns and knives strapped beneath the clothes. Then I'm out the secret hatch through the roof that Jackson showed me last night, shimmying down the hidden steps and cutouts until I'm back on the ground.

It fucking figures that the *one* night I'm not in my apartment, right where I need to be to stay close to Portia, I'm not.

My body screams the entire sprint to the nightclub. I'd come away from the earlier fight in decent shape, considering my odds, but my torso, neck, and arms are bruised to shit. My arms are clawed up like I got into a fight with a cat and then there's the pesky bullet wound on my shoulder, cleaned and taped over with gauze.

The hoodie hides it all, though, so aside from looking tiny in large, black clothes that cover me up more than a nun in church compared with what everyone else in the club is wearing, I don't stand out too much.

"Portia?" I breathlessly ask the bartender—James, I think—while also looking around for any sign of the thugs. My eyes catch on something purple and shiny further down and behind the bar. The lights in the club reflect off of the person, making them stand out like a disco ball and instantly drawing my focus.

I don't even wait for him to answer me, jogging down the line and pushing through the drunk customers to get a closer look. Portia straightens and slides shots across the bar to her current customers with a smile. Her skirt and bra look more like a purple swimsuit with a layer of dangling silver scales. She looks like a mermaid between her outfit and makeup, and I can clearly see that she's uninjured with the amount of exposed, unmarked skin she has on display.

"Portia!" I call out above the music and the crowd.

She turns and beams at me, flouncing over while spinning a wink at someone as she passes them. "Rae! I'm glad you're okay. But should you really be here right now?"

"You're glad *I'm* okay?! What happened? I came to make sure *you* were okay."

"Oh." She shrugs and starts making a drink. For who, I'm not sure, but it seems more like a defense mechanism to keep herself busy. Like she can't sit still for a second to talk about something as serious as what almost happened. "I just asked them to leave."

I stare at her in disbelief. When she doesn't elaborate, I take a deep breath. "And they, what? Just did as you asked and left?"

She hums under her breath, adding something else to her concoction, and then shakes it and pours out two glasses of neon green liquid. "I asked nicely," she finally concedes, as if that makes all the sense in the world.

They knew she knew me. They'd heard her *talking* to me while they were trying to find me. And she just...asked them to leave, and they did without a fight? Without kidnapping her?

Wait.

I reach over the counter and grab her wrist to get her full attention. "Porsh. Are you...?" I don't say it aloud.

There's a flash of something *real* in her expression, and then like the flick of a switch, she's smiling and innocent again. "That's all it was, Rae. I'm glad you're okay, but you may not want to hang around here for a bit. I can tell everyone you quit, so if they come asking again, that's all they'll hear."

She's gentle but firm when she pulls away from me. I don't fight her, even though I could have held on. I'm not looking to back her into a corner to talk to me. I'm trying to look out for her, and yet she's somehow the one looking after me. How the hell did that happen?

Portia turns away and serves up the drinks to a couple of girls at the bar. I watch her in silence as I stew over what she told me. I have to be right. I know she's sweet, but there is *no* way she talked herself out of that situation. And I see no sign of injury to indicate that she somehow fought them.

But they are gone like she said.

And she doesn't look the least bit ruffled.

I narrow my eyes at her and try to look past the show of innocence. Now that I'm looking hard enough, I can see it. It's exactly that. A show.

All of her expressions, the way she moves, it's an act. I have to be paying attention and looking for it, but I can see it for a split second here and there where her mask slips.

I move around the bar and take her hand when she finishes closing out someone's tab. "We need to talk," I tell her, giving her a *look* that shows I mean business. She blinks at me and nods, letting me guide her by the hand into the back hallway until we're in Elias's office.

I close and lock the door behind her.

She watches me quietly. Her face is calm and otherwise blank, so I have no idea what she thinks I'm bringing her back here for.

"Tell me what actually happened." She opens her mouth, and I hold up my hand to stop her. "Not that bullshit line about being *nice* and just asking. I know who sent them, and they wouldn't have left just like that. I appreciate you looking out for me, but I need to look out for you too, in case those guys come back." I pause and then cock my head the slightest amount. "*Will* they come back?"

She smiles and turns away from me to the chairs in front of the desk, then spins and drops back over the nearest armchair. Her silver stiletto heels bounce over the edge as she stretches her arms over her head.

"I didn't lie to you. I did ask them nicely to leave. My requests just carry a bit more...oomph...to them."

I knew it.

I raise an eyebrow. "Oomph. As in, an extra special ability to what? Tell people what to do?"

She hums and picks at the scales over her skirt. "Something like that." Her forest green eyes slide back up to my face. "I'm sure you already know all about things like that. Elias wouldn't have let you stay or work here otherwise."

"Are you saying everyone who works at Hype has a gift?"

Portia shrugs. "Almost everyone. Those who don't, know about it, though."

I didn't realize Elias kept his staff and tenants exclusively to other gifted people or those who know about us. So, nearly everyone working here has a gift? That gives me a whole new perspective of the club.

Portia smiles and nods at my sudden realization, then flips her legs over the arm to bounce back onto her feet. "Right. So, what can you do?"

Turn objects to ash. Take down buildings. Break a person apart from the inside out.

Yeah.

No big deal. Definitely not villain-esque.

"I'd rather not talk about it. It's the reason I'm running from those guys that came looking for me, so it'd be better if you didn't know."

"Well, those guys shouldn't be coming back here. If anyone else comes in, I can talk to them too."

"What exactly did you say?" I pause and quickly add, "Wait. Is it something you can turn off and on? If you say it to me, will it affect me?"

Portia giggles and shakes her head, sending her long brown locks swaying back over her shoulders. "I can turn it on when I want to use it. I just told them you weren't here. And to leave and never come back."

I chew on my lip. This means I'll be safe from them, but they could send others. That's not what worries me, though. What if they, or others, while talking to those guys, realize that Portia used a gift on them? "Do they remember that you said something when you use your gift on them? Would they be able to figure out what happened?"

"Well..." She tangles her fingers. "Not usually. Definitely not non-gifted. But it has happened before with others like us. I'm not sure if it's based on their gift's strength or if something else breaks them free of it."

"Breaks them free?"

"My command wears off once they realize it for what it is. So, if they figure out what I did, it stops working."

Shit on a stick.

If that happens, they won't come back for me next time.

They'll come for Portia too. They would love to have a gift like hers at their disposal.

Any other time I've been found by Gifted Enterprise, I've split. It isn't worth the risk of being captured or killed by them. This is a big world, and there are plenty of other places I can be. I don't have roots anywhere, so the world is my oyster and all that shit.

But now? I can't leave Portia. Not when I'm the reason she could be captured and taken in by the people who messed me up. She may not be as innocent as she appears, but there's still something pure and *good* about her that I can't let them tarnish.

If only Elias wasn't gone.

Though, I guess that's not my only reason for wanting to stay. Even though I haven't been here long, this place has felt more like a home than anywhere else has so far. I'm starting to make friends, I have a good place to stay and a way to make money, and I've made more progress here than anywhere else.

I sigh and rub my temples over the headache beginning to build. I need sleep. And I need a plan to keep us both safe.

I don't like the answer that comes because I'm not used to depending on others, but this is about more than just me now.

It's time to visit that friend of Elias's. And until then...

"All right. You can't go back to your apartment. There's too big of a risk that when they find out what you did, they'll come here and follow you home when no one else is around." I move through the room, opening drawers and cabinets in my hunt.

She rolls her eyes at me, and I try to contain my annoyance. "I can take care of myself. I'll be fine."

She doesn't know, I reason with myself with my teeth clenched. She has no idea who Gifted Enterprise is and what they would do to her. How they would break her into pieces just so they could remold her into something of their own creation.

"Not with them. Trust me, Portia. I've been their prisoner before. You *can't* let them take you. I can't let that happen. Please, just...just humor me with this. I won't be able to sleep again if you don't." I don't even care if I'm being dramatic. Elias would kill me if anything happened to her.

I would lose my mind if I let anything happen to her too.

Portia keeps watching me tear the office apart. "What are you looking for?"

I slam another desk drawer closed. "Keys to the apartments in case there's an open one you can stay in."

She moves to a short, wooden cabinet behind the desk, opens a door, and then enters a combination into a safe. It clicks open on the first try. Portia holds up a key card and grins. "He's too predictable sometimes."

I have a feeling that's not inclusive of just anyone.

"Good. You can crash there until I get this handled. Keep a low profile until then, and I'll let you know when it's safe."

"I can help you."

No. Absolutely not.

"I'd rather know that you're safe here. If everyone here has a gift, then put them all on high alert. Look out for each other. Don't let it slip to anyone who they are until these guys are off of our backs."

Frowning, she checks the clock in the room. "Last call has already been announced. I'll head up now to check out my new home."

I nod and silently apologize to Elias for the mess in his office. From what I know of him, he might have an aneurysm if he sees it. "I'll walk you there so I know where it is and show you mine."

I rap against Apartment 148B, where Elias's friend and designated contact point lives. It's one of those modern, sleek style buildings that fancy business people usually live out of. There's a lobby area, restaurant, gym, and pool all on the first floor. I had to actually check in as a guest at the front desk and receive approval from the tenant to be allowed access upstairs.

I wonder why Portia isn't staying in a place like this. I'm sure Elias would pay for it, considering all of his resources.

Then again, it's a good twelve blocks from the nightclub and a decent walk.

Now that his friend knows I'm here, thanks to the front desk, I'm expecting the door to open right away.

It doesn't.

I knock again harder.

"One second! One second! Don't break the door down!"

I wasn't banging on the door *that* hard, was I?

It swings open, revealing a guy with messy black hair and ash grey highlights around my age. He nearly collapses against the door jamb with a grin. "Ah, if it isn't Miss Raegan of Ruin. Ruination? No, ruin." He snaps his fingers and points at me. "Catchier to keep it short."

My blood chills. "What did you call me?"

"Oh! Just a little nickname I've been working on since I heard about your"—he wiggles his fingers at me—"gift from Eli."

I swallow, struggling with the lump in my throat at what that could mean. "Are you...Kit?" I take a gamble from the word scribbled on the paper with the address.

"That's me! Short for Kittredge, but what the hell kind of name is that, am I right? Eli said that Kit fits me, though, so that's what I go by now."

"Er, right. Can I come in, Kit?"

"Sure, sure." He steps back and waves me in. The entryway is tiled, with a narrow table and mirror on one side and a narrow door on the other. "Can I get you something to eat? Drink?" he calls over his shoulder as I follow him further inside to the living room.

"Thanks, but I shouldn't be long. What gift did Elias tell you I have?" I ask while I take in the room. There are dog beds and toys filling the room, and even then, there's fur coating the couches. I look around for a dog or dogs, but no one comes running out of the open doors off the living room.

Kit spins around and collapses into the couch, which seems more fluff than substance because it swallows him up like a bean bag. His grin widens, and I notice the sharp point of his canines. Did he file them down like that, or was he born that way? "Just the cool power to destroy. Anything. And everything."

My stomach drops. How? And from Europe, no less? I'm too anxious to sit anywhere and keep myself standing at the edge of the sitting area. "And what makes him think that's my gift?" I try to keep my voice calm and nonchalant.

"The Seer person he's with out there. Said you were in trouble tonight. Well, that Portia was in trouble when Eli asked about her, and he wound up seeing what you were up to instead. Since, you know, you're what led to Portia being in trouble."

Fuck a duck.

"What do you mean he 'saw' me?"

He shrugs and kicks his bare feet up and over the coffee table. "The Seer can share what they see, when they see it. So, he watched most of it. Like a movie in his head." He points to the side of his head and then cocks it to the side. "Eli also saw you coming here to tell me about Portia. He said the Seer didn't see any issues with Portia for at least another couple of weeks, so he should be wrapped up with his project by then to come home. She'll be safe in the apartment you put her in."

"Oh." I sit in the armchair so I can process all of that.

Elias knows what my gift is now. He actually watched me use it.

On people. He's seen me for the monster that I am, and instead of rushing home to keep me away from Portia, he's still leaving her in my care for a few weeks.

He must be crazy.

Kit lets me sit in silence for all of thirty seconds before he bounces back to his feet. "I'm surprised you're here so early, though. I knew you were coming, but I figured you'd try to get some more sleep first. You must care about Portia a lot that you came straight here after. That's really sweet. I like you." He's talking a mile a minute with chihuahua energy, and I just stare blankly at him.

"Um. Yeah." I stand too. "Sorry to have wasted your time since you already know everything."

"No worries at all. You had to come. Since you didn't know I knew. Oh, and I have to give you something." He digs into his cargo pockets, working through different ones until he pulls a slip of paper out with some chicken-scratch writing on it. "Eli asked me to give you this information. Said it was your next lead. This guy is going to be at that address next Friday. He said you should look into him."

I take the piece of paper from Kit and memorize it just in case, then shove it in my pocket. "Thanks. I'm going to assume this nugget of information came from the Seer as well?"

Kit laughs and leads me back to the door. "Something like that."

I'm not sure what that means, but I don't push for more. He's stretching and yawning so wide he could catch butterflies, and I instantly feel bad for coming over so early in the morning.

I step out his door and turn to look one last time over my shoulder. "Thanks again. And sorry for the early morning visit."

"No problem at all, Raegan of Ruin."

"Don't call me that," I growl.

He smirks and closes the door.

Chapter Sixteen

RAEGAN

I SPEND THE NEXT couple of days at the library researching the man on the paper from Elias via Kit. Turns out he's a congressman, which is lucky for me because the internet is bursting with information about him.

A man in his fifties, been in the government for half of his life, and well-liked by his constituents. I had to Google that word; I'm not gonna lie. Government and the legal system were not something we went into great detail in understanding on the island. And the streets didn't teach it either.

His wife passed away from cancer seven years ago, and he's been somewhat of a popular bachelor since. He was even named sexiest man of the year by his state last year, which is apparently a thing. For every party and event he attends, he has a different girl on his arm. The standard seems to be young, blonde, and pretty.

He crossed the underage line at least once and was called out on it in a scandal four years ago. Seems he's been more careful since then, and he's played it off as helping law and political science students experience work and life as a congressman in a short-term work study. It explains why he rotates through the women so quickly and why they're all so young.

The rest…either the people like him enough to turn a blind eye, or he's got good support to keep his name from being smeared in the media.

Which probably brings this all back to Gifted Enterprise.

I knew that they must have had ties to the government to keep all of their experiments under wraps and out of any red tape, but seeing it still leaves a bad taste in my mouth.

After the third day of staring blearily at the computer screen—seriously, I don't know how people can stare at a screen every day—I've got Congressman Joe all figured out.

It helps that he's had enough interviews stored on the internet for literally *anyone* to access that I know everything from his address and general schedule to his likes and dislikes.

Including the party happening this Friday at the city mayor's house on the beach. It's his annual end of summer bash that's open to the public. Security will be tight, I'm sure, but it also means that among the hundreds of guests that usually appear, I will easily blend in.

Now all I need is a flowery, summer dress and a backstory.

"So, what are you studying at school?"

A brown-haired, brown-eyed guest, who I've guessed is in his thirties, takes his place at my side as I stare out at the ocean. My heels are gone, lost somewhere at the base of the deck so my feet could sink into the warm reserves of the sand for what's left of the sun's heat now that it's slipped below the horizon.

There's a dusky glow over the water still. I love watching the transition to night as the light inevitably gives in and sinks into the blanket of darkness.

I blink to break myself free of the trance I'd been in. I bring the champagne flute filled with some fruity thing or other to my lips, and I set my gaze over the rim to finally give full attention to the guest who's been almost constantly in my shadow since I arrived.

At first, I'd given in to his attentions and flirted back to keep up appearances that I knew someone here and fit in. But this is the fourth time he's sought me out to restart our conversation after I'd excused myself.

He's keeping me away from the congressman. I can't let this entire afternoon be in vain when Elias specifically mentioned this day. There's still the rest of the night to go, but the hours of pretending to fit in here are already taking a toll on me.

I lick my lips so as not to waste what little alcohol the drink has in it and force myself to smile. "Business law," I recite based on the university major that the congressman seems to use as his excuse for his hunting ground of young women.

"That's wonderful. I'm an attorney, you know. If you ever need an internship closer to your field of study, I'd love to help out." He smiles, and that's when I can't stop seeing the Ken doll. He looks like he had been the model for it because even his expression is spot-on.

Wide smile with bright white teeth and looking like plastic.

My stomach takes this opportunity to growl at him to back off.

His brow pinches with concern. "Didn't you eat anything? I'm sure there's still some left. Or the dessert should be out by now."

"I did." I laugh softly behind my hand. "I suppose that wasn't enough, though. Or I'm just hungry for dessert."

I *am* hungry for dessert, but I'm not sure how much I trust what they'll be bringing out. None of the food was edible. There was shit on boards that looked like cat food. And servings like octopus balls. Really? If that's what the rich eat, then I'll pass and take a greasy burger or pizza any day of the week.

"Come on, then." He jerks his head back to the beach house. "Let's see what they have."

"Sure." I smile back. My face is going to be sore for days after how long I've had to keep my face smiling like this.

I follow him back up the beach and grab my heels on the way in to the mayor's lavish mansion. The tables are spread with desserts now of all shapes and colors. I don't recognize most, but I spot some original cheesecake with cherries, and yup, that's exactly what I'm going to eat.

My body won't be thrilled that *that* is the only thing it's gotten in the last day, but hey, beggars can't be choosers. And I'm nearly to the beggary status now.

"There you are!" someone calls out behind us and then chuckles.

I turn and blink when it's Congressman Joe slapping his hand on

Ken doll's shoulder. "I've been needing to speak with you. Where have you been all day?" he continues.

Ken's gaze lands on mine as he smiles at me. The congressman follows his look to me and his eyebrows shoot up to his hairline.

"Oh, I see. Entertaining a date, perhaps?" He moves around Ken doll and extends his hand out between us.

I try for a shy smile, which seems to work considering how the congressman's polite smile sharpens in response, and reach for his hand. Rather than shake my hand when he has it in his grasp, he tugs me forward and plants a kiss on the back of it.

"It's a pleasure to meet someone as...delectable as you, my dear," Joe tries and fails to deliver seductively. Or maybe I'm too obsessed with Aiden's voice that anyone else's just falls flat.

The gasp that leaves my lips at the sudden jolt is real, and Ken doll takes that as his cue to step between us. "We were just discussing her new internship with me," he says, his voice strained as he looks at my hand still in the congressman's hold.

Joe gives me another once-over from head to toe, pausing not-so-subtly on any exposed skin. His smile borders on leery when he's finished. "A law student as well?"

My mouth opens to counter Ken's claim that I was already his intern. It would never work considering my false identity doesn't actually exist, let alone go to the local university, but they're both too wrapped up in whatever dick-measuring contest is happening between them to notice.

"Yes, business law. But I needed to get her fed before we could continue that conversation. It seems she didn't have enough to eat earlier."

"I see. Or the earlier food wasn't to your tastes...was it, dear?"

I pull my hand free of his, which he thankfully relents to without complaint. I'm not completely sure how to answer his question safely. Is it rude to admit that was the case? It's not like he's the actual host. I want to stay on his good side to see what more I can learn from him, though, and it seems safe enough to agree with his observation for now.

"Sorry, but...not really," I admit softly.

Joe grins and wraps his arm around my shoulders. I have to fight back the knee-jerk reaction to stiffen at his overly-familiar touch, but he doesn't seem to notice. "Don't worry, my dear. The mayor tends to go overboard at these events with the eclectic menu, so there's nothing for you to be sorry about." I nod slowly, too focused on his touch to pay his words much attention. "A pretty thing like you can't only eat the fluffy desserts that are left. My residence is a few streets away from here, and my cook can whip up something more suited to your tastes if you'd like."

My head snaps up at the same time as Ken doll's.

"Oh, I couldn't—"

"Hey, wait just a minute, Joe. She and I were—"

"—about to discuss the internship, I know. We'll eat something quick and be right back within the hour. I'll have her back to you before you know it," the congressman schmoozes with practiced ease. His face tilts down so he can turn his creepy smile on me. "What do you say..." His sentence hangs there for a few seconds until I realize what he's asking for.

"Rebecca," I answer with my false identity I came up with.

"Rebecca," he repeats. "The party is still far from over, and I'm sure you'll need something more substantial to eat in the meantime. I'll bring you back as soon as you've eaten, on my honor."

I look between the congressman and Ken doll, suddenly unsure of the situation I've found myself in. This was supposed to be a reconnaissance mission. Keep an eye on who Joe talks to. Listen in on any conversations I can. Look for any hints or clues that might lead to a connection with GE.

But being invited to his place?

What if it's a trap?

Yes, but for a helpless college law student he *just* met. It's not like he had this prepared in advance. If I tried to reschedule to give myself time to prepare with weapons, it would give him the same opportunity. At least doing this spur of the moment on both sides gives me more of a chance to see him with his guard down.

I could ask to use the restroom and maybe snoop around a bit. See if I can find anything there on GE.

Perfect.

Best case, he feeds me and brings me back here exactly as he promised. He does believe I have someone waiting here for me, at least, so it's not like he would do anything to make me disappear. Still, I know a slimeball when I see one.

Worst case is that he tries to take advantage of me.

Unfortunately, I have experience with that, and I can handle it.

Ken still looks annoyed that I'm being taken away, but I note he doesn't protest any further after Joe's promise to bring me back within the hour. That should be comforting that he doesn't plan to kidnap or kill me, but I need one more safeguard to be sure.

"Okay," I acquiesce softly. "I really appreciate it, Sir. I need to tell the friend I came with that I'll be at your place for the next hour, though, so she doesn't worry or leave without me. Do you mind if I let her know to wait for me?"

His face doesn't falter at the mention of my "friend," which puts me more at ease. Good. Whatever his intentions are, he isn't worried about bringing me back on time and well enough for me to go home with my friend. And he'll believe someone is here waiting for me and would report that I hadn't returned after going with him.

"Of course. I'll call my driver to pull up out front and you can meet us there once you've spoken with your friend." His arm drops from my shoulders to give me room.

I offer him and Ken a smile and then hurry off to pretend looking through the crowd for my *friend*. I slip into the restroom to pretend I found her in there and then make my way to the front door.

The black SUV smells of leather and fresh polish. Every shift in the seat causes an audible creak, and I can barely breathe to keep from fidgeting too much.

What would normally have two rows of seats in the back instead has two bench seats facing one another, and a black divider wall between us and the driver.

He smiles at me once I've buckled myself in for the short, two-minute trip to his home. Large, ornate gates slowly open when we approach, and then we drive around a brick circle to the front door.

I move to open my door, but Joe places a hand on my lap. I bite down my instinctual reaction to flinch, but enough comes through that I can tell he noticed. I try to laugh it off. "Sorry, I'm a bit nervous coming to a congressman's home. Especially one as nice as this."

Joe chuckles and pats my leg. "Don't worry, my dear. It's nothing special. I just wanted you to know that my driver will be around to open your door for you," he explains just as his driver opens his door first, even though he'd been seated on the passenger side.

He exits out his door, and I wait for the driver to open mine.

Relax.

He's on a time limit and he knows it. People are expecting me back. Whatever intention he has for bringing me here, it can't be anything too terrible. And I can't pass up the opportunity to find out why Elias wants me looking into this man. I need to find that connection before we head back to the party.

The driver prompts me to walk up the front steps to where a butler is waiting for me at the door.

"Please, this way, Ma'am. Mr. Tabershire has asked that you wait for him in the lounge while he places your food order in the kitchens."

He guides me to one of the many rooms off the main hallway through double doors. The room is about the size of my living room and kitchen at Elias's apartment combined, so its size isn't overly daunting. The style and contents are more so, between the heavy maroon drapes tied with golden rope on either side of the massive window taking up one wall, to the built-in, mahogany book shelves that fill in the other three walls with more books than I've seen in one place aside from a public library. The furniture is all the same, shining dark wood, with tight fabrics spread over the sofa chairs and couches.

The seating area is arranged around a gas fireplace, while a desk is settled in the back corner with a couple wooden chairs.

I head straight for the desk, convinced I may spot something of value within the papers laying haphazardly across it without a care in the world.

"Ah, Rebecca." I pause in place, even though I'm steps away from the desk and my goal. "Please, sit over here while we wait."

Damn.

I try to peer at the contents from my current position, but after a brief scan, nothing sticks out at me from this distance. I need to get closer to the desk and I need more time.

"Oh, okay." He's standing at the edge of the sitting area. "Actually, I am a bit thirsty. Would you mind—"

"Curtis!" Joe shouts out before I can finish. The assumed-butler appears in the doorway as if he'd been standing at the ready just outside of it for this exact purpose. "Some drinks, if you would."

"Of course, Sir." Curtis looks at me. "What would the lady like?"

My teeth bite down on my inner cheek in frustration. Right. He has house servants to get these things for him. Why did I assume Joe would get me a drink?

Then why did he go to the kitchens to order my food?

Food he apparently decided on without asking me.

"Just a water, please," I answer.

"Nonsense." Joe waves a hand at my reply. "We're still celebrating the end of summer and going right back to the party. A champagne will do. I saw her drinking some at the mayor's house."

Curtis nods and exits without another glance my way.

It shouldn't matter that he disregarded my request like that. I don't plan on drinking either option anyway. But the implication that I don't have a choice stirs up old memories that coil tightly around me.

Memories of being forced to do things. Of being told how I

should act or feel. Of all choices being taken from me until the only choice I could make was *his*.

I force my stiffened body over to the sitting area and take a seat on one side of the sofa.

I need to steer my thoughts away from Gordon. Especially now. I know I fit the image of the girls he takes advantage of. Is that how there are so many? He jumps at the first opportunity to lure them in?

"Rebecca." Joe's voice is keyed down low, but it's how close it sounded that startles me.

I glance over to find him seated right next to me, but the firm cushion barely moved when he sat.

He strokes the side of my face. My teeth clench to stop myself from moving away.

"You're a beautiful woman. I can see the fire in you, even though you're doing your best to stay polite. I like that. You've learned some control over the...unfortunate emotions that women have to deal with."

I grip the edge of the sofa.

"That's my good pet. How should I reward you this time?"

Blood rushes in my ears as my heart thumps wildly. It feels like my skin is stretched too tight and I need to claw a hole in it to make some room. The world around me begins to spin, but Joe continues on, taking my silence for whatever he believes as implicit approval for him to keep going.

"I wanted to talk to you about that internship opportunity. I understand you were already thinking about taking one with Steve, but I'd like you to reconsider being my intern instead."

His words are barely there. Like words spoken behind a pane of glass that I could make out if I concentrated hard enough, but I'm only able to pick out bits and pieces instead.

I need to get a grip on myself.

Gordon is dead.

This is a non-gifted human. I can use my gift if it gets too bad.

But his words are so much like Gordon's were. I hadn't counted on that.

"Going to school for a degree in law, and then going on to a law school, it can be a challenging road. You're going to encounter professors you don't like, who don't like you. You're going to be overwhelmed in your workload and tests. There are hundreds of thousands of nuances in laws and regulations that you'll have to familiarize yourself with. In short, it's going to be difficult."

The hand on my face moves and air fills my lungs at the space. But then, he rests his hand on my exposed knee and my entire body tenses before I can hide it. I try to laugh it off nervously. "I knew all of that when choosing my degree."

"What I'm offering is a chance to...smooth out any potential bumps in your road. Pave that road, so you can learn what you need to without the fear. The stress. The drama. I can get you to that degree, with some effort on your end of course." His fingers start to climb up my thigh until they reach the hem of my beach dress.

Nope.

I can't do this.

This man...he's too much like Gordon.

I can feel panic beginning to accelerate my heart rate and make my palms sweat. I won't be a victim again. I'll never be a victim. This is *my* choice.

"You understand what I'm asking, Rebecca. Don't you?"

I'm struggling to keep my gift from bursting out of me as it spits and hisses in my gut. He has no idea the danger he's in, and I can't even speak to tell him that while all of my attention is zeroed in on keeping my gift contained.

The sound of something hard rolling into the room grabs both of our attention as we look up to see what it is. A black ball spins toward us, and then smoke shoots out on either side. The doors to the room slam shut.

"What the hell is this?" Joe yells and stands.

I kick it away and cover my mouth, but I can taste it on my tongue and burning the back of my throat.

My vision swims, and everything goes dark.

Chapter Seventeen

RAEGAN

"Kill him before I lose my patience with you, pet."

"I-I can't. Why are you asking me to do this?" I cry out. My hands are already shaking from the full day of training he's put me through. I'm exhausted. I'm not sure how I'm still standing, but he dragged someone in while I was finishing my last exercise.

The guy is bound and gagged in a chair with a machine on wheels next to him and wires attached across his chest and extremities. We're in the large gymnasium where I've spent the last month on my own with only Gordon's company. We train from the moment my alarm goes off until he decides he's satisfied for the day and leaves.

"You can, and you will," Gordon responds flatly while noting something on his tablet.

"Who is he? Why do you want him dead?" I push further.

Gordon sighs and lowers his tablet. "He's no one. A failed lab rat.

But you can make his existence worthwhile. Show me how your gift works on people and then his life will have meant something."

No one. The same words he's been calling me.

Worthless.

"No."

"No?"

"I won't do it. I'm not killing anyone with my gift. Anything but that."

"You killed Vera easily enough."

"That wasn't—"

Gordon cuts me off with the wave of his hand. "I don't care what sob story you've sold yourself on. You killed your friend with your own hands and have no one to blame but yourself. Killing this stranger who means nothing to you is pale in comparison to the monster you pretend you're not."

My hands fist and shake. "I'm not a monster."

He scowls and snatches a handful of my hair, yanking it back. "You are whatever the fuck I say you are, pet. Now, kill him, or I'll kill one of your friends."

Gordon jerks me back before releasing me. I stumble and catch myself, but he's occupied poking a finger at his tablet repeatedly. He turns the screen toward me.

The boys' room fills the screen. It's angled from the top corner some-where, so the entire room is in view. Only Jackson is in it, floating his origami animals around in different formations to practice with his gift.

"Kill the lab rat, or I'll take this one out. He's about as useful as a fan and hasn't shown any progress in his training. All of your friends have been struggling with compliance, in fact. It'd be better for Gifted

Enterprise to put them down before they age out. All except for the one who can mute gifts." Gordon lifts a two-way radio to his lips. "Prepare to terminate subject 1-3-6-5 on my mark."

A red dot appears on the side of Jack's face.

"No!" I leap at Gordon, but fall through him when he activates his gift. I've tried attacking him before, but this is how it always ends. With his gift, he's untouchable. And I can't hurt him if I can't touch him. "Please, wait."

"Ready..." Gordon speaks into the radio again.

Jackson looks up. The red dot is now centered on his forehead, but that's not what has Gordon and I stopping to stare. He's looking directly at the camera, and what looks like the origin of the laser, and he smirks.

For the first time, Gordon looks surprised.

It brings a smile to my face, until Gordon sees that and his face darkens. His thumb compresses the radio button to talk, and I lunge for his arm.

"NO! I'll do it! I'll do it! Stop!"

He wrenches his arm away and pushes the button down again. "Hold for fifteen minutes. If you don't hear from me by then, shoot him." Gordon sets the tablet in the basket on the machine. "Do it. Now."

I hurry over to the boy seated in the chair. His eyes are wide with fear as he tries to plead with me through the gag.

"I'm sorry. I'm so, so sorry," I choke out and pull his gag down.

"He was going to kill me anyway. Please just...make it quick."

I have no idea how to make it quick, but I hope he's gone before he can feel my gift. "What's your name?" I whisper as my hands encircle his arm.

"Caleb. Caleb Stone."

My eyes blur with tears at what I have to do next. I really will be a killer after this. And once it starts, will it stop?

But it sounds like Gordon's already done with my boys. If this can keep them alive and safe until Aiden can get them free...

"You're a monster." Gordon's voice echoes in my head.

Yes. I am.

I shove all of my gift through my hands and into Caleb. He screams the second my gift touches him, and his screaming continues even as I push harder and harder to finish it.

I don't stop until the screaming ends and the machine sounds on a single, low tone.

Gordon grabs my face and turns it up so he can inspect it. "For someone claiming not to be a monster, you sure took your time with that kill. Hands on the arm to start instead of somewhere vital too. Hmph."

"Call them off." My voice cracks, but I don't care. All that matters is he tells whoever is on the other side of that radio not to shoot Jack.

He checks his watch. "This is cutting it close. I'm not entirely pleased with you, pet. I hate to be questioned. I hate to repeat myself."

Panic builds in a paralyzing grip on my lungs as time ticks away and he makes no move to call off the hit.

"Consider this your last warning," he continues, his voice cold and dark. The back of his hand caresses my cheek, and I flinch at the contact. "I can find better use for your mouth than talking back if it happens again."

"Please," I beg with my eyes downcast.

He scoffs, and finally, I hear the click of the radio. "Stand down."

A tiny sob of relief bursts free involuntarily, and I drop my face against my hands to try to hide it.

Thank goodness. Jack...

The taste of smoke is thick on my tongue as I come to. My body coughs on instinct, trying to drive whatever smoke or gas it inhaled out of my lungs before my brain can come back online. Between the flavor in my mouth and the dark memory still clinging to my mind like thick cobwebs, my stomach turns and clenches in warning.

Please don't throw up.

That is the worst feeling. And it puts me at a disadvantage while I try to figure out what predicament I'm in now.

The last I remember, I was at Joe's house. Did he do this? I tried to take the right precautions, but that doesn't always mean it's enough. This entire hunt for Gifted Enterprise has been trial and error for me of what works and what gets me in trouble.

"We really should stop bumping into each other like this, beautiful."

Kellan's arms are crossed over his chest, his dark shirt tight and stretched over his chest as usual, while black markings scrawl up his neck and down his arms. He's in jeans and boots, and his long brown hair is pushed behind one ear and comfortably reaching past his shoulders. His blue-green eyes check out the little dress I'm wearing.

It's short, white, and covered in large sporadic blue flowers. The dress makes me think of innocence and sweet fun, which are words I haven't been associated with in a long time.

I won't admit that I'm embarrassed to have him catch me wearing something like this. I feel...pretty. And weak.

Not that his opinion on how I look matters. I should be focusing more on how I passed out next to the congressman and woke up to Kellan in a kitchen.

The sheer size and grandeur of the room screams money and matches what little I saw of Joe's estate. Still there, then.

I attempt to lift my hands but face resistance. I finally take stock of myself. I'm zip-tied to a wooden chair.

"Why am I tied up?" I demand more heatedly than normal. I can't promise I have my emotions completely under control, and seeing him doesn't make dealing with them any easier. Gordon used all four guys against me in my year with him, and those memories are now fresh in my mind after that unplanned nap.

"How did you find out about this one?" Aiden asks, stepping forward out of the shadows of the room to reveal himself. He's dressed in a black suit, jacket buttons undone and revealing a flash of a weapon on one side.

Rather than answer Aiden, I look around the kitchen for Joe.

"He's incapacitated in another room." Aiden walks closer again and stops in front of me with his arms folded. "Now, how did you discover he was a part of them?"

What is this? Are they interrogating me?

Well, I was found at Joe's place in a dress. Sitting next to him on a sofa while he had his hand on me. And Aiden has claimed that he thinks I work for GE.

Fuck.

This does look bad.

I try for a loose shrug, as if that can make me seem less guilty of whatever ideas Aiden's floating around about me. "I'm undercover looking for some information."

Kellan scowls in the background, but Aiden talks back.

"Mm, right. Undercover. So, you didn't just so happen to be at a known GE board member elect's home, wearing *that,* and chatting like good pals when we showed up? Or did you somehow know we were planning to interrogate him and you're here for his protection?"

"No! I'm here to snoop around. That's it, I swear."

His eyes harden. "And how did you plan to do that with a house full of his staff around?"

My mouth opens and closes like a fish out of water. I didn't plan for so many people being here, sure, but if I had just gotten to that desk when he wasn't in the room... "Pee break. It's a big place and easy to get lost in. Besides, I saw some papers on the desk in the room we were in. That would have been easy enough to look at if he left the room."

"Pee break?" Aiden scoffs. "It looked more like you were preparing to fuck him for the information when we showed up."

I freeze.

They saw...

Kellan slams his fist back into the kitchen cabinet behind him, breaking the door and letting it crash to the counter and floor. "You know he coerces young women to fuck him? He uses them like his own personal whore at his beck and call, and then throws what's left to the curb after he's done with them."

I knew. Not the details or everything, but I'd figured with the rotation of interns and how he'd started his spiel on me.

"He finds the troubled girls. The ones who have trauma in their past or seem broken in some way. That's how he gets in their heads. How he controls them. He manipulates them into being his play things." Kellan keeps going, getting angrier by the second, but it's

Aiden I'm more concerned with.

His eyes narrow on me when my body stiffens.

How did the congressman know? No, he couldn't have. I showed up at that party and he *happened* to meet me because I was with a friend of his. So, he couldn't have known about my past. About what happened on that island.

Then I remember the words that reminded me so much of things Gordon used to say. His hand on my face. My thigh. The nausea at his touch. At feeling like I wasn't in control.

Like the other times.

"Kellan." Aiden tries to cut him off with a slashing look.

Kellan pauses and must see something on my face, because his twists with rage. "Did he touch you?!" He storms over to me, and I try to shift back, but the chair and bindings keep my hands from going anywhere.

"Stop!" I take a deep breath. I'm here. I'm...as whole as I've been in a while. Gordon is dead. And if this guy is part of GE, then I'll rid the world of him too somehow.

I'm able to take another calming breath at that reminder. I'm fine. "No, he didn't. Just...I don't need to hear any more of it."

I'm not going to admit what that man had done. It's my business, not theirs.

Aiden sighs. "All right, cut her loose and get her far enough away from here that she won't come back."

There's a second of relief that he might believe me for once, and then that drops like a rock. "Wait, what?"

Kellan takes a knife from the block on the kitchen island and moves around me to slice away at the zip ties.

"We came here for the congressman and to get information from him, not you," Aiden reasons matter-of-factly.

"Let me stay to hear what you get out of him too. Otherwise, my whole plan was just wasted." I rub my wrists once they're free and stand. "You've got masks or something, right?"

Aiden's chocolate eyes sweep over my dress, making me self-conscious over it again in less than ten minutes. "He'll be blindfolded, but he knows your voice. And I know you won't be able to stop yourself from saying anything. Whether it would be to rat us out or ask him a question, I can't take that risk."

"I won't."

He strides over to me so quickly that I back up until I hit a wall. "You were always good at finding and pushing my buttons, Raegan. You knew how to get under my skin and around my orders just enough without actually crossing the line. What makes you think I can trust you won't do that again now?"

His breath is hot in the air between us as he stirs up old memories. I remember his kiss, and what I'd done to earn that kiss by doing something without his permission.

The intense need to feel that way again, to feel something other than the crap that's been filling my head today, rises up in my chest. I trail my fingers down his silk tie. It's smooth and cool beneath my fingertips. Like luxury embodied in a simple accessory. And here he is, wearing it to interrogate and possibly torture a man.

It shouldn't be as sexy as it is.

He snatches my wrist and presses me against the wall until I finally bring my eyes to his. "What game do you think you're playing? You're not sticking around until I know you're taking orders from *me* and not them. I'm done playing nice." His tone is low to keep this between us, but it only makes it come out like a dark promise that makes my toes curl.

His breath fans across my face, and my body becomes acutely aware of his close proximity. He's practically panting with the need to control me. To put me in my place.

And I get a thrill out of acting out again to see what he'll do. Just how far will he take his threats? I'm curious of what he's offering—I mean, threatening—me with if I do what I want anyway to snoop around this place while they're busy with Joe.

It's a nice distraction from everything else today, and I'm here for it.

"Playing nice? When have you ever played nice with me? When you lied to everyone about me getting off the island after hitting me over the head?"

"I don't mean to interrupt," Kellan remarks beyond Aiden, "but we have an interrogation to finish before everyone wakes up."

Aiden and I hold each other's stares for another few seconds, just breathing in the thick air between us, before he releases my wrist and pushes off the wall. He adjusts the cuffs on his sleeves and walks away.

I close my eyes and inhale shakily. I forgot how dangerous it is to get so close to any of them. Once I'm sure that I have my shit together, I open them to find Kellan watching me with an odd look on his face.

"What?"

"Time to get you somewhere far from here."

"Kell, wait. Let me stay to do some more digging. I can't leave here empty-handed."

He shakes his head. "Sorry, beautiful. I'd love to trust you, but this isn't the time to test that." He swoops forward and grabs me before I can bolt, scooping me in his arms and holding me tightly against him. Even my attempted wiggles to escape are no match for his strength.

Kellan runs me out of the door in the kitchen, going a direction I don't recognize and through some woods I didn't even know was in the area. The side of my face is pressed against his chest, so I'm breathing mostly him while we're moving. All I can breathe, hear, and smell is Kellan.

I keep trying to push, shove, or wriggle against him to find a weak spot in his hold, but we just keep getting further and further from the congressman's home. "Kell!" I scream to get his attention, muffled as it may be.

He keeps going like he has some destination in mind, and then finally slows when we are deep in the woods. Kellan releases me back to my feet and thankfully catches my wrist before I fall on my ass.

He pulls me in and pushes his finger beneath my chin. It's apparently become nighttime while I was unconscious, so his eyes are dark as he studies me with more serious intensity than I'm used to.

"Are you sure he didn't do anything to you?"

I jerk my chin away and step back in an instant before he can read whatever reaction my body might give him. "I told you. I'm fine. You should be more worried with how pissed I am that you guys ruined my plans to get information on him. Are you at least going to share what you find out with me?"

Kellan runs his fingers through his hair. My eyes get caught on the muscle in his arm as it flexes in that movement. "You know we can't do that. You still need to prove to us that we can trust you." He catches me looking and smirks when I hurriedly pretend I *wasn't* just drooling over his body. "I wish it was as simple as us just working together again, beautiful. Really. But you have some answers to give us still."

Right.

I scuff my foot against the ground and, when I feel the grass and dirt underfoot, I realize one of my heels is missing. "Shit! Really? And you dropped my shoe?"

He raises one brow at me. "You some kind of fancy girl now?"

"No, you prick. I'm supposed to return them and this dress to get my money back. I only have—" I bite my tongue and look away.

Kell cocks his head and responds with a low rumble of his own. "Only have what? Are you running out of funds, beautiful?"

"You know what? It's none of your business. Where did you take me anyway? How do you know I won't just walk back to the estate and still ruin your plans to make it fair?"

He frowns at my refusal, but thankfully lets it go. Then it twists into a grin. "Your sense of direction is still terrible, so I made sure we're far enough away that I'm not worried. You're more likely to wander to other neighborhoods than find your way back." He points to the left. "There's a bus stop about a mile that way and it's your closest chance of getting out of these woods. Here." He pulls out the knife he'd stolen from the kitchen and cuts an arrow pointing up into the bark. It's not a great job, and the knife is fucked, but I guess I can see it.

I'm not sure why I would need it though, unless it's too late for buses. "Kell, what time is it?" I ask slowly as realization starts sinking in on what might happen.

"It's late for this neighborhood." Kellan stalks around me.

Shit.

"Wait—"

"Sweet dreams, beautiful."
Knocked out again.

Chapter Eighteen

Raegan

"And then I had to walk to the bus stop and take three buses to get back to the city. With one shoe." I jab my chopsticks into the pork fried rice to break out a chunk that I can shovel into my mouth. "Mm, ma god," I moan behind my hand and then swallow. "This is so good."

Portia giggles and leans back in her fluffy purple butterfly chair, her legs crossed while she holds her own container of Chinese food. Her dark brown hair is tied back in a high ponytail, her eyes and cheekbones accentuated with bright orange makeup and glitter, while bubblegum pink tinted lip gloss is smeared over her lips.

She's wearing only a strappy bralette—which her breasts are fit to burst out of—and shiny but spandex-fitting, orange mini-shorts.

"I told you to come over to eat any time. I can order you some food when I order out at night, too, if you want."

I'm busy filling my face with the yummy goodness to answer right away and shrug instead. I'm not used to relying on anyone. Thinking of contacting her, or even Elias, is a conscious effort and definitely not my gut reaction. Which is usually what I go with.

Yet, here I am, gabbing away to Portia like we've been friends forever now that she's moved in to Elias's apartment and the one right next to mine. She'd had some of her friends in the bar pack up her things at her previous apartment so she could make Elias's modern and monochromatic one feel more like home.

I'm *really* interested in seeing his reaction when he comes home and sees it.

"So anyway," she continues when I'm too busy inhaling food to speak. "That was Aiden who knocked you out and left you there?"

"Kellan," I correct with a mouthful behind the back of my hand.

"Kellan. Got it. And he does the scaley thing, right?"

I nod while hurrying to finish my current bite. "Yup. I'm not sure what to call it because he's not invulnerable since he does get injured. It's more...crazy regeneration that goes into overdrive to protect him once it's activated? And then he uses that to beat people bloody, so he turns his defensive gift into an offensive one." I cock my head to the side as I recall the other times I'd seen him use it. "He might get stronger too. Or he could just be that strong, I'm not sure."

"That sounds sick! I wish I could do more with my gift than just tell people what to do."

"Porsh. I *wish* I could tell people what to do. You know how handy that'd be with Gifted Enterprise? Hell, even with Aiden. And *Dane*." My eating slows to a halt at that thought. There isn't much I could, or would, tell Dane to do. I'd use that gift more as protection to keep him from *not* trying to kill me.

I know I almost let him do it. And I would again if stuck in the same situation, because there's nothing I can say or do to fix it. But I would rather spend my life taking down the organization that did this to us, to Vera, if I had the choice.

She hunkers back down in her chair like she's settling in for story time. "Oooh! Yeah. Tell me about Dane. This sounds like it's going to be juicy."

My lips twitch automatically in response to her behavior and I shake my head at myself for falling for this girl so easily. I swear she has more than just the ability to tell people what to do. She exudes contagious energy that sucks me in and makes me never want to leave.

"It's a long story."

She rolls her eyes and then claps her hands at me. "And I'm a night owl whose night has just started. So whooo, whooo, is Dane?" She hoots.

I laugh at her antics and set my food aside. I've never opened up to anyone about something real before. Not since the guys before Vera's death. But then I met Elias, and his help has been invaluable. And now Portia's somehow weaseled her way in too. I realize then that I care about both of them. And I think...they care about me too. I feel like I finally have others I can trust and confide in. Even if it's just these two people, it feels...good.

"Well, we all pretty much grew up together on that island where GE had kidnapped us to. I think we were there for..." I try to count the possible years in my head, but it's difficult when we had no holidays, birthdays, or seasons to use as benchmarks.

"...I think eight years? Ish? Anyway, we all became close because they all shared a bunkroom, and I was right across the hall. But then, we started learning more about why we were on the island and what they were trying to do with us. We thought we were helping people. Or we would be helping to make the world a better place with what we could do."

I rub my arms as the memories come back at speed in the forefront of my mind. " I found out that we were just lab rats. Either they wanted to control us, or they wanted to find a way to steal or replicate our gifts. We already had our suspicions before that, but just as we were digging into it together, something happened, and I...killed one of us. Dane's sister. That's why he hates me."

Portia's mouth drops open. It closes, then opens again.

Shit. Why did I just say that?

I'm getting twitchy the longer she stays silent and shoot upright to my feet. "I should go."

"No!" She almost jumps out of her chair and then falls back in it. "Sorry, I didn't mean to gawp at you like an orange karp."

A what-now?

"I just can't believe you killed his *sister*," she continues, and my nerves just spit and frazzle even more. "Why did you do it? Did she try to kill you first? Did she go all batshit cray cray under all the lab testing? Did she pull a Luke Skywalker and go to the dark side?"

"I think that was Anakin..."

"Who's that?"

"Never mind. And yeah, it was something like that," I give her. The chances of her talking to one of the guys about this are slim, and the last thing I want to do is lose the one friend I have. And a friend who feeds me, at that.

"Which one? I don't remember all of the reasons I gave." She bounces in her chair and her hair swings behind her.

"Cinderella!" A booming voice echoes out in the hallway. "CIN-DERELLA!"

I look to the door and frown.

It couldn't be...

"Is that Prince Charming?" Portia hops from her seat and starts toward her door. I grab her arm to stop her.

"Wait," I hiss and move in front of her. "I have an idea of who it might be, but in case I'm wrong, go hide in your bedroom."

"I'll be your backup." She picks up a fork from the coffee table and nods seriously at me like she believes she will take this person on with only a kitchen utensil.

"At least go behind the couch so they can't see you."

Her mouth opens like she realized something, and then she nods. "Got it. Sneak attack."

"CINDERELLLLLLA!!!" His voice continues back down the hall in our direction.

I turn, blocking Portia's view of the door, and take both of her hands, and fork, in mine. "No attacking unless I give a signal, okay? I'm just going to check this out. If it's GE, I need you to escape out a window. Otherwise, just stay behind the couch until I say it's okay to come out."

"A window?" she squeaks. "There aren't any fire escapes out of our windows."

I start moving her behind the couch. "Let's hope it doesn't get to that point then."

She kneels, and when I bring a finger to my lips to remind her to be quiet, she mimics me and nods.

"CinderELLLLA!!"

I snag one of my knives from the table and move to the door to peek through the peephole. It's too small to make anything out other than a dark figure stomping up and down the hallway.

Knife at the ready by my side, I open the door and shift into the doorway so that the apartment is blocked.

Kellan grins at me as he walks back down the hallway toward me. Two fingers lift up the strap of the missing heel that had been left behind at the congressman's house. His blue-green eyes rake over me, and it's only then that I remember what I'm wearing. A sexy navy-blue romper that Portia let me borrow while my dress and regular clothes are getting washed.

I cross my arms over my chest, keeping my knife in the grip of my hand. "What are you doing?"

He stops with his arm leaning against the side of the doorframe above me so he can cover me in his shadow. "I'm doing the bit from that movie. The girl loses her shoe. Then the guy shouts her name over and over again for her to come out so he can bring it to her."

I burst out laughing. Then his face scrunches like he missed the punchline, and I laugh even harder. He thinks that's the movie.

"Look, beautiful, I'm glad seeing me has made you so happy—"

I put a hand up. "Hold up. I'm laughing because you're an idiot. Who mixes up *Cinderella* and *A Streetcar Named Desire*?"

Kellan doesn't even look upset or embarrassed. His grin stays put even as I call him out. "My mistake. I forgot you were such a movie buff."

"Me too."

There's a long pause where we both stare at each other, getting lost in the past, when his eyes suddenly dart behind me. I turn to look just as Portia walks up behind me with her fork.

"Hello! Are you the Kellan one? Can I stab you with my fork?

Pretty please?"

"Portia!"

Kellan bursts into laughter. "Absolutely…"

Her face glows with excitement, and she steps forward.

"…not," he finishes sternly, but with his lips still spread wide. He looks back at me. "I'd be surprised that you have friends like this, but…no. This seems about right."

Portia blows air out, sending her stray hairs into the air. "Worth a shot."

I turn my body at an angle to slightly face her without putting my back to Kellan. "You don't just stab him to see his scales. It still hurts him."

"Aw, beautiful. I didn't know you cared," he murmurs into my ear, and his long beard tickles my shoulder.

I swat him back, and he moves out of reach, but maintains his position against the door.

Portia's looking between the two of us with a mischievous smirk on her lips, and I give her a look. "What?" she asks with a teasing grin.

"Can we have a minute?"

"Oh. Sure, sure. If you need a bed though, don't forget yours is next door. I hate washing sheets because then I have to make the bed after."

"We don't need one of those. I just need a minute to see what he wants and then he'll be gone."

She chuckles and waves to Kellan before heading back to her chair in the living room. It isn't much privacy, but this is her apartment, and she would probably get me to tell her what happened here anyway, so I let it go.

Kellan's gaze is trained on me when I turn back around, and a small part of me wonders if he'd checked out Portia. She's gorgeous, showing a ton of skin, and fearless. All amazing qualities.

What if Portia liked what she saw now that she has a face to his name? My heart grows heavy, and I frown at the feeling.

He grabs my chin and forces my eyes to meet his.

"What're you thinking about?" his deep voice drawls, and warmth spreads through my limbs.

"Why're you here, Kellan? We keep having...less than happy encounters, and yet you're back again. Glutton for the fight?"

He smirks at me. "With you? Always." My insides clench in a delicious way that I can't think about when he's keeping such direct eye contact with me. He drops my chin and lifts the long, lost shoe again. "I'm here with a peace offering. And a request."

I start reaching for my heel back and then pause when he finishes. "What kind of request?"

"Come out with me tonight. For old time's sake. Let's go blow off some steam together and have some fun."

My laugh is cold and short. "You're kidding. Every time I'm out with you lately, you have a habit of leaving me stranded somewhere. Where are you planning on ditching me this time?"

Kellan chuckles and loops the strap over my hand anyway for me to take. "Aw, that was all harmless. And necessary," he adds, giving me a look. "I swear I won't do that tonight, though. I really just want to have a good time. No drama. No bullshit. Just you and me. Whaddya say?"

"Mm...still no." His smirk shrinks but doesn't completely fall off his face. "Thing is. I don't trust you. Any of you. This could be some sort of trap for all I know. Why would you suddenly want to spend time with me or invite me to have fun?"

He leans in close again. "Why are you so afraid of having fun with me again?"

"I'm not afraid." I'm staring at his lips as they breathe on mine before my eyes jump back up to his.

"Then prove it."

The world falls away as we look at each other. There's no apartment, no GE, and no bad history between us. I'm just here with Kellan in a silent standoff with my blood singing and my head swimming. A burning ache in my chest drives me to close the distance between us, but my head still has enough sense about it that I avoid leaning into him.

His beard tickles my chin, and I grab what's hanging off his face. "Fine. But you have to clean yourself up first. And not tonight because I'm having a girls' night."

Kellan grins and strokes his beard when my hand falls away. "Deal. I'll pick you up tomorrow night at nine. Lookin' my best."

Smiling, I roll my eyes at him. "It's not a date, so don't try getting all fancy. I just don't need to see you looking like the yeti anymore." I step back to grab ahold of the door.

"See you tomorrow, Cinderella," he says with a roguish grin.

I shut the door and smile. Then I turn and remember that I'm not alone here.

Portia's beaming as she leans forward and clutches the edge of her fluffy chair. "Ooh boy, Rae. We still have so much to catch up on. I need to know what all of that was about. And you still have to finish telling me about the other guys and why you murdered Dane's sister."

Right.

Just that.

The sun glares at me as it breaches the horizon. I squint up at the wide window over the couch I'm sprawled on and note that Portia has no window covering. Nada. When I turn my face toward where her bedroom is, I can hear her breathing soundly even though her room is just as bright.

Lucky.

I close my eyes and groan softly at the thundering beat of a headache and the way I still feel buzzed. I roll slowly and then use my hands to push myself off of the couch to stand. I grab my knives and stumble to her door, deciding I'd rather ride this out in my bed with blackout shades so I can sleep for another eight hours. I check the time on my phone and it confirms we'd only gone to sleep a couple hours ago after filling each other in on our pasts. Or what Portia remembers of hers, at least.

I promised to help her figure all of that out once Gifted Enterprise has been destroyed.

The door to my apartment falls open beneath my weight when I try to lean on it after entering my code, and I nearly fall on my face. If I reach the ground, I'll likely park it there until at least the drunkenness has subsided. I drop my knives and phone on the kitchen counter and blindly make my way to my room in the dark.

"Is this some pathetic walk of shame that I'm witnessing?"

My soul jolts out of my body, and I crash back into the counter so hard that I know my back will bruise. "Fuck!"

"If I'd known you were out doing exactly that, I wouldn't have wasted my time waiting for you. I didn't realize that had a higher priority than taking down your enemies. If so, then I shouldn't have worried."

I don't know what's worse. The arrogant and venomous *filth* coming out of Aiden's mouth or the smooth cadence of his voice that would make me believe he's trying to seduce me if I was dumb enough to ignore what he's actually saying.

I straighten and find Aiden sitting back on the couch so he has a perfect view of the door. He has one ankle resting across his knee, and his fingers are clasped together, resting on top.

For the first time since I've seen him in this city, he's not in a suit. Instead, he looks almost human, wearing gray sweatpants and a black V-neck shirt that reveals a glimpse of his chest.

"Then get the fuck out! I didn't invite you over."

He shifts forward to lean on his knees. "Were you doing that? Fucking someone?"

My mouth drops open at the gall of this man. Then it closes when a thought occurs to me. "Are you *jealous*?"

He scoffs and stands. "Of course not. I'm trying to gauge your level of commitment to getting in our way or if you're...distracted." Aiden slowly moves around the coffee table. I watch his every step but can't find it in myself to move away as he closes the distance between us. Moving away from him would be like admitting defeat. It would show him weakness.

I hold my ground as his feet nearly brush against mine when he finally stops. "I didn't realize I played such a big factor in your plans. Am I screwing them up that well?" I smile at that, and he counters with a frown.

"You are slowing us down. I have to believe that's intentional." One of his hands grasps the counter on one side of me and my heart rate spikes as the smell of cinnamon hits me. "If you cared about taking down GE like you say, you wouldn't have time for *meeting* people. Unless..." He grips my face. "Unless you're working for *them* and just pop in enough to interrupt or distract us."

I shove at him so he releases the counter, and I get a breath of non-cinnamon-scented air again. "I'm confused. Am I too distracted fucking other men to take down GE, or am I working for them and me having a personal life is somehow distracting you?"

His face gets in mine like he thinks he can intimidate me.

He can, by the way.

We're almost pressed up against each other now. My nipples harden, and I'm grateful I have pasties on in this skimpy romper to stop them from poking into him and giving away my body's betraying reaction to him.

"I'm only going to ask you this one last time. Are you working for *them*?" he asks softly, his eyes searching mine for the answer.

It shouldn't sting that he might actually believe it. That they all might, except for Jackson. They wouldn't if they knew the truth. If they knew what GE did to me, what *he* did to me after Vera's death. And what I did to protect them.

Tell them.

I freeze when the thought occurs.

No.

I'll never tell anyone what Gordon made me do in that year with him.

"No," I breathe.

Aiden watches my lips when I answer, then brings his gaze back to mine. His long fingers trail up the side of my face, pushing my hair aside. He leans in close, his lips hovering over mine, and my breath catches.

Is he going to kiss me?

Do I want him to?

He was my first kiss, and I've compared every kiss since then to his. That's one memory that has never faded in the years that have passed. My body arches into his on reflex, as if it's seeking that same heat, the same rush as that first kiss.

But can I do that? Could he mean it?

Of course, he wouldn't. He's playing you.

Still, I don't move or fight it.

His lips stop so close to mine I can taste him.

"Liar," he hisses. He grabs my wrists and pins them behind me with one hand, and I watch a wide metal bracelet around his wrist transform into a blade that he grips and holds to my neck. "I know your secret, Raegan."

My eyes widen, and I stop breathing.

He couldn't.

"No."

His brown eyes look pitch black as he glares down at me with contempt. "I do. I found out while we were still on the island."

I can't breathe. Fuck, I can't breathe. My chest constricts tighter and tighter, and I might see dots in my vision, but it's too dark in here to know for sure.

Was that why he left me on the island? Did he somehow see one of the things I did for Gordon? Is he disgusted by me? Does he hate me for what I did?

I start to slump in his grasp. He frowns and shifts the blade from my skin.

He knows.

I can't pretend it never happened if someone knows.

It means it's real.

I fall to the ground and try to drag air in through my lungs, but it feels like I'm getting nothing.

Aiden crouches in front of me and almost looks concerned when he grabs my shoulders and shakes me so I look at him. "You've been accused of working for GE before and never freaked out like this. What am I missing? *Breathe*, Raegan."

My hands grab for his arms automatically like I might draw strength from him. I pant over the floor and squeeze my eyes shut while struggling to regain control.

He picks me up, and I cling to him, if only to keep myself *here* and *present* with him as my anchor. I'm set down on the couch and then he opens the curtains and window. The cool morning breeze sweeps in, and I feel like what air I breathed that time actually worked. I jump toward the window, sticking my head out of it and breathing in deeply. Again. And again.

My body is trembling when I bring myself back to sit on the couch.

"Why would knowing about your birth certificate scare you so much?"

I'm still trying to breathe right again, but my eyes snap to his in confusion.

"Birth certificate?"

His eyes narrow. "Your secret," he repeats.

"What are you talking about?"

"I found your birth certificate. You were born on the island."

I breathe a sigh of relief.

He doesn't know.

"So?" He's sitting on my coffee table and watching me like I'm the biggest puzzle for him to solve.

I try to ignore the crack in my psyche for what almost happened. "I'm not sure what you found, but I wasn't born on the island. I was raised by my Gram in Alaska. As far from the islands as you can get."

He huffs and shakes his head. "You're a great actress, I'll give you that. I stole the birth certificate and validated it here. There is no Raegan LaRoux that ever lived in Alaska. Or any of the states for that matter. I checked. Which means everything you told us was a lie. You weren't kidnapped like the rest of us. You were *born* there. Probably conditioned since birth, too."

"Stop it!" I snarl and jab a finger into his chest. "You don't get to find a piece of paper and accuse me of something like that. I didn't lie to you. And you don't get to erase the years I had with my gram just because you don't believe me. I *know* my past. That piece of paper is the lie."

He snatches my wrist. "Oh really? Then what happened to your parents?"

"Car accident when I was little. Or didn't you look into them from my birth certificate?"

"Their names were redacted." Well, there you go. Suspicious as fuck. "Why did they have pictures of you on that very island as a little kid?" He yanks something from his pocket and holds it up for me to see. It's a photo that's worn around the edges and dirty, like it's been dragged through the dirt and seen things. A little blonde girl, no more than four or five, waves her arms and grins widely. Behind her is the mansion we'd all lived in for eight years.

My anger stutters when I look at the girl's face.

It's me.

My hair, my eyes, my expression.

What. The. Fuck.

"I...I don't know." He gives me a look, and I tighten my lips. "But I'm not lying. I *know* I was in Alaska and lived there with Gram. And I was taken from her."

His brow furrows, and I silently will him to believe me. There was no way I'd been brainwashed or raised on that island. I *remember* being taken.

"What else?" he asks instead, pocketing the picture of me.

"What do you mean?" I ask distractedly, my eyes still on the pocket as if I can see the picture there while wondering why he didn't just give it to me. What use does he have for it now?

"What other secret do you have that made you have a panic attack? Is it about Vera?"

My heart rate picks up again at the reminder. "No."

It's wishful thinking he would be satisfied with that and move on. But, of course not.

"Gifted Enterprise?" he presses on.

I squeeze my eyes shut and my breathing shallows.

"Raegan..."

I jump back and open my eyes before his hand reaches my leg. "Please. Stop asking. It's...personal. It doesn't matter."

"Then let me—"

"No!" I shout reflexively.

Besides, it has nothing to do with them. Or Vera.

Just me.

And Gifted Enterprise.

It's between us.

His brows pinch as he studies me. At last, he sighs and leans back. "Back to the other matter, I think you believe what you're saying, but it doesn't explain the birth certificate or the pictures."

He stands and moves to touch his wrist where a sleeve normally is, then clears his throat when he must realize he's not in his suit. "Until I know one way or the other, it'll be best if you stay out of our way. And stay away from Kellan and Jackson."

CHAPTER NINETEEN

RAEGAN

"ETHAN!" I SHOUT TO one of the bartenders at Hype who Portia has given her seal of approval on. The nightclub is filled to the brim tonight. The dance floor is a mass of bodies writhing to the beat, and it's exactly where I want to be tonight. Lost in a sea of people and consumed by the music.

But first, alcohol.

Ethan's blond head pops up from his conversation with a customer and he gives me a wave. He says something else to them and then jogs down the counter. "Rae, right? Weren't you supposed to be avoiding this place?"

I shrug and offer him a smirk while perching an arm on the bar. "I'm sure they think I've abandoned this place as a hangout by now. Sticking around isn't my usual MO."

"Oh?" His eyebrows raise, and he looks me up and down. "And

what is?"

"Dancing and drinking until my feet give out. And then falling into whoever's arms and bed is available that morning," I purr, leaning closer and letting charged silence fall between us.

Ethan swallows so hard his Adam's apple bobs. His eyes shift down my dress before scrambling back to my face. I grin at him, and he starts brushing his fingers through his hair.

"It's another one of those nights, so can I start it off with a couple shots? I've got a bit of dancing and drinking to get in so I can catch up to the other guests here."

He expels a breath and smiles. "Of course."

Ethan slides two large shots over to me. I don't miss his fingers brushing against mine before he pulls away and then takes hold of his shots. I raise an eyebrow and half a smile at that.

"You think I was going to let you take those alone? What kind of bartender do you take me for?" he teases with a grin.

Mine mirrors his when I raise the first shot between us, which he obligingly clinks his with.

"To dancing and drinking."

"And fucking," I add, then down each shot. "Thanks. Time to dance!"

He waves me off, and I immediately begin prying my way through the throng of dancers to the head of the dance floor.

My body picks up the beat like second nature, and I close my eyes, giving in completely until I'm nothing but the music.

The stress from the last couple of weeks, the demons in my head torturing me over that birth certificate, the anger and confusion with Aiden, Kellan, Jackson, and Dane; I let it all go as I move, like sweating out a fever but releasing my pain through physical exertion and surrender.

I don't even notice who I'm dancing around or against as I move.

Musk and motor oil break through the nothingness I'd wrapped myself in before fingers firmly grip my hips and tug me back against a hard body.

"Sexy as you look up here, beautiful, you're coming with me," Kellan growls into my neck.

I open my eyes and look around me. I've moved onto one of the stages to dance, apparently, but there's an odd bubble of space around the platform that I heavily suspect Kellan had something to do with.

Stay away from Kellan.

You were born on the island.

Aiden's voice still echoes in my head. If dancing doesn't fix my woes, then more drinking will. Followed by sex that's hopefully good enough to keep me distracted and feeling good until I fall asleep.

"Let me go," I snarl and throw my elbow back at him. He doesn't bother blocking it and grunts but keeps his hold of me. I wiggle and try to pull away from him, but none of it does any good.

"You promised me a night of fun, and I'm here to collect. Or did you forget your promise so easily?"

I pause my struggle with an internal *oh shit* and turn my head. Kellan's scruffy beard and messy hair are gone. His beard is trimmed and neat. His deep brown hair is tied up in a knot at the back of his head and out of his face.

He looks... fucking good.

No sign of the Yeti.

His blue-green eyes twinkle dangerously at me, and my lips part, but I'm too afraid to speak in case I say something stupid that gives away what his new look has done to me.

Kellan flashes me a cocky smirk when I still haven't answered him, and I realize I've been not-so-casually checking him out this entire time. So much for hiding it.

"I know. I look good. The others are thrilled too, though I have to say I like your reaction the best," he murmurs. One of his hands slides down my hip to the hem of my skirt and then he strokes his thumb in a lazy circle against my thigh.

My core pulses at the contact, and I shiver involuntarily against him, which only widens the arrogant look on his face. It's enough to snap me out of the thrall I'd been trapped in.

I grab his hand and throw it off of my leg. "Shut up, Kell. You just look like an actual human being now, and I'm shocked by what was still under that bush you had."

He laughs and turns me around to face him. "Now, now. There's no need to be embarrassed. And as much as I'd love to keep your ass grinding against my dick for the rest of the evening, I did promise to join in on some racing, and you promised to be my partner in crime for the night."

One moment, I'm dancing; and the next, I'm dangling over him with my face crashing into his lower back. "What are you doing?!" I scream and beat my fists into his back. "I can walk, you son of a bitch!"

His arm wraps around the back of my knees while another clamps around the bottom of my skirt.

"Let's keep our promises tonight, yeah?" He hops off the plat-form and my face smacks into his back again.

"Argh!" I cry out and grab my nose. Downside of him being

nothing but pure muscle. Hitting him actually hurts me more than him. Especially with my face.

He makes quick work of getting us to the exit. Then we stop abruptly, and I curse again while protecting my face.

"Put her down." I hear Ethan's voice and shove against Kellan's body so I can try to see around him and what's going on.

Ethan and one of the club bouncers block the exit.

"Sorry, fellas, but no can do. She and I have a date tonight. Right, beautiful?"

"She didn't say anything to me about that earlier," Ethan argues.

Kellan's body stiffens.

Great.

"Oh?" he asks almost casually, but I recognize the dark undertone of a threat in his voice. "And just who the fuck are you?"

"I'm her friend," Ethan replies, and I breathe a sigh of relief. Then he continues, and I smack my forehead against Kellan. "And you aren't leaving Hype with her."

"Ethan—" I try to cut in, but Kellan pinches my thigh, and I jump and cry out in his grip.

Asshole.

"Show me what you've got, then. I can spare a few minutes. I'll even give you a break and only fight with one hand." He releases the hand behind my knees.

"Kellan, stop." I punch his back as hard as I can.

He laughs again. "Keep doing that, beautiful. I could really use the back massage to warm me up."

Oh yeah? I shove my hand down the back of his pants and pinch his ass, nails included.

He moans obscenely and then bites my thigh. "Fuck, do you really want to be doing this here in front of them? I'm all for sex in public, but I didn't think you'd be into having people watch."

"Does nothing bother you?" I grumble. I push myself around to look at Ethan upside down. "Sorry about him. I'm fine, I promise. I can handle him."

Ethan frowns. "You know each other?"

"Unfortunately," I answer, and Kellan's grip tightens. I'm going to be paying for that later. "I'm okay. I'll see you later."

Kellan's chest rumbles through his back against me in what I'm sure is him growling, but Ethan finally nods and steps aside with the bouncer. We don't move right away and a trickle of worry slides down my back. What is he doing? I wish I could see his expression.

"Kell?" I prompt after at least a minute of silence.

He moves finally, and we're through the door to his car. He opens the passenger door and then sets me down on my feet. I'm thankful he keeps his hands on me as all the blood takes its time draining from my head, and I struggle to balance myself.

"Get in," he barks, then moves around the car to his seat.

There's a second of temptation to run.

Just a second, but I remember that I did promise to have fun with him tonight. They may be fine breaking promises, but I've never broken any of mine. And I won't start now.

I take my seat and check around me for a seatbelt. "Of course not," I mutter under my breath.

The door is barely closed before I fall back into my seat when Kellan takes off.

"That guy wants to fuck you," he bites out like I've pissed in his cereal.

I shift myself more comfortably in the seat and cling to the door handle. "So? Maybe I want to fuck him."

He rips his gaze from the road to look at me in a mixture of pain and anger. "Do you?"

My first instinct is to snap back 'yes,' whether I mean it or not just to piss him off. I'm still furious over Aiden's accusations and him still not believing me after I've been honest with him every time he's asked. But Kellan isn't Aiden. That and the pain in his eyes stops me.

"Maybe. I don't know. What does it matter?"

"What do you mean, 'maybe'?"

"I mean, if I'm looking to have sex one night to feel good and forget about life for a while, then he's on the table," I snap, annoyed with him pushing this. What I've done, and still do, to cope with my past is none of their business anymore.

He turns back to the road before we rear-end a line of cars. He swiftly turns us down a side road and takes a winding path that quickly has me lost.

"I thought this was supposed to be a night of fun. If you can't hold up your end of the deal, I'm out."

His knuckles loosen on the wheel, and he tosses a quick glance my way, then sighs. "You're right. Let's go break some rules, like old times." He cracks a smile, which is like a quarter of his usual grin, but it's a start.

My eyes roll at the mention of our old shenanigans on the island. "I'd hardly compare something like this to the little pranks we did when we were younger."

Kellan's smile widens. "You've gotta up the stakes the older you get, or else it's too easy and not fun anymore."

"For you, maybe." I look over at him. "Why not bring one of the others with you? Why me?"

"Aside from the obvious that you had always been my partner in crime before?" He shifts gears and we speed on to the highway. Weren't we going to the airport for street racing?

"Aiden hates that I do any of this at all. He says we have enough people after us to then have to worry about cops and law enforcement up our asses if I ever get caught. Jackson isn't into this sort of fun and though he might go along with it for me, he'd probably use his gift to cheat and make it end faster. And Dane, well, he can't come down from his tower in case GE finds out where we've been hiding him from them."

"Hiding him?"

Kellan raises an eyebrow and glances over at me. "You don't know?"

I cross my arms and glare at him. "Why would I know anything? I haven't seen or heard from you since you all left me on that island. Not until I came to this city, at least."

"About that...I didn't know you were still on the island. Aiden couldn't find you and assumed you'd left when another boat was gone. For years after we got away, I thought that was exactly what you'd done."

"Why would you think I'd actually leave all of you?"

He gives me an *are you kidding me* look and, yeah, okay. Good point.

"I hated you then. I thought you'd lied to us the entire time. You killing Vera and then leaving the island without us? It was all the proof I needed to see that everything we'd had together was a lie."

I open my mouth to protest. "Let me finish," he cuts in. "I was angry with everyone back then. I got into fights all the time, drank and smoked, and did a whole host of bad shit until Aiden finally reined me in. Even then, I didn't slow down. I just got smarter with how I did it. Then, sometime after Jackson came back, he said something to me. He told me that he didn't think you'd gotten off the island. You hadn't left us behind. Because he'd searched the country for you, and he couldn't find any sign you existed. None.

"Then I thought about what that might mean. That we may have left you behind and you might still be under their control. Or worse, dead. I was a miserable fuck after that. So, when you came back here...when I saw you again and knew you were alive, I was so fucking relieved. And angry. With myself for not trying to find you sooner. And also with you. Because you still owe us all an explanation for Vera. I was too emotional to listen to you then, but I'm ready now. I want—no, I *need*—to know why. Was any of it real?"

My heart is hammering in my chest as he confesses his side of the story, just like Jackson had. He hadn't known either. I suspected as much after Jackson's story, and now this merely corroborates it.

Aiden is the one who actually left me behind.

"Yes." My voice is choked from the damn emotions congesting my throat.

"How much of it?"

"All of it."

"Did you hate Vera?"

"No."

"Will you tell me what happened?"

"No."

His jaw ticks. "Fine. Did someone force you to do it?"

"Kellan, I don't—"

"I'm almost done and then I'll drop it. Just answer the question," he pushes.

"No." My voice strains at the confession. "No one forced me to do it."

"Did you plan it?"

"No."

"So, it was an accident?"

"Yes...and no."

"What the hell does that mean?" he growls in frustration.

"I really don't want to talk about it. Please stop asking questions. Fun time, remember?"

He gives me a sideways glance. "You're going to have to tell us all what happened eventually, you know that, right, beautiful? There's no way we can all just hang out like old times again with that hanging between us."

I draw a slow breath and exhale, then say in a calm voice, "I don't expect things to go back to normal between us ever again either. I'll leave you all alone once GE is destroyed."

Kellan smirks and shakes his head, but doesn't say anything.

The car pulls up next to another on the highway and Kellan leans over me to the handle on the door to crank the window down. My heart jumps at the contact as he nearly lays himself across my lap.

"You ready?" he shouts through the open window to the driver in the other car.

The driver gives him a thumbs up. Kellan shoots me a devilish grin. "Are you ready?"

I grip the bar under my seat and the handle to my door and try to press back into my seat. None of it will save me if we crash or flip, but I still feel better for it. I can at least pretend I tried not to die, all for seeing the wildness in Kellan's gaze that echoes and beats in my chest in response. I feel alive and reckless. My life is literally in his hands now, and it sends a shot of adrenaline pumping through my veins and pulling at my face until I have a grin as crazed as his on.

"Smoke him."

His grin sharpens. "As you wish. Give us a countdown, beautiful."

I hold my hand out the window and count down from three, then throw my hand forward to signal the start of the race.

We speed forward at the same time. A car appears in front of us and Kellan slams on the brakes while our opponent passes us. He swerves into the other lane, zipping us by other cars and then flying into another lane when a stretch of road opens up.

The two cars zigzag between traffic in a dangerous but mesmerizing dance. This is nothing like the clear drag of the last race, where Kellan easily swept passed his opponent in seconds and it was over. This is part skill and part luck.

The wind whips through the car from our two open windows and my hair blows wild around me. My cheeks are flushed, and I hold my breath as we make lane change after lane change at breakneck speeds on a highway that's running over the city.

The lanes narrow from four to two, and Kellan downshifts when we get stuck behind a tractor-trailer. The other car is somewhere in front, but our line of sight is gone and there's a steady line of cars in the lane to our right.

Kellan curses and checks all the mirrors, then dives us into the breakdown lane and drops gears to send us flying forward. The other car must see us coming and cuts into the breakdown lane before we can sneak past. But the fast lane is open and we graze by the car in front, so there's only pavement stretched before us.

I gasp when I'm thrown back in the seat from the sudden acceleration. We drive neck and neck with the other car as it tries to find an opening to push in front of us, but Kell keeps us nosing ahead.

A mile marker flashes at us and Kellan whoops into the night air. He slows us down to a more normal speed and lets the other car merge in front of him.

He flashes a grin at me once we glide down an off-ramp and stop at a red light at the bottom. The light darkens his already-tanned skin in an ominous, reddish glow.

He looks like the devil right now, seated by my side and grinning at me like he's just won my soul in this race.

With the way my heart is beating out of my chest and I'm panting for oxygen, maybe he did. Because I am not in control of my body at this moment. My fingers shake as I retract them from the stranglehold I'd had them in on their designated spots. "Wow," is all I manage with a breathless laugh.

"You liked that?" Kellan chuckles and turns us onto the street when the light switches to green.

"That was insane." I grin back. "How did you know where the end of the race was?"

"It's the next five-mile marker from wherever we start. Why? Do you want to give it a go next?" He pops his eyebrows at me, and I roll my eyes.

"Definitely not. I can barely drive. I learned enough to get a car from point A to point B without crashing, but it's not good, and they were all automatic. They weren't my cars, so if they got scratched up a bit, it didn't matter."

He stops the car in the middle of the road. The person behind us honks and shouts out the window at us, but Kellan's focus is solely trained on me.

"How about a driving lesson, then?"

Chapter Twenty

RAEGAN

I balk, and his grin widens. "Don't worry, I can start slow. No street racing for you tonight."

I scoff. "That's slow?"

"It is for me. We can always try a bit of racing if you're up to it once you figure out the clutch."

"What's a clutch?"

The car behind us screeches its tires as it takes off around us, the guy waving the bird out the window. As if either of us gives a shit. Kellan doesn't even bother to turn his way.

"All right, get out." There's a second of dread that he's kicking me out and leaving me on the side of the road again. Considering the good night so far, it'd be about right to happen now. But then he opens his door and steps out, and I realize he means to switch.

I release a breath and hesitantly pull the latch on my door to swing it open.

It's not that I don't want to drive cars. I just know that I'm never going to own one, so why bother? I've lasted this long on buses, taxis, and walking.

I snap my head up to find him leaning against the hood of the car with an outstretched arm on the open door. "What? You nervous?"

I stand and freeze when I realize I'm now trapped between him and the car. "No. I just don't need to drive."

Kellan crowds me back against the car. "Bullshit." His breath is hot against my face as I'm trapped in his blue-green gaze. "We only fear what we don't know. So, face it. Learn it. *Own* it. Then you'll never be afraid again."

"It's not that simple."

"Isn't it? Have you tried?"

I duck under his arm, and he turns, his gaze following me all the way around the car with an intensity that I can feel burning into me. I pull the lever beneath the seat to move it until my feet can at least touch the pedals.

Kellan sits and throws his seat all the way back so he can stretch his long legs out as much as the dash will allow before his shins hit it. He throws an arm behind the headrest like he is lounging and about to take a nap, then tilts his face to look at me with his signature smirk.

"Ready?"

I look from the shifter to the *three* pedals on the floor. I'd been happy enough to learn that one pedal meant go and the other stop. What is the third one for?

As if reading my mind, or maybe the confusion on my face, Kellan starts his training. "The third pedal is the clutch. You use that to manually shift gears for better control of the car." He leans over and uses his hands to show me how my feet should look on the pedals when shifting gears, when to use the shifter, and what feels like an oversimplified explanation of what looks so complicated.

"Now, give it a try."

I do, and the car grinds beneath my feet when I can't get the timing right. I cringe at the sound and peek over at him, expecting him to be annoyed or pissed that I'm hurting his car. Instead, he's contemplative and rubbing at his beard. He snaps his fingers and then looks at me. "Stop the car. I've got a better idea."

Before the car comes to a complete stop, he hops out and strides to the driver's side to open my door.

"What are you—" I start, but he waves me out. Disappointment and relief swirl in my chest as I do what he asks. I turn away to move back over to the passenger side, but he grabs my wrist.

"Don't go anywhere." He fixes the seat back for his legs, then raises the steering wheel up. Kellan crooks his finger at me and curls it in. "C'mere."

I stare at his lap and then back up at him. "You're joking."

"It's the best way for you to learn. You can feel how and when I do it and then try it yourself."

I scrunch my nose. "I think everyone else in the world who learned how to drive one of these things would disagree. They all learned another way."

"Well, they took weeks or months to learn it. I'm teaching you in one night. Now, get in here, beautiful. I promise I won't bite."

The whites of his teeth are so large in his grin that it's hard to believe him. And for whatever reason, I do anyway.

I duck down and grab the roof of the car as I find my seat in his lap. His hands guide my hips where he wants me and then he jerks the seat forward until my feet reach the pedals and his knees are bunched on either side of the wheel. It can't be comfortable for him, but I'm more focused on the fact that he's surrounding me on three sides.

It's so cramped that his chest is flush against my back, and his breath is constant behind my ear and neck. His knees box me in, and I'm acutely aware of my short dress riding up as my ass presses firmly into his lap.

"Put your feet on mine," he rumbles in his deep voice. Liquid heat pools between my legs, and I pray my dress and underwear will keep that secret. I do as he asks, my feet curling around his ankles, and then he moves his hand under mine on the shifter. He shuts the door and puts us back in neutral. "Now, close your eyes."

I turn to look at him with surprise. "Why?"

Kellan smirks at me. "Because I don't want you watching what I'm doing. You need to feel it. Let the car tell you when it needs to shift and then do it."

Swallowing, I manage a small nod, then close my eyes. Now I feel even closer to him. All I can feel and smell is Kellan around me. My skin tingles at the close contact and I take a deep breath to get my body under control. His beard tickles my ear and I shiver just as his foot drops on the clutch. My foot falls with his, and then both feet and my hand are moving.

The car steadily increases speed, and I notice after a couple of shifts I can hear and feel it when the car needs to shift. Kellan's body moves so smoothly and mine follows along with his as we move to higher gears and then back down repeatedly.

"Now, you try. Don't open your eyes. I'll steer. And I'll tell you whether we're going faster or slower."

"You'd better not crash us into a wall or the water, Kell."

He chuckles and I can feel it vibrate from his chest to my back. "Go when you're ready."

I push his foot down and start going through the motions we'd done like a coordinated dance. Kellan guides me with the speed, and I'm pleased when there's no grinding noise with any of my shifts.

I'm midway through another gear change when Kellan's curse and tone snap my eyes open. "Fuck." I jump and screw up the shift. The gears grind until Kellan steps in to take over. He swings us around and that's when I notice we're at the abandoned airport. And there are red and blue lights heading our way.

"Shit," I agree. "Should I crawl over to the other seat?"

Kellan reaches between my legs and the seat flies back with me going with it. "No time. Just hold on tight."

I'm trapped between his arms and legs as he thrusts the car into its highest gear to speed us away from the airport where we'd likely been trespassing. We're back in the city quickly, but two police cruisers stay in sight behind us. Kellan starts whipping us down smaller one-way roads, winding us left and right into shorter streets to try and lose them.

A third cruiser almost crashes into the back wheel of our car from out of nowhere, but Kellan yanks on the emergency brake and then shoots us away from him. We jump over a curb and hear metal snap and scrape against the concrete, then drop back over the other side of the median to drive back in the opposite direction.

We weave through the city in a way only someone who knows the streets inside out could do, turning down roads I couldn't even see were there until we'd disappeared down their unlit alleys.

After a while, Kellan drives down another alley. "We'll hide here," he starts, moving his foot to the brake and then cursing when the car makes no move to stop. He wrenches the emergency brake to slow us down, but the solid building wall at the end is closing in faster than the brake will slow us down.

"Kell!" I cry out in panic.

"Pull your knees up!" he bellows, then flips us around and crushes me into the seat. His body covers mine, and his hand pins my neck to the back of the seat.

The car smashes into the wall, and I release a choked scream as the hood bunches up like an accordion and the windshield shatters. I wait for the dashboard to squish us both, but the car groans and then quiets.

I'm struggling to breathe, and I'm terrified when Kellan doesn't move. "Kell? Kellan?!" My hands are stuck between my chest and his, my body pinned to the seat and my neck still captured in his hand. I'm immobilized.

He doesn't answer and the panic claws up my chest and into my throat. "Kellan! Wake up! I know you're alive, you prick!" Tears are clogging my voice, and I curse them for weakening it when it's the only thing I can use to try waking him up. Because he can't be dead. His gift wouldn't allow it.

Right?

The longer he stays quiet, the more I struggle under him to do anything I can to wake him up. "This isn't funny, Kell. *Move.* Say something. *Please.*"

He's not breathing.

I should hear or feel him breathing over me, but there's not the slightest movement of his chest.

"No, no, no. Kell, you can't do this. You're invincible, right?! Wake the fuck up!"

Is it because the car is crushed too much into him that it's not letting his body heal? He always had to take anything stuck in his body out before his body could heal, so is that why? Then, how am I supposed to get the car out of him to heal if I'm trapped?

I struggle against him. Even if it means pushing him further back into the car, if I can shift enough that his body has some room from the car, then maybe...

I keep wiggling and throwing my body back and forth against his.

How long can he stay like this without dying?

He can't die.

He *can't*.

I just got him back. We were figuring things out. I was having fun again.

Everything I've done has been to protect him and the others. So, he can't die when I've been fighting for him all this time.

"Please, Kell," I beg again, imploring him to move. "Don't leave me."

A sob slips free, and I give one final shove.

Then he groans, and his body shifts over mine.

"Kellan!" I croak out.

He pulls away from me as much as he can in this overly-tight space, his shoulders and head ducked down from the roof, and he winces at the movement. His blue-green eyes rake over me with worry. "Are you okay?" He releases my neck and starts searching my body with his hands for signs of injury.

I suck in oxygen now that my airflow is no longer restricted and hurriedly wipe the tears from my face. "I think so."

I'm so relieved he's alive that it's taking everything in me not to descend into bawling madness. I turn my focus on making sure he gets himself healed so I don't do exactly that.

Kellan's knees are on the floor in front of the seat, and the dash of the car is embedded in his back. I can't even see his lower legs or feet beneath the crumpled mess. It's like it gobbled him up.

"Oh shit, Kell." I reach for his back, and he grabs my hand.

"I'm good. Hurt like a bitch, and I hit my head, but my gift's starting to take over."

Starting to. It can't heal him while the car is still in him, though. "Get out of the car so you can heal already," I snap at him when he doesn't do it right away and still seems focused on looking me over. "I told you I'm fine."

He smirks at my tone and grabs my chin, so I look at him. "Worried about me, beautiful?"

"Of course, I am!" I yell at him. "Get out!"

He finally relents and shoves the door open. It screeches on its hinges and fights him, but once it's open, he pulls himself out, and I get a clear view of the damage to his lower back and his legs. They're bloody and mangled, and my chest constricts tightly.

He pants on his hands and knees on the ground just outside of the car, and I can see the fine tremble in his muscles as he struggles to keep himself upright until his gift kicks in now that the car's no longer in the way of his flesh healing. He rips his shirt off and out of the way and picks out any remaining bits of glass in his back and arms.

His body slowly begins to stitch itself back together, his ankles and feet straightening, and golden scales filling in over the freshly healed skin.

I don't breathe again until every last injury is healed and reflecting moonlight from his hard exterior.

And then I'm breathless for an entirely new reason.

I've seen Kell injured numerous times before, but it was always a wound here or there. It's never affected most of his body at once.

The bits of skin I can see through the tears in his pants and his exposed lower legs and feet are covered in golden scales. They continue up either side of his torso, but the skin from his abdomen up his chest is more of a solid pale gold. The scales along his sides stretch to cover his arms to the back of his hands and then up his neck and along the sides of his face.

His eyes are dark and feral. He looks almost...draconic.

He effortlessly rips the door off the car and leans in over me. "Let me see you." His voice is deeper than usual, like a rumble echoing from a deep chamber in his chest.

I shiver at the sound of it.

He offers me his hand, and I let him guide me carefully out of the car until I'm leaning against it. He works his way down every inch of my exposed skin while I'm mesmerized by his scales fading away before me. Kellan presses his forehead to mine and exhales. "I don't see anything. Did I crush you?"

I tilt my face up to his while keeping the contact with our foreheads until we're staring into each other's eyes.

He saved my life.

He could have let me die in that wreck. He could have protected himself instead.

But he took every injury for me. He risked his life, took every bit of pain I know he feels, and is still looking me over in case I have so much as a scratch.

He protected me.

Like he always used to.

The feelings I tried to push away since seeing him again break free in a rush of warmth and desire. It will never work out between us after what I've done.

But I can't deny what's between us anymore.

Not after that.

My hands move up his shirt to curl around the back of his neck. His eyes heat, but he doesn't move or say anything.

I ignore the betrayal and distrust that's supposed to be between us when I pull his lips to mine.

I ignore Aiden's accusation when I sink my tongue between his lips and his fingers tangle into my hair and grip tight.

I ignore the past and anything else that might hinder this moment.

All I know is that I want him. I have wanted him since I knew what it meant to want someone.

And I'm not holding myself back anymore.

Fuck the consequences.

We snap at the same time, clawing at each other like animals. It's all teeth and nails and tongue as we take what we want with abandon.

I sink my nails into his back and drag them down, drawing a pleasured groan from deep in his chest. His teeth find the crook of my neck. Every nibble, every firm suck shoots an electric current of desire straight to my core. I grind my hips against him to sate the pulsing need there, but it isn't enough.

He tugs at the top of my dress and then rips the front open with a snarl when it doesn't give easily. I cry out from the force of it that I'm sure will leave a bruise, but I couldn't give a fuck right now. My breasts spill free, and he drops his head to ravish them while I lean back and moan. I pull his hair tie free and tangle my hands in his soft locks, pulling and grasping at them.

I grab his hair to pull him up, and he growls and wraps his hand around my throat before he gives me a brutal kiss that takes my breath away.

Following the grooves of his abdomen downward, I rip open the button on his pants and tug them down. His cock springs free, and I wrap my hand around the hard, hot length.

I need him now. It's as if I'm afraid that this moment might end at any second, and if I don't have him inside of me, I might never get the chance again.

Kellan breaks the kiss and looks like he might say something, so I jump up and wrap my legs around his waist, lining myself up with him.

"Don't stop," I pant, my voice thick with desire. "Fuck me, Kellan. Make me feel you tomorrow and the next day and the day after that."

He groans and pushes me back against the car. "Fuck, beautiful. That's music to my ears." His hand tightens on my neck while the other hand has a bruising grip on my hip.

Kellan thrusts into me in a single stroke, wringing a garbled scream from my throat. I'm wet enough to ease his passage, but he's thick, and I still have to adjust to his size before he drags his shaft back to the tip and slams into me again. My nails dig into his shoulder to hold on tight as he relentlessly fucks me against his car.

His hand on my neck cuts off my screaming and black spots edge my vision while he gives and takes pleasure like it's his mission.

My entire body clenches and coils at record speed, and my orgasm crashes through me. I collapse against the car where his hand and dick have me pinned, feeling like a ragdoll as I catch my breath. Kellan collars my neck and crushes our lips together.

I kiss him back in a breathless frenzy as his hips circle inside me, and I tremble from the stimulation.

He carefully moves us to the back of the car. I whimper when he pulls free of me and sets me on my feet. Kellan chuckles and spins me around, planting my hands on the trunk and positioning me just right for his height with my knees on the bumper. "Don't worry, beautiful. I'm not finished with you yet," he murmurs his heated promise into the back of my neck and bites down just as he drives into me again from behind.

My breasts flatten against the cold metal of the trunk when he holds the back of my neck. I push my ass up and back into him, meeting his thrusts so that we're matching each other stroke for stroke. He shifts a little, and a wanton moan flies past my lips as his dick runs over the sensitive area that makes my toes curl and my legs spasm.

He laughs softly. "Is that where you like it?"

I struggle to nod my head in his grip.

He grunts, keeping himself positioned to hit that spot. Then his fingers drag some of my leaking slick up to my clit and tease it until I can feel another orgasm rushing up on me again.

"Oh god. Yes! Fuuuuck, Kellan!"

"That's it, beautiful. Come for me again like a good girl."

He speeds up, and my heart stops with the intensity of the orgasm that nearly washes me away with it.

Kellan swears as he follows behind me.

We don't move for what feels like an eternity after that.

It takes until my body finally stops twitching and the rush of heat subsiding for my brain to come back online.

Shit.

This was a mistake.

One that felt *amazing*, but a mistake all the same.

Aiden is going to kill me.

Doing this was selfish of me.

"Don't," Kellan warns.

"What?"

"Don't second-guess it. Don't get in your head." His thumb strokes across the back of my neck, which he has yet to let go of.

"How did you—"

Kellan turns me around so we're facing each other, his arms on either side of me on the back of the car. "Your body told me." He brings his thumb and pointer finger to my nipple and pinches it, eliciting a gasp from my lips. "Whatever you're thinking, stop. You can lie to yourself, but your body doesn't lie to me, remember?"

He kisses me slowly, but with no less heat than before. I can feel my body unfurling under his touch like a blooming flower. It doesn't even feel like my own then. Like it's his to command.

My heart flutters in my chest when his lips leave mine and, for once, I'm at a loss for words. What can I say when my body so clearly answers him all on its own?

When I opt to keep my mouth shut this time, Kellan grins and helps to fix my dress, but there's no amount of sewing that can be done to restore it for Portia. I'll have to dip into my funds to buy her a new one.

Kellan pulls his shirt back on and fixes what's left of his pants, before he ties his hair back up and out of his face. He looks over the car and gives it a pat. "Sorry, girl. I'll get you fixed up."

"How far away from the club are we?"

"Other side of town."

Crap. I am not walking all the way back, and taxis aren't out this late at night.

"Don't worry, I'll call us a ride."

I nearly snap my neck with how fast I look over at him. "Not Aiden."

He raises his brows. "Oh? And why not?"

I cross my arms over my chest and try to feign nonchalance. "Other than the fact that he still hates me? If he finds out about what just happened..."

He grins like this is all so funny, and I want to punch him for it. "What? You think he'd hate you more? Do you care how much he hates you?"

"I think he'd join Dane in trying to get rid of me," I snap back.

He shakes his head. "Neither of them actually wants that. Give them more time."

Kellan doesn't know what Aiden did to make sure I stayed on the island.

"Call Jackson, then," he says. "He'll come if you call."

"I don't have his number."

He laughs and steps up close to me. "I'm sure you do. Go on. If I call, he'll ignore me."

I pull my phone out of the hidden pocket and check my contacts, where I only expect to see Elias's and Portia's names.

Jackson's name is above hers.

Ugh. Stalker.

CHAPTER TWENTY-ONE

RAEGAN

THE SOUND OF A motor grabs our attention and Kellan quickly shifts between me and the alleyway entrance. I'm about to push him aside, but he moves before I can touch him and howls with laughter. He claps his hands like he's enjoying a performance.

A sleek black car rolls down the alley toward us and stops a few feet away from Kellan. His hand is already gliding across the hood as he approaches the driver's door that opens, then he grabs the top of the door. "You ask him first or just steal it?"

Jackson emerges from the low-profile car. His hood is up, but I can still feel his gaze on me before he answers Kellan. "Stole it." He shrugs like it's no big deal. "He wasn't using it, and I don't have a car."

He steps around the door while Kellan is busy cackling and taking a seat behind the wheel. Jack pushes his hood back and stops in front of me. My breath stalls at the intensity of his blue eyes as they run over me from head to toe. Then they flick over to the trashed car and his body tenses.

His exposed fingertips flex and reach for something under his hoodie, and I grab his arm to stop him.

I don't know what he's about to do, but it can't be anything good with the look in his eyes. "I'm fine," I rush out. "I don't even have a scratch on me."

"What happened?" His tone is relaxed, almost sounding bored, but I know from his body language that he's anything but that. Does Kellan even realize how pissed Jackson is right now?

"We were chased by the cops, and we were going to hide out here, but the brakes weren't working. Kellan shielded me."

Jackson's hand collars my nape and he pulls my forehead to his. "Reckless as always," he murmurs; a smile tugging at the corner of his lips.

A huff of laughter escapes me. "Guess so."

He inhales deeply, and I jump back.

Shit. Do I smell like sex? Would he know? Does it matter if he knows?

My chest clenches, and yes, it matters.

He holds his hand out to me, and I stare at it like it might strike out at me. He waits there with endless patience for me to take it. Like there's no doubt in his mind that I will.

It's that confidence that has me reaching for it. Because when he has zero doubts about it, how can I?

His hand wraps around mine and he tugs me next to him, then his fingers split mine apart until we're holding hands. My heart somersaults in my chest and then burns at my selfishness. Without another word, he walks us over to the car he brought that Kellan's still pawing at.

"Get out. I'm taking her back to her apartment."

Kellan's head pops up and his brow furrows. "And what am I? Chopped liver?"

Jackson slips his free hand into his hoodie pocket and tilts his head while still smiling at Kell. "You made this mess. You can clean it up."

How easily I forget that Jackson's just as much of an asshole as the others. He just never directs it toward me.

Kell stands, and his height forces Jackson to angle his face up to maintain eye contact. He's definitely the tallest of the bunch and at least three inches taller than Jackson. Which says a lot about me, considering I have to look up to see Jackson.

Jack's gaze moves down Kellan like he's cataloging every detail and piecing things together. He's always been exceedingly observant, and I know that he sees evidence of what happened between Kell and I.

My hand squeezes his, and he turns to look at me without hesitation.

"Jack, he literally broke his body to save mine. I won't leave him here."

"All right," he concedes smoothly, then his smile sharpens into a smirk, and he presses a kiss against my cheek. Kellan growls behind him, and I swallow roughly.

I'm in so much fucking trouble.

This is why I should have just kept sex to a nameless stranger at the club.

Would it have been as mind-blowing as what I had with Kellan? Absolutely not.

But what the fuck am I supposed to do with this?

I sigh when Jackson pulls away and Kellan doesn't stop glaring at him. Time to put on my big girl panties. "Enough with whatever the two of you think is going on here." I pull my hand away from Jack's and walk around the car to the passenger seat. "I'll make one thing perfectly clear. I don't belong to anyone."

I shut my door and am pleased when the other two pile in without another word. Jackson climbs behind the driver's seat in the back and Kellan takes point, as expected, being the street racer.

The ride to the club is quiet, save for Kellan touching every possible button in the car like a kid in a candy shop.

"So, whose ride is this?" I finally ask.

"Aiden's," Kellan replies with a wolfish grin. "He never lets us drive it. But he hardly does either, so fuck knows why he doesn't share."

Ice slides through my veins. *It's okay. There's no way he'll be able to tell I was in his car.*

"How are you guys going to get the smushed-up car out of the alley?"

Kellan checks the rearview mirror to look at Jack. "You up for flying it back to the shop?"

"Aiden's car can drag it back. I'll keep it light," he answers, which means he'll use his gift to float the car while Aiden's moves it.

Kell snickers and swings the wheel to the right, only for the car to peel that way in a tight turn. He whistles and then guns it. "The control on this car is insane. Let's see what else it can do while we have it."

Jackson chuckles in the back seat, and I roll my eyes. "No cops this time, Kellan. I doubt Aiden will appreciate his car returned in the same shape as yours."

Somehow, we make it back in one piece to the club.

"Thanks for the ride and the night out," I say while unbuckling my seatbelt. Then I hear the other car door open, and both Kellan and Jackson get out. "What are you doing?"

"Walking you up," Kellan answers with a grin. Jackson slips through the shadows around the back of the building and Kell adds, "And scouting out that your apartment's clear."

"I lasted five years on my own, Kell. I don't need you guys looking after me."

He steps up onto the sidewalk and wraps his arm around my back, pulling me close. "If I'm being honest, I'd hoped we could continue our night here." He nips at my ear, and I gasp. "Since I need to go back for my ride, we'll rain check. But this is the end of our date night and the proper thing to do is to walk you to your room, isn't it?"

I'm about to argue again that this wasn't a date, but I'm so tired from everything that happened that I just sigh instead.

Kellan's hand drops to my waist. We walk inside together and up the stairs to my apartment. Jackson's nowhere to be seen in the hallway, but I'm sure he's nearby.

"Well, good night—"

Kell grips my hips and backs me into my door and kisses me.

His mouth and tongue are scorching as he burns me from the inside out. My hands are forced to cling to his shirt while my knees wobble and threaten to give out. I can feel the outline of his dick through his pants against my stomach, and I clench my thighs when my body dampens eagerly for it like the thirsty bitch it is.

I shove him back, and he chuckles, then licks his lips like the prick *he* is.

I get even wetter.

"Sweet dreams, beautiful."

I flip him off and push the code into the door so I can slam it in his face.

I take a deep breath and then turn to face my apartment. I'm expecting Jackson to be standing somewhere, but after checking my bedroom and the bathroom, there's no sign of him.

Well, not completely.

On the kitchen counter are multiple guns, magazines, knives of different shapes and sizes, and a first-aid kit.

There's a folded note lying in front.

The note reads, *I've got your back. Always.*

My phone rings on the counter next to me while I'm reviewing my notes on Joe. It's the standard ringtone, which tells me immediately that it's not Portia, so I pick it up to check the caller ID.

It's an unknown number.

The only numbers in my phone are Elias, Portia, and Jackson anyway, so that doesn't mean a whole lot, but they're also the only ones who have this number.

Wait. Except for Joe.

I'd called his office, listed on his website, and left a message with the secretary when I'd gotten back to my apartment the next day. I'd pretended to be freaking out and checking on what happened to the congressman. The secretary had been confused and said nothing was wrong, but she would pass my message on to him.

That was two days ago.

Since Aiden and the others won't be sharing any information they gathered from him, I needed to keep up the charade as Rebecca and get back to work on the assignment Elias gave me. As far as Joe is concerned, we were both attacked and I disappeared.

At least, that's what I hope he's thinking since I had nothing to do with the interrogation that followed, as much as I wanted to.

"Hello?" I answer softly, pretending to be Rebecca just in case.

"Rebecca? It's Joe Tabershire."

"Oh, Congressman! Are you all right? What happened?" I ask, feigning breathlessness for the innocent act.

"I'm more concerned with what happened to you. Are you okay, my dear?"

"I'm fine. Just a bit shaken up. I remember talking with you about the internship and then smoke, and the next thing I knew, I was waking up in the woods. I had to walk to a bus stop to get home and then I called the police. But when they said they checked in with you, nothing was wrong."

He chuckles through the line. "Just a prank from a friend. He didn't realize I'd had anyone with me, so I'm sorry you had to experience that."

I freeze at the lie. Is he trying to keep up appearances for Rebecca and the press, maybe? "Oh," is all I can think to say back.

"Please, let me make it up to you. I have some time this afternoon and we can pick up where we left off. I can have a car pick you up from the university around 2:30?"

I check the time on my phone. That should give me enough time to make a quick pit stop at the drug store and then bus hop my way to the university for the pick-up. "Okay. Yeah, that would be great.

Thank you."

"I'll see you soon, my dear," he says and ends the call.

I hop from my seat at the kitchen counter and grab the cash I have. I'm not going in empty-handed this time. Before things can get too bad, I'll slip crushed up sleeping pills in his drink. We need to have enough alcohol before that so I can convince him we'd slept together and I had to leave to get back to the dorms. That'll give me a small window to snoop for information.

The butler greets me at the door again with a polite smile. There's no sign or tell from him of what happened the last time I was here. He doesn't seem flustered or upset in the least that he'd been made unconscious a few days ago by unknown assailants.

Was this sort of thing not unheard of for public figures? Or do they always keep these events quiet from others?

He leads me to the same lounge as the last time. Congressman Joe is leaning back in his chair behind the immaculate and carved desk in the corner, his feet crossed at the ankles, while laughing into his phone as music plays softly in the background.

"Excuse me, it looks like my guest has arrived. I'll call you back." He hangs up and places his cell phone on the desk.

"Rebecca! I'm pleased that you did actually come back here."

"Well, I'll admit I was a bit nervous."

Joe grins, but it's darker than the ones he's given me before. "Of course, you would be. I've decided this time to cut to the chase so I don't miss you again."

Miss me?

My gut tightens.

Something's wrong.

I tuck my hands behind my back and start calling on my gift, hoping that I'm wrong but making sure I'm prepared if I'm right. My gut usually is.

The double doors to the room close behind me, and I hear the firm click of a lock.

"What's going on?"

His eyes practically twinkle when I ask that. "Please, have a seat." He waves his hand at one of the seats in front of him.

"No thanks," I reply bluntly. I can't keep up the act when all the red flags and alarms are going off.

"Oh? And where are you going after this? I must say, we have a lot to catch up about. But which one of us will have more questions?" His grin twists to something ugly. "I'll start, since you seem confused. I know your real name is Raegan, and that you belong to Gifted Enterprise."

I freeze.

"I'm sure you're wondering how I found that out. Well, you could say that bringing you in has been my assignment for a few weeks now. I had no idea how I was going to find a single girl in this city, and yet who would have guessed that you would show up in my sights at the mayor's party?"

The volume of the music goes up and I realize there's someone else in the room with us. I look around, then move to the side of his desk where a child is chained by the neck to his desk. And she's singing.

I raise my arm to grab at her chain, but it feels heavy and warm and barely moves. "What the—" My lids droop for a second and then I snap them back open. Joe's grinning at me from his chair, his chin propped on his fingers as he watches me like a shark waiting for me to tire of swimming.

"I got a bit of insurance from GE when they learned who had broken into my home and questioned me. I had to tell them some things, of course, but nothing that GE can't get around. This little girl is trained to put anyone to sleep who's a threat to me. Not that we won't fix that, my dear, but I think it's better we have this conversation when your gift is a bit more...settled. And yes, I know about that too. Quite a terrifying one, but useful if it's in the right hands."

My lids close again, and I stumble into one of the chairs.

He stands, towering over me where I'm leaning on the chair to stay upright. "It's nothing personal, dear. You see, I need to bring you in as my first test to Gifted Enterprise in order to earn my spot on the board. Apparently, there's someone there who really wants you back. But now that I know about you, I promise, I can look out for you."

He moves around the desk toward me, and I stumble back, grabbing onto each piece of furniture I can to keep me upright. "Thankfully, GE has the resources available to fix my home security footage that had been tampered with. They know exactly who interrupted me last time, and they've assembled a team to exterminate them now, so there will be no more interruptions for us."

My eyes fly open and adrenaline surges through me, trying to shove the drowsiness from my limbs. He checks the watch on his wrist and hums. "Should be about done now, so we'll have plenty of time to chat once I've moved us to a new location."

No!

I reach into my gift and yank it out, not caring where it sits so long as it overpowers the sluggishness and disintegrates anything I touch. I run for the large window and slap my hands against it. It turns to dust at my fingertips in seconds and then I'm launching myself through it and sprinting as fast as I can to a running car so I can force the person to drive it back into the city. I can only hope they're at that big tower that Jack had pointed out to me and not somewhere else.

Please. Don't let me be too late.

Chapter Twenty-Two

AIDEN

THE LAST MEMBER OF my team finishes his piece in time to round out the hour mark of our meeting. It's my policy that every meeting must be done within an hour to not waste anyone's time. Mine, in particular.

While I rebuilt this organization after taking it over and am its biggest supporter, it doesn't mean I actually enjoy doing the business and politics side of things.

I'll make the decisions and fund what is needed. Otherwise, I've hired a team to run the rest of it for me.

I might have tried to do more if my brothers would have gotten more involved. But each one of them made it clear they had no interest in running a business or the Guild with me.

"If I may," Parker, one of the team members voted in to help me run the Guild, cuts in as the others are preparing to leave.

"What is it?"

"A few of our newest members have been offered work and a place to stay at the Hype nightclub, owned by Elias Thorton." My eye twitches at the implication that I didn't know who owned that nightclub.

"Your point, Parker?"

"Well, I wasn't sure if I should be talking them into staying with us. They'd be greater assets here—"

"Let them do what they want," I cut in before he can finish and piss me off. "The Guild isn't here to collect and use people like us. Our primary goal is their protection. Providing them with work options is next so they have a purpose and means for living *if they choose it.*"

Elias's nightclub was here before the Guild was a speck in my mind. But it's not sustainable for the growing number of gifted people flocking to this city. There are only so many jobs to do in one little nightclub. How does Elias plan to help the others who come once he has no work for them? The Guild was created with growth and scalability in mind. It will last far longer than Hype.

Parker nods and murmurs an apology. The rest are shuffling about, speaking among themselves.

I stand and button my jacket, then pass the others by to leave the room first.

My walk to the elevators takes me through the great hall, where ten-seater tables are lined up one after another with room for up to five hundred people.

The Guild membership is sitting around a hundred and fifty since its rebirth two years ago. Two years since Jack came to me and the others and asked for help taking down his mentor, who had been using gifted people to spread his influence and power. He was a mini version of GE all on his own, and once Jackson learned what he was doing, we were forced to kill him.

It left us with hundreds of gifted people and the Tower to look after, and so we repurposed it into what it was originally promised to be, using the resources left behind.

After we escaped the island, I always planned on finding a way to fight back. It's our responsibility as ones who have survived them to do so. It took more convincing of the others, but after we found out Dane was being hunted and that they'd never stop coming for us, it left us with no choice anyway. They'll never let us, or any other gifted person, live unless they are under their control.

We've been able to stay off their radar by running the business side as a temp agency and keeping the use of gifts hidden during the jobs, but there's always the risk that something will slip.

A few members wave or smile at me, to which I offer polite nods in return. I catch Cassandra breaking off mid-conversation once she spots me and then hurrying my way.

I pick up my pace.

The elevator door opens, and I jab my finger for the Loft. She's running now with her hand up, like she thinks I'll actually stop the elevator for her even after I've repeatedly told her that I'm not interested.

My hand presses against the cold steel of the elevator, and I use my metal manipulation gift to shut the doors faster than normal. I keep them shut even after she tries ringing the elevator again, and then exhale when I'm finally lifted away from that floor.

I'm more irritable today than usual.

No, that's not entirely accurate. I've been in a bad mood since

Raegan suddenly appeared in our city out of the blue.

That was no coincidence either. I'd bet my Aston Martin on it that Jackson finally found and led her here. And then gave her a reason to stick around.

My hand rubs subconsciously across the front of my jacket over the inner pocket where I keep the picture of her hidden. I showed the others her birth certificate, but this? I've kept it to myself and on my person almost every day since I found it on the island.

The lights in the library flicker in warning that it's time to pack up and return to our rooms. The sound of books slamming shut, wooden chairs moving, and chatter among the students who'd been studying in here peaks as they start to leave.

I wait patiently in an aisle of dusty old books no one has bothered to look at or read in years. The room goes dark within minutes, and then the hazy glow of the automatic lights embedded on the ends of the aisles adds an eerie light and darker shadows.

There's a light giggle that I instantly recognize and confirms my suspicions.

Raegan, Kellan, and Dane were whispering with one another over something. Since Raegan is the smallest and quietest of the three, she would be the most likely one they'd choose to do whatever task or prank they'd thought up.

I should be annoyed with them for risking themselves like this. For risking her, *most of all.*

But my heart is racing in anticipation of catching her like this. It's become a sort of game between the two of us. I give her rules and boundaries to follow. She pushes them. I get her alone to scold her.

I try to tell myself it's silly and I should stop this. But every time I confront her, it feels like I'm getting that much closer to something that I want. Something I need. I need to feel that way again. To keep going with this game to see where it leads. Because maybe at the end, I'll find myself and what I feel like I've been searching for.

I listen carefully to Raegan's movements, following a few aisles behind so she doesn't notice me, and wait until she arrives at her destination.

Adult movies.

There are only so many books and movies that GE has approved for us to watch and stock on the island. But there are also some that the staff have brought in with them to share, just for them.

Movies aren't my thing. I prefer to get lost in a book that teaches me things. Business things. Learning about numbers, strategy, people...that's all information I plan to use one day.

It doesn't mean I won't watch some scenes here or there, though, when the movie is on in the room.

I step up behind her. I'm not trying to be overly quiet now so I don't startle her, but she's so engrossed in her search that she doesn't notice me anyway.

I clear my throat.

Raegan jumps and spins around, crashing back into the shelves hard enough that a few loose movies tumble and crash to the floor. She opens her mouth, and I quickly slap my hand across it.

Her blue eyes widen in surprise. I wait a little bit longer and then drop my hand.

"Aiden," she murmurs breathlessly, and the sound of my name on her lips goes straight to my dick.

I know the way she feels about me. And the way I feel about her.

But I also know she has feelings for the others too.

Any of us giving in to those feelings means certain downfall of our little group. It's best to keep it all at bay until I can figure out how this entanglement we've gotten ourselves in won't be the end of us.

Logic tells me that's the best course of action.

But it feels weak when she looks at me like this. When her striking, big blue eyes are looking up at me like I will punish her with more than words, and rather than looking scared by that idea, she looks curious. Maybe even excited.

I've never touched her before like that, but I can't deny that the temptation hasn't been there each time. And somehow, she can sense it. Like we're both waiting for me to make up my mind and act on it, but she'll push me into it if she has to.

I almost reach out to touch her, but I shift at the last second to grip the shelf by her shoulder instead. "Do I want to know what you're up to this time?" I ask softly.

She swallows. The motion travels down her exposed throat, down to where her hands are clasped together at her chest.

"I'm looking for a dirty movie," she confesses. "Kell and Dane want to watch one, and I told them I'd watch it with them."

My grip on the shelf tightens. Absolutely not.

Are they both making their move? Am I too late?

This isn't a race.

But if it was, if the others aren't going to wait anymore, where do I stack up?

I lean closer. Even in the dim glow of the aisle lights, I can see the flush of heat beneath her cheeks. She reacts so easily to me. It's intoxicating.

"I told you not to do things without letting me know first. So I can make sure none of you end up caught or in trouble," I remind her on

a soft chastisement.

Her lips curl into a smile and she strokes her hands down my shirt. Even though they stop at a safe distance, I can almost imagine the feel of her touch continuing downward until I'm hard as a rock in my shorts. "I know," she starts in a soft teasing voice. "It was just a simple movie, Aiden. I didn't want to bother you with it."

The spark of wildness in her eyes tells me she knows exactly what she's doing.

I grab her wrists in one hand to keep her from touching me again. "Did I say not to bother me if it was trivial?"

She licks her lips and then breathes out, "No."

I nod. "Good."

"So, can I get the movie now?"

"No."

Raegan's face flickers to surprise and then her nose scrunches in annoyance. "Wait, why not? You're here with me now to watch my back."

I push her back into the shelves, bringing a squeak from her lips, and I realize I'm still gripping her wrists. But I don't let go.

I have her trapped against the shelves so she has nowhere to go, and no hands to stop me, though I know she wouldn't. That's not the point.

"Why?" she asks again softly when I still haven't answered her. She's pushing me again. Making me act or do things I'd normally hold myself back on.

So, I answer her.

My lips crash into hers, feeding this building need inside that I've been denying for so long. I've been holding myself back out of fear for what it would do within the group. Of what it would do to her to have to choose one of us.

But I can't let her watch that movie with the others. I can't take that risk of losing her to them either.

I slide my tongue along the part of her lips, and she opens them without hesitation. I cup her face and bring us closer together. Her hands grab desperately at my shirt and a moan pulls from her chest through our kiss.

I'm just as desperate to feel her. Every stroke of tongue, every press of our lips, even our hands grabbing and pulling at each other is never enough.

She feels better than anything I could have ever imagined. She tastes sweet and tart at once, and the rushing need to claim her in every way burns through my veins.

More movies fall from the shelves in our avarice.

It reminds me to slow down. To draw this out so it imprints on my memory if this doesn't work out. If she doesn't choose me.

When I finally draw back, I pull away enough to put some air between us. My hands at some point moved to either side of her face, and I bring them back as well while we both pant to catch our breaths.

Raegan touches her lips, which are swollen and perfect from our kiss, and then she looks at me. "That was...I mean, you...wow."

Her reaction brings a smile to my lips, even as the reality of what I've done begins to sink in. It's too late to take it back now, though.

I want to do it again. And again. And I don't want to stop.

I step back from her before I give in.

"Aiden?"

"We shouldn't do this here. Get back to the room and tell the others a teacher stayed behind and you weren't able to get the movie."

She chews on her lip. "What about you? Aren't you coming back with me?"

"Jack's meeting me here in an hour anyway so we can go through the records room again. It's safer for me to hang out here until he shows up than to go through the hallways more than necessary. I'll clean this up while I wait." I point out the mess around us.

Raegan nods. "I could stay and help you?"

I turn and settle my palm across her lower back and start walking her back to the door. "We won't be long. Jack just stands guard to watch my back and I want to look through the files myself. If you and the other two watch a movie, we'll be back before it's over."

She stops at the door to smile at me. "Okay. I'll see you in a bit, then."

"In a bit," I confirm, then close the door behind her.

The elevator dings when it finally reaches the top, and I drop my hand. I found her birth certificate in the records room that night. And rather than telling the others what I found, I hid it from them so I could look into it more on my own first. I didn't want to *worry* them. I chose my feelings for Raegan over my brothers. What if I'd told them and we'd been more careful around her? We could have warned Vera to not be alone with her. But I didn't. And I have to live with that guilt.

I take another few calming breaths and then flash my tattoo at the scanner to open the doors. Then the face scanner to get into the Loft.

Kellan's sprawled on the couch to my left, one arm and one leg hooked over the back of it and his other arm dangling off the side with an empty bottle in hand. His feet and chest are bare, with only black sweatpants covering his lower half. His hair is shorter, cut shoulder-length.

His trimmed facial hair is what ticks me off.

I've tried getting him to clean up for *years*.

Years.

Raegan is back for a few weeks and he does it without complaint. I don't know if it was by her request or he suddenly felt self-conscious, but there you have it.

Prick.

Kellan's sudden change is proof of why she needs to stay away from him. I can't trust she isn't here to hurt one of us again until I find out more. Until I have my answers, I can't trust her to get close again to the others. I already failed us when Vera was killed.

I failed Dane.

Last time, I let my feelings for her cloud my judgment.

I refuse to allow something like that to happen again to any of us. She's far more dangerous to us than anyone at GE.

Even knowing she could wind up as the enemy, I still crave every glare, every sharp-tongued jab, anything she'll give me. Love, hate, anything so long as it's just for me.

I've avoided her as much as possible while she's been here. Tried to scare her away. Threatened her with her secret. Anything to make her leave before I can't control myself anymore.

I'd hoped to get answers when I confronted her, and instead, I only got more questions. What is she hiding? More than what happened with Vera, there's something else she's not saying. She's a complex puzzle, but I need more time and information to solve it.

Then I witness Kellan and Jackson coming home with genuine smiles and peaceful expressions I haven't seen them wear in years, and jealousy burns through my veins like lava. Here I am, trying to get to the truth for everyone's safety, and they're hopping right back into old habits and feelings without a second thought.

"Got a problem with Kellan?"

Dane's voice snaps me out of my thoughts. I'm standing over the couch glaring down at Kellan, which is probably what prompted the question.

I pull my gaze away from him to seek out Dane, who's sitting at his desk surrounded by monitors like a bird in his nest. "He stole my Aston Martin last night for a joy ride," I tell him instead. I know it was him because he messed up all of my settings. And I fell into my seat because it was so far back, it was almost in the back seat.

"Could've been Jackson," he adds, though he's only aiming accusations his way since Jack has made it clear he's on Raegan's side.

"Where is he?" I glance around the room and the sliding doors to the balcony, but there's no sign of him.

Dane grunts. "Said he could smell a storm on the wind and that he was going to seek it out."

I look out the windows at the bright, blue sky with hardly a cloud in it.

"A literal storm or GE?"

"Mm, yes. He tells me everything," is his sarcastic but distracted reply.

I stalk over to his nest and scan the monitors to see what he's working on. "No luck on the island?" I guess based on the satellite maps of oceans all over the world.

Once the congressman informed us in our interrogation session that there are new islands being used like the one we'd been on, it's been our sole focus on finding them. Those should lead us to more information on who and where the board of directors are, and most importantly, there will be a lot of gifted people to rescue.

If it's not too late for them.

"Jesus fucking fuck!" Dane shouts and slams his fingers down on the keyboard.

I raise my eyebrows in surprise. Since he's been isolated in the Loft, he'd taken on a crazy number of online classes, some legitimate and some offered through the dark web, to master hacking. It was his way of helping us since he couldn't physically leave, and so far, it's been beyond useful. I'd also thought he had mastered it, because there was almost nowhere he couldn't go.

"Something wrong?"

"Someone's fucking with me. I'm trying to hack into the satellite images over the Caribbean Sea and the Gulf of Mexico areas, but every time I think I'm in, I get kicked back out."

"Are you sure you were actually in?"

Dane spins around in his chair and scowls at me. "Of course, I was. Someone is deliberately letting me spend hours getting in and then changing it the second I get through, so I have to start all over again."

Hm. "Sounds like you're on to something in that area. Do any of the regular online maps show what's there?"

"They don't show anything out of the ordinary, though the images aren't clear enough to even see what's on the islands they do show."

"You think there are more islands?"

He shrugs. "It's just a hunch."

I rub my hand over my mouth. The time it would take to fly or boat around and island hop until we found the right ones would be too long and would alert GE.

"Just keep trying and let me know what you come up with. If not, we may have to find another way—"

The lights cut out, covering us in darkness.

Chapter Twenty-Three

AIDEN

When the backup generators don't kick on immediately, I unbutton my suit jacket and reach for the handle strapped to my back beneath it. As I pull the handle out, the metal unfurls. I snap it at the ground and the pieces all straighten at once into a long sword.

"Get Kellan, get your cuff, and throw on a hoodie," I order softly. "Then meet at the exit hatch."

Dane's fingers fly over his keyboard as he locks everything down and deletes any local files, then he jumps out of his chair to get Kellan. I run to my room to don more metal.

A spray of gunfire attacks the windows and Kellan roars in pain.

I grab two of my thick broad swords that are a foot in width each and put them side by side between me and the windows. I focus on their shape, using my gift to bend the metal at will until the two swords become one large metal shield with their pommels turned into a handle.

Bullets clang against it as I grit my teeth and lift it before running back into the main room to look for the others.

They're both waiting for me at the escape hatch on the floor, crouched behind the coffee table. Dane's wearing a hoodie with the hood up to hide any distinguishable features and his hand is glowing against Kellan's chest. Kellan's hunched over Dane should any bullets get through. His scales are on full display.

Dane can block someone from using their gift or he can turn the gift on full through touch. The former part is what GE is most likely after, but the latter...well, only Kellan's gift has benefited from it so far.

"Get through the hatch!" I shout. "I'm right behind you."

Kellan yanks the hatch open and waits for Dane to drop down first. He looks at me like he might wait for me to make it over to them.

I snap, "Go! Dane needs you at the bottom when he gets there."

Priority one is to get Dane out without anyone realizing he's been here this whole time or with us.

Two is getting the Guild members to safety and hoping that GE doesn't realize there are gifted people here.

Three is the safety of Kellan and I, and making sure Jackson is safe.

Raegan's face appears in my mind, and I shake my head.

Crouching behind the table, I re-curl my sword back to its whip-like form, then sit on the edge of the hatch and grab the handle to pull it down over me when I drop. The shield rests over me as I fall down the long, winding slide we had made when the building was renovated. It goes halfway down the Tower to the Guild's main floor and dumps me onto my feet in the kitchen's storage closet.

Dane's holding Kellan's upper arm to keep the scales activated while they stand by the door to wait for me.

"We should go for a sneak attack," Dane starts. "I'll cancel their gift and you can knock them out."

Kellan growls and shrugs his arm away, starting his one-hour time limit with his impenetrable body. After the scales appear, he has an hour with them before they retreat and he's vulnerable again without some rest. "It sounds like there are too many. Hide here while Aiden and I take them out. We can't let them see you."

"Someone could find him here when we aren't looking," I consider aloud. "He stays with one of us."

"You take him then. I'm going to go bulldoze through them all." Kellan throws open the door and runs out of it.

I curse his brashness and hand Dane a dagger. I split my shield into a halberd and a smaller shield and give the latter to him as well. "Watch my back. Don't go far or chase after people."

He clenches his jaw but nods. It's difficult for him to be a primary target by GE, especially with a gift that doesn't let him fight back himself. But there are other ways he can fight, so long as he doesn't get separated from us.

We walk out the door and through the kitchens into the great hall where chaos has broken out in the massive, three-story room.

It's gifted fighting against gifted, with only the clothing separating GE from Guild members. Our members are being dragged or carried away and my hands clench over my weapons.

It looks like our secret's out.

Or was it already out somehow and that's why they're here?

I hook the halberd across my back and snap my whip sword out. Then I flip it up and swing it at the first line of GE fighters. The blade slashes across them and knocks them down. I keep the edge blunt so I'm not cutting everyone in half, but injuring them enough to keep them out of the fight.

I keep moving through the hall taking out anyone in my way, but it's never fast enough. I stop one Guild member from being taken, only for two more to be whisked away. For as many as I've taken down, another swarm floods in until we're outnumbered three to one.

Most of the gifted here don't use their abilities to fight. The difference in skill and training between the Guild and GE is glaring, and I know we will lose if we keep fighting.

"Code Blue!" I shout out. "Code Blue!"

Our members start to move when they can, mobilizing as they've been instructed for that escape plan. But too many are still stuck in a fight and can't turn their backs.

I pull the extra metal from my sword back into my other hand and mold them into throwing knives. I start targeting the fighters keeping the Guild members from escaping, either taking them down or distracting them enough for our members to get the upper hand.

I'm forced to change the halberd into more knives, and then the remaining metal on my body until only my sword is left.

Kellan's in the thick of them, knocking through them two at a time. But a circle is closing in around him. His chest heaves with exertion, and it's only a matter of time before his skin reverts and he'll be vulnerable again.

"Dane." I turn to check on him for the hundredth time and freeze when he's not there.

Sharp pain sears into my shoulder, and I fall to the ground. A man steps forward with a spear of ice in his hand as he readies to throw another one. I yank my whip sword behind me. Where it would normally curl and fall short, I curve it back and sharpen the blade, then score it across his chest and shatter the ice.

The man screams and falls back. I hurriedly search for Dane where he's fighting off two men who have blocked him off from getting back to me.

I pull the ice from my shoulder and push back to my feet to start toward him, but the ice man yells behind me, and I spin around, flicking my wrist up in time for my sword to crash into the next spear of ice.

Fuck. I don't have time for this. I'm not losing anyone else in our group.

I whip my sword out and sharpen the blades. It crashes back to the ground and cuts the floor in the impact. "I don't have all day. Let's go."

He starts conjuring and throwing ice at me left and right. Damn it, do I wish I could conjure metal like that. I swing my sword back and forth in a tiring but effective maneuver to keep cutting through his ice until he's tapped out.

I throw my sword one last time and stretch it thin so it reaches him and cuts his head clean off.

I try not to kill them if I can help it, but if he's going to get in the way of me getting Dane back or helping Kellan, then it's an easy choice to make.

Screaming erupts behind me, and I pivot hard as Raegan ravages the two men who had Dane from behind. They drop to the ground with skin so fractured and split it looks like parched dirt in a desert with blood running through the cracks.

She doesn't even give them a second more notice before she's rummaging through their gear and pulling two guns out. She tosses one at Dane and runs toward the crowd around Kellan without waiting to see if Dane would catch it or not.

He does, but he stares at it and the men at his feet.

"Dane, move!" I snap at him. Gunfire echoes behind me as Raegan takes on the men surrounding Kellan while I wait for Dane to catch up to me. When I turn around, I notice the large group of GE fighters who I'd been blocking from the Guild members is long gone. Probably while I'd been distracted by the ice guy, dammit.

Our members should be gone by now though.

I grab Dane to make sure he stays with me and because I'm not sure if Raegan saving his life will qualify her for a free pass from him right now. We start working through the crowd around Kellan when a voice cuts through the fighting.

And then everything stops.

Everyone steps back. I look at Dane, who is as confused as I am, and then we push through to Kellan's side. Raegan is standing in front of him. I turn to snap at her for running blindly to him without backup, but the words catch in my throat at her pale face. It reminds me of how she looked when I confronted her about her secret. I swing my head around to look for the cause.

"Ah, pet. How I've missed you," a man says as he steps through the parted fighters. Then he comes into the light and recognition dawns on me. He was one of the scientists on the island. He ran the tests on us and made us complete different exercises for his research.

Gordon?

"You're supposed to be dead," Raegan whispers fearfully. I look back to her and her body's taken on a full tremble.

"On. Your. Knees," Gordon demands slowly.

She drops to her knees instantly, and a sob slips free.

What.

The.

Fuck.

The scientist walks confidently up to Raegan and then he strokes the side of her face. My muscles clench with anger and the desire to intervene, but I force the urge at bay to wait for the right moment.

It's like there's no one else in the room but them right now. All of us are just flies on the wall as she stares up at him and he smiles down at her. His finger curls under her chin and lifts it so she's looking right at him, and I catch tears sliding down her face.

It's him.

I don't know what or how, but he's the reason she freaked out.

"You're so weak right now without me, it's pitiful," Gordon murmurs with disgust.

Raegan grimaces and then she keels over and vomits at his feet. The scientist sneers and steps back.

"Disgusting. I think we'll have to start from scratch, if you're even worth the trouble."

Kellan's on his feet again, though his scales are gone, and rushing toward him with a roar. "GET AWAY FROM HER!" He throws his body into a swing aimed square in Gordon's face.

His fist flies through him and Kell stumbles off balance.

Gordon ignores him and the way Kellan's body literally fell *through* him and snatches the back of Raegan's hair to drag her back up on her knees again to look at him. "You're dirty and worthless and—"

She spits on him. Rage twists and contorts his face, and my feet move before I can think. Then he shrieks and releases her.

A throwing knife is embedded in his wrist and his other hand grips around it. We all—except Raegan who's still staring at the ground—look up.

Jackson has an entire host of knives hovering in the air behind him. He flicks his hand forward and they sail down at their targets on their directed paths. Everyone screams and runs for it, Gordon included, as the knives follow their every twist and turn until they find their homes or they make it out the door and Jackson's eyesight.

He jumps off one of the wooden beams and barely slows himself before he lands next to Raegan.

Jackson and Kellan help her up to her feet. Her face is blank. Empty.

That man abused her on the island. Before Vera's death? After?

Does it matter?

He is marked for death either way.

I glance over to Dane to read his reaction to all of this. He's glaring at her, but he's also not attacking or aiming his gun at her either.

At least there's that.

"Jackson, where were—" I start, but he cuts me off.

"Safe house. We'll talk at the safe house."

It's a good idea if anyone else is around. We can regroup, check in with the Guild, and figure out what in the actual fuck just happened.

The safe house is a mini version of our Loft hidden in a disgusting building no one would ever think to look twice at.

It's where I saw Raegan for the first time in five years, sneaking through the back door like a thief in the night.

Now she's sitting on our couch with her arms wrapped around her legs and a haunted look on her face that's been there since we left the Guild. My mood borders on murderous the longer I see it.

I should have attacked him sooner. As soon as I realized what that was, I shouldn't have waited.

That won't happen next time.

Kellan brings her a cup of water, which she takes with a barely audible 'thank you,' as she stares at nothing. Or at least nothing we can see. She doesn't even move when Kell tries to offer her a warm washcloth and then wipes any remnants of her bile from her face and clothes himself.

I grab some gauze to wrap my shoulder before joining them on the large sectional couch.

Dane's *still* staring at her.

The entire walk back, he watched her like a hawk. Now that we're all seated in the living room, he hasn't taken his eyes off her. But now his expression is unreadable.

Jackson is perched on the back of the couch on the other side of Raegan from Kellan, a throwing star flipping between his fingers while leaning his face on his other hand. He's scratched up and bruised as if he'd been in a scuffle, but none of us has brought it up yet.

No one has said anything yet.

To give Raegan more time, I focus on the other catastrophes of the day.

"Any ideas on how they found us?" I finally start. When no one answers right away, I turn my focus on Jackson. "What happened to you?"

He smiles and shrugs. "You know what they say. You go looking for trouble and you usually find it."

I frown to show my complete lack of amusement, but he isn't bothered in the slightest.

"It was a trap, actually. I was ambushed. I think to keep me busy while they attacked the Guild." He shoots me a look that tells me he has more to say later and I give the barest of nods so he knows I understand.

"Did they want Dane?" Kell asks, tossing the washcloth on the table and leaning back into the cushions with one arm stretched above where Raegan sits.

"I don't think they realized who I was when they tried to grab me. They may have just assumed I was another member of the Guild, is all," Dane answers.

"So, an attack on us? Or a snatch and grab of more gifted people?" I muse aloud.

"You," Raegan chimes in, and I practically jump to attention. The fear is gone from her eyes, but her face is guarded now instead. Her blue eyes latch on to me and my blood heats. "That was courtesy of the congressman. You remember him, Aiden? The man I was gathering information from before you kicked me out?"

I scoff at that, pleased by the flicker of annoyance she sends my way. I'll gladly take that over her haunted look. If I have to push her and be the bad guy to snap her out of that trance she was in, so be it. "Gathering information for *you*, maybe. Don't try to pretend anything you were doing was for our benefit."

"At least having me there only puts me in danger. Apparently, you guys know a bunch of other gifted people and you just led GE straight to them."

My jaw ticks at her brazenness, but I feed on it too. "How are you so sure it was that scum and not someone else?" I challenge back.

"Because I was in his office with him when he told me."

There's a pregnant pause as we absorb what she's said.

Kellan grabs her arm. "Alone?!"

She throws her legs to the ground and tries to tug her arm away, but his grip is too tight. "Of course, alone. I'm always alone."

"What if he—"

I interrupt Kellan, "Is he dead?" If she left him dead in his office with evidence all over the place, then we needed to be working on a clean-up *now*. The last person she got information from ended up with a knife in his skull.

Raegan finally yanks her arm free and then crosses them. "I left as soon as I heard he had a hit out on you from GE. He said you might be dead already, so I didn't stick around."

"Why?" Dane speaks up. "Why drop what you're doing just because you hear we might be in trouble?"

I decide against pointing out that 'dropping what she was doing' was putting herself at risk against someone I doubt she realizes has some pull at GE and focus instead on how Dane's eyeing her with confusion like he thinks he might figure her out in one night. It's laughable, but I wait to see how she answers him.

She bites her lower lip as she realizes what she's admitted to.

She cares about us. For all of the betrayal and enemies talk we've been throwing around at each other, there's no other explanation for her coming to our aid and abandoning her own mission.

"I wasn't going to let them kill you, that's all," she tries to brush off. The four of us watch her intently, and I know none of us are fooled by it.

Rather than let that train of thought continue, she sends her ire back my way.

"By the way, your home invasion stunt has awarded him a child chained to his desk and brainwashed to protect him."

Shock ripples through me, followed by anger.

"I'll handle it," I swear to her. I'll save the child and get them the help they need, if it's not too late. Then, I'll gut that piece of shit *and* Gordon and bring them to her to hang on her wall. The scientist hasn't done anything specifically, but he was on the island. That and something about him has me wanting to shred him to pieces.

Raegan sets her empty cup down and stands. "Don't worry, I'll take care of it. Just thought you should know."

Kellan scowls from the couch and stands to block her way. "No. Stay away from him. I mean it."

She jabs a finger into his chest, which I'm sure hurts her more than him. "You don't tell me what to do. *No one* does," she snarls. There's a glimpse of fear in her eyes again, but she blinks and it's gone.

His face falls like something just clicked for him, and he lets her pass.

Rae walks right by him, but I keep watching Kellan's face darken with rage the longer whatever is on his mind stews.

"You apparently all know where I live, so you know where to find me if you need me." She waves and leaves, and we're left with more questions than answers.

Again.

Jackson stands and walks across the back of the couch, then hops off and opens the window.

"Following her home?"

He turns to me and nods. "I'll fill you in once I know she's safe."

Then he's gone.

"What's the matter with you?" Dane aims at Kellan.

He turns to look at Dane and then at me as well. "There's more to what happened on that island than she's letting on."

"No shit, dumbass. She still hasn't explained why she *murdered my sister*."

"Then we need to get her to tell us what happened! I won't believe she just did it on a whim. And whatever the fuck was going on with that guy has something to do with it. So, stop pretending you're going to hurt her and help us figure this shit out!"

"Then how do you explain the birth certificate, Kell?! She's been one of them all along. There's no need to hunt for another explanation, because *we have it*," Dane snarls.

"No. She's not theirs. Why would she be fighting them then? Coming to help us? You're too blinded by what happened to Vera that you won't see what's right in front of you!"

"Of fucking course I am! That's not something I'm ever going to let go of. She killed my sister. She's gone. Forever. So, sorry I'm not going to rush to help her. You saw her obeying that guy's orders. What more proof do you need than that?"

Kellan swipes his hand at a dining chair and throws it across the room. "Did you miss *everything else*? She didn't want to be near him! She *threw up* at the sight of him."

"What if she was the agent they sent to kill your parents and sister? Would you still defend her then?" Dane spits out.

Kellan freezes. "Don't bring them into this."

That's it. I step between them. "We need to focus on getting the Guild members back."

They're quietly seething at each other, chests heaving as they catch their breaths from the screaming match. Dane caves first, going to his nest of computers to work.

Kellan's glare follows him there, then pins on me. "And what about Raegan?"

I want answers as much as he does, but I can't admit that in front of Dane yet. He'll do something stupid like storm off where GE can easily pluck him off the streets as they've been trying to do since we escaped. I have to keep him safe and out of GE's hands. I owe him that.

"What about her?"

He steps toward me, finger shoved into my chest. "Why did you tell me she made it off the island? You left her behind and alone to face fuck knows what for five years while we had each other. What if that's when he got to her? Did you think about that? You owe her more than anyone to find out the truth."

Fuck.

My chest tightens as the idea takes root.

He grabs a jacket from the wall and storms out, slamming the door.

Dane looks up from his desk with a scowl directed at the door.

I give it an hour before I head out myself.

Kellan isn't the only one seeking answers tonight.

CHAPTER TWENTY-FOUR

RAEGAN

Hype is packed by the time I get back. I'm ragged and worn with blood still spattered on my clothes and now soggy as well. The storm must have rolled in soon after we got to the safe house, because it was raining the entire way back. Thankfully, my stalker shadow was nearby after only a few minutes in the freezing rain, and then the rain simply fell around me for the rest of my walk.

I force my way up to the bar and almost collapse against it. "Porsh!" I groan aloud before the music in the room swallows it up.

She appears like a damn fairy godmother in her colorful skirt and netted top, all covered in glitter. On her back are sheer purple butterfly wings. One might think it would look silly in a nightclub, but the outfit brings it all together and she pulls it off.

"Rae?! What happened? Are you okay? You look terrible!"

I huff from where my chin is resting on my arm on the counter.

"Gee, thanks friend."

She squats so we're face-to-face and studies me. "You look like you've seen a ghost."

Panic flares in my chest, and I squash it back down. None of that.

"I did," I mutter. I can't think about him right now. I need to forget everything that happened tonight. Just enough so I can get some sleep and then I'll figure shit out in the morning. I know if I try to sleep now, though, I'll only wind up trapped by nightmares.

"I don't want to talk about it now. I need drinks. Lots of drinks. Shots."

Portia smiles and strokes my hair. It's not in a condescending way like I feel it would be with others. It's warm and sweet. "I've got you, Rae Rae. We'll get you fixed up."

She turns and shouts down the bar. "Ethan! Give my girl that cheeseburger you just brought back!"

"I don't want to take his food," I mumble, and she runs her fingers across my head again.

"Come on. I have a change of clothes in the back you can use to clean up." Portia brings me back to the employee room and helps me change and fix my hair and makeup so I don't look like a wet, bloody mess anymore.

Once we're back out to the bar, she brings me to a spot where a plate of food is waiting for me. My stomach growls when the smell hits me.

"Wow, what happened to you?" Ethan asks worriedly.

I lift my head and frown, tucking hair behind my ear. "You're really making a girl feel good about herself, Ethan."

"Sorry, I didn't mean it like that. Just...are you all right?"

"I'm alive and here, aren't I?"

And isn't that the truth? I should count my blessings for that right now. For Jackson showing up in time.

Ethan knocks his knuckles on the counter. "Well, let me know if there's anything else I can get you."

I force a smile that I'm still not ready to feel on my face and nod. Then I shovel in my burger like I haven't eaten all day. Wait, maybe I haven't.

Portia gets back to taking orders until my plate is cleared of the large cheeseburger and fries and then returns with an entire tray of shots. "Let me know if you want me to walk you back to your room once you're sufficiently trashed."

"I'll be all right. The apartment's just upstairs," I say, and she laughs.

"We'll see. Have some fun, girl, so you can fill me in on everything tomorrow."

I take the shots one after another, flipping the glasses over each time one is emptied. I lose count of how many I've done, but once the warmth of liquor slides under my skin like a blanket and bees begin to buzz in my head, I know I'm good.

I head out onto the dance floor to release some of my stress and anxiety and leave it behind.

I dance until my body is hot and languid, my mind dark and spinning. I have no idea who I'm dancing with, only that I'm lost in the crowd as another slave to the music.

My current dance partner breathes on the back of my neck with their closeness, and I grind back into them and throw my head back into their shoulder, eyes closed. I'm pulled taut against them. Their hands roam down my thighs.

I'm dizzy and clumsy, so when I start to push away from them before this goes too far, it's a weak attempt, and I'm tugged back in place. "No," I mumble, pushing at the person's—a man's—chest as I turn to see who it is. I just want to dance. And then pass out alone in my bed.

"I've got you, sweetheart." The man leers at me and yanks me back against him.

"Don't touch her," a smooth, male voice threatens from behind me. I'm pulled away from the first guy and stumble into a firm body. The smell of cinnamon fills my nose, and I inhale deeply. It's familiar, but I can't place it while my head's still spinning from all the movement.

I should be getting away from this one too, though.

"Hey! Find your own girl! This one's mine tonight," the first guy yells, grabbing my wrist.

I push off the second guy while trying to simultaneously free my wrist, which results in me flailing with the uncoordinated effort. The second one wraps an arm around my shoulders to secure me back against him, then extends his other arm toward the first man.

There's a flash of metal that reflects the colored lights changing above the dance floor. I blink to clear my vision. Is he holding a blade against the guy's neck?

Hang on.

I drag my head back to look at my current captor.

Aiden.

The first guy drops my wrist and curses. "What the fuck? It's just a chick." He backs up and disappears through the crowd. The blade shortens until it disappears up Aiden's sleeve.

A giggle tickles up my throat, and I slap a hand over my mouth, even though it doesn't stop it from coming out. Somewhere deep down, I know I should be concerned over what's going on, but the idea that Aiden came to the nightclub to dance with me is hilarious.

Did I already fall asleep and this is a dream?

He frowns at me, but doesn't say anything. Then he's walking us through the throng of dancers and I realize he's not here to dance. He's making me leave.

"Hey!" I shout and try to twist out of his hold, but he propels us to the back of the club.

"Are you too drunk to walk up the stairs or do I have to carry you?"

"I'm not leaving—"

My stomach drops when I'm lifted unexpectedly, and I scream and throw my arms around him in a panic that I'm falling.

Aiden scoffs at my reaction, and I would snark at him for it if him running up the stairs with me didn't give me the spins. I bury my face in his neck and close my eyes, willing my stomach to cooperate. His cinnamon scent helps.

I don't poke my head up until we stop and there's beeping, like the sound of entering a code to enter my apartment. I don't know what his plan for me is, but I'm just drunk enough that the idea of sleeping with Aiden to end my night doesn't sound terrible. I can't think of a better distraction.

He sets me down as soon as the door closes behind us, then grabs my shoulders in a punishing grip. "What the fuck are you doing?! We all get attacked and *this* is what you do right after?"

I smile slyly and slide my hands up his dress shirt under his jacket. "What? You jealous?" I giggle again at the joke that would be, and then at the rise I knew I'd get out of him when he seizes my wrists and pulls them off of him.

"What's the matter with you?"

I twist my wrists out from his grasp and then wrap them around his neck and press against him. "What's the matter with you? It's just a bit of fun."

Aiden shoves my hips back, but I grab his tie and pull him with me. I hit the wall and gasp. "Tell me about what happened with Gordon. What happened to you after I left you on the island," he demands angrily.

That man's name out of his mouth pierces through the alcohol and makes my stomach turn. My entire plan to forget him flies out the window as I'm forced to remember that he's alive. He's here. No. *No!*

I shove Aiden back. "Get out! You're ruining everything!"

He snarls and reaches for me, but I dive to the ground and crawl away from him. I grab my shoe from the ground to chuck back at him.

Aiden curses, but it distracts him for hardly a second before he flips me onto my back. I throw my hands and legs at him, hitting and clawing at him in my struggle. He swears again when I knee him in his thigh, just shy of my intended target. His legs pin mine down and then he wrangles my wrists over my head in one hand.

"Just tell me and I'll let you go. I need to know."

"Why? So *you* can sleep better at night?" I spit out at him. "I don't owe you any-fucking-thing, Aiden. You want to see all the scars I've got? You want to make sure I've been punished enough for what I've done? Because I promise you, I have. Does that make you feel better?"

Tears leak down the sides of my face to the floor as the pain and memories I'd tried to hold back start hammering their way back out.

My lungs tighten until I feel like I can't breathe. I'm going to be swallowed whole by the darkness creeping back into my mind and waiting to consume me.

My eyes squeeze shut. I can't see him looking at me anymore. I can't let him see all of my broken pieces as I begin to shatter.

Warm breath fans across my face, and I angle toward it instinctively. Lips touch mine, and time comes to a standstill.

The kiss is soft, almost comforting, before his lips coax mine apart. My body tingles and heats with every slow and deliberate stroke of his tongue. It's like he's breathing life back into me, and the darkness recedes from my mind.

I return his kiss with greater fervor, seeking to banish the thoughts that will drown me until I'm only heat and desire. I barely graze against him, and he snaps free of the kiss.

Aiden releases me and stands, leaving me bereft and angry. His hand rubs across his mouth as he stares at me in shock. "I shouldn't have—" he starts as I push back to my feet and wobble a little. Then I slap him.

He scowls and grabs the back of my neck to yank me against him. Our lips smash together in hate or passion, I can't tell, because now we're scrambling at each other with bruising grips and scraping claws. I'm desperate to feel his skin against mine and tear his shirt wide, the buttons snapping and popping and falling to the floor while my hands are busy running up and down his chiseled abs and chest.

His hand in my hair tightens hard enough to bring fresh tears to my eyes, and I dig my nails into his chest in return.

He lifts me up and my legs wrap around his waist without hesitation as I grind against him and push deeper into our kiss. There's nothing soft or nice about it. We're a clash of teeth and tongues and a battle of wills as we each fight to consume the other first. My hands scrape at his back and slide through his hair like I have to mark and touch every inch of him.

We swing around the room, and he crashes me back into a mirror on the wall that shatters. My dress blocks most of the damage, but shallow cuts nick my upper back, and I groan into his mouth as the bit of pain mixes with pleasure.

There's no more room in me for anything but, and I'd happily drown in this feeling every night rather than where I'd been about to go.

We're moving again, this time to the small table against the wall like he means to sit me on it, and the knick-knacks that Elias had on there for aesthetic are swept aside and shatter on the ground. My ankles lock behind him as he leans forward, crowding me against the wall and table. I rub my hungry pussy against him.

My fingers scramble for the button on his pants. Our kiss breaks and it's like a spell is broken and the realization of what he's doing kicks in. Frustration swells in my chest when he steps back and shakes his head.

I drop my legs back to the ground and throw my entire body into shoving at him. "That's right. Leave. I hate you anyway. I'll just go find someone else downstairs who can *actually* give me what I need."

His face darkens, likely with the same hate he has for me. Aiden stalks forward and then we're kissing again. I'm confused as fuck, but not totally complaining, as we're thrown back into a kissing frenzy that has us moving to the bedroom. He lifts me up and carries me over to the bed, then covers me with his body.

He grabs my hands and locks them above me and my body arches and curls up against his.

Something cool and hard slithers around my wrist and I pull away from it. The jingle of a chain answers, and my eyes snap open.

Aiden smirks above me and slides off the side of the bed. "I've left your one arm free if you need to finish before going to sleep. But the only one getting you off tonight is yourself."

I look up and find one of my wrists handcuffed to the bed. Except it's no ordinary handcuff, because it's chained directly *into* the bed. Like it's a part of the bed.

Because that's exactly what it was before Aiden created a handcuff from the metal frame.

"You fucking bastard!" I snarl at him, and his smirk widens.

"Have a good night and we'll chat some other time when you aren't drowning in alcohol." He walks over to the bedroom door, and I snatch the lamp on the bedside table and chuck it at him.

He laughs and closes the door in time for it to smash against it.

A knocking noise rouses me from sleep, and I groan, hoping it'll go away. "Knock, knock!" a soft voice sings through my bedroom door.

The door opens, and I open my eyes as Portia pokes her head through.

"If there's a guy in here, cover up because I'm coming in for my Rae Rae!" she calls out. Then she gasps and rushes over to the head of the bed. "What happened to your bed?" Her eyes widen and she looks at me in awe. "Was it that good?"

I roll onto my back and cover my eyes with the back of my

arm. "You know, when we traded codes to get into each other's apartments for emergencies, this isn't what I meant." It comes out grumpier than I intended, but I'm still spitting and hissing internally at what happened with Aiden last night.

At myself for letting it get as far as it did.

At him for stopping it.

Ugh. I hate him so much.

She sits on the edge of the bed and *tsks* at me. "Nonsense. You love my visits. I brought you water and medicine for the hangover. I also snagged us some breakfast sandwiches."

My arm flops back onto the bed, and I look at her like she's the fucking moon goddess. "You're right. I fucking love you. Don't ever leave me."

She smiles, but there's a tinge of sadness to it that sets off alarm bells. She hands over the cup of water and pain relief without a word.

I sit up and take them, then jump on that look before she can get away with it. "What was that look? Please tell me that you aren't actually thinking of leaving here."

Portia sits on the bed with me, legs crossed while holding her ankles. "I don't know yet. What was it like traveling on your own the last couple of years?"

"It was hard, Porsh. I never knew where I would be eating or sleeping some nights. You can meet some people who will take advantage of you the first chance they get."

She chews on her bottom lip. "But weren't there fun times? Didn't you feel...free?"

I frown. That's not...really how I would have put my time hopping around from one place to the next. "What's this really about?

Why do you want to leave?"

"Well, I've been here for two years and haven't gotten a single memory back. I was thinking...maybe if I went off and explored a bit, something might bring them back. Or I might remember something." She fidgets in her spot. "I've been leaning on Elias too much and it feels like I've become...trapped. And then when your goons showed up, I'm trapped even more between the club and this apartment."

My heart sinks in my chest. This is all my fault. If I hadn't come here, she wouldn't have to worry about GE. She was only brought to their attention because of me.

"No. That's not what I meant, Rae!" She leans forward and puts her hands on my legs. "I'm so happy I've met you. And it was like this before you showed up. Elias just made things so...easy. And I thought I was happy with that. But now that he's been gone for a bit, I realize that I've been using him as my crutch. An excuse to not go out in the world and discover who I am."

"Let me go with you, then." I grab her hands in mine. I don't want to lose her friendship. And I know how bad the world can be out there. At least if I'm with her, I could help protect her.

Or would I just draw more danger to her?

"Or wait until I deal with GE, and then we can go together," I amend.

Portia shakes her head. "I think I need to go before Elias comes back. Because...I don't know if I'll be able to leave if he's here," she adds, her face flushing at the admission.

My face splits into a grin. I try to keep my cool, but inside, I'm cackling. "You like him, then?" I'd suspected when she was upset he'd left, but I didn't want to put my hopes there. It could have been wishful thinking after learning about Elias's secret crush and how sweet they would be together. At least the two of them can give me hope for nice relationships.

She smiles, embarrassed, but her voice is strong when she answers. "Yup. A lot. Too much."

Cue internal screaming.

I clear my throat. "I see. Well, have you talked to him about it?"

"About liking him?"

I grin at her. "No, I meant about wanting to go see the world. I guess that, too, but I'm sure if you asked him, he would help you with that. Maybe even go with you. Just...don't go rushing off too soon, yeah?"

Portia smiles and tucks her hair behind her ear. "All right. I'll think on it some more." She pauses. "So? Where's the man I saw bring you upstairs last night? And why is half of your headboard gone?"

I chug the cup of water until it's empty and set it on the nightstand. "That was Aiden ruining my night."

Portia crosses her arms over her chest. "That was rude." She inhales sharply. "Wait, so then did you two—" She points at the headboard.

"No! We didn't. I mean...we almost, but then we remembered we hate each other, so he handcuffed me to the bed and left me. I turned it to dust of course, but I was so angry that I overshot it a bit."

She snickers and falls back on the bed, spreading her arms out wide. "Handcuffing you sounds like foreplay to me. Or, so I've heard at least."

Heard?

"Portia..." I drawl slowly.

She hides behind her hands.

"Have you had sex?"

Her ears turn bright red and she shakes her head while still covering her face.

I pull her hands away. "Don't be embarrassed. If that's your choice, then it's nothing to be ashamed of."

"Well...I mean. I could have and I just don't remember."

Ah, right.

"Does anything ring a bell when you're...flicking the bean?"

"What bean?" She looks at me, puzzled.

"You know." I bring my hand between my legs. "Petting the kitty. Playing the clitar." Portia stares at me, confused. "Well, shit. You need to start on that first anyway. Otherwise, how are you going to know what you like? Or don't like."

I toss the blankets off of me and some fall on Portia's legs. She grabs them and pulls them up to snuggle in. "All right, first things first. I have a little girl to rescue from an evil man. Then I can give you a little sex one-oh-one class. How's that?"

I strip the dress off of me and start tugging on my black pants and shirt.

"A little girl?" She pops upright. "Let me help too. I'll get the girl and you can distract the guy. Then you don't have to worry about her while you're busy."

A refusal pauses on my lips as I consider her plan. Her gift really would come in handy for the little girl. She can stop her from putting us to sleep and get her out before either of them gets hurt. Leaving me alone with Joe.

A smile forms on my face and Portia bounces on the bed. "Is that a yes? I can help?"

"Just this once, okay? The girl sings people to sleep, so you'll need to make her stop singing and then get her to go with you to safety. Bring her back here and I'll pick her up after to get her some help."

I try not to think about how my available help is most likely Aiden until Elias comes back. It feels like that trip is taking for-fuck-ing-ever. Or maybe I'm just annoyed by how quickly I've come to rely on him even when I still barely know him.

"Got it." She grins like the Cheshire cat and then hops off the bed. "You can tell me the full plan while we eat."

After breakfast and hashing out the plan, I load up on guns and knives and give her one of each just in case as well. I shut my door and turn the handle out of ingrained paranoia that it's locked behind me, then turn to stride down the hallway. A single set of heavy steps echo up the staircase, and I tuck Portia behind me at the top, pulling out one of my knives.

"Hey, beautiful. Where are you off to while the sun's still up?"

I tuck the knife away and scoff. "I could say the same to you. I thought vampires couldn't be out in sunlight."

Kellan's grin sharpens to expose his rows of white teeth. "You got a thing for vampires?"

"No."

"Oh, so just me then?"

Portia giggles behind me, and I roll my eyes.

"What do you want, Kell? I'm a bit busy right now."

He leans back against the stair rail and extracts a box of cigarettes from his pocket and picks one out to stick between his lips. He reaches for the lighter, and I snatch the cigarette and toss it.

He frowns at me. "Those are expensive, you know."

"They'd be cheaper if you quit," I counter.

Kellan laughs and runs his finger over the other cigarettes in the box. "Are we going to keep doing this?"

"So long as I'm standing here, yes. Or I can walk away and leave you to it."

He laughs and shakes his head at me, but pockets the pack and lighter. "You win this one, beautiful."

I raise a surprised eyebrow. "Oh? And why is that?"

"Because I'm coming with you." His gaze drops down to Portia and then back to me. "Though I didn't think you'd have company for this mission."

"How do you know what I'm even doing?"

"Come on, beautiful. You told us last night that you were going to save the girl. I knew it would be the first thing on your mind once you got some sleep, if you didn't try going out last night. But Jackson made sure you didn't leave Hype or your apartment to do that, so here I am, to pick you up and drive you there."

My brain glitches.

Did Jackson see what happened with Aiden last night? Did he watch me drunk dancing with strangers?

Portia squeezes my hand, and I jerk back to the present. "I've already got all the help I need, but thanks anyway."

I start down the stairs and he grabs my elbow.

"I'm helping whether you want it or not. You pushed all of the blame for what happened on Aiden, but I was there too. I'm just as guilty. It's my responsibility to fix this too."

"Having someone watch your back while you're with the icky congressman would make me feel better," Portia adds in.

"Fine. But if you mess this plan up for us, Kellan, then whatever trust we've been building back between us? Gone. Never coming back. Don't fuck that up."

He grins and drops a kiss on my temple. "I've missed you too, beautiful."

Portia 'awws' behind me, and I flush and start hurrying down the stairs before either of them can see.

I'm half expecting the congressman's house to be difficult to break into, but after hopping the brick wall around the back of the property and Portia using her gift to convince one of the staff to let us in and gather the staff in the kitchen, we make it inside without much difficulty.

Having her on the team really does make the plan run smoothly.

It's the first time I see, or notice, her using her gift. It's so...understated?

I'm not sure if that's the best way to describe it, but considering the flashiness and impact of my gift and the ones I've seen, I wouldn't realize she had a gift even while she used it unless I knew about it.

It's perfect.

Even Kellan looks at Portia more warily afterward, now that he realizes what she can do. I smile with pride at my friend. She looks excited and wired over helping and I have to calm her down so we don't stick out too much.

Kinda hard to do when Kellan is as large as he is, and Portia is scantily dressed in neon pink.

We walk through the hall and pause in front of the lounge double doors where I'd seen the little girl last. There's no guarantee that she's still here and hasn't been moved, but we'll search the entire house if we have to.

"Remember, Portia. Don't even look at him. As soon as we see the girl, make sure she doesn't sing and then get her out of here and back to the car."

She nods. Kellan steps up behind me so close I can feel his body heat. Having him here with me, on my side, is a comfort I never realized I needed until now. I've always done things alone, where I never had to count on anyone else and worry about them betraying me or having their own agenda. He's here for the same reason as me. And I know he won't let anything happen to us.

It's a different sort of strength that flows through me in that knowledge. I straighten with a dark smile.

"Let's do this."

I open the door and raise my gun to aim it at the chair behind the desk. Not to actually shoot but it's a good threat that will hopefully keep him under control from a distance. The chair behind the desk is turned away from us. I slowly move around the desk, keeping my gun trained on the chair. Empty.

"She's not here."

"Beautiful, please tell me you checked his schedule today to know where he was going to be at this time," Kellan drawls with his hands on his hips.

"Wait," Portia speaks up before I can find something to say that doesn't admit to how that's exactly what I didn't do in my rush to get this done. She fingers along the ridge of one of the wooden panels below the bookcases. "There's a small gap on this side." She pushes against it and nothing happens.

"You're thinking it's a hidden door?" I ask and move to stand next to her. I can feel the small gap when I run my finger over it and shrug. "Kell?"

He cracks his knuckles and stalks up behind us. We move aside and he knocks on the wall. There's a hollow echo behind it, which erases any doubt that it's hiding something. "If anyone is in there, back up, close your eyes and cover your head."

Singing starts up, and we all look at each other.

"Portia, can you make her stop?"

Her green eyes are worried. "I've never tried when I can't see them."

"Just give it a try and we'll see what happens."

She nods and touches her hand to the door, then leans her forehead against it and closes her eyes. "It's okay. You're safe with us. Stop singing."

We wait a beat, but the singing continues, and my body grows heavy.

Portia tries again, "Stop singing. STOP SINGING."

The girl's singing doesn't falter, and I pull Portia away from the panel, then give Kellan a nod to go ahead.

Kellan waits a few seconds and then his fist flies through the panel. His hand comes out bloody and battered, but it heals quickly enough and then he's pounding more holes in until he can yank the false door off.

The singing crescendos, and we drop to our knees. Portia crawls through the opening and pets the girl's hair until she looks up.

"Stop singing," she commands softly.

The little girl's lips snap shut. Portia smiles softly at her. "You're safe now. No one's going to hurt you." She offers her hand out to the girl, and she stares at it. We all wait without a word, and finally, the girl reaches out and takes it.

CHAPTER TWENTY-FIVE

RAEGAN

"THANKS FOR YOUR HELP," I murmur to Kellan as we walk side by side out of the back of Hype and into the alleyway.

After the little girl fell asleep in Portia's bed, we decided it was best for Portia to look after her while Aiden arranges for a trusted contact to come pick her up. Portia can keep her calm, if need be, until then. It also means I can avoid going to the safe house and having to face Aiden. Or Dane. Or Jackson.

Apparently, only Kellan is safe right now.

The thought makes me laugh at myself. None of them are safe for me. I'm in trouble with each and every one of them. In multiple ways.

Kell crosses his arms and eyes me like he can pry the secrets from me with one look. "We had to come all the way out here for you to thank me?"

"No, but I didn't want to wake the girl up."

"And the hallway wasn't good enough?" he asks with a raised brow.

I shake my head. "I wanted privacy too."

I can hear how weak that sounds when we both know that my room is right next to Portia's. It would have been no trouble to go there if privacy is all I wanted.

But my apartment is still a mess from last night. Glass litters the floor, as does broken décor and whatever else had been on most surfaces in the living area. Then there's the missing half of my headboard that would raise questions.

He doesn't prompt me again with words. Just a look.

"You're hiding something," he accuses.

I grab his shirt, and he willingly shifts closer at my nonverbal request. "I'm hiding a lot of things," I purr.

His hands smack against the building on either side of me as he leans over me. "Yes, you are," he agrees roughly.

My fingers glide through his hair and then I pull his head down to close the distance between us. He's hesitant in the kiss at first, like he might try to pull away to finish our conversation, but I bite his lip hard enough to taste blood.

He growls and grabs the back of my neck in a bruising grip. His other hand rips at the button on my jeans and he slams me against the wall, his hand coming up just fast enough to cushion my head from what was likely to be a concussive blow.

The jarring motion shoots a thrill of excitement through me, and I grip his hair tighter. The knot in it loosens and tendrils start to fall around his face and my hands. His beard scratches and tickles across my face, and I suck on his upper lip and shiver at the feel of his stiff bristles against my tongue.

Kellan cups my sex, and I drop my head back to gasp for air. His mouth travels down my jaw and neck, marking me with teeth and hickeys that I know I'll pay for later. His other hand starts rubbing and then sliding between my already wet pussy. He hisses when he feels me.

"So fucking wet. Is this for the danger or all for me?" he asks in a husky tone as his facial hair prickles up my neck to my ear.

My cunt clenches in response.

"You. Both. I don't know." I jerk my hips into his hand to seek more friction, and he chuckles. He knows exactly what I need, but he doesn't change pace or stop his steady strokes from my entrance to my clit. I might go insane if I don't get more.

I grab his wrist and try to grind better against him. His hand leaves my pants, and I whimper at the loss. He grabs my wrists in one hand, then shoves my pants and underwear down just below my ass.

Kellan drops to his knees and drags his tongue across my slick, then circles and sucks my clit so hard that I convulse against him.

"Fuck!" I cry out at the overstimulation and melt back into him as his tongue works miracles. My legs tremble, and I begin to sink down onto his face.

He pulls away just as I'm about to come, and I almost sob. He starts wrenching at my boots to come off, and I rush to help him rid me of them and my clothes. It doesn't matter that we're outside and someone could walk out of the building or down the alley.

Kellan throws my legs over his shoulders and hoists me up and back against the building, then buries his face between my legs again.

My calves tighten, and I grip his hair as moans rip from my throat. My entire body is taut as a bowstring and then it snaps. The orgasm explodes through me, taking anything and everything with it in a riptide.

"Fuck, that was beautiful." Kellan shimmies me down until I'm straddling his suddenly bare waist and my arms are around his neck. He kisses me hard and fast, forcing me back against the building until there's nowhere to run from him as he devours my pleasure.

He presses against my entrance and I push back into him, needing him inside me so I can feel complete. He thrusts inside in one fell swoop, flattening us against the building until he might come out the other side.

My arms and legs cling to him at the rigorous pace he's set.

It's hard and fast and everything I need.

I feel like I'll be swept away if I don't hold on tighter to him. My face drops to his shoulder, and I bite down hard.

"That's right, beautiful. Mark me as yours. Because you're fucking mine, do you hear me? I'm not making the same mistake twice. Now, come for me again and strangle my dick with your sweet pussy."

His words work like a charm, lighting me on fire and then throwing me off the cliff to spiral once more. My inner walls clamp down on him, and he curses and pushes through it until he slams into me one final time for his release.

I remain curled up over his shoulder as I catch my breath. The afterglow buzzes under my skin, and I smile into his shirt until his last words and their meaning filter back through.

He sets me down, but his hands don't leave me. "No. Not again, beautiful. If this is going to be a recurring thing, then out with it so I can put it behind us."

I grab my clothes to start pulling them back on. "There is no us,

Kell. This is just sex. No mine. No yours. I don't belong to anyone. If you can't handle that, then this isn't going to be a recurring thing."

Kellan slams his fist into the building, and I jump. "Bullshit! You're lying to yourself if you think we're just fuck buddies." He crowds me and grips my arms. "You're throwing your walls back up because you're scared. I don't know what you think I'll say or do if you tell me the truth, but I'm not going anywhere, beautiful. You're not going to scare me away. Let me in."

His blue-green eyes lock on mine with such openness and determination that I can't look away.

"I can't," I whisper. His grip loosens, and I take that opportunity to duck away and run back into the building.

Cleaning my apartment as a distraction from Kellan doesn't work the way I'd hoped. First off, the apartment is small and barely has anything in it, so it's primarily me sweeping the broken things into the trash. Anything that's larger that I can't save or easily toss, I use my gift to destroy and sweep up the rest. Which means I'm now down a bedframe and headboard, but at least the reason isn't as obvious as before.

The second reason it doesn't work is that cleaning doesn't require much thought and my mind keeps going back to the conversation anyway.

If Kellan thinks we're in some sort of relationship, then I need to stop being with him. As soon as I have the congressman and Elias is back to watch Portia, I'll be gone. I can't be with anyone like that.

Besides, I have a mission.

My phone pings, and I check it, assuming it's Portia. Jack's name fills the screen instead, and I open the text.

> Claudia is picking up the girl. She'll take care of her.

If that message came from anyone else, I might not believe them. But if Jackson says she's good, then I won't question it.

I text Portia that I'll be over in five, then finish getting ready and let myself into her apartment. She's sitting in her butterfly chair with a pack of Twizzlers in her lap and a pair of earbuds in.

I frown and tug one of her headphones free.

"Listening to music like that while alone in your apartment isn't a good idea when we're still on high alert," I chastise softly.

She peers at me. "Then how should I listen to music?"

I snag a Twizzler from her pack and flop down on her couch. "Keep a headphone out of one ear. Or listen to it through a speaker at a low volume so it's just background noise but not so loud that you can't hear someone in the hallway."

She scrunches her face. "I wouldn't be able to hear the music at all if it's that low."

"Then make sure I'm here with you when you want to listen to music. Did you even hear my text?"

She snatches her phone up to check it. Well, that answers that. "Claudia? Have you met her before?"

"No, but Jackson says she's good and I trust him. Has she woken up at all?"

"No. I've checked on her a couple of times, but she's completely out."

"Poor girl is probably exhausted after everything she's been through."

A gentle knock echoes from the door, and I hop up from my seat. "I'll get it." I wrap my hand around my gun and flick the safety off. I open the door just enough to fit my head through, then fix my foot on the floor behind it to block it from being opened any further.

The woman standing there is tall and thin. Her long, dark hair reaches past her hips. She's wearing jeans and a simple boat neck shirt. And while she does have some light makeup on, it looks natural and friendly. Her eyes twinkle when her lips lift into a smile.

"Hello there! I'm Claudia." She extends her hand out to me.

I take it slowly. She gives me a firm, but short handshake. "May I come in? Aiden sent me and I think it's best if we talk about what you need with some privacy. Are you Raegan or Portia?"

"Raegan," I answer. "Did Aiden tell you what this was about?"

"He did." Her eyes sweep over the apartment as she enters. "Is she here?"

"Isabel's sleeping right now," Portia says from her chair. "Are you going to be able to help her?"

Claudia smiles warmly at her. "You must be Portia. You know, we could really use someone with your talents at the Guild. I heard how you were able to get the girl here without any trouble or causing more harm to her. That's a real gift you have."

Portia perks up in her seat. "What's the Guild?"

The woman looks at me, but I shake my head. I don't know much about it either, aside from Elias mentioning it that one time.

Her brow furrows, and she taps her finger against her chin as she seems to study us from a new perspective. "How do you know Aiden? I assumed you were prospective Guild members."

"It's a long story."

"I see." She nods. "Well, you could call the Guild a community of gifted people. It's where we can be around others like us. It—Well, up until last night, it was a safe place where we didn't have to worry about being hunted or used."

"You mean the building that was attacked last night?" I ask to confirm. I thought it was a coincidence the guys lived in the same building that Elias had pointed out as the Guild. Businesses fill the first few floors and then apartments in the stories above.

"Yes, that's right. Everyone who lived there is a part of the Guild."

So the building was a hot spot for GE to attack and steal as many people as they could. "Where did everyone go after the attack?"

Claudia studies me for a moment. She must decide I'm trust-worthy for some reason, because she tells me. "The bunker. There are floors underground that are more heavily guarded and can still fit everyone, though it's tight. They will stay there until it's safe to return to the Tower. Which won't be long, I hear. Just a few more security precautions will be put in place."

"So, what does Aiden have to do with the Guild?"

There's a long pause before she answers. "He's the Guild Master." Portia and I stare at her blankly, and she adds, "The leader of the Guild. He runs it."

Oh.

"He created it?"

"Well, not exactly. He took over when the man who started it was killed two years ago."

Ah. "Gifted Enterprise?" I guess.

Her face pales. "No. Uh, you should really talk to Aiden about it. It's not my place."

"What's your place in the Guild?" Portia chimes in. I'm still trying to figure out why she's so worried about telling me how Aiden became the leader of it. Did he kill the founder? Like a coup d'état? Is that how they have so much money for cars, a safehouse, and that fancy Loft? And where do the other guys fit in with this Guild?

"I'm the head of the rehabilitation team for gifted who were brainwashed or are suffering in any way from their time with GE." Her smile returns while directing it to Portia. "Your gift would be really great on the team if you'd be interested."

"Um…" Portia looks my way and then back to Claudia. "Thanks. I'll think about it."

"Of course. If you're just finding out about the Guild now, then I'm sure you have more questions you'd like answered first. If you ask Aiden, he can fill you in or direct you to one of the board members."

"Why isn't Aiden staying with the Guild if he's the leader? Are you sure he didn't abandon you?" I cut in.

Her expression hardens. "Of course not," she replies crisply. Like my insult to Aiden offended her on his behalf. "He recognized that they've become a target and is distancing himself to protect the rest of the Guild."

Hm. Sure he is.

I know firsthand that he's not above abandoning others to protect himself and his brothers.

"We all know that it's a dangerous time for us now. GE isn't the only group or people who are a threat to us. He's doing his best to keep us all as safe as possible and we're doing our best to support each other," she continues. Then her voice lowers to a more serious tone. "I don't think it'll be long before the rest of the world knows about us at this point."

Chapter Twenty-Six

RAEGAN

I spend my afternoon running through shops to expand my wardrobe. I can only borrow so many bright, glittery, or sequined clothes from Portia before enough is enough. I'm still low on funds, so I buy a couple things here and there and then steal the rest.

I'm not proud of it, but a girl's gotta do what she's gotta do. Especially when she doesn't exist on paper to ever qualify for a legitimate job. That and because holding a job for more than a month usually equals GE finding me.

I use my gift to remove the tags and anti-theft devices and stuff the stolen goods into my existing bag from the store. Once I've snagged enough outfits for a week, I call it quits. I'm not greedy and that's more clothing than I've owned in a long time. I also hate shopping.

As I'm walking down the sidewalk back toward Hype and my apartment, the distinct feeling of being watched creeps between my shoulder blades and up my neck. I cautiously check my surroundings, but only see people going about their day.

It's late afternoon and the streets are still busy.

I frown and keep walking as I scan around me to look for anything out of the ordinary. If I am being followed, the last thing I want to do is lead them back to where I'm staying. Better to draw them out and get rid of them first.

I take a few side streets away from Hype just in case, zigzagging and making sure the feeling of being watched doesn't subside. Then I twist down a less popular shopping district with no cars and walking paths only. There's no one around, so I drop my bags and ready my gift in both hands.

Something moves out of the corner of my eye, and I jerk my head toward it.

Sitting on top of a light pole is Jackson. He's in his usual gear. Hood up, so I can't see his face, one knee bent and foot on the pole while the other dangles off of it.

He lifts a knife and whips it at me.

I'm shocked for half a second before self-preservation kicks in, and I duck and cover. It sails behind me.

"Jack, what—" I start after he misses, then look up in time to see three more knives shooting my way. I drop to the ground and then jump when I hear a thud behind me.

The knives are frozen in the air about a foot off the ground. The air shimmers, and a man lies there. Each knife is buried deep in fatal locations.

Was he the one following me all of this time?

I bend over to get a better look at the guy, but he's not familiar. Then I swing back up and around to chew Jackson out for the knives and my nose brushes against cotton. I startle backward, my foot tripping over the guy, but Jack grabs my arms and pulls me back upright.

"Excuse me, little one." He straightens me out and shifts me to the side. He then waves his hand and the body lifts a foot off the ground. Jackson turns and walks down a tiny alley between two shops with the body floating after him.

I follow too. Because I'm owed an explanation, damn it.

Jack drops the guy to the ground and squats to start rummaging through his pockets. The stench of death punches me in the nose and I cover my mouth before I choke on it. It's only after he's down that I see the other bodies already here. Four, including the previously invisible guy. But it looks like the others aren't so fresh.

"Do you mind explaining what's going on here?"

He slides his knives out of the body and wipes them on the guy's clothes, then tucks them away wherever they go beneath his hoodie. He walks back to me, then nudges me to keep walking with him out of the alley. "Come on. It's best not to hang around dead bodies during the day."

"Well, no shit. Are you just going to leave them here?" I argue, but my body does exactly as he directed anyway.

"For now. I'll come back for them later if someone else doesn't find them first."

"Wouldn't that be a problem if someone does exactly that?"

He shrugs. "Not really. There's nothing to lead cops back to us."

We're back on the shopping street and Jackson angles us back to my bags. He uses his gift to lift the bags and holds his hand over his shoulder until they gently fall into it.

"What about GE? They'll know it was us."

"They know we're here now. No point hiding anymore."

I cross my arms and study him. I feel like there's something else I'm missing that he's holding back on. His piercing blue eyes are twinkling back at me through the shadow of his hood, and the angle's just right in the sun that I can see his smiling face. "Okay, well, throwing the knives at me like that was not appreciated."

His smile stretches as he chuckles. "I was testing your trust in me." He turns and starts walking away. With my bags. "It still needs a lot of work, by the way," he calls over his shoulder.

"Hey! Where are you taking my stuff?" I call and hurry after him.

"To your apartment. Isn't that where you were headed with them?"

"You're coming back with me?"

His head tilts to the side as he looks over at me. "Do you not want me to?"

"No, it's not that. It's just...usually, you pop in and out. Or you're apparently there and I have no idea," I add with a *look*.

Jackson laughs softly.

"About that...I appreciate you looking out for me and saving me three times now."

The time at the docks, when Gordon appeared, and now today.

There's a tiny smirk at the corner of his lips and now I'm wondering if it hasn't been more than three times. I haven't been attacked since the docks other than today. Have there been more I don't know about?

Shit. I hope not. Here I was thinking how well I was doing even after they discovered I'm here and now I'm doubting everything I thought I knew.

"Anyway, I lasted five years without any help. I swear I can take care of myself. I'm sure you have other things to do..." I drift off as we enter Hype and I wave at the staff cleaning and preparing the club to open soon.

We head up the stairs to my apartment and I open it to let us both inside. Thankfully, I'd cleaned the mess this morning that had been made last night.

Ugh. Don't think about it.

Jackson brings my bags right into my room and sets them on the bed. I'm not sure if nerves make me feel like he stares at the missing headboard, because when he turns back, he doesn't say a word or look confused or curious.

I hope he didn't notice.

Fuck me.

"Raegan."

Jackson's suddenly standing right in front of me, his hood down and cerulean gaze locked on me. It's almost disconcerting how he looks at me so intensely. Like the rest of the world doesn't exist anymore, and I'm the one and only thing he sees.

His hair is as black as his clothes, which only makes his eyes pop that much more.

"There is nothing more important to me than you. I will do whatever it takes to make sure you're safe." His fingers push my blonde hair behind my ear and continue down my neck. A shiver snakes from my neck directly between my thighs at the sensual contact and his words.

"I've been looking into how Gifted Enterprise found you here. I'd been careful to cover up any trail of you and yet they showed up anyway. Between that and eliminating the smaller units they sent in to take you, I've been a bit busy. So, I'm sorry if I haven't been around much."

His hand settles against my neck and his thumb strokes over my pulse like he's desperate to feel it beat and push against him.

I reach up to place my hands over his and close my eyes. I sigh and lean into his hand. "From the sounds of it, you've been around me plenty," I start softly, thinking both of him going behind my back to kill people for me as well as watching over me when I'm unaware. "But I'd rather see you when you're around or know that you're there."

I open my eyes as he smiles and pulls his hand away to dig into his hoodie pocket. He extracts a paper crane and then gently fixes its shape and holds it in the palm of his hand. He blows behind it and it lifts and flies the short distance to me, where I catch it.

"I'll send you one of these if I'm around then, but can't be seen."

My chest aches as I caress the little paper crane and all of the good memories it brings back. "I'd prefer you in person when you can, but I like this if you can't."

Smirking, Jackson whispers in my ear, "I doubt you'd want me to interrupt if you're in the middle of something with Kellan." He shifts back just enough to see my face and his smirk deepens. "Or Aiden," he adds in a teasing tone.

Fuuuuuuck.

I push him back and turn away from him to stare at the kitchen counter. My face feels like a hundred degrees, and internally, I chide myself for it. What am I embarrassed for? It was just sex. Aiden was...well, that was a mistake. But he kissed me first. Did Jackson see that? Why do I care so much that he saw all of that?

Ugh. I've been going around dancing and having sex while Jackson's been protecting me for *weeks*. I feel like a complete asshole.

What does he see in me, after watching all of that, that he sees worth protecting?

My hair is dragged over the front of my shoulder, exposing my neck. Jackson's breath warms my skin as he chuckles behind me.

"Did you watch?"

"No." I turn my head over my shoulder to look at him expectantly for more. He just shrugs and smiles at me. "I wasn't invited," he adds, like that explains everything.

Except it explains *nothing* and has my heart hammering in my chest. Is he saying he wants to be invited? With the others? *What does he mean?*

But I'm too chicken shit to ask and swallow the questions down.

As if he can sense my nerves on the entire topic, he steps back to give me some breathing room and tucks his hands away into his hoodie pocket. It's like a foot comes off my lungs and they can finally expand to full capacity again. Jackson's relaxed demeanor lulls me back into feeling calm.

I can do this.

Push that knowledge to the side for later so I don't act like a complete idiot in front of him. With the others, I'm like my usual strong and confident self. But with Jack, all my walls come down and I'm just a girl in a big world trying to survive one day at a time. I want to bury myself under that hoodie and hide away from the world with him, where I know he'll keep me safe.

"I was actually on my way to you to bring you something today."

"What is it?" I ask, curiosity piqued.

Jackson reaches under his hoodie and whips out a folded paper. And now I'm convinced he must have all sorts of hooks and pockets and things on the inside of it. Or he's a magician.

My hand closes over it, but he doesn't let go right away.

"I found out who told GE you were here."

"Who? You mean someone ratted me out?" I thought I'd slipped up somewhere.

Jack nods slowly and then releases it.

I stare at it, then unfold it. It's an article in some fancy newsletter I've never heard of, but the main picture grabs my attention first. It's of Elias and I walking into the gala.

Shit. I should have worn a mask the moment we left Hype.

The article barely mentions the photograph. What it does include is *my name*. How would the photographers have gotten my name? I was just Elias's date that night.

I skim through the rest of it and check the back, then look up at Jack in confusion. "Who gave them my name?"

"Dane."

My heart seizes and the article crumples in my clenched fist.

I can understand him hating me and trying to get his revenge. But to involve *them*? To put everyone else in this city at risk? Hype? Aiden's Guild? His brothers?

Going after me is one thing.

Putting everyone else I care about at risk, and other innocents around them, is going too far. Even if Jackson foiled his first attempt at taking me out, did he become a coward in our time apart that he would resort to having his enemy take the revenge for him?

A cold hand grips the back of my neck, and I shudder. I didn't realize I'd closed my eyes and begun to shake with rage at Dane's selfishness. My eyes open. Jackson's watching me. Waiting to see what I'll do next.

"You're sure it was him?" I growl out.

His eyes clock mine, like he's reading my every emotion deep down in my soul through them. "It was him," he confirms without an ounce of doubt.

My gift stirs and grows heated in my gut. I feel it trying to force its way out. To consume me in it so I can destroy everything and everyone around me until my fury is abated. I struggle to keep it contained, even as the darkness in me crows about justice.

I'm sure now that he's the reason behind the attack on the beach. The reason that Congressman Joe was assigned to bring me in. Why Gordon showed up at the Tower.

He's so far gone in his need for revenge that he's stopped caring about who else he hurts. He's become a danger to Jackson and the others. To this city and the other gifted people hiding in it.

"Would you stand by if I killed him?" I ask Jackson. He says he has my back. That I'm the most important person to him. But would he stand by my side if I went after one of his brothers?

He doesn't seem shocked or upset by my question. His expression hasn't changed at all aside from looking...interested. In me. In whatever I'm about to say or do. He cocks his head to the side. "Is that what you really want?"

"Just answer the question," I snap back. Because I have no fucking clue what I want to do right now.

His eyes darken, and he closes in on me. I take a half step back, but he's faster and takes my face in his hand. His fingertips are ice against my heated skin. I'm sure he can feel my gift burning beneath the surface and so close to coming out that a flicker of worry pierces through the rage at him touching me right now.

"I know you, little one. Perhaps better than you know yourself right now." I open my mouth to argue, but he continues before I can get a word in. "I will stand by you and whatever you decide to do."

He kisses my forehead, and my heart stutters out of its raging beat.

It's not as clear-cut of an answer as I'd hoped for, but I suppose it's enough.

"Let's go, then."

Chapter Twenty-Seven

RAEGAN

The long walk—because neither of us owns a car—gives me a lot of time to think and stew over what I will do when I get there. Jackson doesn't say a word the entire time.

I almost get on his case for it, until I look over at him and notice how his eyes are constantly moving around us. He seems relaxed walking beside me, but a tension in his face gives away how alert he is to our surroundings.

My words die on my tongue, and I settle more into the quiet between us.

Even now, on our way for me to do who-knows-what to his brother, he's watching out for me. I was just too busy rampaging within my head to notice.

We're not even halfway there when I admit to myself that I'm not on my way there to attack Dane. At least not physically.

I was blinded by anger with the news of what he'd done when it first hit me, thinking that the only way to protect the others in this city was to get rid of him, but who was I kidding?

As furious as I am with the stupid decision he made, I could never consciously hurt him. I'm the one who hurt him this badly in the first place.

I still care about him.

I miss what we used to have and who he used to be.

If anyone is to blame for why he is who he is now, it's me.

My temper and gift cool and fizzle out and are replaced with annoyance and surface anger at his stupidity. Jackson gives me a look as I take a deep breath and I wonder if he somehow sensed the change in me.

While I've decided that I'm not going to kill or maim Dane, I'm no pushover and have plenty of anger I can still throw his way to make sure he doesn't do something so foolish again. And I'll throw some Aiden's way if he knows about it.

I shove the door open when we get there. Jackson stands just behind me like an ominous shadow for anyone who may try to get near me and it bolsters my confidence.

The three others are seated around the dining room table, having a meeting since there's no food on the table, and they all snap to attention when they see me. Kellan looks at Jackson over my shoulder and then back to me. He looks annoyed and broody. Whether that's still from me running away this morning or at this sudden intrusion with Jack at my back, I can't tell.

Aiden just looks confused, and Dane looks pissed by my appearance in his home.

Perfect.

I storm up to the table and focus all of my attention on Dane.

"You're a rat bastard and a real piece of shit, you know that?" I grab a pen off the table and chuck it at him.

He swipes it away and sneers at me. "Oh yeah? You finally ready to tell everyone the truth about how you feel?"

"What's this about?" Aiden tries to interject, but I ignore him and lean over Kellan to point my finger at Dane.

"How about you tell everyone the truth about what *you* did? How you told GE that I'm here and how I've been getting followed and attacked for *weeks*, because of *you*? How you put everyone else in this city in danger by drawing GE here?" I bang my fist against the table in emphasis.

A chair screeches back on the floor and Kellan's suddenly towering over me. "You did *what*?!" he snarls and grabs Dane by the collar of his shirt.

"Let him go, Kellan," Aiden orders and stands from his seat.

Kellan and I turn our heads simultaneously to look at him.

"Did you know?" Kellan whispers threateningly.

I step back out of Kellan's way as he holds Dane in one hand and Aiden's glare on his other side.

"Of course not. But I want to hear it from Dane if it's even true before you go trusting her over your own brother," Aiden counters back.

We all look at Dane, who isn't even trying to break free of Kellan. He slashes a hateful look at Jackson. "You're a motherfucking traitor, Jack. I knew she would be trouble from the moment she showed up here, and that's all she has been. Look at us!" He waves his arms out at the room.

Even I can see the divide between them. Kellan and Jackson defending me on one side, Aiden and Dane on the other.

They're looking at each other with distrust, hate, and contempt. Nothing like how we all were together on the island. Was this all because of me? Because I'm in the same city as them?

I'm the villain.

This isn't what I wanted. I was supposed to keep my distance from them and focus on my mission, and now it looks like I'm tearing them apart.

No matter what I do, everything I touch gets destroyed.

My throat thickens at the realization.

Aiden's studying the room like me, eyes landing on Kellan and then Jackson with a deepening frown before it falls on me.

"Did. You. Do. It?" Kellan spits at him.

Dane glares at him. "I did. She'd do it to any of us. As soon as she killed the informant we had, I knew I needed to get rid of her. I just tipped GE off with her name and a picture in one of the newsletters I know some of them read." His anger swings my way. "No one else was supposed to get hurt," he snaps.

Kellan's face and fist tighten with rage. A sharp stab of panic hits me that he might actually beat the shit out of Dane for this. Dane seems to realize it too, because his hands are glowing and gripping Kellan's forearm to block his gift from coming out.

"That's enough. Put him down." Aiden has a sword in his hand out of nowhere and it lengthens until it rests against Kellan's neck. With his gift muted by Dane, the blade nicks his skin and a tear of blood drips free. But the wound, even as tiny as it is, doesn't heal.

What is happening?!

"What do you want, little one?" Jackson whispers in my ear so only I can hear him.

"Not this," I breathe out, and I can feel his smile brush against me.

Kellan curses when a throwing star embeds into his wrist so deeply that I gasp. His hand snaps open, like the tendon keeping his hand closed was cut suddenly, and Dane drops to the ground.

He yanks the star free and relief floods me when his body immediately heals it.

I run to Kellan and check his wrist and neck, and then glower at Aiden until he puts the sword away. "Are you okay?" I ask him, and he grins at me.

"Aw. Were you worried about me, beautiful?" He strokes my hair through his fingers, and I stubbornly remind myself not to liquefy under his touch. He wants more from me than I'm willing to give. I can't let that continue.

I push away from him, though not unkindly, and smirk at him instead. "Just making sure you didn't lose the use of your hand. I'm sure you need it," I tease, though he catches my real meaning behind it and laughs.

"Damn right, I do."

"What the fuck are you two going on about?" Dane grumbles and turns to me. "So? You came here to rat me out. What now?"

"Now, it's out in the open and we put it behind us." Aiden steps forward, and I grind my teeth.

"You're fucking joking. He sold me out to GE and is the reason they're even here. He put your Guild and everyone else hiding from them on their radar. And I'm just supposed to let that go?" I demand angrily. "There's no taking back what he's done!"

I think of Portia. Elias, Kit, Ethan, and everyone else at Hype. Hell, I don't even know anyone at this Guild other than Claudia and now Isabel being there, but doesn't Aiden care *at all* that Dane is the reason they're all at risk now?

"We're never going to beat them like this. Us or you, Raegan," he growls at me. "If we're going to get rid of them for good, we need to work together."

I stare at him in shock.

"I thought we could ignore you, but that's clearly not the case. We keep getting in each other's way and slowing the other down. It's a win-win. We'll all be on the same team and look out for one another." He shoots a look over at Dane, before returning his attention to me. "And we'll be working together on the same plan. There's nothing we can do now to fix what Dane did, other than having us help keep them off your back. Dane is also their number one target for his gift, so you'll get closer to them just by being around him."

He finishes his speech and I just shake my head at him. It would never work. Dane would sell me out again to GE, to Gordon, in a heartbeat if I were close to them. And the others...it's clear now that I only make things worse between them. I won't be the reason they're torn apart. They're supposed to stick together.

With Elias's resources, I don't need Aiden or the guys to help me take down GE. As soon as he comes back, we can brainstorm our next plan of attack. I can keep moving forward without destroying the people I care about the most.

"What does that mean?" Aiden questions, his voice tight with irritation.

"No," I answer firmly. "We can't work together."

His brow furrows. "Why not?"

I look around the room at the others. At the people who mean more to me than they will ever realize. It gives me the strength to do what's necessary to keep them together. "I already have a partner I'm working with. Besides, you don't trust me. We can never be a team if we don't trust each other."

"Who? And we can put aside our differences and trust in that we all want GE gone. It's a common goal that we're working toward. Trust in that."

Dane cuts in, "I don't want her here either. I'm not working with her."

"See? Not happening." I give him a saccharine smile and turn back to the door.

There's no deal or offer he can make me to join sides now that I've seen the damage I cause them.

It's better if I do this without them.

Sighing, I lean against my apartment door. I'm not entirely sure how I feel that went. Instead of coming back feeling relieved or satisfied with any revenge on Dane, I just feel empty. And lonely.

Jackson patiently watches me as I put myself back together. He'd followed me out of the safe house and all the way back without a word.

My shadow. My protector. My personal god of death.

He knew exactly what I needed when everything was going to hell in a handbasket and did it without hesitation.

He said he knew me better than I knew myself. Can I even doubt that anymore?

His hood is back down again now that we're alone, but his eyes are no less intense out of the shadow. There's a dark heat in his expression that calls to me. I want to bathe in it and feel it in the way he touches me.

"What do you want?" he asks so softly that I'm not sure how I actually heard the words that barely grazed past his lips.

My heart thumps and squeezes in my chest, and my breathing shallows.

"You," I breathe in an exhale.

He's on me in less than a heartbeat. I'm mid-gasp when his mouth covers mine, and then it's game over.

His kiss is demanding. Eccentric. Insatiable.

I can taste the obsession on his tongue. Feel his devotion in his touch as his hands hold either side of my head. It's almost too much. I'm drowning in him as he fills me up and saturates me with the endless depth of his need for me.

I cling to his hoodie for support when my body threatens to give out under the headiness of his kiss. His hands grasp my wrists and our lips smack apart with how quickly he pulls them away. Our foreheads and the sides of our noses stay joined as we pant.

"Wait."

I release his hoodie when he tugs on my hands. His cerulean eyes never stray from mine, leaving me doubtless that he won't be gone from me for long.

Jackson carefully drags his hoodie over his head. The motion is slow and drawn out while he maintains eye contact with me for as long as possible. It feels like a strip tease, even if it's only a hoodie. But it's *Jackson's* hoodie.

What does he look like underneath it now, all grown up?

I'm half-kidding to myself that I'll see he has a demon's torso from making a deal with death to be its reaper.

The hoodie finally drops from his head and onto his arms and then he carefully extracts those as well. Jackson's lips tug into a cocky smirk when he tosses the hoodie to the floor. It drops like it's weighted with lead and clatters with the sound of metal.

Holy fuck.

He wears that all the time?

I check out what he's wearing underneath and, surprise, surprise. It's a black shirt.

"Is black your favorite color?" I tease to break some of the sexual tension in the room.

He chuckles and bends down to unlace his boots and heel them off. "I could ask the same of you. But I already know why you wear it so often."

I follow this dance we're doing and remove my boots and socks. Then put all the weapons I had on me on the counter. "Tell me."

Jack circles me like a predator. "You wear it trying to blend in at night. Because you think bad deeds can only happen in the dark."

"Don't they?"

He stops behind me. Natural instinct screams at me to turn around. Never let a predator see my back. My pulse sledgehammers. I clench my hands at my sides and try to relax, but my breathing only quickens when my hair shifts over my shoulder, and I feel him drawing closer to me.

"No." His voice is dripped in darkness and sin, and I shiver in anticipation. He's not even touching me and my underwear is soaked. "Some of the worst things happen in the daylight. By the very people you think you can trust. People who wear masks far better than any real monsters."

He plants his hands on my hips and pins me back against him. His hard length digs into me, and I writhe into it.

"Why do you wear black then?" I pant, trying to keep playing the game but failing miserably with how desperately I want him to keep touching me. His hands play across my every curve, stroking up my inner thigh and slipping up my shirt. It's like he's using his hands to memorize every line of my body by touch alone.

It's intoxicating.

Empowering.

"So that my enemies never see me bleed," he finally answers me. His tongue paints a line up my carotid artery to my ear. "An enemy who never appears injured, no matter what you do, is terrifying."

"Jackson," I beg.

His teeth scrape across my pulse as he drags my shirt up over my breasts. The clasp comes undone and then both of his hands find and grab them. My nipples are tugged and teased and pinched and my hips squirm harder against him.

I'm yanked back tightly into him and gasp with surprise, because I can feel both of his hands still higher up. Nothing keeps them still, but I can feel it. Then a soft, teasing pressure tickles through my pants at the apex of my thighs, and I jolt in shock, as much as the invisible band at my hips allows me.

Jackson chuckles into my skin. The invisible wind or hand or whatever it is continues to caress and fondle me through my pants until my legs shake. The band around my hips and Jackson's hold on me keep me from falling. I'd be putty on the floor without them.

"I want you so badly, Raegan. I've always—" He hesitates for a moment and I'm afraid he might actually throw the L-word out and I'll go running for the hills. He hums under his breath. "—wanted you," he finishes. "Do you feel what you do to me?"

The pressure on my clit intensifies just as the invisible hold on my hips keeps me from running away when it becomes too much at once.

"Oh God. Jackson. I'm going to come."

Everything comes to a crashing halt when he releases me. My orgasm, which had been creeping up my back and preparing to detonate, deflates and flies out of reach. Frustration replaces it and I whirl around at him.

"What happened? Why did you stop?" I demand on a breathless exhale.

"I'm yours, little one, but not like this." He steps up to me so I have to crane my neck back to look at him. "I'm not just going to be your distraction like you're doing with Kellan. When you're ready for me, really ready to take my leash, then you can have all of me."

He kisses me, and I fight him at first, still pissed at what I just lost, but his tongue wipes away the anger and I sink into him. His arms cocoon me, and I fall deeper into his kiss like quicksand. Or tar. Smooth and dark and impossible to get free of once you've been touched by it.

Jackson breaks off the kiss and plants a gentle one on my forehead while I re-orient myself with where I am. He slips his hoodie back on and throws his hood back up, tucks his feet into his boots without tying them, then leaves my apartment.

I collapse into the nearest chair, leaning back and taking my hand to my clit, hoping I can stir my orgasm back around.

I keep forgetting that while Jackson was always there for me, and still clearly is, he was never less of an asshole than the others.

Chapter Twenty-Eight

RAEGAN

Congressman Joe has gone into hiding.

It's only been a day since we rescued the little girl—Isabel—from his home. It may be too early to make that call, but when I checked with his public schedule where he was supposed to be appearing, he never showed.

Does his sudden disappearance mean he's gone to GE to regroup? Should I be more worried about what kidnap attempt he'll try next? Will he involve other brainwashed gifted people the longer this drags on until he finally has me?

He knows who I am now. Any of my attempts at learning more about him risk me falling into one of his traps. But is there any other way right now? He's my only lead, and he clearly has the ear of the board as a potential member.

Regardless, I have to find him first.

And I do have an idea. One that Portia, Kellan, and Jackson will hate, but it'll work. I can set myself up as bait. He needs me as a step in his initiation process or whatever to become a board member, so I know he hasn't stopped trying to find me as well. That means I'll just need to make myself more readily...kidnappable.

My pen scribbles across the notepad with possible ideas and locations where I'd most likely be spotted and appear vulnerable. I add a note in the corner that Jackson and Kellan need to be distracted with something else.

I'll also need a plan for how to get away once he has me and I have information that will guide me to other board members.

Loud scratching echoes from my apartment door. I pull my gun from its holster and aim it there while slowly approaching it.

I peek through the peephole.

No one's there.

My skin crawls, and I shudder. A ghost, perhaps? What if that invisible guy wasn't dead?

No, he was dead.

There's a small whine, and I look down through the hole as much as I can. A dog?

I open the door partway, gun still ready in one hand, and see that it really is a dog scratching at my door.

He's only a foot and a half high, but his coloring is beautiful. Light gray with mottled black and white. His face and legs have tan and then a white chest.

"Wrong door, puppy. This isn't your home."

I check up and down the hallway to make sure no one will jump out and surprise me while I'm distracted and then squat down to hold out my hand for him to sniff. "Can I pet you? You look *so* soft."

The dog woofs softly, then rushes between me and the door to hurry inside my apartment.

"Shit, hey!" I spin around and hunt for where he went. I catch him biting the throw blanket on the back of the couch and gasp. "Stop that! No! Bad dog!"

He gives me an odd look, and then he's growing and changing. His limbs lengthen, snout sinks in, and the fur recedes. I stare open-mouthed at a naked Kit on my couch, the blanket barely covering him from his torso to his upper thighs.

"What the hell?"

He grins at me and pops up just enough from the couch to wrap the rest of the blanket around his ass before falling back into it. "Surprise!" he shouts with his hands out.

The dog toys in his apartment. The abundance of dog fur. His playful energy. And I hadn't seen a dog while I was there. "You're the dog," I say aloud as it all clicks together.

"I'm *a* dog. Not sure I can count myself as *the* dog."

"So, you're a shifter, then."

"Yup!"

"Well, that explains a lot." I sigh and set my gun back on the counter. "Why did you show up as the dog? I could've shot you."

He pouts. The resemblance smacks me in the face, and I can't believe I didn't realize it the first time I met him. "You'd shoot a doggy?"

"Of course not. Not on purpose, at least. I wasn't expecting anyone."

Kit stands, using one hand to hold the blanket in place while his other hand starts touching anything and everything in the room while he walks around. "It's safer for me to travel as a dog. Less chance someone might recognize me. And people are nicer to me and give me pets and lovings."

"Oh. I didn't realize you were on the run. Who's looking for you?" I lean my elbow back on the counter and follow him as he openly scopes out my apartment. Everything in it belongs to Elias and came with it, aside from the clothes I stole and a few personal items in the bedroom, so I'm not sure what he could be looking for.

He shrugs. "Oh, you know. Nefarious folks."

His attention zeroes in on my notepad, and I slap my hand over it. He chuckles and keeps moving.

"So, why are you here?"

"That's a bad idea." He waves his finger behind him toward my notes. "Very, very bad. But I know we don't know each other well enough for you to listen to me that easily. Oh!" His fist hits his open palm and the blanket drops to the ground. "I know what might convince you to wait!"

"Kit!" I slap my hand over my eyes before I accidentally see something I don't want. "Blanket!"

"Oh. Whoops!" He hops back over to me. A quick check ensures that he's covered again before I drop my hand. Kit leans against the back of the stool next to mine and grins playfully at me. "Guess what happy news I have?"

"What?"

"Guess! Guess! It's part of the game."

I roll my eyes, smiling. "Fine. You know where the congressman is." His excitement turns to confusion. "What? That's my main goal right now, so it'd be pretty happy news if you knew where he went."

"You mean the guy Eli told you to pick up last week?"

"Yeah. That one."

He drums his fingers against the cool metal under his hands. "Nope. Thought you had him. Guess again."

"I did, but...well, it's complicated."

Kit bounces impatiently. "Got it. Complicated. Now, guess!"

"Uh..."

"Eli's on his way home!" he bursts out.

Relief washes through me, and I sink in my seat with an exhale. Have the two weeks passed already? Thank fuck.

"That's...really good news. Great news."

Yes. No more relying on Aiden or the guys for anything. He can help me find the congressman. And make sure I have a solid escape plan.

Finally, I can make progress on GE.

Excitement and relief mix in my chest. There's a tinge of something else too, but I push it aside. This is for the best. For everyone.

"Right?!" he responds excitedly. "He should be here in the morning sometime."

"In the morning? That fast?"

"He actually left, like, I think this morning or last night, but it's a long flight and they have to stop and re-fuel and all that. But yeah."

"Great. Great..." How quickly could he find the congressman? Would I be able to take down the board soon after that and finish this once and for all?

I lean back on the counter. "So, was that the news you came here to tell me?"

"Hm?"

"The reason why you're here."

"Oh! No, I just thought you'd like to know that."

He looks pleased with himself and then smiles blankly at me while

I stare at him expectantly. A minute passes.

"So....?" Still nothing. "Kit. What else did you have to tell me that you came here for?"

His mouth parts and then he scratches behind his ear. "Right. I heard about the attack at the Tower the other day and how some people like us were taken."

It was four people last I'd heard, but they hadn't been recovered yet. I wonder idly if Aiden has slept at all while searching for them.

"I'm a good tracker. Not just because I'm a dog. Well, maybe because of that, but I've been able to pick up scents before that others like me haven't. I thought I'd give it a go and see what happened."

"And? Did you find them?"

"I couldn't tell. There was no way I could get close enough to the building. But I was able to follow a trail from someone that smelled...wrong." He maneuvers around me to slide the notepad in front of him and writes an address. "I can't guarantee they're still there or not, but I would bet a peanut butter rawhide that they'd at least been there."

I can't put all of my hope that they haven't been moved already, but there could be more clues inside. Or, if the building is cleared out, Kit could sniff for another trail.

Next comes the hard part.

Telling Aiden.

As much as I'd like to do this on my own to help others like me, there's no way I can take on an entire building of GE goons. It's likely to have a security system in place too. Even if I could take out a decent amount of them before the alarm is raised, I'd still be outmanned and outgunned if any of them have non-tactile gifts.

"Thank you for doing that."

Kit grins at me and shrugs. "I'm glad I could help. Let me know if you need any more sniffing done. As long as there's no fighting involved. I don't do fighting. Just sniffing and pets."

I laugh, feeling lighter from the good news he's brought me. "Got it. I'll let you know."

He shifts back and rubs against my shins and waits. I give him the pets he's looking for with a smile. He's not just soft. He's like baby blanket soft that you want to rub your face in. I stroke his fur a few more times and then pull back. He licks my hand and trots to the door, which I open to let him out, and he runs out of view.

I head out immediately to give the news to the others. We may not be on the best of terms, but I'd never withhold information that could save people over personal grudges.

There's an eerie quiet on the streets as I take the quickest shortcut I know to the safe house. It's normal this time of night for the activity to have slowed down, but it's never empty like this.

It feels like the city is holding its breath.

My hands fist as unease settles in my gut. I wore a hoodie before I left with the cooler chill in the air tonight. I'm grateful for the small temperature drop so I can tuck my hair back and pull the hood over my head.

I scan the street, checking around the corner before I move in case I'm being followed again.

I make it to the safe house without incident, which should tell me that I'm being paranoid, but I still can't shake the feeling that something is wrong. I head inside, using the combination Jackson gave me to gain access without having to knock and hope that they'll let me in when they see it's me.

I walk right in and close the door behind me.

A chair crashes against a desk as Dane rushes upright. He has a gun in his hand, which I'd take personally if their last home hadn't just been attacked. I see when he realizes it's just me. And when he still doesn't drop the gun.

Okay. I take it personally now too.

"How did you get in here? You can't just waltz in any time you fucking please."

Aiden's standing behind him in his little circle of monitors. His face is drawn in concentration as he studies the screens. At Dane's reaction, he doesn't even bother looking at me. It's like he doesn't register me as a threat worth watching. Even though I walked right into their current home.

I bristle at being ignored, but then his hand flies out and smacks Dane in the back of the head. "Quit whining and keep working, Dane," he demands without breaking eye contact with the screens. "Raegan, if you're here to tell me that you've reconsidered joining us, then this may be a bad time."

Dane sends me another death glare warning and then sets his gun down within reach on the desk. He returns to his seat and the keyboard and starts clicking through cameras around the city. He has apparently tapped into every store, ATM, and even traffic light camera in this city for his personal viewing.

The monitors all shift with each click, each displaying a different camera and moving across the screens as he works through them.

I should just hand them the address and leave. Because I'm *not* joining them.

But curiosity gets the better of my pride.

"What's going on?"

Aiden's dark brown eyes finally deign to flick my way, then return to the screen nearest him when a new camera view appears. "Is that a yes? That you've changed your mind? That you'll take orders from me without complaint?"

I snort and walk over to the tech corner to see it for myself. "Of course not. I have a possible location for where your people were taken and thought you'd like to check it out."

That gets their attention, and they both turn around to look at me.

"And what makes you think they're there? Do you even know what any of them look like?" Aiden questions derisively.

"I have a..." I hesitate to say the word 'friend'. The only person I would call that is Portia. She's the only one I've opened up to. Well, more than anyone else lately. She still doesn't know the darkest parts of me, but she's the closest I've let anyone get in a long time. "An ally. He's a shifter and he tracked one of their scents to this place."

Aiden sighs and straightens, running his hand through his finger-length brown hair. It makes the hairs stick up in funny angles that should look stupid and lazy. I bite my inner cheek in annoyance when it only makes him look sexier.

Ugh.

"Do you think we haven't already thought of that? We have shifters in the Guild. They're the most common type of gifted out there right now."

I imagine what it might be like to shift into a giant bear or wolf and take a bite out of Aiden. The picture makes me smirk.

His eyes narrow at me.

"All right then." I shrug nonchalantly. "I'll just throw the address out and wish you luck on your search."

I walk back to the door. The feel of his stare on my back makes my skin prickle. I reach for the door handle and grab it.

I'm expecting Aiden to stop me. But Dane's voice calls out to me. "Just give me the damn address." He's pushed his chair back and has his hand out expectantly.

I look over my shoulder at him. "Really?"

Dane scoffs and Aiden shakes his head before returning to scanning the camera views.

"You think we're actually going to ignore a possible lead to our Guild mates? Aiden's just being a dick."

"When isn't he?"

Dane's lips twitch at the corners, and I *might* be about to glimpse a smile from him, but then his face drops like a sack of potatoes. He jerks his fingers back to bring my attention to his still empty hand. "Let's see it, then."

"Tell me what's going on that has you eyeballing every camera in the city."

"Now, who's being the dick?" Aiden croons.

I roll my eyes and stalk over to them. "I didn't say I wouldn't give you the address unless you told me. I'm just curious. I noticed something was off on my way over and seeing you two like this has me wondering if I need my knives out when I leave."

"Did you see anyone?"

"You mean, people? Not really. Maybe two or three. I know it's late, but the city isn't usually this dead."

Dane and Aiden share a look. Then Dane taps on the keyboard

and a live feed from another camera flips on in the monitor above his. Kellan's fighting three people in black in an alley somewhere. The view changes to another street, where Jackson's floating a body behind him.

My hand reaches instinctively to my gun. "Are you guys being attacked again?"

"No. But Gifted Enterprise is scattered around the city for something tonight. Kellan and Jackson went out to get some answers. And lessen their forces just in case," Aiden replies.

I frown and look more closely at each of the monitors around us. There are people in the same black get up in nearly half of the screens. I don't know the city well enough to tell where most are, but I recognize a few.

"Isn't that girl your friend?" Dane points out.

I spin around to the one he's pointing at on one of the higher monitors behind us. "Shit," I mutter and pull out my phone to call her.

"Move this to the bigger screen and add any other cameras in the area," Aiden tells Dane. He moves it within a couple keystrokes, and I have to turn around to follow it. The rest of the street appears in different angles and heights, and I actually see her walk from one monitor to the next before the phone picks up.

"Hey, Rae! How's the hunt?" Portia's clear and sweet tone carries through my speaker. It's loud enough that Dane's eyes darken when he looks between my phone and the scantily clad girl walking across his monitors.

Aiden's eyeing me too, probably hoping his look can drill me for answers on what 'hunt' I'm on. Portia knows that I'm trying to take care of Congressman Joe once and for all. And that he's been AWOL for about thirty-six hours now.

"It's slow progress. What are you doing out?"

She's been careful for two weeks to keep inside Hype between her apartment and the club. The only time she's been out was with Kellan and I to save Isabel. But it's...I check the time on my phone and frown. I hadn't realized how late it actually was.

"Did you bug me or something?" Her head swivels back and forth to look around her, and she laughs.

"Of course not. Dane saw you on his cameras and alerted me."

"Oh? Is Dane stalking me, then?" I should laugh at the joke, but my heart trips when I see him watching her steadily on his screen.

Dane scoffs and keeps eyeing the monitors. "I'm trying to reduce her casualties by association," he answers caustically.

The jab stakes me in the heart and leaves me winded. Portia's attitude sings through the phone back to me, and I try to remind myself that I do have at least one person on my side who's *not* an asshole. "Um, wow. He sounds better with his mouth closed."

I laugh at her insult to play off that what he said didn't affect me.

"Ignore him," she continues. Yup. She didn't believe me. "I'm picking up some food and then heading right back to my apartment at the club. I'll call you as soon as I'm back."

"Okay. Please be safe, Portia. I've seen some goons tonight, so I don't want them to stumble across you while you're out. Food and then straight back."

"Aye, aye, Captain!" she cheers and then hangs up.

I stare at her on the screen as she enters one of the twenty-four-hour restaurants we have in the city.

How far away is that from here? Would I make it there in good time? But it's a solid forty-five-minute walk from here to Hype, and that restaurant is in the opposite direction. I'm an hour away on foot.

It'd be better to watch her here to make sure she's okay than try to head over there now.

"She shouldn't be out alone right now," Dane mutters under his breath while looking back to the other screens now that she's inside a building and out of sight.

It feels like I'm being chastised as a bad friend. Probably because that's exactly what he's doing. He's reminding me that I'm the bad guy. I may try to be good or fool myself that I'm on the side of good, but I'm the catalyst for disaster.

Their group of brotherhood is falling apart because of me.

Their Guild has been running for years, but suddenly I show up and they've been found and attacked.

People are always dying around me.

The criticism hits home. "I'm not her keeper. She can do whatever and go wherever she wants. She knows the risks right now."

I'm not her prison guard. I'm her friend. If she wants to go out, then she has every right to do that. It's just my responsibility now to make sure she's safe.

I pull the address from my pocket and slap it on the desk next to him. "Here."

Dane pulls the address up on his computer and then Aiden lifts the piece of paper in his hand to peer at it more closely.

"This isn't a place we've looked at already. Who is this ally of yours?" he asks coolly. Aiden's trying to act unbothered, but I can tell he doesn't like that I have people helping me out that he doesn't know about.

"Wouldn't you like to know?"

He pins me with a look. "Yes. I would. That's why I asked."

I shrug and check back on the screen to see Portia heading back to the club. I smirk back at him and pretend to zip my lips closed. "Sorry. My lips are sealed."

"We should send a scouting team to this location now. If they have as many personnel out wandering the city tonight, it might be less guarded," Dane interrupts us and circles to face us in his gaming chair.

Aiden nods. "I'll call in whoever's available. The last group didn't get in that long ago and needs to sleep or they'll just be putting themselves at risk."

"I can offer my services as a helping hand this once. Just to help rescue the people taken because of Joe."

"Who the fuck is Joe?" Dane snarls.

"No," Aiden answers at the same time as Dane. "I can't trust you in the field yet until I can see you're able to follow my command." Then he answers Dane, "He's the congressman that Raegan cozied up to and who's currently got GE on the attack after us."

Dane's expression turns murderous, and I shoot a glare at them. "What you *meant* to say, asshole, is that he's the guy you let walk after you and Kellan broke into his home to question him. So, he's out for revenge on you two for *your* fuckup."

Aiden's eyes narrow. "At least I didn't try to fuck him for the information."

Oh.

Oh.

My vision blurs to red, and I hear the crack of my hand sweeping across his face. My hand pulses and tingles at the contact as blood rushes to my palm.

Fury and pain blend in a toxic combination. My gift hisses and spits in my gut, and then it begins to fade and fall out of my reach. It's still there, but it's like a clear, steel wall has been erected around it. I feel hollow and empty without it, and panic begins to backfill that void.

I blink out of my head to find Dane's grabbed my upper arm and his hand is emitting white light between us. He's blocking my gift.

Aiden's hands are balled into fists, and a red mark is blooming on his cheek.

"Fuck. You," I utter darkly with as much venom and hatred as possible. I step back and then glare at Dane when he doesn't let go. We're both trapped in a stare-off of wills and unspoken threats.

Me being around them is like a ticking time bomb.

All I bring with me is chaos and destruction.

I am the villain in this story.

He finally releases me, and I storm out.

Chapter Twenty-Nine

RAEGAN

I scrub myself clean with such voracity that my skin burns bright pink under the scalding heat of the shower. Washing my hair is no less violent. I attack my body with soaps like it was the one who destroyed me with a single sentence. Whether he knows it or not, Aiden saw through to my weakest link and plucked it out with so much contempt that my sanity almost crumpled to ash at his feet.

He can't know the truth.

But it's terrifying how close he came to it.

Seeing my weakness and attacking it must be his true superpower, because no one else has ever come that close. He knows exactly how to dig under my skin and get to me no matter how many walls I've erected to keep others out.

I hate him.

I *hate* him.

Hot tears glide down my cheeks as I slam my fist into the shower tiles repeatedly. My body slides down the wall to a heap at the bottom. I curl my head between my legs and let grief over what I'd lost and who I've had to become consume me in silence.

My hands and feet are tight and wrinkled when I shut the water off and drag myself out. My skin is overheated, so I lie naked on the bathroom floor to cool down. Not that it's much, considering the bathroom has become a sauna so thick I can hardly see a thing.

Once I feel strong enough to move again, I open the door and inhale the cool air of my apartment. I'm tempted to call Kellan over tonight. As a big *fuck you* to Aiden. And then Jackson's words about using him as just a distraction filter into my mind, and I abandon that idea. I never meant to use him like that. Either of them.

They deserve better than that.

Better than me.

At least I have Portia.

Wrapping a towel around myself, I move to hunt down my cell phone. Huh, no missed calls or messages. She was supposed to call me when she got home over an hour ago.

I press call and start fixing my hair. It rings to voicemail. I try it again. Voicemail.

Did she fall asleep? I know I saw her walking back into the building.

I dress quickly and step out my door, then knock on hers. I'm not expecting an answer if she's sleeping so, I enter in the code and then let myself in.

The apartment is dark.

Portia hates the dark.

I flick on the light and stare at the open room.

There's a bag on the floor and a note on the table. Dread grips my heart as I run to it and snatch it up.

> *Rae, I'm sorry for doing this without any warning. I need to get away for a bit to clear my head. I don't know how long I will be or where I'm going, but I promise I'll call you once I've settled in somewhere so I can fill you in on everything. Hopefully, you can come visit me then and you'll have vanquished the evil GE guys so we can celebrate! I know you'll win. Stay strong and kick some ass.*
>
> *Love You!! Xoxoxo*
> *Portia*

I read the letter again and chew on my lips. I thought she would wait for me. Or Elias, at least.

Elias will be home tomorrow. Is that why?

Hurt that she'd leave with a note rather than saying goodbye aches in my chest.

But then I think better of it.

She's safer away from me. I need to get my shit figured out and done before I can go see her and help her like I promised I would.

I sigh and tuck her note into my pocket just as my phone rings. Portia's name flashes on the screen, and I smile.

Well, that didn't take long. At least we can still stay in touch while she's on her journey.

"Miss me already?" I tease when the call connects.

"Oh, I do," a male voice replies instead. Alarm hits me like a lightning strike.

"Where's Portia?" I demand, my hand gripping the phone like it's this person's neck when I find them. "Who is this?"

"She's here. And I'm your good friend, Joe. Have you missed me while I've been gone? I hear you've been looking for me."

I fight to keep my voice calm and even. Of all people, how and why did he pick Portia? *Because of you. By association.* "I have. Now, let her go. I can meet you wherever you want. You can bring Portia and I'll go with you without a fuss. No weapons. No fighting. I swear it."

He chuckles and it feels like bugs crawling under my skin. "Well, that does sound like a nice deal. To *you*, maybe. However, I saw what this girl is capable of when I played back the tapes in my office the day you *stole from me*. You have someone who belongs to me. I'll have her back first. I'm being fined per day that she's gone by the ingrates at GE, so she must be returned promptly and unharmed."

Unharmed? What the fuck does he think we're doing to her? This man is deranged if he believes he treated her best.

"Fine," I lie. I have no fucking clue how I will trick him into believing I have that girl with me, but I can work out the details later. All that matters is arranging a time and a place for me to rescue Portia before anything happens to her.

"I knew you could be reasonable. Bring the girl and yourself, alone of course, and then I'll release your friend."

"It feels a bit like I'm losing out on this deal, trading two for one."

"My dear Raegan, there is no winning for you any longer. Either you come with me and I'll take care of you, and I can promise that is as close to a win as you can get, or Gordon gets you back."

My blood chills, and nausea rakes up my throat.

"That's what I thought. You have two days. I'll text you the location with just enough time for you to get there, so be ready."

"I want to talk to her. Put Portia on the phone so I know you actually have her."

"She's still sleeping soundly, and I'd hate to interrupt that. I'll be sure to give you a ring when she's up though."

The call ends before I can ask anything more. I stare ahead as my mind wheels over what to do. I would never turn Isabel back over to him or GE, let alone any other child. All I can think of is a dressed up and painted mannequin in my seat and pray that fools him enough to get out of his car so I can attack him.

There's a high chance he'll have guards or more help from GE, so I'll have to take them down too.

I need to make sure I'm locked and loaded with weapons before I go. I'm sure Jackson will lend me more if I ask for them, as long as I don't ask for anything that would make him take notice something is off.

I spin around to go back to my apartment and slam into a hard body.

"Just where do you think you're going, beautiful?"

I blink up in surprise at Kellan. Jackson leans against the wall behind him.

"When did—"

"Oh, sometime during your call with that sleazy piece of shit." My eyes widen and he nods. "Yeah, I heard him. And all about your little deal. That is a hard *fuck no*. You aren't turning yourself in. I have a feeling you'd do some self-sacrificial shit for that friend of yours and the chance to take that guy out."

"But—"

"No," he growls savagely.

I try to storm out the door around him, but Jackson side-steps in front of the door.

"We came to check on you after all the GE activity tonight, little one." His head angles. "It looks like that was the right call."

Kellan steps up behind me, blocking me between them. "We're going back to the safe house and we'll figure this out. Together. We're not losing you again."

My chest burns at his words. I want them so badly it hurts. But Aiden's words are still fresh in my mind, and I refuse to let them waste their time and attention on me anymore.

"I'm not getting anyone else involved in my mess," I argue hotly. "She's my friend. I'm the one who let her come with me to his house where he spotted her. He also wants me for whatever fucked up reason. Point is, none of that has anything to do with you. Get out of my way."

I try to duck out the side, but Kellan blocks me with his arm.

"It has everything to do with us," Jackson counters in his low, haunting voice.

"Are you going to behave, or do I have to carry you?" Kellan asks.

"If you think I'm going to take any help from that *dick*, Aiden, or that Dane would ever help me, then you're crazy and—Argh! Put me down!" I beat my hands against Kellan's back where I'm once again hanging over the back of his shoulder.

I call on my gift, ready to fight them both if I have to, to get away. There's no reason for them to get involved in this. I can take care of it myself.

Jackson *tsks* from behind me and gathers my hair in his hands. "If we're planning on rescuing your friend as soon as possible, it's not a good idea to waste your gift on Kell." He twists my hair and secures it with something at the back of my neck. His fingers trail from the bun up my neck to my jaw, where he tilts it to the side, so we're eye to eye.

"If you think either of us are going to let you go at anything alone again, then we're not the crazy ones."

The heat of my gift dies to a simmer and then peters out.

"One hour," I concede quietly. "If that time is spent bickering and not finding Portia, then I'm leaving and doing it myself."

Jack smiles, and Kellan chuckles beneath me.

I take that as agreement when they don't argue with me.

Even if it kind of feels like that might not be the case.

I draw a deep breath to ready myself before we walk into the vulture's nest. The safe house. But it's where both Aiden and Dane circle me with words that cut and pick and tear me to shreds, so it seems fitting.

I'm dressed to the nines for war, which should be clue enough for them that I'm not here for verbal annihilation like last time.

We stopped at Kit's apartment so I could send a message to Elias straight away as I'd promised I would if anything happened to Portia. When he didn't answer, I'd been forced to write a quick note and shove it under his door.

"What are we waiting for?" Kell teases me with a wink and throws the door open.

It bangs against the wall, and Dane's head pops up from his desk as he scrambles for his gun. His eyes are half-lidded like he'd been passed the fuck out.

Aiden appears down the hallway.

Naked.

And dripping wet.

"You'd both better have an explanation for what she's doing here. I just kicked her out a few hours ago." Aiden doesn't even bother trying to cover himself up. He stands there without shame, his arms folded, staring us down with disapproval.

It's an internal battle to keep my eyes above his hips. I mean, I hate his guts so it's not like I'm doing this out of any respect or kindness. I just don't want him to catch me and *think* it means something. Then I'd never hear the end of it.

Dane's put the gun down and is rubbing at his eyes while yawning. It reminds me of a grumpy cat that's annoyed for having his nap disturbed.

"Some of us need sleep to function," he grumbles and then gets caught in another yawn. The usual snarky tone he's been using around me is dull and sleepy. And almost cute.

Almost.

"*She*," I start, finding a point on the wall above Aiden's shoulder to stare at, "is here to cash in on one of the many favors you owe her." His brows lift in surprise. "Oh, and you did not kick me out. I left because I was done with the conversation."

He smirks at me and my arms quiver with the need to knock it off his face.

"Did you? Or was it something I said?"

"Nothing you say can make me do anything."

Aiden looks almost smug at that, and I add sharply, "Did you plan on me slapping you, too?"

Kellan whistles and laughs. "Did she now?"

Aiden merely shrugs. "You could've done better."

"Oh yeah? Come over here and I'll make sure I do it right this time. Maybe the other side so it matches." I step forward and start to raise my hand at my side.

Jackson steps in front of me. His blue eyes catch mine and my focus pulls completely to him. I drop my hand. "I wouldn't normally interrupt, but you have more important things to be doing, little one."

Portia.

I take a deep breath to settle my anger with Aiden. For now, at least.

Dane scoffs from his computer chair. "Like what?"

Well, I guess he's awake now, because that harsh tone of voice is back.

"Get dressed," Kellan tells Aiden. He plants his hand down on the back of the couch and then uses it to launch himself over and onto the cushions. "We'll fill you in when I don't have to stare at your shriveled-up cock and balls."

My eyes inadvertently fall to fact-check what Kellan's said. They are *not* shriveled. His long dick is hanging at half-mast as if we'd interrupted him while he'd been showering and he hasn't been distracted enough to lose it completely yet.

I look back up to his face and he's staring right at me.

Of-fucking-course he caught me.

"Hurry up," I snap at him, then move to lean forward against the back of the couch. I can't sit down or sit still until Portia's back and safe.

Jackson hops up on the back of the couch. He tosses an orange my way out of nowhere, and I catch it on reflex. "Eat."

I tear open the skin in pieces and drop it on the floor as a later gift and surprise for Aiden. Even though my stomach is twisted in knots, I force myself to eat the fruit.

Dane eventually joins us in the living room and sits on the furthest end of the couch from me. He kicks his socks up on the coffee table and leans into the couch, his hands burying themselves in his front hoodie pocket.

For once, we're all quiet.

It's almost like old times, if not for the layer of tension radiating between us all and reminding me that those times are long gone.

Aiden stands at the edge of the living area. He's dressed in military-esque clothing that accentuates the muscles in his biceps and makes my mouth water. "All right, Jackson. You tell us what happened."

"Why him?" I burst out before I can stop myself.

"Because he'll get straight to the point."

Jackson chuckles and leans his face against his fist. "Her friend, Portia, was kidnapped by the congressman."

"And we're going after her, I presume?"

"We? No, I just need your help to find her. I'll get her back myself," I answer first.

Aiden casts his gaze over Kellan and Jackson, then lands on me. "That may have been your plan, but it's not the one they'll follow. *We* will assist you in getting her back."

"I get Jack and Kellan going in to help me, but why would you?"

He scoffs and crosses his arms while widening his stance. "I don't expect you to understand, but I'll stand by my brothers if they're running into danger to make sure we all come home. I'll do whatever it takes to make sure we stick together."

"Not to mention our Guild mates might be held where she is," Dane adds. I notice he refuses to look at me during this conversation as if he's pretending I'm not actually here.

Which is...fine. It's better than being held at gunpoint.

He stands and returns to his U-shape desk of monitors. "I'll start checking cameras around your building tonight to see if I can follow them."

Aiden nods and pulls his phone out. "I'll call the scout team back in to rest and be on standby to go back out."

A ringtone sounds and we look expectantly at Aiden's phone. Then they look at me and I realize my pocket is vibrating. There's only one person it could be.

I yank my phone out and flip it open.

"Portia?!"

Screaming pierces through the speaker into my ear and echoes in the room.

CHAPTER THIRTY

RAEGAN

"Portia! *Portia*!" My voice cracks.

"Such a shame she woke up so quickly," Joe says over her screams. "But it is morning and as good a time as any to get started."

"Stop hurting her! You gave me two days."

"Of course, and you'll have them. However, our mutual friends would like to learn more about her while she's here. She's refusing to answer any of their questions. So, really, this is her doing. I must say, she's stronger than she looks."

"Anyone who touches her is dead," I bite out. "And I won't be using a gun to do it. Tell that to everyone if they want to live. You'll all leave her alone until I come for the swap."

Joe chuckles. "If you so happen to turn the girl and yourself over sooner, you can cut her time here short. Tick Tock."

Portia's screams are cut off when the connection ends.

"No, no," I breathe and dial her back. It rings again and again, and then cuts over to voicemail. I try again.

And again.

"Portia." My voice comes out in a pained whisper. I'm tempted to chuck the phone at the wall, but it's my only connection and hope for her. I steady my grip on it and shove it back in my pocket to take away that temptation.

A gaping pit of rage swirls in my gut. I close my eyes and feed it with more and more until my skin is brimming with it.

Someone touches my shoulder and I snarl at them. Dane watches me solemnly. "Put your gift away. Now isn't the time."

I look at my hands. My arms. All of my exposed skin has a soft reddish glow. I didn't even realize I'd activated my gift.

The others are standing and staring at me as well.

"Did you find her?"

"Not yet."

I can't sit around here waiting while she's being tortured. "Call me when you do." I tug away from his grip and turn to the door.

Jackson somehow beats me to it. "Where are you going? The hour's not up yet."

"I can't just stand around doing nothing while she's being tortured! I'm leaving."

"To go where?"

For once, his calmness doesn't soothe me. It has the opposite effect. I have to *go*. *Now*. Portia has been there for me since the first time we met. She's listened to all of my crazy stories, supported me in any of my choices, and never once judged me for anything I said or did. The girl has the biggest heart, and I can't let her lose that because of me.

She deserves so much more from me. I've been selfish dealing with my own problems and asking her to wait for me to help her with hers.

I should have done more. To help her. To keep her safe.

"I'll check every building in this city if I have to," I snap. "I have to try."

"You'll be wasting your time and energy," Aiden chastises. "Wait here, get sleep if you need to, and we'll wake you when we've found something."

"You think I can *sleep* after hearing that? You think I'm just going to roll over and do nothing?"

"The alternative is you burning yourself out until you're useless to us when the time actually comes."

"I won't." He's not wrong. I could easily do that if I don't control my gift and let it run wild. I finally reel it in, leashing it.

I look to Jack, who's still standing in front of the door. He tilts his head and smirks at me. I take it that he's not planning on budging from his spot, but then he side-steps from the door. That was un-nervingly easy. I'm shocked he's letting me go, but he's always been able to read me well. He must see how determined I am and that they can't stop me.

I grab the door and wrench it open.

Elias storms inside and surveys the room. His slate eyes fall back on me. "Well?"

His dirty blond hair is in disarray and his suit is unbuttoned and wrinkled. His face is tight and dark, and he's working a five-o-clock shadow along his face and neck. There are dark circles under his eyes.

Another guy steps inside behind him. He's tall and lean, but his jacket clings to his arms to show off that he's no pushover. His skin is like milk chocolate, and his eyes and hair are both dark. He keeps his gaze on the room and the others in it.

"We haven't found her yet," I admit. There'd be no point trying to lie to him with his gift, though I wouldn't ever lie to him about Portia regardless. I'd hoped to have her back before he returned.

"Where have we looked so far? Do we have any information on GE-owned locations in a fifty-mile radius?"

Aiden doesn't look all too pleased with Elias standing in his apartment. The others don't seem to care less, but I can tell there's something between them. They know each other. If Aiden tries to kick him out, I'll punch him.

"Dane, get back to the computer and keep following those cameras. We'll narrow down the direction and area and we can cross reference it with a list of Gifted Enterprise-owned buildings."

Dane follows Aiden's direction by immediately returning to his seat. "I was able to pick up the car they took her in from Hype," he says. "I'll see how far I can follow them."

Elias turns to the other guy he brought with him. "Start pulling the list of properties they own while he's doing that, Noah."

The guy, Noah, nods and then his eyes flick over to me.

"That won't be necessary," Elias says, as if understanding what that simple eye movement meant.

Noah grunts and moves to the dining table to set down a simple briefcase. He pulls out a laptop and powers it on.

"What won't be necessary?" I question since it obviously involved me.

"It's nothing," Elias replies and I frown at him. "He doesn't know or trust you and thinks you may be involved. He'd like to check your memories to be certain this isn't some sort of trap."

Kellan whistles and strolls over to sit at the dining table with Noah. His back is to me while Noah sits at the end, but I notice that he's casually placed himself between us. "Checking memories, huh? That's a crazy gift. Is it like sorting through a file cabinet? Or like a long movie?"

Noah ignores him and instead pins me with another stare. "You show up out of nowhere, find out Elias's weakness, and then within hours of him coming home, she's suddenly taken?" He pauses as that sinks in. "Too much of a coincidence."

"I didn't—"

"I know," Elias cuts in. He gives Noah a look. "I already vouched for her. There's nothing more to discuss on that."

I'm still frozen with shock that Elias said he vouched for me. He doesn't know me, not really. Or anything about my past. Seeing the truth can't be enough for him to know who I am.

Elias gives me a small smile, almost like he can read my mind and is trying to comfort me.

Ugh, stop it.

I owe this man so much.

"Do it."

Kellan, Noah, and Elias all look at me. Aiden and Dane glance over too, but they're mostly focused on cycling through cameras in the city. "Read my mind or my memories or whatever. I'll do whatever it takes to get Portia back."

Noah looks surprised and then smirks at Elias, who shrugs. "If that's what she wants."

Noah stands and we meet each other halfway. Jackson's suddenly leaning against the dining room table and watching Noah in a 'hurt-her-and-die' kind of way. Kellan's turned in his seat, his body tense.

"You don't have to do this, beautiful. You don't owe him shit."

"I do. For Portia." There's a hushed argument happening between Dane and Aiden, but I give my attention to Noah in front of me. "Do you get to pick and choose what you see?"

"For the most part. It's like rewinding a tape. I can move quickly through it or stop and let it play out."

I draw in a deep breath. "Okay." Noah's hand comes up to reach toward my face. "Does it hurt?" I ask quickly, and he pauses.

"Not at all. Just close your eyes and it'll be over before you know it." His tone is soothing, but it doesn't calm me as much as having Kellan within arm's reach of him and Jackson right there.

"Just look at the stuff that has to do with Portia. I only met her a month ago, so you don't need to dig any further than that."

"What if you plotted to get to Elias before you came here?"

"Fine. Check a couple of months back then."

"Close your eyes," Noah commands softly.

His hand covers my eyes and gently hugs the sides of my head with his thumb and fingers. Then, just as quickly, it's gone and I'm blinking up at him in confusion.

"Is something wrong?"

Dane and Aiden have joined the crowd around us.

"It's already done." Noah nods to Elias. "She's clear." Something else passes between them. I bite my lip with worry. He wouldn't have pried and looked at anything else, would he?

He offers me a small smile, which is the first one I've seen on his face since he arrived. Is that a good thing or bad?

"Hear that?" Kellan aims at Dane and Aiden. "Clear. No GE secret agent."

Dane scowls at me. "Just because she's innocent of this incident doesn't prove anything else." He stalks back to his chair and plays the next camera footage.

Aiden's studying me, but jury's out on which side he's on. "Let's get back to work."

As much as I'd rather avoid them, I join in the camera hunt. There are enough monitors that we can split them up to check and get through them faster. As soon as the car Portia's in leaves the current camera's frame, Dane spins up cameras in the area in thirty-second loops for us to check.

We call out the camera name at the bottom when we see her, and he plays it through until she disappears again. And so on.

"That's it. We're out of cameras." Dane freezes the last frame of the car on his screen. "They've left the city, and I don't know of any cameras in that area for at least a half mile after that."

"Noah got the list of every building owned by Gifted Enterprise and their subsidiaries within fifty miles." Elias hands Dane a USB drive. "Can you filter it to that area?"

Dane plugs it in, drops the list onto a map, and then circles the area. The list decreases to three spots. "We've got a house, a warehouse, and a butcher shop."

My stomach drops at the last one. I fucking hope it's not there.

"Mm, wait a minute," Dane hums. "The warehouse is the address you just gave us."

"Did you guys check it out?" I ask.

"Not yet. The scouts we had out were finishing up the last location before I called them in to rest." Aiden puts his phone to his ear. "I'm sending you a new location. Secure the area around it and then hold it. We'll be there as soon as we can to move in together."

He then texts the address over.

I start checking my weapons to make sure I'm locked and loaded. No matter how much I wear, it never feels like it's enough. What if I'm a bullet or a knife shy?

Then use your gift, I remind myself.

Elias hangs up the phone call he made as well and looks between Aiden and the others. "Do you have any weapons Noah and I can use? My teams will be meeting us there as well. We can come up with our plan while your team secures the perimeter."

Jackson smiles and waves them after him down the hallway. "This way."

CHAPTER THIRTY-ONE

DANE

THE BEAT-UP SEDAN WE'RE forced to take clunks again, and I wonder for the hundredth time if we'll even make it to the warehouse. It's old and rusted with half of the dashboard pulled apart or missing. The seats are cracked and torn. Everything is manual, from the transmission to the windows and seats. The only music option is an old AM/FM radio and cassette player.

Neither of them works.

Which means, Aiden and I are stuck in silence.

Which *means,* I'm bitching and moaning the entire drive to fill it.

"Kellan's being a prick. I bet the car he's driving at least has a working fucking radio." I twist the knob for the stations and the dial moves back and forth across the numbers.

There's the briefest buzzing noise, and I crank the volume up. "Come on," I mutter and try to fine-tune the spot I'm on to get something back.

The sound fizzles out. "Piece of shit!" I yell and punch it.

I crane my neck to look at the back seat, which is seatless, to search for something metal. The floor is filled with junk and random auto parts. Like Kellan used this car as his trash pile while working on another car. Probably the car he's in with Jackson and Raegan.

We could have all squeezed into one car if three people didn't mind not having a seat, but it was unanimous that we wanted to split up and have our own seats.

I try not to think about how the new guy had viewed Raegan's memories. Or how he'd supposedly "cleared" her of any ties to GE. At least as it relates to her friend. I don't think about what that might mean or that there's a chance Raegan is actually keeping something from us to explain what happened.

If she were innocent, she would have denied it.

She would tell me *why* she betrayed Vera. Why she betrayed *me*.

"Oh no." My sister chuckles from behind me.

I jump at the unexpected visitor and hurriedly check the room to make sure she's the only other one in it. "Fuck's sake, Vera!"

She grins and plops herself down on my bed next to me. "What? Didn't you hear me come in? You're lucky it was just me and not one of the others, then. What would they say if they saw you writing this—" she waves her hand at the notebook on my lap, struggling to find the right word before she finishes lamely— "stuff."

I slam the notebook closed. She merely smirks at me and shrugs. "You can't give her that. A corny written confession is already a terrible idea. But having movie references in there?" She throws her head back to laugh.

I shove at her, and she falls back on the bed, which sparks another burst of laughter. "Shut it. I think she'd like it. She's coming over to watch a movie tonight after her session ends, and I was hoping..."

My sister pushes herself back up and roughs up my hair. I smack her hand away, annoyed as always when she does that, and work to fix it. "You're adorable, Dane. But you know that you aren't the only one in your little group who has a crush on her, right?"

Kellan does, too. We bicker about it when the others aren't around, because he keeps pushing boundaries with her in front of us to prove that she likes him more. Always pulling pranks together, and the way he uses his gift as a counter to hers means he gets to hold and hug her when she's feeling vulnerable about her own gift.

But he doesn't have what she and I share. He doesn't know all of our inside jokes and moments we've shared binging movies and shows together. Or how she'll open up to me. Really talk to me. More than the others, I'm sure.

And the other night, when we were watching a movie with an unexpected moment between the two main characters, we looked at each other at the same time. The world just...froze. She began to lean toward me. We were hardly an inch away, face-to-face, and I thought...we almost...

And then Kellan burst through the door after his last session had ended and we'd jumped apart.

It's all I can think about now. This is our first movie night since then, and I don't want to fuck it up this time.

"I know. Kellan hasn't been hiding it from anyone but her."

Vera rolls her eyes. "Right. Just him."

Aiden hasn't said or done anything I've noticed to indicate otherwise. And Jackson...well, it's hard for anyone to know what he's thinking. He mostly keeps his thoughts to himself. He and Aiden have been busy with their sneaking around to learn more about GE's plans for us. I doubt they've had time to worry about crushes.

I surreptitiously check the clock to see how much time is left before Raegan shows. Any minute now. "Well, you're a girl, Ver. If girls don't like letters, then what do they like?" I ask in a rush.

She scoffs and hops off my bed. "They like action. Just kiss her, Dane. Stop beating around the bush and making up excuses."

"Fine. Then...do me a favor?"

"For a return one, right?"

"Yeah. Whatever. Just...keep Kellan away from here for a few hours, okay?"

"And what the hell am I supposed to do to keep him occupied?" she gripes. "We don't have that much in common, Dane."

"I don't know. Figure something out. Challenge him to something."

The door opens and Raegan smiles at me and then Vera when she walks in. "Hey! Are you watching the movie with us tonight too, Vera?"

Ver gives Raegan a coy smile. "Oh, no. I was just leaving." She turns and bends to whisper in my ear, "You owe me, little brother. But I am rooting for you. Go get some." She ruffles my hair again and I curse at her, but she dashes away too quickly for me to counterattack. "Bye, Rae. Don't forget, we have to chat. Sooner than later," she adds with a wink and then slips out of the room.

Raegan looks confusedly at me. "Did I miss something?"

My fingers comb through my hair to fix the second mess of it my sister made, and I hope that I don't look like a complete mess. "No. Ignore her," I grumble.

Raegan chews on her lip, looking concerned. I drop the mood Vera put me in and focus instead on Rae. On the time we finally have alone together.

My lips turn up to a smile, and I stand to give her a playful nudge. "Really, don't worry about it. Did you pick out tonight's movie?"

She raises her hands in front of her to show the movie she checked out from the manor library. It's a horror film, which means she'll be burying her face in my shirt for eighty percent of it.

Perfect.

I didn't work up the courage that night to make my move, and now I'm glad I hadn't. I trusted her. Cared about her. Liked her. I really fucking liked her. I would have done anything back then to make her happy. To protect her.

When I found out that she was the reason my sister was dead, it was like a dagger to the heart.

My sister, who had rooted for us to be together, who had tried to help me make it happen with her...

How could she have done that to Vera? *Why* would she do that? And why won't she tell me *any-fucking-thing* about what happened other than admitting that she killed her? What else is she hiding?

The only explanation is that she was conspiring with GE the entire time, getting close to us to report on what we were looking into, and then Vera must have found out and Raegan killed her before she could tell us. That's the only thing that makes sense.

I can't accept anything else.

And Raegan doesn't seem willing to give me any alternatives anyway.

What has been driving me *crazy* since she showed back up is that she's acting like the Raegan on the island. Harder and angrier, yes, but I can still see the girl I'd fallen for beneath it all.

Of course, she's the same. She was playing you before, and she's playing all of you again now.

But then why is she fighting against Gifted Enterprise? Who is Gordon to her? Why did she react like that when she saw him again? Why is GE so interested in getting her back if she's part of them?

What should all make sense and click into place isn't adding up now that she's here. It all made sense in my head as I thought I'd figured it all out. Now that she's here, everything's fucked.

I actually feel *guilty* for telling GE she was here. I'd been pissed when I heard she killed the goon that Kellan and Jackson had been interrogating. I assumed she wanted him dead before he spilled any more information about GE, and that was how she was covering it up. So, I went to take matters into my own hands.

Then when I held a gun to her head...I couldn't do it. I didn't have my answers. But most of all...I couldn't while she looked at me like that. Like she forgave me for what I was doing. Like she'd given up.

I moved on to my next plan after that. Between my brothers keeping a closer eye on me to make sure I didn't leave the Tower again and me knowing I wouldn't be able to pull the trigger, I outsourced. She's a part of GE, right? So why not have them pick her up and remove her from town?

It was an impulsive move. One I did out of anger at myself for not getting any answers or taking my revenge when it was right in front of me.

I regretted it almost immediately.

But once that picture was submitted to the paper, there was no taking it back.

I hadn't considered that GE would stick around. That sending that picture would put a spotlight on this city and put everyone else in danger.

After everything I've done to try and help my brothers, it never feels like it's enough. All I do is make it worse. By being hunted for my gift. By being impulsive. And angry. And bitter. And now this.

I'm at fault for Guild members being taken.

I'm the fucking idiot.

And Raegan made me realize that.

It's all I can think about now. What I've done and that she's fucking *right*. I'm pissed at myself for making such a dumb, impulsive decision. And I'm pissed that *she's* the one who called me out on it.

I'm supposed to be one of the good guys. Protecting others like us. *She's* supposed to be the enemy. The one working with GE who doesn't care about others like us.

Fuck.

I throw my head back against the hard headrest and release an exasperated sigh. "Does your phone have music?"

"I'm not wasting the battery in case we need it." Aiden keeps his eyes focused on the line of traffic in front of us.

"I need it."

He scoffs at me. "We should talk about our plan when we get there."

I roll my window down to let in the fresh air and honks of the city. We need to get to the outskirts and then it'll be clear sailing. I perch my elbow on the door and subconsciously tug my hood down further. A habitual check any time I leave our space.

I suspect they have access to the satellites and cameras available. It's the only explanation for how they find me so quickly if I ever go outside.

Just before we got off the island, Aiden and Jackson found out about the students turned lab rats. How they were trying to extract the gifts out of their blood to be used somehow. After GE kept showing up when I'd appear outside, we figured out that they must want my gift. I'm obviously non-compliant to their attempted indoctrination, so all that's left is to take my blood and use it. We can't let them have the power to turn off and on people's gifts at their will. So, I stick to the plan of staying inside the Tower. Raegan was the exception. And now, because Aiden's too paranoid for me to be left alone at the safehouse if this is a trap meant to get me alone.

I don't mind because I hate being cooped up inside. I want to fight. To get my hands dirty and take out some of this pent-up rage on the people responsible for everything that went wrong in our lives. Instead, I'm a burden to my brothers. They have to protect me like I'm a defenseless prize. I hate that. They already looked out for me after Vera's death. They've put up with my foul attitude that has been my constant partner for years.

Learning computers and the internet has eased some of that guilt, but it's not enough for me. I should be there when they take the organization down. I want to know everyone involved in what happened to Vera.

"We already have a plan. Kellan's group is going after the asshat politician, you and I are checking for our missing people, and Elias is going straight in and out once they have Portia."

I almost sneered at Raegan that I told her so. That she brought nothing but trouble to those around her. I know I'm an asshole and completely capable of saying shit like that if I want to. But for whatever reason, I held my tongue on it. I hate her for what she did to Vera. For betraying me. For pretending to care about me. About us. She doesn't deserve me holding my tongue.

But I did it anyway and I think that pisses me off most of all.

Because maybe things aren't as clear cut as I thought.

My fingers tap against the side of the door in tune to a favorite song to distract myself.

"I need you to stick by me this time. Last time we got separated and you were almost taken, even if they didn't realize who you were."

I blow out a breath. My foot starts moving to the same beat in my head, popping up and down with my heel. There's no carpet in here, so my boot hits the metal floor with a deep clang. Aiden presses his lips together in annoyance, but doesn't say anything.

I drop my heel back down and leave it there.

I may enjoy pissing the others off, but not Aiden. I owe him my life. I'll forever owe him that debt for what he's done, and what he's given up, for me.

As soon as we learned that GE had sent an elite group specifically to hunt me down and take me back by any means necessary, Aiden has hardly left my side. He had a chance at another life when we got back from the island. Instead, he chose to be stuck with me.

"I know the drill."

"I didn't say anything earlier but...I'm also keeping an eye out for that man who came to the Guild and spoke to Raegan. Gordon."

My brows knit as I stare outside while remembering that moment. "Why?" My stomach is uneasy recalling what happened, my chest tight.

"Because we're looking for people higher up the food chain and he seems to fit that bill, doesn't he?"

He's not wrong, but I also know it's more than that. Aiden's targeting him because of Raegan. I don't argue with him. Gordon may be our ticket to the board and answers about Raegan.

And Vera.

Pain burns the back of my throat and my hand starts to shake. I clench my hands before Aiden can notice and swallow the pain back down.

I *will* get answers.

Whatever it takes.

She deserves her brother knowing what happened to her and why. Then I'll know exactly what to do to bring her justice.

The last light turns green, and Aiden guns it. Or, he tries to. His foot drops to the floor with the clutch out and the car barely increases its speed. It apparently needs to gain traction, because it finally starts to move. Aiden shoves it in gear and then jams the clutch again while the car struggles to gain momentum.

Kellan's definitely playing a joke on us. There's no way he uses this car for street racing. Even its parts aren't worth it.

We eventually make it to the car's final fifth gear and cruise down empty side streets. Aiden turns on the GPS on his phone as we start zigzagging through side streets and getting further from the city.

The car slows to a crawl and bumps and jerks when we turn off onto a dirt road. I grab the roof out my window and grimace as we feel every rock and divot in the road. We park next to Kellan's ride, and I give it a long once-over.

"I fucking knew it."

Kellan gets out and jerks his seat forward to let Jackson out of the back. He turns with a wild and crazy grin. "What's that? Sour about your ride, Rapunzel?"

I scowl at the annoying nickname he's pegged me with. "Were you hoping this piece of shit died on the drive? At least have a working radio if you're going to offer a car."

He laughs and slams his door shut after Jackson's out. "Sorry I didn't have any options to your taste, Princess. It's the best I could do on short notice. Unless you wanted to have Aiden cozy up to you on your bike. He's the one who refused to take his shiny Aston Martin out for the run."

Aiden waves at the woods and lack of road around us. "My car is not going on missions in the middle of nowhere for it to get scratched to hell."

Noah pulls up beside us in a navy truck with Elias in the passenger's seat and parks.

"Everyone shut up," Raegan snaps at us. "Let's go save Portia and the others before you give away that we're here."

We catch up with the scout team at the perimeter in the trees to let them know we're here and to have them watch our backs. We need to know that enemies aren't going to be pouring in from behind us so we can keep our focus forward.

We divide into the planned groups and go to our assigned doors. We'll be entering from different spots in the building to hopefully take out many people at once before an alarm is raised. We don't want anyone calling for backup or we're screwed.

Aiden's hand grips the locked door handle at our door. It only takes a couple seconds for his gift to rearrange the metal lock to open. We slip inside, and I close and lock it behind us.

The room is dark. There's a light on further inside that reflects enough off the walls to give us faint outlines. We creep forward one after the other. There are footsteps in the next room shuffling back and forth. A guard, most likely.

We clear the current room and peer into the next, which looks like an industrial kitchen. The guard is making a circle around the large, metal island in the middle. His hands rest on his gun as he makes another round and yawns.

As soon as he turns his back on us, I make my move.

I slip through the door and keep low, being careful not to scuff my boots on the concrete floor. Before he turns the corner, I jump and throw my arm around his throat and squeeze his airway. My gift activates to mute whatever power he may have so it's just his body against mine.

It feels fucking *good* to use my gift against the enemy. To feel the drain of his gift leaving his body so that he's an easier target. This is how I can fight. I can make a difference in the battle with GE and all of their gifted soldiers. If only I could use it on more than one goon at a time.

I use my body weight to pull him back into me and drag him back.

The guard scrambles at my arms and then reaches for his gun. Aiden grabs and disfigures it. I squeeze tighter and tighter. His body begins to sag, and I wait until I know he's out. I switch my hold under his arms and Aiden takes his feet. We drag him to the backside of the island and Aiden uses his gift to cuff his wrists to the metal table.

"What are you doing?" Aiden shoots to me in a harsh whisper when we're crouched down.

I shake my head and start forward. We can talk after. I promised to stick by him, but I've been practicing self-defense and grappling skills from Kellan. I'm not here to be babysat.

I'm here to fight.

We're not just facing grunts anymore. Anyone who's here knows exactly what they're involved in. If we can incapacitate them without killing them for questioning, then fine. If not, I'll have no regrets.

The next room is the one with the light on as it shines through the open double doors on the other side. Low murmuring tells me there are at least two people there. We approach the doorway, but stay behind the open door for cover.

He holds up four fingers, and I nod. Four men.

I pull the gun from the back of my pants and begin screwing on the suppressor from my pocket. It's not ideal for stealth, but if all four are gifted, we could use the advantage.

As I ready my weapon and adjust my grip, Aiden pulls his whip sword out. He had to keep the metal on him light for this mission, but I hardly ever see him going into a fight without that one weapon. It's made up of diamond-shaped metal blades hinged together and attached to a hilt so it can curve and move like a metal whip. Aiden's gift enables him to control every part of the metal, from forcing it not to hinge and become a sword, to lengthening, shortening, sharpening, and directing exactly where it will go.

It's a dangerous weapon already, but in Aiden's hands?

Guaranteed death for any who dare stand against him.

We share a nod and then burst into the room.

The four men are sitting at a table together in the center of the room with drinks in hand.

I fire two rounds in rapid succession on the man sitting closest to the door. Then I re-aim my gun on my next target opposite my first.

I pull the trigger twice again, but this guy has the extra seconds to react and dives to the ground. I run and jump on the table, aiming on the other side. Gunfire erupts from the semi-automatic he has through the table. I leap off of it. I shoot repeatedly, aiming for him under the table when I land before he can turn his gun on me.

The gun clatters to the ground. I fire one more time to be sure he's gone and then check on Aiden.

His sword slashes across his opponent's throat and then whips back down and lengthens at the same time to reach the fourth man. He tries to dodge it, but Aiden adjusts the direction and three of the diamond blades at the end plunge into him.

He whips the sword back to himself so the end curls at his feet.

Another door opens. I aim the gun at the middle of the doorway, but a blue merle Australian shepherd dog trots in instead. I sigh and lower my gun.

Elias and Noah had brought this dog along for whatever reason. I can't imagine why someone would bring a pet on a mission, until he sniffs across the floor like a bloodhound. Elias and Noah follow him in. Noah eyes the carnage in the room with a look of mild approval. Elias, on the other hand, is pale and looks away as soon as he spots the first body.

The dog whines and paws at the floor in the corner. Elias is the fastest to move to him. Either he's desperate to find Portia or to get out of this room. Or both.

He starts feeling along the walls and hitting it. The floors are square concrete slabs, so there are lines between each slab. The dog is pawing at one of the lines.

"Secret passage?" I guess. Aiden has these built into the Tower and our safe house, so I'm familiar with hidden spots.

"Kit smells her through there. We just need to find out how to open it."

That's good news. If Portia is down there, then the others will be there as well.

If they're here at all.

Noah strides across the slab and then squats and presses down on something. The slab drops a few inches and then glides back, revealing stairs. "I checked the memories of everyone we came across to get a better layout of this place," he explains coolly without looking up at anyone.

He doesn't wait for any of us to make sure we're ready or to check if anyone's at the bottom before he rushes down. Elias and the dog take off after him. We follow behind. The hallway ends at a T cross-section.

The dog sniffs in each direction and chooses a side. "We'll go this way; you take the other side," Elias directs.

We head down our side of the hallway, clearing room after room. The walls are glossy white, and the floors a polished concrete. It smells like chemicals and cleaning products. Most of the rooms are empty. Either it's too early for the staff to be here or they're concentrated elsewhere.

Aiden grabs the handle of the last door, forcefully unlocking it as he had all the others, and pulls it open.

Our Guild members are there, along with a few others I don't recognize. They're sitting or lying on hard benches along either side of the room. There's a drain along the back wall and a hose and that's it.

"Aiden? Dane?" one of our members, Sheila, gasps.

Aiden steps into the room to look them over. I keep watch just outside the door.

"Is anyone injured?" he asks her.

"Richard might have a broken wrist. The rest are just scratches and bruises."

"There's a team waiting outside to get you back to the Tower. Dane and I will get you there, but we need to move fast and quiet."

Everyone murmurs their understanding and shuffles to their feet. I take point while Aiden takes the rear. A crash sounds down the opposite end of the hallway in one of the rooms. There's yelling and more sounds of fighting. My skin crawls with the need to go help the others, but we made it clear in our planning that each group would stick to its own goals. As soon as we have this group clear of the building, Aiden and I can come back.

I hurry up the stairs and back through the kitchen to the door we came in. The way is thankfully clear, but I can hear more fighting underway up here. I unlock the door and yank it open. One of our guys is already there with a couple of others to collect everyone. I step back and hold the door open, ushering everyone out.

I twist back to talk to Aiden and frown when my feet don't turn with me. Something thick and tacky holds them down.

"Aiden," I warn. The last rescue is stuck at the threshold with one foot sinking into the concrete. I shove them over, sending them toppling out the door with enough force that his foot yanks free, leaving his shoe behind.

I catch myself against the door frame before I fall onto the floor that's starting to suck my feet down like quicksand. I slam the door shut.

Thank fuck.

At least we got them out.

I turn and curse that I'm trapped with my back to the enemy. Aiden's trying to cut through the ground to free himself with his whip sword, then turns his sword on the guy causing this when that doesn't work.

The goon jumps back. As soon as his hands break contact with the floor, the concrete hardens. I fire my gun at him to push him back even further, and Aiden chips away at the concrete at his feet until he's free. He does the same for me while I keep the goon back.

We chase him into the kitchen, avoiding the guy still passed out, and I climb onto the island. I run across it and launch myself at him, tackling him to the ground. My gift hums and glows as I block his gift from surfacing.

I press a hand against his chest and aim my gun at his head.

Something flies at me, and Aiden's sword bats it away. He runs past me to the next room. The ring of metal echoes, and there's a grunt.

My finger tightens on the trigger.

"Wait, wait! I have information. I know things—"

I slam the butt of my gun against the side of his head to knock him out.

"Fine. But not right now." I take off after Aiden and find him fighting back three others simultaneously. I pick one and shoot, but my gun clicks empty.

I drop the magazine and reach for another in my pocket.

A flash of blonde out of the corner of my eye grabs my attention in a chokehold. I lurch around in time as a slender figure turns the corner.

My pulse roars in my ears, drowning out the sound of anything else.

It couldn't be.

It's impossible. I must be seeing things, or someone is playing a

trick on me.
   I don't think.
   I run.

Chapter Thirty-Two

RAEGAN

Jackson makes quick work of the lock and then we're in. My nose wrinkles the moment I cross the threshold. It smells like metal and old urine.

It doesn't take too much of a guess to figure out what they've been using this place for.

"I'm burning it down," I grumble as we walk into a large empty truck bay.

Kellan laughs and throws his fist into his hand. "I'm in."

A small smile curves Jackson's lips that tells me he's on board as well.

Perfect.

I cup my hands around my mouth and shout into the empty space. "Joe!" My voice echoes and carries through the building just as I'd hoped. It's our job to draw the congressman to us and act as a distraction while the others are on stealth and rescue.

We're the perfect team for that job between the three of us.

"Hey, Joe! I'm here early for our deal!"

A guard appears in the doorway. "Hey, what're you doing here?"

"I have a meeting with the congressman. Can you—" The man falls dead on the ground. "Or not."

"He'll come out," Jack reassures me as he plucks his knife from the man's eye. "I'm sure of it."

Kellan sticks close to my side. When I give him a look for it, he raises an eyebrow with a cocky grin. "What is it, beautiful? Is my nearness distracting you?"

"I said you could watch my back. What I don't need is you up my ass the entire time." It comes out harsher than I intended, but I'm antsy for this to be over with. I need to know that Portia is safe and okay. I need to make sure we all get out of this in one piece. And the congressman must die.

Jackson slips his hand around mine and squeezes, then lets go. He knows exactly what's running through my mind. I take the small comfort and wrap it around my heart. She will make it out of this.

Kellan's grin remains stuck on his face, and he leans in close, his large hand rubbing down my back. "I can't wait to see you use that fire on them. Let me know if I should just stand back to enjoy the show if these ungifted goons are all we're going to be up against."

"Don't jinx it," I mutter back at him.

We move into the next room and the sight lining the wall terrifies me.

Row upon stacked row of cages.

There must be a hundred of them.

Cages.

For humans.

Gifted people like us. Being treated like feral animals.

"They're here," Jackson murmurs under his breath. He nods at Kellan and then slips away between one of the rows of floor-to-ceiling cages.

Clapping echoes further down the dark aisle. Kellan and I stop.

"I'm impressed. You found me faster than I thought." Joe appears around the corner at the end of the aisle. Three others follow after him.

He *tsks* as they continue to close the distance between us, stopping a few feet away. "But you didn't bring the girl. And you brought others with you." He shakes his head sadly. "I know you can do better than that."

I ignore him and study the people with him. The guy and girl on his left look around my age and bored to be here. The man on his right is giving me a sinister smile and a serious case of the creeps.

He can die first.

I grab my gun and fire at him to do exactly that. The faster I take these guys down, the sooner I can make sure Portia is safe. I don't have time for idle chit-chat.

The bullets slow before they reach him and then turn and shoot back at me.

Fuck.

Kellan dives in front of me and takes them both in the chest.

"Kell!"

He doesn't budge from his spot planted before me and digs them each out to drop them on the concrete floor.

"Not a fucking chance," he growls, flicking the second bullet away.

Jackson appears out of the shadows behind the guy. Knives are vibrating in the air ready for the attack.

Only...they don't.

The guy on Joe's right laughs and steps back and to the side so he has us all in front of him. "Good try, but I control all things metal. Your knives and bullets won't work on me."

Some of the knives start to turn to aim back at Jackson. They all quiver in the air between them in an invisible battle of wills.

Something crashes into Kellan and knocks him off balance. Again from the other side. And again. Then the girl appears in front of him. "Come on, big guy. Let's see if you can even land a punch."

Kellan reaches for her. I gasp as the third person with Joe disappears and reappears between us. He drives a blade through Kellan's back.

"No!"

He coughs out blood, and I lunge for the guy. He vanishes with his blade. I touch Kell's back and only exhale after his body stitches itself back together.

"Get back, beautiful. They're focused on me and I want to keep it that way," he grunts out. "Just focus on your target."

I wish he didn't have to get hurt for his armor to activate, but at least at this rate, he'll be impervious to any of their attacks soon. "Don't die, Kellan," I murmur to him.

"I knew you cared." Grinning, Kell takes off down another aisle. Speed Girl laughs and runs after him.

Her partner stares at me. I shift my stance to prepare for him to attack, and he frowns. He doesn't seem to be having fun like the girl is. More like he's resigned to this task.

"You don't have to do this."

"You know that we do." Then he disappears.

I tense, looking around me for him to appear out of nowhere again. Kellan shouts in pain, and I spin in that direction. Why did he go to Kellan and not me?

"That's better. Now you and I can go discuss our next steps." Joe straightens his tie and then turns to walk away. "Come on then, dear. We can speak in my office and out of their way."

"Yeah right," I mutter, raising my gun. I pull the trigger. It pauses halfway there, and I let out a frustrated growl. Jackson and his opponent, who are throwing and dodging knives between each other around the room, are stopped again.

Jack's hand is out and aimed at me, and I notice then some of his knives were on their way to me while I was distracted by the stopped bullet. The metal guy smirks and flicks his fingers. Jackson grunts, and then the knives aimed at me drop to the ground.

Joe turns the corner out of sight.

I start after him when my gun is ripped from my hands. My stash of knives and daggers from my boots up to my shirt fly out and then they're all pointing at me.

"Not so fast," the other guy crows.

Jackson slams his fist into his face and the metal clatters to the ground. "Go!" His gravelly voice urges as he strikes the guy again and again.

I run after Joe, praying Jackson will be okay.

I race down the next corridor. There are no windows and no lights, so it's dark and quiet. Even the fighting in the last room is distant and muted. "Joe?" I call out. He wouldn't have left already, right? If I lose him here, the chance of finding him again so easily is slim to none. "Joe!" I yell out again.

I'm sure if he hears me, he'll stop so he can have that chat he wanted.

The skin on the back of my neck prickles, and I begin to turn when something large slams into the side of my head and I'm knocked to the ground. My vision goes black until I hit the ground. I groan as pain ravages my head.

Fuck me. Is he trying to kill me?

Joe chuckles and grabs my wrist. Something cold closes around it and clicks shut.

Even though my gift wasn't active, I can feel it.

The void in my gut where it used to be. Like the heat from my body has been sucked away and I'm only a cold shell.

"W-what..." I struggle to form the words through the pounding in my head.

He flips me onto my back and straddles me. I jerk under him, but he grabs my head and slams it against the ground until I'm seeing stars. If he knocks me out, it's all over.

I claw my way out of the darkness and cling to my surroundings to keep me here. The unforgiving concrete beneath me. The chill of my body from losing my gift. The distant sounds of fighting still ongoing. Joe's heavy breathing above me. His clammy hands wrapped around my throat.

"It would really be best for you to sleep now, my dear. Then I can get us both out of here somewhere safe for us to talk."

I try to speak, but his hands block my windpipe, and all I can manage is a grunt. I grab at his arms to try pulling him off. I reach for my gift, even though a part of me knows it's gone, but survival instinct makes me try it anyway. It's like dipping a scoop into a bucket of ice cream and coming up empty. I scrape at it anyway, desperate for any sign of lingering power.

Losing my gift or lack of air brings tears to my eyes.

He smiles when he sees them. "Do you like the cuff? I don't enjoy making you powerless when your gift is what makes you so special, but it's a necessary thing until I can trust you. It's just a prototype of what's coming from Gifted Enterprise. They still had some blood from that boy they want so much and finally figured out how they can use it. Now all they need is more of it."

Fuck.

Dane!

How? After Vera died, they shouldn't be able to do anything with whatever blood they had left of his.

"Thank you for bringing him, by the way. At least with him, they'll be less concerned over the loss of the little girl. He's the biggest prize they could hope for. So, this did all work out in the end."

I beat my hands against his arms, his chest, trying to break his hold on me. My hand feels something cold in his front pocket and I yank it free. I stab the pen into his thigh with all of my strength. He screams and releases me. I kick and shove him off of me, then scramble away into one of the rooms.

I push the door closed behind me as I struggle back to my feet. My head is still swimming with pain, but I keep moving. I have no idea where Dane and Aiden are right now or if he's already been taken. All I know is that I need to get to them and make sure no one gets their hands on him.

The door flies open, and I jump behind the desk in the room. I grab the drawers and throw them open to search for anything to use as a weapon. I grab a letter opener and hide it behind my back as Joe stalks toward me, backing me into the corner of the tight office.

"You're only making this worse for yourself," he bites out, all pretense of the friendly congressman gone. He shoves the office chair away, and I take that moment to slash at his throat. It cuts across his shoulder and chin instead, but it's enough to distract him while I work my other hand against the cuff.

I've done this more times than I'd care to admit in my time after the island, but it takes some amount of focus and time to do it.

I push harder on my thumb and grit my teeth until it finally pops. I wrench the cuff off my wrist.

My gift floods through me like wildfire in my veins. It burns and feels amazing at the same time. Joe's eyes widen.

He turns to run, and I climb onto the desk and then jump on his back to knock him down. He twists and tries to throw me off of him, but I grab his face in my hands.

Joe releases a blood-curdling scream as my gift decimates him from the inside. It isn't long before his face cracks, then splits apart and oozes blood. "This is for Portia. And Isabel. And every girl you've taken advantage of and thrown away like trash, you piece of shit."

He's still screaming as blood leaks from his eyes. I don't relent even when his breathing stops. I push my gift into him more and more, feeding on his pain and the way he falls apart beneath my touch. It's like his true self is being exposed the longer I hold on. And it's only right that others see him as he truly was.

"You've got him, beautiful." My face snaps up, but I don't let go. Kellan's covered in his golden scales as he gazes down at me, his face solemn. "He's dead."

I can't even recognize Joe as human anymore.

I shudder and release him, withdrawing my gift back into me.

Jackson steps up next to Kellan, and I gasp at the blood spattered over his face and hands.

He helps me to my feet and strokes the side of my face, spreading the blood on his hands over my cheek, but I couldn't care less while I'm lost in his manic gaze that both terrifies and excites me.

I hold his wrist and his pulse greets me with the pounding force of a warm drum on speed.

My touch snaps something in him, and he descends on me. Jackson kisses me like a starved animal. I barely keep up with his demands while he draws me tight against his body.

This is different from the last time we kissed. His control is shattered. Nothing left but the beast.

Kellan growls and rips us apart. "Enough."

Jack's eyes darken and cut over to Kellan and my heart stutters in my chest.

"He's right," I rush out. "We need to find Dane."

They break out of their glaring contest to look at me. Kellan's the one to ask, "Why?"

"This was a trap for him too. We have to make sure he's safe or else…" I trail off.

"Shit. Let's go, then. They should be out by now." Kellan wraps me in his arms and leans down to whisper in my ear, "I'll save your kiss for later then, beautiful."

Flushed, I huff and push out of his arms. "We need to hurry."

I give one last disgusted look at Joe and then remember the cuff. I turn back into the room and grab it, then run past the others back from where we came.

A wave of nausea slows me down, and I stumble off-balance. Jack and Kellan each grab an arm to steady me.

"Fuck, is that blood?" Kellan's voice echoes through my pounding headache.

I open my eyes to Jack holding out his fingers bathed in a vibrant red.

"It's not deep," he surmises calmly. "But she's probably concussed."

"We need to get her out of here."

"No! I need to know that Dane's safe. I'm not going anywhere until I see him."

"One of us can—" Kell tries again, but I start walking.

"I told you. I'm going to find Dane."

He curses, then catches up with me. Jackson flanks my other side. Even though I'm not looking at him, I can feel his gaze boring into me. I get the general feeling that he's waiting for any sign of weakness from me before he takes over, so I make sure to focus on every step and keep moving.

We pass the metal guy on our way. I'd worry he might wake up if not for the cut throat and pool of blood he's in. I look around for the other two. One of the aisles has the cages fallen over in a heap.

"They're gone," Kell explains. "Once the girl got hurt, he grabbed her and left."

I'm surprised at the relief I feel from hearing that. They were on the other side, so I shouldn't care what happened to them. But there was something...different about them. And what the guy said...if he was supposed to be brainwashed, then GE had let him go too soon.

The sound of metal screeching across metal reaches us, and I hurry in that direction.

"Dane!" A brief pause and then again. "Dane!"

My heart jumps into my throat. Kellan bulldozes through the next door and it flies into someone on the other side. Aiden whips his sword at the only other person in the room and slices it across his chest. He snakes it back and stabs it through the man.

The rest of the room is littered with bodies. Dane is nowhere in sight. Has Aiden been fighting them off alone all this time?

"What happened?" I ask first.

"We got the others out and were attacked before we could leave too." He wipes his face with his sleeve.

"And Portia?"

"Out too. With the others."

"Where the fuck did Dane go then?" Kellan snaps.

"He was right behind me and then he was just gone."

Shit.

"We have to find him or we're all fucked." They look at me. "I'll tell you after we get him back."

Aiden nods. "He was back here last."

"I'll go ahead." Jack doesn't wait for a reply and uses his gift to speed him along.

The three of us run to catch up as fast as we can, but my head injury slows me down after the initial burst of adrenaline. Kellan notices and drops his speed while Aiden looks between us with his brow furrowed.

"Keep going. I'll catch up."

"I'm not leaving you behind. Let me carry you, beautiful."

"We could be running into another fight and you'll need your hands. I'll be right behind you."

"Here!" Jackson barks out from an open door. He disappears behind it and we rush over. It's a stairwell leading up. Kellan flips my legs up and cradles me to his chest before I have the chance to protest.

The steps are jarring, even though he takes them slower than I know he could, and I'm forced to close my eyes and lean into him to control the queasiness that the jerking movement causes. We make it to the end and a door that must lead to the roof since there was no second floor.

Kellan puts me back on my feet, and we ready our gifts, then storm through the door.

Dane is standing in the middle of the roof with his back to us. Jackson is a step behind him and to the side, staring forward as well.

I sprint to his side, which makes me still in reach of Dane, and peer across the roof to discover what they're both staring at.

There's a helicopter preparing to take off, but it's the person standing in front of it and staring back at us that seizes my muscles with shock.

She's average height, dressed like every other goon, and her blonde hair is short and wavy. There's a scar from the side of her forehead like a V that then joins and continues through one eye and to her cheekbone.

Vera.

Oh.

Fuck.

BONUS SCENE
TATTOOS - DANE POV

Two years before the events of Ravage

A door slams, and I jerk upright in a daze, reaching instinctively for my gun before my eyes open fully.

"Get your shoes on. We're going out!" Kellan announces, his heavy boots pounding on the hardwood floor of the Loft.

I release the weapon and scrub my face with both hands, groaning at stiff muscles from sleeping at my desk again.

Sunlight beams through the windows, highlighting the mess of renovation work I should probably get back to. Since Jack's been off stalking GE, Aiden is restructuring the Guild, and Kellan goes out to fuck-knows-where, it hasn't been a high priority of mine to start painting just for me.

"What the fuck are you talking about?" I mutter.

He blows past me to the hallway and shoves my bedroom door open.

That wakes me up.

"Hey!" I jump from my chair and run after him. A hoodie hits me in the face as I round the corner to look inside.

"Put that on."

I yank it out of my way and glare at him. "I'm not doing any-fuck-ing-thing until you tell me what's going on. Where's Aiden? You know I can't just go out."

"Where do you think, Rapunzel? Downstairs in his office that he lives in more than here."

Clicking my tongue, I cross my arms over my chest and widen my stance in the doorway, blocking his exit. "Yeah, and we both know why that is. Unless you want to take some of the paperwork and tasks off his plate, I don't want to hear it."

Kellan snorts and stands in front of me, raising a forty-ounce liquor bottle to his lips and guzzling it down. The asshole is almost a foot taller than me, so I'm forced to shift my scowl upward while he swallows half the bottle in seconds. Once he's polished it off, he wipes his mouth with the back of his arm and shoots me an intoxicated grin. "Relax. I'm not criticizing, just saying. Maybe I miss the guy."

Sure, he does.

"You still haven't answered my question about where you think we're going."

He leans down with a smirk. "We're getting tattoos," he breathes, the stink of alcohol filling the air between us, and I reel back, stepping into the hallway. Kellan takes that opportunity to push through with a raucous laugh.

"I can't leave," I remind him again through gritted teeth.

"I'll keep you safe, princess. Just keep your hood up and we'll be fine once we're inside."

"Kell-"

A cabinet door crashes shut. "I obviously can't get a tattoo without you, and I'm getting a tattoo. A lot of them. So, let's cut to the chase. You've been cooped up in here too long by yourself and need to get out. I need to stop my gift from interfering. This is a win-win."

"But Aiden-"

"-won't even realize we left."

Scoffing, I shake my head. "Until he sees your tattoos."

Kellan unscrews the lid on his newest bottle of alcohol. "How's that saying go? Better to ask forgiveness...?"

I shouldn't even entertain this idea. There's plenty to do here in the Loft between painting and then laying the new floors. Or working on my computer skills. I've already put Aiden through enough trouble. I shouldn't go out of my way to possibly make things worse.

I shouldn't.

Fuck.

"How far away is it?"

Kellan's face splits in a wide grin. "Five minutes by car." He twirls his keys around his finger, and I snatch them.

"I'll drive." I don't care that alcohol doesn't affect him as much as it does others. If anything, the drink just makes him take more risks. That's the last thing I need if we're trying to make this trip and any future tattoo trip successful. "But I'm calling Aiden. I'm not going behind his back like some dick."

He shrugs, his wild grin still firmly in place. "Whatever makes you happy, Rapunzel."

It takes seconds to throw on a hoodie and shove my shoes on before we're in the elevator to take us down to the parking garage. I call Aiden on the way, my free hand pinching anxiously at the fabric inside my kangaroo pocket where Kell can't see.

Aiden answers on the second ring. "What's wrong?"

"Nothing. Kell and I are going out to get tattoos. It's around the block, but we'll drive, and I'll keep my hood up. We can make sure we're far enough in the tattoo parlor to avoid any outside cameras while we're there."

It doesn't matter that I've tried to consider every concern Aiden will have in advance. He still pauses on the line, likely running through the couple scenarios I've thought of and about a hundred others.

The silence stretches between us, and my fidgeting intensifies. The elevator rings when we reach the basement level for the underground parking.

"Text me the address. We'll need to get you a mask if you go there again. Your hood can only cover so much."

Relief swirls in my chest, and I nod even though he can't see it. "Right."

"Let me know when you get there and when you're headed back," he adds.

Kellan leans over the phone at my ear. "Yes, mom!"

The call disconnects.

I pin him with a look, and he chuckles before leading the way to one of his cars. He says it's a special year and model, but all I see is a beat-up, black sedan.

"Text Aiden the address." I open the driver's door and sit, readjusting the seat forward to a normal person's position.

"Done," he says with a final tap on his phone. "Take the South exit, and I'll guide you from there."

To his credit, it takes less than five minutes to get there. I tug my hood further forward, casting my gaze to the sidewalk when I get out of the car, and stride purposefully inside without waiting for Kell. Bells jingle above the door as we walk inside, and it isn't until I'm a good six feet in at the check-in desk that I look up.

It's a small parlor, with only two tattoo chairs in the middle with carts beside them, and the walls are covered in a collage of sketches and clients with their tattoos.

"Welcome! What can we do for you today?" The woman behind the desk smiles warmly at us, nudging her glasses further up her nose as she slowly takes in Kellan's height.

"Tattoos, I hope," Kellan answers with a grin.

"For both of you?" she asks, swinging her gaze to me for confirmation.

It hadn't occurred to me that I could get one while waiting too, but why the hell not? I'm already here. "Yeah."

She scans the book in front of her, dragging her finger down the page and then flipping it. "We just had a cancelation this afternoon, so Pete and I should be able to help you today, depending on its size. Do you each know what you want?"

Kellan strips his leather jacket and shirt off, tossing them on one of the chairs along the storefront window. The woman stares at his exposed chest and arms, and I'm about to roll my eyes when I see that it's not *him* she's staring at. She's not flustered or gawping like the others do; she's eyeing his unmarred skin like an artist finding the possibilities on a blank canvas.

"I want a sleeve of tattoos on this arm. I don't care what's in it, as long as this shoulder has dragon scales," Kellan explains with his hand, pointing out where he wants it.

"Well, we can see how far we get today, but you may have to come back to finish it, if that's okay?"

"Of course." He shoots me a sharp grin. "We can come back as many times as it takes."

I release an annoyed huff, but don't contradict him.

"And you?" she directs my way.

I shrug. If I'd had more notice, maybe I could have thought of something, but right now I'm blank. "I'm not sure."

She nods, as if it's completely normal for a customer to want a tattoo without knowing what they want. "Pete can talk to you to get a feel for what you might like and then put some quick sketches together for you to choose from."

Perfect.

"Now then, if you'll come with me to my chair, we can chat about your sleeve," she says to Kellan and moves around the desk.

Oh. Wait.

Kellan's teeth flash behind his dark beard. "Actually, I'm a bit nervous. Can he and I sit close enough to hold hands?"

"Oh! Yes, of course!" She places a hand over her chest and smiles reassuringly at him. "We have a numbing cream we can spread on the area if you'd like."

"His hand is all I need," Kellan replies easily.

Her eyes soften on a low "aww", and I clench my teeth together, trying to remind myself that this was the point of him inviting me.

A guy walks out from the back—Pete, I'm guessing—and once

the woman explains our *situation*, they move the chairs closer.

Kellan plops into his seat without additional prompting, then swings his arm out at me. "Come on, princess. Take my hand."

My jaw ticks as it takes everything in me to not lash out at his antics.

I sit in the other chair and glare at his offered hand, tempted to refuse and make the bastard watch me get a tattoo instead.

"Take. Myyy hand. Take my whole...heart...too..." Kell starts singing, and I cave.

"For fuck's sake," I grumble, grabbing his hand to shut him up.

He laughs and wraps his hand around mine.

"I knew you loved me."

Prick.

Acknowledgements

Thank you so much for reading Ravage and taking a chance on a debut author! I hope you enjoyed the story and look forward to the next book in the series.

My biggest thanks goes to my writing friends, who I've been writing with for fun these last ten years. You all have inspired me to write better and keep writing, even if we take long breaks in between because life happens. And when I told you I planned to publish a book, you encouraged me and gave the best feedback. Thank you for your support and kind words (and constructive criticism!).

Shoutout to Steph and Zee, my editors who helped polish my story and words. You're both amazing.

Thank you to my beta readers for your reactions and feedback! I've gone back to re-read your notes to keep me going when the words I write don't feel good enough.

Finally, a big thanks to my family members for listening to all my updates I was overly excited to share.

Want to receive a bonus scene?

Or maybe stay up to date on the newest releases?

How about early access to ARC or giveaway opportunities?

Sign up for A. L. Rook's newsletter to stay in the know of all things

Rook's books.

Scan or click the QR code below, or go to the website to sign up

@

www.alrookauthor.com

Join the A. L. Rook Reader Group on Facebook

The Rookery

@

www.facebook.com/groups/rookery

Or scan the QR code below

STALKING LINKS

amazon.com/stores/author/B0CYQJ2GWL

facebook.com/groups/rookery

instagram.com/alrookauthor

tiktok.com/@alrookauthor

WEBSITE: https://www.alrookauthor.com

NEWSLETTER: https://subscribepage.io/rooknewsletter

SPOTIFY: https://open.spotify.com/user/31g47djeh3oqclz7y
yaag2hwvtom?si=ca7e308dc7ec4b2c

FB PAGE: https://www.facebook.com/61557109453545/

About the Author

A.L. Rook is an avid reader and has been dreaming of becoming an author since the first grade. She's been thinking up and writing stories ever since. Her favorite stories are dark contemporary or fantasy romance with strong characters that leave a lasting impression. When not drinking exorbitant amounts of coffee while writing, she can be found reading, binge-watching various shows, or traveling.

If you want to stay up to date on release dates, news, or for a chance at extra teasers and giveaways, follow Rook on her socials and join her newsletter.